THE QUEENSBLOOD CROWN

DARKLING SOULS BOOK TWO

ALEX BREE

DARKLING SOULS TWO
THE
QUEENSBLOOD
CROWN
ALEX BREE

CONTENT WARNING

This is a dark fantasy story about monsters with content that may not be suitable for all readers. For a complete content list, please visit the author's website at www.alexbreewrites.com.

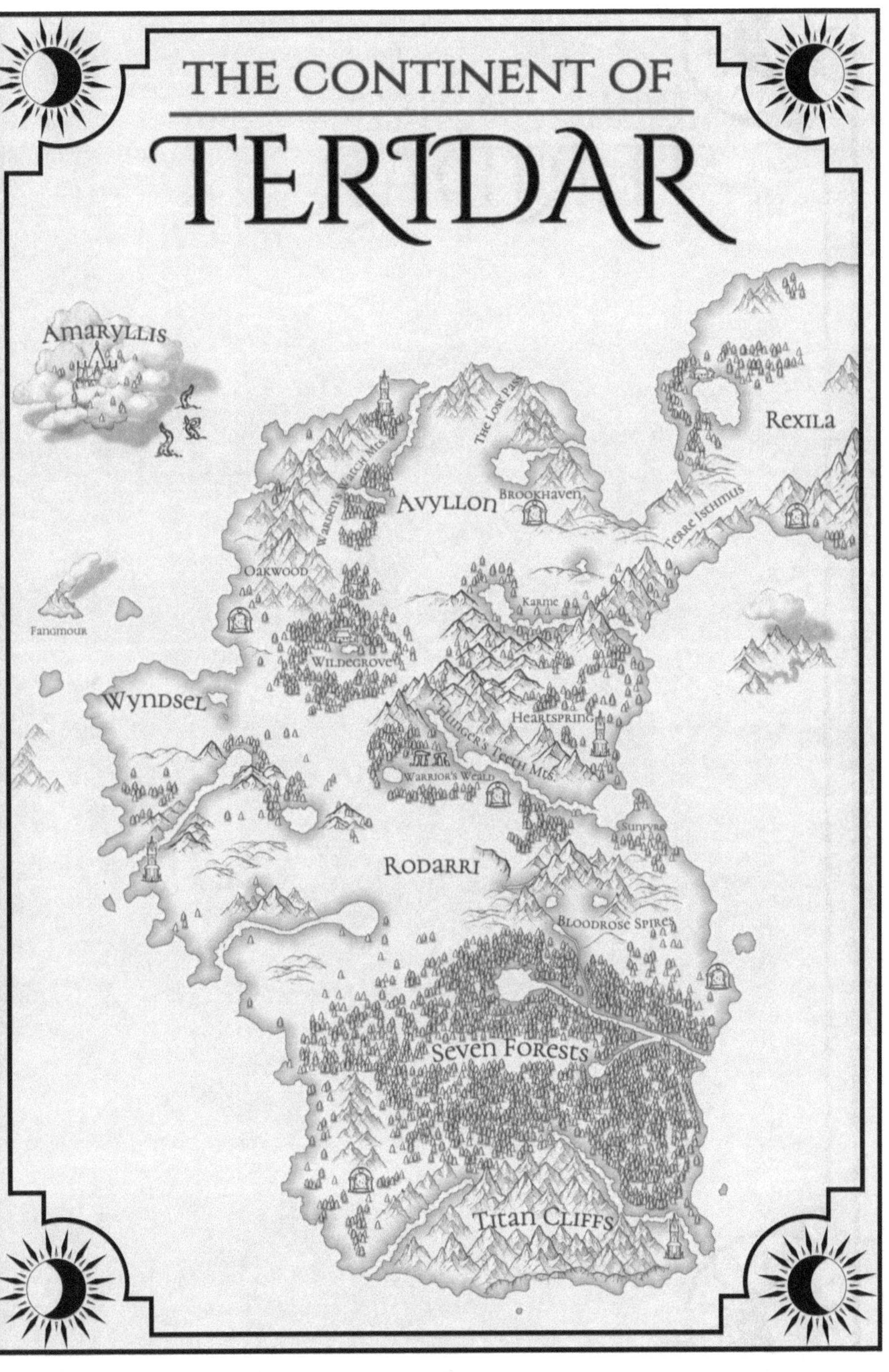

THE CONTINENT OF
TERIDAR
Amaryllis
Rexila
The Lost Pass
Avyllon
Brookhaven
Terre Isthmus
Oakwood
Karne
Fangmour
Wildegrove
Heartspring
Wyndsel
Hunger's Teeth Mts.
Warrior's Weald
Sunfyre
Rodarri
Bloodrose Spires
Seven Forests
Titan Cliffs

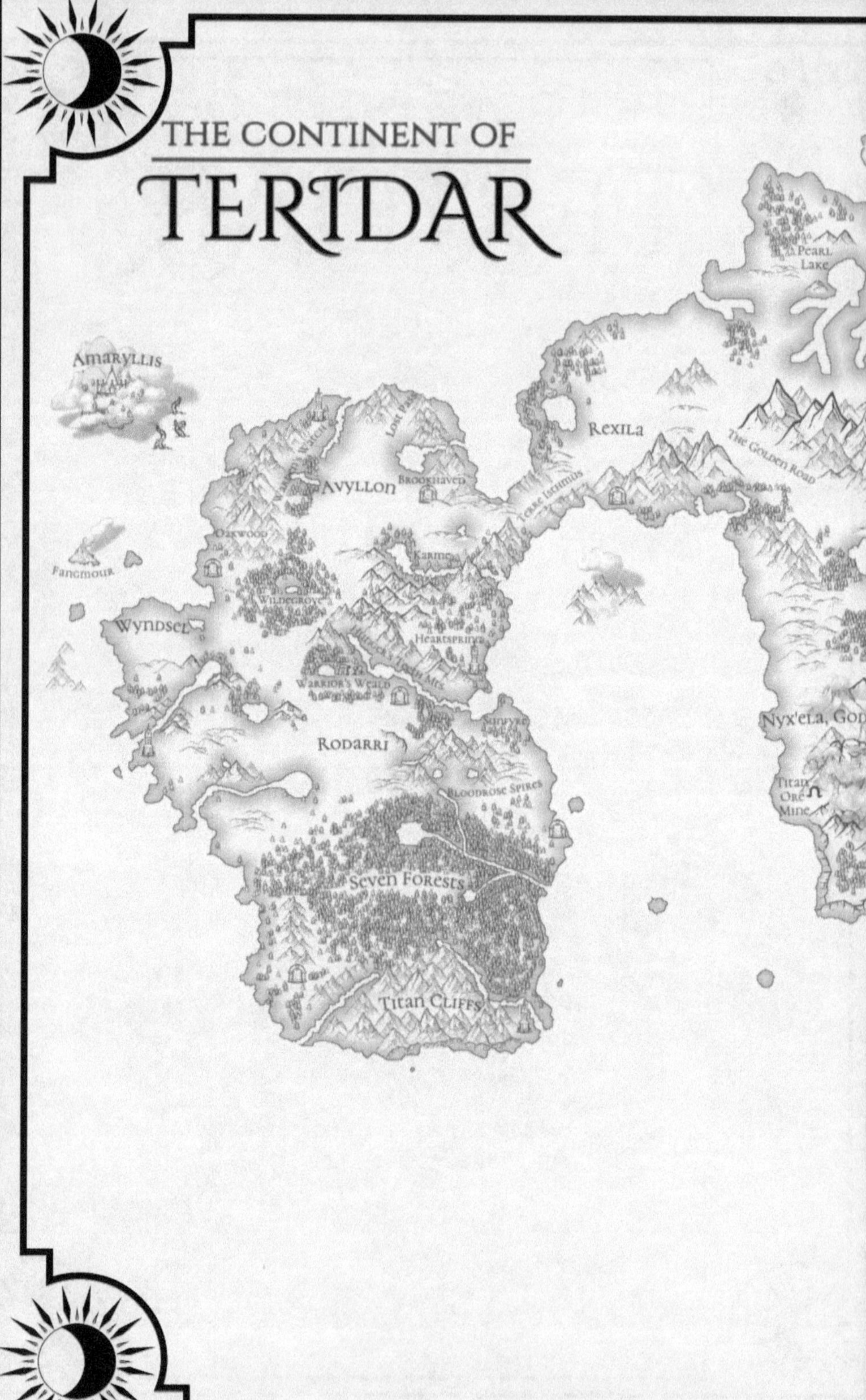

THE CONTINENT OF
TERIDAR
Amaryllis
Pearl Lake
Rexila
The Golden Road
Lost Pass
Avyllon
Brookhaven
Terre Isthmus
Oakwood
Karmo
Fangmour
Wildegrove
Wyndsel
Heartspring
Warrior's Weald
Nyx'ela, God
Sunfyre
Titan Ore Mine
Rodarri
Bloodrose Spires
Seven Forests
Titan Cliffs

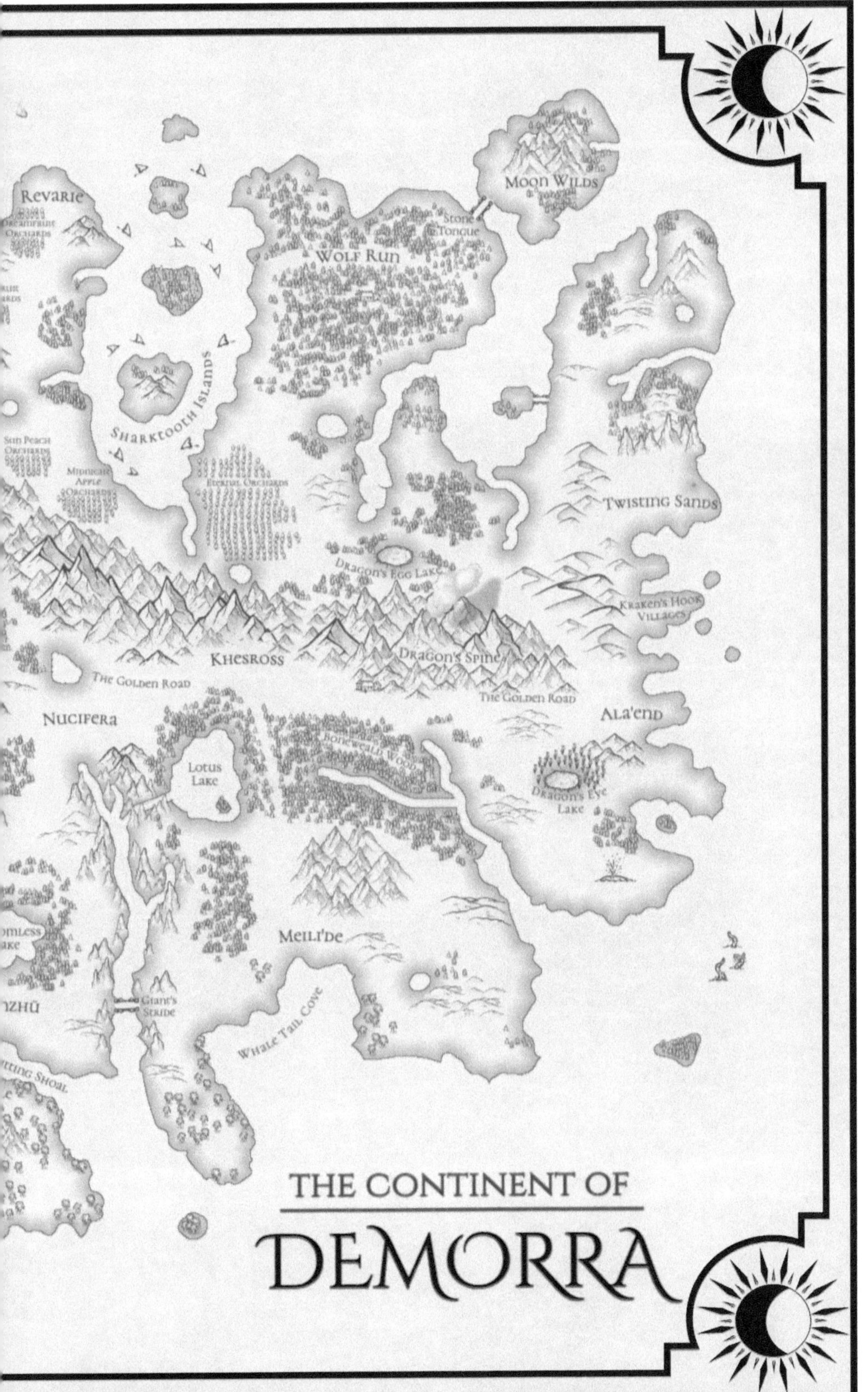
Moon Wilds
Revarie
Dreamfruit Orchards
Stone Tongue
Wolf Run
Sharktooth Islands
Sun Peach Orchards
Midnight Apple Orchards
Eternal Orchards
Twisting Sands
Dragon's Egg Lake
Kraken's Hook Villages
Khesross
Dragon's Spine
The Golden Road
The Golden Road
Nucifera
Ala'end
Lotus Lake
Boneweald Wood
Dragon's Eye Lake
Bottomless Lake
Meili'de
Hūzhū
Giant's Stride
Whale Tail Cove
Spitting Shoal
THE CONTINENT OF
DEMORRA

DARKLING SOULS

Hers is a story of vengeance. There are no heroes, no villains. No right or wrong. If you're looking for a tale of shining knights standing against the tides of evil, move along. This story tells of captives who suffered too long and too great that their souls were corrupted by violence, and what they do when they take their freedom.

Death is only the beginning.

PART ONE

THE BEGINNING
CHAPTER ONE

Death is only the beginning.

*— LAST JOURNAL ENTRY OF QUEEN VITTORIA
NIGHTFLAME LENORE, FIRST QUEENSBLOOD OF
RODARRI. THE DAY OF HER ASCENSION. 1 N.T.C.*

*1152 N.T.C. Five days after the Avyllon summit. Castle Rodarr,
Rodarri.*

Queen Rianne Charlotte Lenore, sacred Queensblood of
Rodarri, crumpled a royal proclamation in her fist. Ink
stained her fingertips and angry tears dripped onto her
pearl-encrusted lace wedding gown. She prepared to die.
The continent and its army of monsters had declared war on the
invading foreign emperor at the Avyllon summit, quietly sealing
Rianne's impending ascension. Her blood would replenish and
protect the land, and she would join her ancestors beyond the idyllic
veil of death.

A cursed hagshit lie. In life we're kept in gilded cages ripe for rutting and sacrificing, and in death we suffer for eternity.

She dared not speak those words aloud, even here alone in her chambers. Her breath came hot, and she steadied herself against her vanity. Once, Rianne was the most devout believer in those lies, but now she knew better—ascension was no more than an execution, and there was no peace in death for the angry souls of the queens whose bones and spirits haunted the wretched ravine.

Queens be with me.

Tears spotted her journal pages, obscuring her final words. Her heart twisted into a knot. She'd never gotten the chance to tell Rhydian goodbye. The man who'd made her hope for a future beyond these senseless deaths.

Just as well. The Warbringer planned to steal her and her kin away from here, and if Rhydian knew what the king planned... he'd tear down the castle walls to save her. The guards would kill him, or he would succumb to his curse and go mad with rage and kill them all. Both ended with his death, and he was worth so much more than a violent and needless demise.

Her breath caught. She leaned her head against the pages and sobbed as her heart shattered. Mourning the life with him she'd never have, she slipped to the floor, surrounded by her pooling skirts until her mind grew numb.

A pink dawn rose, painting the sky with pastel blooms and brushstrokes, the last she'd ever see. At eighteen, Rianne would be one of the youngest ascended queens in the history of Rodarri. Married to her people, and dead too young.

Ancient whispers slithered into her ear.

You will join us soon.

"Go away!" Rianne grabbed a glass orb from the vanity and hurled it at the wall, and it shattered.

Free us.
We will have vengeance.
The kings will die. The kings, they will all die! The
kings shall die by blood and flame and claw, the
kings of old shall die! Oh, how the kings shall die.

"Please stop," Rianne whispered, wrapping her arms around her legs, rocking back and forth.

She squeezed her teary eyes shut, but the whispers wouldn't cease. They never did.

The end is almost here.
It will be over soon.
Death is only the beginning.

The door to her room burst open, and her sister, Jordyn, stormed inside wearing a gown with a skirt cut into butterfly wings and painted to mimic stained glass. Rianne wiped her eyes and struggled to stand, unable to put weight on her injured leg—a warning from King Cavendar to not attempt another escape. She could still feel the cold bite of his blade driving through her thigh.

"They can't do this," Jordyn said. "It ends the firstblood line. You're the eldest daughter of the eldest daughter going back to Queen Vittoria. And it's... too soon." Jordyn's eyes welled with tears.

Rianne drew her sister into a hug and squeezed her tightly. At fifteen, Jordyn bore the same fair skin, light brown hair, and pale eyes as she did, but hints of curves already filled out her gown, unlike Rianne, who caught the withering sickness as a child. A bolt of pain ran through what remained of Rianne's heart. Jordyn would grow to be a great beauty, and Rianne would never see it. She blinked the tears away.

The High Seer's warning drifted through her thoughts. "*Who you think you must become and who you can choose to be are not the same.*" She wished she'd listened better when she had the chance.

Jordyn pulled away. "They can't... You were supposed to live so much longer. We were supposed to run away."

Rianne moved a rogue curl out of Jordyn's eyes. "This was the fate I was born to. We tried to speak up, to run, and we failed."

Jordyn glanced away, picking at the cerulean and periwinkle jewels on her gown. "You could *return*."

Rianne winced. "No queen has returned in three hundred years. It's just a cruel lie and look at me." She pulled at the opulent fabric hanging limply around her willowy shape and touched the dark circles under her eyes. "I'm weak."

Return. As if a queen could return to life once she was beheaded. A cruel joke. A vile lie. No, those whispering spirits of the queens were trapped in that awful ravine for eternity, and soon she would join them.

"Do you think Rhyd—"

King Cavendar entered the room and cut Jordyn off, scowling. "Leave us."

The crown was slipping off his head, and the thick robes cut into his wrists. She hated that they may have once shared kin. Centuries ago, the kings' line and Queensblood may have been related. The truth had been lost to time, but now, they couldn't have been further apart.

Jordyn hesitated, but the dark glint in the king's eye cowed her, and she slipped out of the room with a final tearful glance at Rianne. The doors closed, leaving the king and Queensblood alone.

Behind Rianne's trained, polite expression, hatred bloomed.

The king stalked her expansive chambers, circling her like a wolf circles an injured deer. He placed his hands on his round stomach. "It's time."

Her lip curled. "You need a willing sacrifice, or the protection won't hold. I know what happened with Queen Rosalindt. You can do the same to me—hold me down and cut off my head, but I won't go willingly." She tilted her chin up, trying to look braver than she felt.

A smile slithered across the king's face. "If you don't, I'll start ascending queens until you do. I'll start with Jordyn."

Panic roiled in her mind, with fear and horror on its heels. Not her little sister... Sweet, young Jordyn. She still wore flower crowns in the gardens and sang when she thought she was alone. Her eyes lit up when she held babies and grew sad with rainy weather.

Sickly vines writhed through Rianne's stomach. "No..."

"If you refuse this, I'll do it. Count on it." His breath smelled of wine and spiced meat.

Resistance wouldn't matter. There was no escape. She'd die either way, and at least going willingly would protect Jordyn. Rianne gritted her teeth at the king taking this one act of rebellion from her when he'd taken everything else, but she bowed her head.

"Good," he said.

She glanced up at him. "When will it be your turn to protect your people? We both know any blood would do."

"And that secret will go to the ravine with you." His lips curled into a smirk.

If only I were stronger, I would make him regret his words and lies. Queens—please someone make him regret it all.

"Now be a good girl and smile," he said.

Rianne glared at the floor, refusing him. He leaned forward and grabbed her thigh, squeezing it tightly through her skirts. A wave of agony ripped through her as he reopened the stab wound she'd received after her last escape attempt. Warm blood leaked down her thigh as she squirmed under his grip, but the king didn't relent.

"I won't ask again." He breathed into her ear. "Unless you prefer your last moments to be in a muzzle?"

The scrape of leather on her cheeks and the smell of hounds haunted Rianne's nightmares. Rianne shook with fear, but she pasted a smile on her face, hating herself all the while.

King Cavendar smiled and with a final squeeze to her leg, released her. He reached up and pulled the white veil over her face—the veil signifying her marriage to her people. "Your blood protects Rodarri, and it'll be over quickly."

"When Rhydian hears of this, he will kill you," she whispered.

The king paused at the door, gripped the frame until his swollen knuckles cracked, and then left without another word.

The whispers lingered at the edges of her senses.

Oh, how the kings shall die.

Two guards entered her chambers, their expressions tight. Rianne limped forward, her thigh burning. Rivulets of blood slipped down her leg. One of the guards pursed his lips but offered her his arm. She took it and made her way out of her room into the queen's quarters, past the dazzling sapphire wading pools, the wild peacocks, and the hanging veils.

She entered the long hall where the other queens lined the walls. Rianne swallowed. She passed cousins, aunts, and other relatives, a mix of emotions on their faces. Sadness. Anger. Shame. Resignation. They'd seen the king beat her, muzzle her, and they had still followed her into the woods to try to escape before the king rounded them all up and dragged them screaming back to the castle. Now, they must watch her die.

Her young cousin, Ella, cried, "Rianne! No. Don't leave." She struggled against her mother's arms.

Rianne swallowed a sob, and instead put on a brave face. Children deserved better than this.

Rianne paused, reaching down to touch her face. "All will be well. Don't fret."

Ella's eyes watered. "How?"

There were no answers she could offer.

"Trust in the queens." Rianne's hand dropped.

Guards escorted her, limping, through the lavish halls and toward the Courtyard of Queens, where the city gathered in the sprawling amphitheater walls overlooking the cursed ravine. Covered in black-vined bloodroses, the ancient stone walls reminiscent of the royal cemeteries. The whole place reminded her of a graveyard. She'd never noticed before. Strange mist swirled near the ravine's edge—her final resting place.

She stepped into the mid-morning sunlight to a roaring crowd. The cheers echoed so loudly she couldn't hear herself think. Long glossy ribbons, flags, and fabrics hung from the austere stone walls. Not even at Theo and Rhydian's trial weeks ago was the crowd this vigorous. They craved her death. The thought made fear creep into her skull as the whispers comforted her.

They will pay.

Rianne stared ahead at the block beside the waiting hooded executioner. Raw, instinctual terror filled every corner of her being and froze her shaking limbs in place. The guards gripped her, her arms tiny in their calloused palms.

"Please no," she whimpered.

No one could hear over the roar of the crowds.

Glancing around wildly, she looked up to the king who sat with his arm slung around Jordyn's shoulders. Her sister tried to pull away, but the king held her close, his gaze never leaving Rianne.

No.

Rianne steeled herself. Ignoring her somersaulting stomach, she locked her fears away and walked the rest of the way to the execution-er's block. The guards released her reddened arms.

This is really happening.

Hands trembling, Rianne pulled back the white funeral veil. She hesitated before the block, preparing to kneel.

Boom.

Boom.

Roaring erupted from the courtyard gates over the din of the crowd. Metal clanked and screeched as something angry slammed against the stones. The castle walls *vibrated*. The crowd quieted, searching for the source of the thunderous noise.

"Rianne!" a voice roared from the locked gates.

The blood drained from her face.

Rhydian.

BREAKNECK
CHAPTER TWO

Rhydian, if you read this, I love you. You gave me life and hope for something more. You are my heart. Remember—you are more than your curse.

— JOURNAL OF QUEEN RIANNE CHARLOTTE
LENORE, THE DAY OF HER ASCENSION, 5 NOVA
1152 N.T.C.

1152 N.T.C. The namesake capital city of Avyllon.

THREE DAYS AGO.

Aurienne fell into a prophetic nightmare. In the vision, Queen Rianne was cut down by phantom executioner's axes. Each time, she reappeared and died again. Copies of her rose to great heights before falling until her many corpses piled up. Her bones shattered into flying sharpened shards as her blood sprayed the assembled people.

Roaring, Rhydian watched, bound in chains of shadows. His eyes glowed redder than a blood eclipse.

Then everything quieted, and the vision changed.

Aurienne found herself alone in the Courtyard of Queens with Rianne, who wore white lace wedding garb, near the executioner's dais. Rianne locked gazes with Aurienne, with wide eyes and quivering lips.

"My life for theirs," the queen whispered.

A blade flew out of nowhere and cut her down, her body falling to the pit.

The scene restarted with Rianne in the courtyard. This time, her white dress was stained with blood. Her eyes drained of fear and filled with anger. Her too-white teeth were stained with blood, and her lips curled into a snarl.

"My life for theirs." Rianne's head fell from her shoulders and rolled into the pit.

It restarted again, a terrible loop with no escape. Rianne floated above the pit wearing a scarlet gown and a gleaming crown of sharpened bones. Head lolling. Pale, with blood spurting from her neck. Her eyes were milky and dead, and bruises darkened her paper-thin skin. Her lips cracked and bled, and silver smoke poured from her wounds. Beneath them, the stones of the courtyard hemorrhaged dark crimson blood, which pooled around Aurienne's ankles. Rianne lifted an executioner's sword crafted from bones, still dripping with blood.

"My life for theirs." Rianne swung the sword at Aurienne, and the nightmarish vision ended with ghastly howling.

"You can't defeat what's coming alone," a distant voice whispered. "The prophecy requires Teridar to stand together. Or fall together."

Aurienne woke screaming, drenched in sweat with crimson blood dripping to her pillow from her eyes and nose.

She ran half-dressed and barefoot through the temple to Rhydian's chambers. Her sentinels tore after her in alarm, but she couldn't slow.

No. No. No.

Skipping stairs, she flew down glistening white corridors. She turned a corner too quickly, lost her footing and slammed into the wall. The impact on her already cracked ribs drove the breath from her. She gasped as she pushed off the wall with her bandaged hand. Clutching her ribs, she raced on, nearly stumbling on a carpet and falling again. Every ticking second changed the visions and fates. Already, it was likely too late.

She pounded her fists on his door.

"Rhydian!"

He opened the door with his sheathed sword in hand.

"Rianne. Ascension," Aurienne panted.

Rhydian darted inside and within seconds shoved his feet into boots, shouldered his pack, and sprinted down the hall.

"Take Adonis, go through the Way!" Aurienne called after him.

Across the hall, Theo's door slammed open.

"They're going to execute Rianne. Go with him," Aurienne urged.

Theo spun back into his room, and in seconds, he was pulling on his coat and boots and racing out.

"Theo... It's too late. He won't..." Aurienne pursed her lips and shook her head.

The prophecy said they'd all fall. Rianne would just be one of the first. Still—she knew she had to warn Rhydian. He was owed those final moments.

Theo's expression hardened. "Fate be damned."

He paused, brushed his fingers under her chin to tilt it up and pressed a whisper of a kiss against her lips before tearing down the hall after Rhydian.

Aurienne touched her lips, watching them race to save a queen destined to die.

The miles flew past. Hooves pounded the road to the Way at breakneck speeds, but Rhydian urged his mount faster. Somewhere behind him, Theo and Adonis chased until they reached a demanding gallop. Trees and mountains raced by, but Rhydian scarcely noticed. The red veil of his Warbringer curse descended, and his vision narrowed to a dark tunnel. Rage built in his chest, a sign his curse was close to awakening.

He rode for the Way like it was a beacon pulling him in. His mind scarcely worked.

Gods.

No.

Don't take her from me.

By the time they reached the Way, the horses were exhausted, but there was no time to rest them. The Way was fifty feet high, a tall slim doorway that four horses could walk through shoulder to shoulder. Rhydian slammed his hand against the Way, but it remained locked, and his palm bounced off the invisible barrier. Translucent iridescent orbs of light swirled and danced inside, taunting him.

Adonis slipped off his horse and with shaking hands began to read the incantation, tracing his hands in a careful pattern in time with the ancient words. Several runes, unseen before, glowed as Adonis read.

Adonis stumbled over a word, and the runes darkened.

"Shadowsucking—" Adonis cursed.

Rhydian clenched his fists, pacing before the Way. He slammed his shoulder against the portal, but his efforts remained unnoticed by the ageless magic. He hefted his ax and swung it at the glass-like barrier as hard as he could, but it bounced off with a clang.

The apprentice sorcerer restarted. His tongue stumbled over a word again, and the runes extinguished.

"You can do this," Theo encouraged, his voice gentle and soothing.

Adonis angrily wiped a tear from his face and bit his lip. "I'm sorry; I'm trying. It's hard without Mathis."

Mathis—the sorcerer who'd sacrificed himself to save them all from the Mooncursed massacre weeks ago, and Adonis' longtime mentor. The massacre where Rhydian had to flee if he didn't want to unleash his curse, the very curse whispering in his mind now. The rancid guilt only fueled his rage, and he hammered his ax against the Way again.

Every second they wasted here, Rianne might die. This infernal gate kept him from her. Rage bubbled in his gut. He couldn't lose her.

Adonis carefully read and traced the patterns until white runes pulsed around the frame of the shimmering light portal. With a flourish of his hand, Adonis finished, but nothing happened.

Fear incited the bloodrage, and Rhydian's curse caressed the corners of his mind. He couldn't stop. Gravel crunched beneath Rhydian's feet as he stalked over to Adonis, who frantically flipped pages and scanned the text. Adonis's eyes widened when he glanced up to see the anger painted on Rhydian's face. Rhydian towered over the young sorcerer, and unable to control his rage, he punched Adonis in the jaw. Adonis crumpled, and Rhydian hauled him up by his shirt.

Sputtering, Adonis grabbed Rhydian's hands in his own. "I'm trying, it's really complicated. I'm so sorry, I've been studying for weeks..."

Theo strode forward, drawing his Sword of Souls with a dark and pained expression haunting his eyes. Rhydian ignored Avyllon's royal successor, though a voice of reason told him he ought to be more wary of the soul-rending sword in Theo's hands. He ignored that voice.

"You better get this hellsdamned Way open, or—"

A bright shimmer emanated from the Way, interrupting Rhydian. All three turned as the Way opened, clearing a path to the other side through a curtain of magic. Bubbles of light, with colors so bright it forced Rhydian to squint and shield his eyes, orbited. Across the short path, there was a dark forest—trees Rhydian recognized as the forest outside Rodarri's capital.

Rhydian dropped Adonis, mounted his horse, and charged forward. In his periphery, Theo and Adonis followed, attempting to keep pace, but Rhydian didn't care. He didn't need them. He'd save her himself.

Emptying his mind, Rhydian urged his horse faster, jumping over heavy underbrush and weaving through towering trees. At the edges of the forest, tall austere walls covered in curling, onyx bloodrose vines came into view. Chest heaving, Rhydian jerked his horse to a stop, wrapped the reins around a nearby tree, and ran toward the portcullis.

Crowds cheered inside the walls, and his heart twisted into a blackened knot. Only an ascension could incense the crowds to such a frenzy. Rhydian charged to the gatehouse, running as fast as his legs could go, praying to all the gods and dark powers he'd make it in time.

Reaching the closed gates, Rhydian peered between the bars to see Rianne standing in the center of the courtyard beside the executioner, garbed in white. The metal squealed beneath his ax and bloodrose petals went flying.

He would die to save her.

ASCENSION
CHAPTER THREE

None would be spared.

— *SCRATCHED INTO THE STONE DAIS BESIDE THE*
COURTYARD OF QUEENS.

1152 N.T.C. The Courtyard of Queens, Castle Rodarr, Rodarri.

Rianne's heart plummeted. She pivoted toward the vine-bound gatehouse where Rhydian hammered the locked gate with a double-bladed ax, metal clanging and squealing against metal, the percussion booming into the amphitheater. The stones shook with his effort. Mortar and dust exploded from the force, but the gate held for now. Guards rushed forward, holding it shut. She'd hoped he wouldn't come, for his sake, for everyone's. His eyes already glowed redder than hot coals, a warning his Warbringer curse would soon overtake him. One death, even accidental, and his fate would be sealed.

"Rhydian, no," she murmured.

Rianne hurried toward him, limping and struggling against her heavy lace skirts. Five steps from the gate, guards blocked her way.

"Rianne!" Rhydian roared.

He shoved his muscled arm through the bars, skin ripping against the rusted metal. The black-thorned bloodroses twined eagerly toward his blood. Theo stabbed and slashed at the guards through the bars, keeping them at bay, protecting the Warbringer.

"Rianne!" Rhydian reached for her, face pressed against the bars, eyes glowing crimson.

"Stop him!" the king commanded.

Rianne glanced at the king, and he tugged Jordyn against him. A flash of steel pressed against her sister's bodice. Rianne choked back a sob.

She reached for Rhydian's fingertips, but her guards held her back, and she was too far away. Rhydian reached for her, blood trickling from his torn skin. The metal gate peeled away from the wall as hinges pulled free, but it wasn't fast enough. Slamming his fist against the bars with a grunt, he started hammering at the walls themselves. Stones fell loose as he opened a small hole beside the gate.

It's too late.

The Darkling Prophecy foretold the continent would fall; that they'd all be devoured by its unrelenting advance. Perhaps she was just one of the first to fall to it. Deep down, she'd always known her fate ended like this. She couldn't save herself, but she might be able to buy Jordyn more time.

Stones tumbled toward her, but he couldn't get free. She glanced at Jordyn again as her sister cried out, the dagger digging in.

Her hand fell against her side as she caught Rhydian's eye. They both knew their time was up.

She whispered, "I'm sorry."

"No," he bellowed, shoving his ax against the growing opening between gate and wall.

"We always knew our time would be short," Rianne said. "I can't let him hurt Jordyn or the others. You should leave so you don't have to watch."

She turned away, limping back to the executioner's block.

An unnatural, guttural roar erupted from the gatehouse. "Rianne!"

The booming thunder of his ax on metal and stone returned with fury. She glanced over her shoulder to glimpse Rhydian wildly attacking the gatehouse, causing the walls to quiver. Stones rolled into the courtyard, as he tried to shove his way through. The curse was taking over, and there was nothing she could do to help him.

She returned to the dais, and the crowds cheered. She stared at the wooden block, black with centuries of queen's blood. Deep groves where the ax had fallen time and time again. Fingernail scratches laced the side in an intricate pattern of dread. Just a few steps away, the ravine dropped into nothingness.

Pain coursed through her leg, but she knelt before the executioner's block.

"Rianne, I'm coming. Rianne, no!"

He was going to die or unleash his curse and go mad. And neither would save her sister from the king's dagger.

"Rhydian—please run," she called, praying he would leave after she was gone.

She swallowed, and tears streamed down her cheeks. Her hands shook as she placed them on the block. The clangs from the gatehouse swelled and echoed.

She glanced at Rhydian and mouthed, "I love you."

"Don't do this. I'll kill you all!" The gate groaned as Rhydian pressed his knee against the metal, ax striking again and again.

The gate began to bend in half. Theo joined his side, driving his shimmering sword into the mortar near the hinges and leaning against it to pry it free. Guards braced benches against the crossbar rods to try and hold the gate shut. Rhydian finally shoved his torso through, swinging his ax wildly.

"Nothing will interrupt the ascension," the king beckoned the executioner.

"Since the first days of Rodarri," the executioner announced, "Queensblood has replenished the land. For over a thousand years, we have experienced peace and prosperity from their noble sacrifice..."

"Rianne!" Rhydian shouted, as dozens of guards swarmed the gatehouse, bracing it to keep him caged.

"Queensblood will protect us with their blood, or their return," the executioner continued.

Her hands trembled as fear traveled up and down her arms. Her vision blurred as her instincts fought her decision. Glancing down, she saw a field of crushed wildflowers rather than the dusty ground and executioner's block. That wasn't right. Rianne's brows drew together in confusion as silver cords reached out of the ravine and wrapped around her arms, yanking her down. She nearly lost her balance as she peered into the yawning abyss. Rianne blinked back tears, and the false images vanished.

The executioner murmured, "It's time."

The words dragged her back to the present where the lustful crowd was already drunk on the promise of blood and violence.

She tried to be brave but felt very small. "Will it hurt?"

He stiffened. "I'll do my best, so it doesn't."

"You made sure the blade is sharp?"

He nodded, his hood obscuring his face. "I'm sorry to be the one to do this."

She peered up at the watercolor sky, committing every color to memory, before she closed her eyes, leaned forward, and placed her neck against the block. Her fingers dug into the cold, ancient wood to keep her hands from trembling. Tears rolled down her cheek and nose. Her breaths came too shallow and too fast, as terror shot through her veins.

Eyes closed and savoring her final memory of a pastel sky, she smelled the tang of copper, the oil of the ax handle, and the phantom kiss of flower petals from the gardens she loved so dearly.

Like a flame hissing under the extinguishing snuffer, her overwhelming emotions cut to consuming numbness. Her thoughts fled her reality.

This can't be real.

This can't be happening.

Is this another nightmare?

She gripped the sides of the block with her frail fingers, ordering herself to keep as still as possible. The executioner could get a cleaner cut that way.

"I'm afraid," she whispered to no one.

Rhydian never stopped sobbing, shouting, fighting as his body pushed half out of the wall—sending guards sprawling. "Rianne, please no. Fuck you all. I'll kill every hellsdamned one of you. Rianne!"

In her final moments, her heart broke. Her pain was over, but his had just begun.

The metallic whoosh of air from a rising ax told her that her time had almost come. Her heart hammered so fast she could taste copper. Her entire body began to shake, and she gripped the wood so hard her knuckles turned white. The second air-splitting hiss came as a final whisper haunted her mind.

Death is only the beginning.

The ax struck true.

Her last memory was not a watercolor sky. Blood. Her headless corpse. Sky. Dirt. Sky. Dirt. Roaring crowds. Her dying eyes glimpsed the edge of the ravine before darkness enveloped her, and she fell.

An eternity later, her head came to rest at the bottom of the ravine with mountains of gleaming bleached bones. Her body bounced off the stone walls before it landed beside her with a loud crunch in the skeletons. So deep, the world of the living faded away, and only the realm of the dead remained.

Silence.

Peace.

Darkness.

A thousand silver eyes snapped open from the shadows. The spirits flew shrieking toward her. If she could, she would have screamed. A final tear rolled down her cheek as pain erupted in her soul.

Pain.

Darkness.

Pain.

Darkness.

Madness
Chapter Four

The last one of you that fell to the madness of the curse caused destruction lasting a thousand years. I should kill you now before it takes you.

— *Grimfall.*

1152 N.T.C. The Courtyard of Queens at Castle Rodarr, Rodarri.

Bitter madness overtook Rhydian as the image of Rianne's execution branded itself into his brain. Her reaching for him. Her screaming. The ax biting into the wood. The white lace of her wedding gown blossoming with blood. Her broken corpse discarded into the pit. The crowds cheering her demise.

Without her, Rhydian's tenuous control over the bloodlust snapped. He raged at the gatehouse in a frenzy of stone chips and dust, roaring. A guard reached for him through the bars, and he snapped the man's arm into pieces then grasped another guard's shirt to slam his head against the metal.

"Tomorrow, Queen Jordyn shall join her sister Rianne in protecting the land," the king announced.

Rhydian snarled. "I'll kill you!"

"Rhydian stop!" Theo grabbed his shirt to yank him back. "She's gone."

Rhydian shoved him, and he went tumbling backwards. Rhydian grabbed the bars with his bare hands and cranked on the metal. Dust poured down as the bars bent, and the stone cracked. Blocks toppled from the walls and ceiling. Arrows flew into the fray, slicing Rhydian's arms.

He had to get to her. To be with her. His entire body burned with his need to get through this gate. The castle would drown in the tidal wave of blood he would bring down upon them all. It would be so easy. One death and he'd be truly gone to the thoughts rattling around his skull. He'd be unstoppable. A wild grin settled on his face.

"There shall be an ascension every day for ten days," the king said. "Everyone return inside while we deal with the Warbringer."

Rhydian pointed to the king, before slamming against the twisted gate. The crude barricade of tables, chairs, and metal bars turned to splinters under Rhydian's ax. He swung for any guards in his reach, each crumpling under his attack. One casualty and he'd claim the powers of death and tear this castle apart until nothing was left but the foundations. He'd turn it all to rubble. He caught a guard's sword with the bottom of his ax and snapped it in half, flinging the blade back through the gate.

"Kill them," the king ordered before disappearing inside, dragging Jordyn by the arm.

Rhydian wedged his boot near the bottom of the gate and rammed his shoulder against it. The gate creaked, and guards on the other side went sprawling. So close. Then he could be with her.

He took a large step back before lunging forward and driving his boot into the twisted metal. The gate flew into the courtyard.

Theo shook him again, knuckles digging into Rhydian's chest. "She's gone, if you want to avenge her, we have to leave now. More guards are coming. We need to go."

Rhydian shoved Theo backwards. "Leave before it's too late. I won't even recognize you."

"I'm not leaving you!" Theo ran his hands through his hair glancing up at the ravaged gatehouse.

Rhydian hardly heard as he stepped into the courtyard. The ravine was calling to him, and he'd get to her... he'd avenge her. He'd kill everyone, and then he'd join her in the darkness at the bottom of the pit so she wouldn't have to be alone. Even if it was hell, they'd face it together. He couldn't stand the thought of her down there for all time. His mind unraveled as rage consumed his senses. His eyes burned with unseen sand, and his nose was scorched by the scent of rage—cinnamon, smoke, and hot pepper. Needles prickled his skin as copper coated his tongue.

Not long now.

With a groan, the gatehouse collapsed behind them, sealing them in. Cracked stones bounced off Rhydian's shoulders as Theo dove against the wall to avoid being crushed. Even though he knew they would both die, he couldn't stop. The curse was breaking him open.

"Rhydian!" Theo gripped his arm, trying to drag him away.

Theo should've left. Rhydian shook him off and stepped further into the courtyard, prepared to swing his ax again. The guards stumbled backward through the debris.

One soldier froze in place, turning ashen upon seeing the Warbringer. His sword fell from his hand. Somewhere in the depths of Rhydian's faraway memories, he knew the man's face. They'd trained and patrolled together as Queensguard. Long days and longer nights, they might've been friends. It didn't matter now.

Rhydian grinned and swung, preparing for the murder that would change him forever.

An immeasurable power yanked him backwards by the collar. His spine hit the dirt, and his ax went flying. The red fog of madness dissipated as his vision swam with stars and the air was compressed from his lungs.

A flash of silver darted in a wide arc, knocking the Rodarri soldiers to the ground. Then it was upon him, grabbing him by the collar again and yanking him across the dirt. Rhydian struggled to suck in a breath as he was dragged backward at alarming speed.

Rubble scraped his back as he flew across the ground. Rhydian reached up to feel what had captured him and found a fist made of iron. Blinking, he tried to clear his vision to see he was being dragged out of the crumbling gatehouse toward the dense tree line. They were through the outer walls in a few moments as rocks and branches raked his back at high speed. The castle grew small in the distance as Theo stumbled after him.

He whipped his head around, glimpsing Grimfall, the elf.

Pulse prickling with adrenaline, he recalled her at the summit dispatching the Mooncursed with ease. Bodies piling around her, and blood flying off her starlight sword. Even in his crazed state, he knew the danger she posed.

Sprinting, she dragged him behind her with unmatched ferocity as if he weighed nothing at all. Her long silver hair flew behind her, and her gray patterned skin blended into the disappearing castle walls.

"Let me go." He snarled as he clawed at her hand.

She mumbled something in a language he didn't understand, and it stoked his rage. He hammered at her leather armor, but his fists bounced off as though she were made of something stronger than stone. Theo stumbled to keep up with her, stuffing his glowing sword into its scabbard.

"Rianne!" he roared, reaching for the shrinking ravine.

Tears of rage rolled down his face as this fucking elf stole his revenge, his final resting place with Rianne from him.

Spine scraping the dirt, she dragged him toward a gatehouse in the outer wall. Arrows stuck into the ground around them from the portcullis overhead. Guards shouted for her to stop, but she drew her glowing sword, and they stumbled away. With a single swing, she drove her blade into the wooden gate. The wood splintered as she twisted her sword, and the gate gave way. Rhydian scrambled to rise, but she was dragging him again before he could find his footing.

Finally in the forest, she released him and sent him tumbling into the brush. She stood between him and Rianne, and he saw only red.

"What in all the hells were you thinking!" Grimfall balled her fists. "It's a miracle your curse hasn't taken you."

"That's the point," Rhydian snapped through gritted teeth. "I want it to take me."

Rhydian twisted and came up swinging. He launched toward her. Theo jumped between them, and Rhydian slammed into the blacksmith. Theo's feet slid through the grass.

Theo pressed his fists against Rhydian's chest, "Get a hold of yourself. Rianne gave her life to save her sister and the others. You promised to save *them*."

The words struck the shard of Rhydian not yet taken by the curse. The pause was enough to find a tenuous handle on his anger. Rhydian spun away from his friend, fighting for a hold on his sanity.

Theo kept his hands up, blocking the elf from Rhydian's sight, protecting Rhydian from the nightmare of what would happen if he attacked Grimfall. He should know better than to pick a fight with someone who measured time by centuries, who'd downed Mooncursed by the dozen at the summit, but the time for wise decisions had gone.

"Rianne begged you not to lose yourself to your curse," Theo said. "If you do this, you'll be betraying her memory. And you can't help the others."

Rhydian bellowed and punched a tree. Bark went flying and the uprooted tree toppled over.

"She's dead!" he shouted.

The memories were burned into the back of his eyelids. Tears in her eyes, reaching for him through the guards. Her limping to the block, grabbing it with her frail hands. The fear written on her face. Her tilting her head up to look at the late dawn sky. The ax coming down. Her body, lost forever into the darkness.

"They killed her!"

Rhydian grabbed a sapling and bent it in half. He grabbed a rose-bush by the roots and ripped it from the soil before kicking down another small tree. The thorns ripped open his skin, but he welcomed the pain. He lifted a small boulder and hurled it into the trees. Small animals scurried away, and birds cawed angrily overhead.

"We need to get farther away—the guards are going to be here soon, and he's not exactly subtle," Theo murmured to the elf.

"I can carry him," she said, irritation dripping from her tone.

Rhydian snarled, and she grinned at him with short, pointed canines. She tossed her hip-length silver hair with a flick of her hand. One hip was cocked, her arms were crossed, and she sported a bored look Rhydian knew was false. Grimfall was probably the most dangerous being on the face of the continent, and he'd be a fool to test her. But gods, he wanted to. Shaking, he turned away.

Fury and rage blanketed the ache of a broken heart as he stalked deeper into the forest.

They walked until Rhydian's feet ached. It didn't matter. His chest still heaved with every breath, his nostrils flaring at the thought of what King Cavender had done—of what he'd do to him in turn. It didn't register that they'd reached a clearing until Grimfall next spoke.

"Warbringer, the curse is nearly upon you," the elf warned. "You need to calm down."

Calm down.

Rhydian spun and swung a fist at her. She dodged easily, swept his legs, and pinned him against the grass. Her knee pressed into his chest. Dry grass crunched under his back as the weight of a mountain pinned him. He dug his fingers into her leg, but she didn't even flinch.

Rutting, hellsdamned elf.

Rhydian snarled up at her, and she growled in return. Flashes of her starlight monster-killing sword peeked out over her shoulder.

"I warned you, Warbringer, don't make me put you down," she

hissed. "If you succumb to this curse, I will end you as I've destroyed every other monster who lost control."

Maybe she should.

Rhydian prepared to launch at her and pound her head into the ground. It was futile, but he'd enjoy trying. He flexed his fingers and tucked his feet under his hips.

Theo knelt beside them, tilting his head to catch her gaze. "Excuse me. The great Grimfall... Uh... Madam... Elf?"

Madam elf?

Rhydian and Grimfall both slowly turned from one another to stare at Theo. The elf's brow lifted incredulously. Rhydian could only gape at how utterly ridiculous his friend sounded, unable to focus on how mad he was.

"Rhydian needs time," Theo said. "He just watched the woman he loves die. Give him a chance."

With a roll of her eyes, she lifted her knee off Rhydian. He pressed up from the crushed grass. He paced in tight circles, seeing red and destroying everything within sight before crumpling in the dirt in a pile.

Theo hesitated, glancing between Rhydian and the elf. "I'll collect Adonis and the horses. Will you..."

"We'll be fine, Theo," she said curtly.

Theo gave her a long look before he disappeared into the trees.

She sat beside him. "I'll ask again, what were you thinking? You nearly killed dozens of people, or more. You almost brought the castle down. Days ago, you told me you'd do anything to fight this curse and now you seem determined to succumb."

"I had to try and save her." Rhydian snapped a twig between his fingers, alternating between volcanically angry and entirely numb. "And then I wanted to be with her."

She said nothing for a long time, and when she spoke her voice was tight. "I'm sorry you couldn't save her."

Rhydian said, "I failed her."

Her expression almost softened. "We can't control everything.

You did what you could. And now you must decide what to do next."

"I want to kill him. That kingshit, King Cavendar. I will dangle his body over the ravine and let Rosalindt and the other queen spirits devour him. Maybe Rianne's spirit will be there too, leading the charge." He glanced at her and saw his red glowing eyes reflected in Grimfall's silver ones.

"Then what?"

He blinked.

"Kill him," she said. "Get your revenge. But then what? What would Rianne have wanted you to do?"

Rhydian stared at the mossy dirt. "I was going to save the rest of the queens. We were going to help them all escape. But I think the king is going to ascend her sister tomorrow."

"If you want to save her sister, then you've got to get a hold of yourself," she said.

Rhydian pressed his hands against his face. "I can't. The curse is hungry, waking. I feel it. I can't best it, not this time. Not without Rianne."

Images of Rianne haunted him. Chasing her through the gardens. Worshiping her body in the wildflowers. Stolen kisses in castle alcoves by candlelight. The touch of her fingers on his face. Her voice in his ear, keeping the curse at bay.

"You dishonor her memory with your weakness," she said.

Rhydian's head snapped up, and, without thinking, he lunged for the elf. She spun, driving her knee into his stomach. He landed in the dirt, hard, sputtering and coughing.

"You have the chance to save her kin, and yet your emotions are robbing you the opportunity," she continued. "If you ever loved Rianne, you would honor her wishes."

Scrambling up, he charged again. The heel of her hand shot out and caught him square in the chest like a battering ram, hard enough to nearly crack his breastbone.

He tumbled backward through the dry grass and thorny brush,

unable to catch his breath. His vision darkened, and his chest was on fire. Finally, he sucked in precious air to sate his burning lungs.

She stood over him. "You have a duty to the living, Warbringer."

He sat up slowly, feeling the fight leave him. His head pounded, full of cursed images he couldn't banish. Rianne *would* be ashamed. She went to her death so bravely to save her sister and the others. He couldn't let her down, and the elf was right. Grimfall was just trying to help him, too, and he was behaving like an animal. He hated himself.

Rhydian glanced at the elf, seeing the glow of his eyes reflected in her own begin to fade. The song of violence in his blood quieted. Now, he was drained and empty.

"I'm sorry," he said softly to Rianne and Grimfall both.

The elf sat beside him, out of reach. "It is much easier to be angry than it is to be heartbroken. I know."

Hot, angry tears flowed.

"Rianne had the heart of a warrior," the elf said. "She faced her death bravely."

"She deserved better than death," Rhydian said miserably.

His world was shattering, and he kept seeing her die. This had to be some horrible nightmare, one he no longer wanted to be part of.

Finally, he lifted his head. "I don't know what to call you. Grimfall?"

"My name is Nesryn."

"Nesryn, once I save them, if I can save them... Would you do me a favor?"

She cocked her head, studying him. "You want me to kill you?"

"Yes," he whispered. "The curse... I can't hold it back anymore."

"When the curse takes root in you, I will end it. It's why I found you." Her hard expression softened. "I thought you meant what you said after the summit. You don't want the power; you want to overcome this."

He shook his head. "It doesn't matter now. I'm going to let it take me to avenge her."

Nesryn leaned forward to meet his gaze. "If the curse overtakes you, it is my sworn duty to destroy you, to destroy any monster who threatens humankind."

She'd said as much before, but he needed to know. He'd avenge Rianne no matter the cost—and the cost would be his sanity. He'd unleash his curse to kill the king and the guards, but the visage of who he'd become after terrified him, and he couldn't stand to hurt the innocent. He had to know she'd end it before it got out of control. He needed her.

His eyes met hers, pleadingly. "Swear it."

"I don't need to—"

"Swear it. Please." He reached out his hand, desperate for this assurance.

She studied it before clasping it with her own, sealing the oath. "I swear to do my duty."

Relief flooded him as he prepared for the end. Soon, it would all be over, and he'd rejoin Rianne in the peaceful gardens beyond the veil of death. Only a few short hours separated him from finding her again. His fears poured out of him as he settled into the acceptance of his fate.

Nesryn stared into the trees. "You may feel done with this world, but I have a feeling the world isn't done with you."

He chuckled darkly, feeling madness prickling the edges of his mind. "After we save the Queensblood, I'm done with it." He caught her gaze. "You were right, before. This world makes monsters of us all."

SINS, ALLIES, ENEMIES

CHAPTER FIVE

1152 N.T.C. The namesake capital city of Avyllon.

Bone runes tumbled through Aurienne's shaking fingers before she released them onto her carved altar. The runes landed in spiraling patterns, promising chaos and bloodshed, but also hope. Not all was lost then. Rodarri was vital to defeating the emperor and surviving the Darkling Prophecy, and Aurienne's intuition told her that Rianne was the key. If only Rhydian and Theo could get there in time.

She prayed telling them wasn't a mistake. The dark oily smudge on her aura nearly had her hesitate to send them straight into the heart of such danger, but she knew Theo would never forgive her if she didn't give his friend his best chance at saving the woman he loved. It was a leap of faith that her goddess would ensure it all worked out.

The bones in her hand ached. Rubbing them idly, she exhaled, trying to ignore the throbbing of her ribs and the stitches tugging at her arm. She glanced toward the mirror across the room, eyes searching for the bruises under the concealing powder on her neck.

Aurienne's divination cards rattled in their spelled box, bringing her attention back to her altar. She removed the cards, flipping through the deck before coming to stop at The Dead Queen. On its face, a woman with silver hair wore a crown of roses and held a great sword.

Who could this be?

She'd assumed it was Rianne, but the silver hair and icy expression on the card didn't match the Queensblood at all.

Golden ink trickled out from a wound on the figure's neck and smeared onto Aurienne's skin. Aurienne rolled the ink between her fingers. A dark portent. Her heart sank as the figure dropped to her knees before falling into a ravine on the face of the card. They hadn't made it. Rianne was dead.

"My life for theirs," Aurienne whispered—thinking back on the horrible vision.

I know how that feels.

She bowed her head. "I'm sorry your fate couldn't be changed."

Taking in a deep breath, Aurienne slipped The Dead Queen back into the deck. She stared at the blazing fire in her room, searching for answers on every ember. Her heart was numb. Even at their first meeting, Aurienne knew Rianne's fate was to die. The magic of that place, the deep tradition of the ascension, and the power of the curse was too great. Rianne had known it too.

While many futures *might* come to pass, once fate settled upon a person, there was no escape. Aurienne's own fate was the same. She was destined to lose this war, destined never to love, and now her soul was doomed unless she found a way to remove the stain from the spirit necromancy. All fates she couldn't escape any more than

Rianne could have been freed from the Queensblood curse. All of Rianne's paths had always led back to an ascension.

Goddess—by the end of this war, will we all be dead?

She removed The King card—the one currently representing Theo. He swung his glowing sword, wearing a serious expression. She touched her lips to the card before pressing it to her forehead.

Please be safe. And please don't hate me.

In the few days since the summit, they'd danced around the tension building between them. Did he resent her for forcing the crown upon him? Did he know she would die to protect him? Would it matter?

She gingerly placed the card back in the deck and returned it to the spelled box before rubbing her throbbing hand. The broken bones hadn't mended yet; none of her injuries had fully healed even with Master Healer Elianna's daily ministrations. She shuddered, desperately trying to push thoughts of the attack away and failing. She bore the marks of these past days on her mind and body and soul.

The knife driving into the meat of her arm.

The icy water rushing up her nose.

The hands upon her neck.

The fists on her body.

Crunching of bones and oozing blood.

The walls began to close in on her. The quiet was deafening. The loneliness crushing. She had to see someone, anyone. Stumbling, she rushed to the door of her chambers and flung it open just a few inches.

Sentinel Kolten immediately straightened. "Are you alright?"

She swallowed. "Yes. Thank you."

Closing the door, she leaned against it, still panting. Her cards rattled in their box again, frantically slamming against the lid.

Stillness settled over the evening. Her heart fluttered against her chest bone.

Goddess protect me.

Whispers filled her chambers. Three voices whispering over the top of one another again and again, reciting her birth prophecy—the darkling souls prophecy.

> *One thousand stars fly as souls unearthed.*
> *The monsters of old roam the earth.*
> *Seer's visions condemn the Darkling War,*
> *Against the enemy from distant shore.*
> *Four pillars lost and the fifth lost by Fate.*
> *Darkened skies fill with howling hate.*
> *The fate of the world hangs by moon's light.*
> *Darkling Souls fight, darkling souls die.*

Visions of battle slammed into her as her soul was dragged from her body into the spectral realm. Steel clashed against steel, sending sparks flying. Theo's dark gleaming sword and Nesryn's starlight sword cut into monsters. The stars were certainly flying.

It was all coming true. The beasts from nightmare stalked across the golden fields encircling Avyllon. Shadows. Mooncursed. Stone giants. Wyrms. Worse. Monsters of old. Her visions condemned the war already, because she sure hadn't been able to save them yet. Enemy from distant shore was Demorra. She'd always wondered whether it would be Arryn or another nation—but their enemy was now clear. The skies were dark with vampires now, making that line true.

But the pillars? What did it mean? Four pillars. A building? Some ancient site that held the key to their salvation or destruction? A metaphor? Were the pillars people? Five heroes to save them? The five nations on the continent?

Aurienne rubbed her temples as the whispers quieted and she returned to her slumped body. She'd wanted to ask Nesryn more about her birth prophecy, but after the summit the elf had vanished.

She pressed her palms against the cool stone floor, trying to steady herself. The emperor would be coming for them all soon, and she'd just sent their savior to Rodarri. And now that Theo and Rhydian tried to stop the ascension, would King Cavendar break the alliance? They needed all five nations of the continent, of that she was sure. A united front was the only way they could survive the might of the empire bearing down on them.

She sighed, heart heavy, as she drew her legs against her chest and rested her chin on her knees. The little red fox crept over the balusters of her balcony to sit beside her, wrapping its tail around its paws. She reached over to stroke its fur, seeking comfort from her companion as she searched the haunting images.

The answer was right there, hidden in her visions, the readings, and the prophecy. If only she knew how to unlock them. Though barely five weeks passed since the Foretelling Rite and nothing was the same, she felt no closer to the answer she sought. Shifting futures, clouded visions, and a failing body thwarted her every effort.

Phantom howls and beating wings echoed. Her head snapped up, rubbing the chills racing down her arms. She'd seen the Moon-cursed attack on the caravan, watched helplessly as the fang and claw tore into her friends. And much worse was on its way to them, Shadows and behemoths and forgotten creatures, if the prophecy and her Foretelling Rite visions were right—and they always were.

Teridar's only protection from those twisted beasts were even darker creatures, whose hunger for blood was unmatched.

Will our own sins, our allies, or our enemies rip us apart first?

Night's Hunger

Chapter Six

The hunter stepped into the night unbound.
He slipped into the dark abyss and drowned.

— Kassia Lora Guara, witch of Wildewood,
divination card reading.

1152 N.T.C. The Hunger's Teeth Mountains, near the Terre Isthmus.

Mooncursed blood dripped from Stellan's vampiric claws, and he stopped to lick the black ichor before it fell to the trampled mud. A shudder ran through him at the divine taste. Narrowing his eyes at the snarling Mooncursed limping toward him and gnashing its serrated teeth, he tilted his head. The titan ore plates screwed into the creature's rib cage scraped against the pebbles as it crawled over the ridge.

Stellan sucked the blood from the end of his claw, savoring every drop. He'd sworn to his last remaining kin, Miella, that he'd protect her homeland against the beasts from the Darkling Prophecy. A task he relished as it permitted him and the thousand vampires bound to him to drink sinful blood without limit. After a millennium in self-imposed prison, their hunger was endless. He'd sworn to protect his family from the Shadows all those years ago, and now magic of the Shadows was back in new form. Twisted, misshapen hybrids of man, wolf, and other creatures—the Mooncursed prowled the edges of Teridar. Throughout the valley, hundreds of vampires were locked in their own battles, bound to his oath. Hundreds more battled across the continent.

Pausing, he brushed a spec of dirt from his silken shirt before inspecting a small tear the beast had pierced into the luxurious fabric. A growl escaped his lips. The beast would die for its transgression.

The sparse trees peppering the slopes echoed with Mooncursed snarls as the night skies darkened with a horde of leathery, vampiric wings—Stellan's kin. Several paces away, Julietta snapped the spine of her own foe.

Stabbing pain speared through Stellan's side, and his head whipped toward a distant peak near the isthmus. One of his kin, Tomas, was in trouble. He could feel it through the curse bond. Leaping forward, Stellan snapped the Mooncursed's neck and tossed its body down the incline without even stopping to siphon the lifeblood.

Unfurling his wings, he took to the skies, following the source of his pain. Over a thousand vampires emerged from their self-imposed prison just weeks ago—and he knew the pain of every single one. Shooting through the clouds, he was joined by others racing to defend their kin.

Then he saw them. Over a dozen creatures snapped at a lone vampire, ripping his flesh with each lunge. Tomas tore the throat from a Mooncursed beast, but another clamped down on his arm and wrenched him away. He spun and clawed at him, but another slashed his back to the spine. Three leapt on Tomas, sinking their fangs into his bronzed flesh. His gleaming blond hair vanished as the Mooncursed piled on top of him, leather armor and silken shirt disappearing beneath fur and fangs.

Stellan beat his wings, the muscles in his back hissing in agony as the ligaments threatened to snap. He wouldn't let those mongrels take one of his from him. They were his responsibility. His charges. It was his fault they were cursed, and he had to protect them.

Stellan swore in a long-forgotten language. Tomas shouldn't have been alone. They never hunted alone. Another few seconds, and he'd reach him—and the Mooncursed wretches would perish under his hatred.

With a shout, Tomas yanked his claws from a Mooncursed's mouth and slashed its neck to the bone. He sank his teeth into the neck of the one biting his arm. Another beast slashed at his chest, and crimson blood oozed through his leather armor. A Mooncursed lunged at him from the shadows, and Tomas knocked it across the clearing.

"Tomas!" Stellan snarled, tucking his wings in tight and diving toward the carnage.

Tomas looked up, onyx eyes gleaming. Another snap of something in his spine, and the anger fell away. Only peace remained for a split second. Tomas disappeared beneath a dozen beasts in a frenzy of fang and claw.

"No!" Stellan roared.

At the last second, close enough he could smell the coppery tang of blood, Stellan unfurled his wings and beat three times. The power of the burst knocked Mooncursed flying. But Tomas was gone. Not enough remained of Tomas to reform and heal. They'd eaten him and dragged away the pieces.

"Tomas!" his cousin, Erelia, cried—falling to her knees.

Stellan pivoted slowly as the other vampires landed all around him.

"Kill them all and bring me the pieces of Tomas." Stellan's voice was hardly a whisper, but it filled the clearing with hate.

The vampires turned on the Mooncursed, attacking with renewed viciousness. Howls and yelps filled the air as they avenged their brother. Julietta, who never strayed far from Stellan's side, ripped a smaller Mooncursed in half. Its spine dangled for a second before she threw it to the others. She threw her head back, howling in delight.

Mooncursed and vampire clashed under a gleaming moon. Half a dozen Mooncursed had died, and another half dozen monstrously large wolfish creatures battled on. A long, shrill howl pierced the night, and without even a moment's hesitation, the beasts turned and ran.

The vampires paused, tilting their heads toward the beating of paws heading northeast. The crackling air signaled magic in the air. The Mooncursed were retreating out of the mountains, down the foothills, and across the isthmus. As one, the bloodied vampires turned toward Stellan.

Four vampires crept closer, laying out chewed pieces of Tomas. Erelia rested her hands upon the gory remnants of their kin, of her brother. Bloody tears wetted her cheeks, as understanding passed between them. The head and heart were still missing. Stellan's shriveled heart pounded as his fangs ached for blood to sate the blackened rage poisoning his veins.

"Bury the pieces," he ordered tightly. "He won't return to us."

Stellan flexed his claws as the others dug into the hard-packed earth. Dirt churned upward as the grave deepened, releasing the scents of rotting vermin, worms, and decomposing leaves. The vampires crawled out of the hole.

"I shall lay him to rest," Stellan said, stepping inside.

Gently, he gathered up the pieces and returned them to the land. He rested his long claws atop Tomas' shredded chest.

I'm sorry for bringing this curse to us. I'm sorry for your pain and that I couldn't protect you. Yet, I am so thankful your fight is over.

Climbing out, he choked on his rage as the others buried the pieces of their companion. It had to be worth it. Even losing precious kin was worth ensuring that Miella was protected. Ancient oaths were sworn to protect their bloodlines, and Miella was his last remaining descendant. He might've failed as a husband and father, but he would keep his promises now.

Stellan's eyes narrowed toward the retreating wolflike-beasts. They'd taken one of his vampires from him. The second to fall in this war.

He watched the creatures run in an unwavering straight line. What had called them back? They fought wildly until death consumed them, so what could control them? Why did they retreat?

Crouching, he lunged into the sky and beat his wings hard to glide over the fleeing Mooncursed. Over the past nights, he'd noticed that they weren't attacking villages, they were running scouting formations.

What are you looking for, mongrels?

Sensing dawn's approach, Stellan landed on a foggy mountain peak bordering the isthmus land bridge to the empire, watching the beasts disappear in the distance. The first fingers of sun lightened the sky, and Stellan backed into a cave. There he waited.

Julietta landed at the mouth of the cave and crept inside. "Tomas is dead."

"I know," he said.

"Why are we doing this for a girl you don't even know?" Julietta gnashed her teeth and dragged her claws through the stone walls. "She's not your daughter. She's a distant relative who barely even shares your blood. We just lost one of our own today. For *them*. The emperor isn't a threat to *us*. We could feed from both sides as the war rages on. We could fly to another land and leave this all behind. So why are we here?"

"We made an oath, Julietta. We became this to protect our families, and however distant, she is our family." He waved his hand toward the surrounding lands. "They'll all die if we don't fight their monsters for them."

Julietta scoffed. "That oath died a long time ago. By betraying us, they turned us into this forever, so now we owe them nothing. You don't have to risk our lives again for people who don't appreciate it. Why cling to the past?"

"We're dead in the ways that matter," he replied. "Our families are all that's left of everything we loved. Miella's not my daughter, but she is my lineage, my legacy. Once that's gone, it's like we never existed. Everything we did will have been for nothing."

"How many more of us will die to fulfill your need for penance?" Her voice was a hiss as she backed deeper into the cave.

Julietta leapt to the ceiling, locking her claws to the stalactites, before wrapping her wings around herself in a leathery cocoon. Erelia and two others joined them. Stellan waited for the hell of daylight.

As dawn broke, Stellan's bloodlust dulled into a distant and painful memory. It should have been a reprieve from endless hunger, but what came next was worse. Humanity returned during his waking daylight hours, reminding him of what he'd once been all those years ago.

The rays of sun were invisible claws, shredding the dark impulses away. He roared and wrapped his wings around himself tighter. The urge to retch nearly overtook him, but he weakly managed to flee to the empty abyss in his mind.

Images of shattered skulls, spurting blood, and dismembered limbs hammered at the walls of his mental prison. He saw every face, heard every scream. Even here, he could taste their fear, sins, and hopes. The last beat of his victims' heart thrummed together in an unending melody of pain. The faces of family long dead, watching him with sadness.

I'm sorry.

Every sin encased him in guilt for the things he'd done each night. It never lasted. When day blurred into night, the hunger returned.

DESPERATE RESCUE
CHAPTER SEVEN

Her time was too short and her duty too great.

— UNKNOWN.

1152 N.T.C. Castle Rodarr, Rodarri.

The Warbringer, immortal elf, and future king of Avyllon crept through the secret passageway leading to the queens' chambers, dripping wet and covered in strands of slimy green moss from their climb up the drainage tunnels.

Rhydian knew this maze of deserted passages inside the castle walls all too well, having traversed them often in his secret trysts with Rianne. Nesryn held up her hand, stilling them. She tilted her head to listen through the walls with supernatural senses. She motioned them forward with a flick of her gray camouflaged hand, and they continued through the dust and cobwebs. It'd taken most of the night to formulate a plan and sneak into the castle. With dawn nearly upon them, they were running out of time to save Jordyn from her ascension.

"Here," Rhydian whispered.

He pointed to the bookcase doorway he and Rianne frequented, and immediately his heart twisted. Phantom sounds of Rianne's skirts swishing against the stone floors haunted him.

"Are you okay?" Theo whispered.

Rhydian gritted his teeth, fighting the cursed urge to slam his friend's head into the wall. The edges of his vision bled crimson again. Nesryn would have to make good on her promise soon.

He shook his head, trying to clear the boiling hiss from his ears. "I'm fine."

Nesryn mumbled something under her breath.

Ignoring her, Rhydian unlatched the door and pushed it open. First light reached into the passageway. He glanced around, checking the normal posts for guards, and found none. The guards must still be searching for him or posted at the Courtyard of Queens. They wouldn't have left the queens unattended and roaming free. Which means they had to have barred the doors from the outside, locking all the queens inside this wing. He slipped out from behind the book-case, with Theo and Nesryn on his heels, and crept down the hall toward the sitting areas and wading pools. Quiet conversation from just over a hundred Queensblood drifted from behind the many sheer curtains.

A group of children huddled in a corner, holding toys that none of them played with. They whispered to one another, wondering if they'd soon join Rianne. Serious conversations were being held by a group of older women who stood near the foun-tains. Those who were Rianne's age didn't speak at all; they embroidered in silence, trying to distract themselves from the inevitable. If Rhydian didn't help them, any one of Rianne's rela-tives could be next.

He stepped around a veil and saw Rianne's aunt, Yllicea, talking in low tones with another of the oldest queens, Tamiira. Both wore opulent gowns in shades of mourning black, their gray hair twisted into long braids. Their blue eyes were swollen and puffy.

"Rhydian?" Yllicea stood, recognizing the longtime Queens-guard. "Oh Rhydian... I volunteered to go for Rianne, I... They... I..."

Rhydian placed a comforting hand on her frail shoulder. "I promised Rianne I would come for you all. I wish I'd done it sooner, but I'm keeping my promise to her now. We have a way out of the castle through the passages."

"We tried escaping before and the guards caught us at the tree line and dragged us back. We... we can't make it."

"You didn't have us before. This—" he gestured to Nesryn, "is Grimfall."

Yllicea's eyes widened. "The story... Shadows rise as grim falls. Death to one. Death to all."

"An elf," another queen whispered.

Nesryn scowled but spoke in that lilting voice with the edge of a titanium dagger, "I promised Rhydian I would help free you. The guards will not be a problem this time."

Yllicea swallowed and glanced at Tamiira.

"I'll succumb to my curse if I have to. You're leaving. Tonight. All of you," Rhydian said.

He didn't have time for this hesitance. They had to go now. He opened his mouth but Nesryn beat him to it.

Nesryn spoke quietly, "You just have to be brave."

Yllicea's expression hardened. "For Rianne."

Rhydian glanced around. "Where's Jordyn?"

"They took her," young Ella said.

Rhydian studied the eight-year-old's face, so young and hopeful. Too young to witness and endure what she had. Poisonous guilt darkened his blood, and he nearly cursed. He was complicit in these crimes. Why hadn't he seen the truth earlier? He should've freed them all the first day he stepped foot in this haunted place.

Rhydian glanced around at the several dozen queens gathering and peering at him from behind pillars. Each one was Rianne's kin, born for death. Adorned. Pampered. Caged. This was his only chance to set right the wrongs he too allowed.

"We're leaving," he announced. "All of us. We'll take the tunnels. Grab what you can, we leave now."

Queens raced to their rooms, wrapping babies in swaddling blankets and fur. Rhydian offered help where he could, holding tiny babies in his massive arms as the mothers gathered what they could carry. Toddlers clung to his legs, and he murmured soothing words to them.

Faces pale, Queens wrapped strips torn from shawls and blankets around their slippers, likely from having been acquainted with the cruel landscape outside their home during their last attempt. The last attempt Rhydian had known nothing about.

By the gods.

He realized that was why King Cavendar refused to allow him to speak with Rianne at the summit last week. The fat fool didn't want Rhydian discovering what had occurred in his absence.

Glancing down, he was caught in the wide-eyed stares of the children clinging to him.

One way or another, the ascensions ended today.

Around him, the queens hefted blankets filled with food and jewels, and within minutes they met Nesryn at the bookcase entrance. He handed off the children, helping them into the passages that snuck through the castle.

Rhydian glanced across the chaos, feeling torn between going after Jordyn and ensuring they all made it out.

"You go for Jordyn," Theo said, clapping Rhydian on the back.

Rhydian gripped his friend's shoulder, unable to express his gratitude.

"The secret passages go past the ravine on the way to the outer walls, and Nesryn and Theo will take you to the woods," Rhydian said to the queens. "I'll get Jordyn on the way out and meet you."

"I should stay with you, Warbringer, in case," the elf whispered.

"Get them to safety first, please. Then..." He felt the pleading in his eyes.

Nesryn grimaced before licking the points of her predatory teeth. Finally, she nodded.

"We don't have much time, her ascension was set for dawn," Yllicea said, alarm painting her words.

With a final look back, he tore ahead of them through tunnels leading toward the Courtyard of Queens. The crowd above was a steady hum filling the narrow corridor that shook the walls. Reaching the secret entrance to the amphitheater, he cracked the door and peered out from beneath.

The high seating surrounded the jagged ravine just beside the executioner's dais. The center of the Courtyard was dusty dirt, and bloodroses grew over the walls and ramparts. Then he saw her. Jordyn's hands were bound behind her, and she struggled against three guards holding her before the dais.

"No! I won't go." Jordyn screamed.

A guard kicked the back of her legs, and she fell to her knees. They held her down as she elbowed and twisted in their grips. A guard gripped the back of her head and pressed it against the block.

"No!" She squirmed.

We're out of time.

Hearing commotion behind him, Nesryn, Theo, and the fleeing queens crouched in the courtyard to the entrance of the deserted tunnels, soothing crying babies, and peering through peepholes to the courtyard. Rhydian pressed his hand against the door.

"Head toward the forest," Rhydian said. "Don't wait for me."

Rhydian hefted his sword and charged across the courtyard.

The executioner faced the ravine with lifted hands. "Arise, our queen arise."

Rhydian's vision turned crimson. Godless bastards. They were his now.

Guards shouted the alarm, but Rhydian had nearly reached Jordyn. Rhydian cracked his hilt into the first guard's face, and he dropped like a stone. The second drew his sword on Rhydian, but he'd already thrown a punch that sent the man tumbling across the stones. Jordyn wriggled free of the third and was running toward the door to the secret passage. Rhydian kicked the man's knee with a sickening crunch, twisting it, and the man fell screaming against the block.

"Run!" Rhydian shouted.

He charged after Jordyn who stopped short with a dozen guards blocking her way to the now-open door. Inside the passage, queens screamed. In his haste, Rhydian had failed to fully close the door—and guards had swarmed inside and were already dragging queens out.

No.

Theo hacked with his steel sword at the guards, and behind him Nesryn disappeared in the darkness of the tunnels. A guard caught Jordyn and dragged her away from the door, screaming.

"Kingshit," Rhydian cursed.

The red veil fully descended over his sight, and his blood sang. Rhydian charged forward, slashing his sword at Jordyn's captors. He railed against his urges, buying time.

No death wounds yet.

Wait 'til she's free.

Shallow cuts.

His curse whispered for more. He hacked off a man's hand, and Jordyn shot away from him. She turned, and Rhydian sliced the rope on her hands. Jordyn picked up a fallen soldier's sword and held it awkwardly, though her expression solidified to stone. A warrior's heart, just like her sister.

Nesryn stepped out of the tunnel, eyeing Rhydian darkly, dragging three guards out behind her. She rolled them into the arena with a twist of her hand and three broken bodies went sprawling, the men groaning in pain, but not lethally harmed. Theo peered over her shoulder, scarlet stained blade aloft.

Dozens of guards poured from the castle, sprinting for them. Rhydian caught Nesryn's cold gray gaze, tracking the firm set of her mouth. He knew she'd protect the queens.

"Not a bad day to die," Rhydian mouthed to her.

He faced the approaching guards and stepped in front of Jordyn. "Go with them," he murmured, twirling his blade.

The Warbringer settled into the familiar stance, readying himself for madness. His mind, for a second, went faraway. He and Rianne were in the garden before he left with the Avyllon caravan. Lazy afternoon rays of sun danced between the trees. Rianne sat on a blanket beside him weaving a crown of wildflowers. She smiled and reached over to touch his face.

She whispered, "I love you. I wish all our days were like this." He felt the whisper of her lips against his. "If my time on the world has to be short, I want every second of it with you."

Then she was gone, and he was staring down an army of soldiers seeking to execute her sister.

"I will die happy knowing I spent every second I could loving you," he whispered back to the memory.

Swords clanged. Metal screeched. As the first four reached him, they were sent rolling backward into the others. More followed. Rhydian gave the first a boot to the chest and dropped to his knees. The crowds cheered and booed. The king was shouting something lost to the din of the amphitheater.

Rhydian spun away, parrying one man's sword toward the other. He whirled his blade in a wicked circle, driving six more back. They rounded him warily, while more raced toward them. He was surrounded.

"Arise, our queen, arise," the executioner intoned. "The Queensblood protect Rodarri with their blood or their blade—as they have for centuries. If you will bless us with your return, arise."

Rhydian snapped a spear in half, smashing the guard in the chest. He hurled the metal-tipped end, and it pinned another guard to the ground screaming. Rhydian dodged an arrow, picked it from the ground and hurled it back. It sank into a man's shoulder. He twirled his sword, waiting for the next charge.

"Arise, our queen, arise."

The guards, one by one, looked over his shoulder and stopped their advance, freezing in their tracks.

Swords fell.

Mouths dropped.

Crowds quieted.

A heavy hush descended upon the crowd as a deathly chill filled the air with needles. Theo lowered his sword, and Nesryn's expression hardened. The queens shuffled out of the passageway with expressions of horror at the ravine behind him. Babies cried. A queen screamed and fainted. Jordyn gasped.

Rhydian sensed predatory eyes on his spine, and the hairs on the back of his neck stood up. He slowly turned toward the ravine, and his Warbringer blood froze at the ghastly sight that was the inspiration for his nightmares to come.

Rianne was crawling out of the ravine.

RETURNED

CHAPTER EIGHT

They held her down, cut off her head.
No longer living, but not yet dead.

— *THE BALLAD OF THE QUEENSBLOOD.*

1152 N.T.C. The Courtyard of Queens at Castle Rodarr, Rodarri.

Death folded around Rianne; drank in everything that she was and took it for its own. All her pain and loss and fear disappeared. Soon her passing joys and fleeting moments of happiness evaporated. Memories were ripped away as angry souls invaded.

Silence. Utter darkness. Nothingness. Oblivion.

Pain.

Nothing.

The hint of light behind a shadow then darkness. Numb silence floating in a void. A faraway echo of a roaring crowd at the hint of the edges of her mind. Then silence. Time didn't exist. She floated in a sea of memories.

Twirling dresses spinning in the grand ballrooms.
Bloodwitches chanting curses in the dead of night.
Secret doors opening and closing.
Queens wielding swords in a burning castle.
The fall of executioners' blades upon pale necks.

The memories all faded, and she felt her grasp on them slipping. She struggled to hold on to herself in the crushing gloom. Silver eyes blinked at her.

Nothing.

Nothing.

Nothing.

Still nothing. It may have been just a second and it may have been an eternity. A dim light faded in and out. Then back to darkness and timelessness and absence. Consciousness was at the edge of her grasp. Existence was just there, beyond the next shadow. Undeath and rebirth came together into a flow of power that combusted and filled the pit.

Thousands of bones were illuminated by the nightmarish powers circling her broken body. Glowing silver energy pulled the broken pieces of her back together and fused them with hellfire. The spirits slithered into her.

If she could feel pain, she would have screamed. Such sensations and emotions were lost to her though.

Underneath the numbness, Rianne knew only rage.

The voices of the other queens spoke to her softly. Before, Rianne would have been terrified at the whispers of the ghosts, but she now knew better. They had been guiding her all along—to her destiny.

There's nothing to fear, not anymore.

Rianne sat up, she turned her head, testing the tenuous connections returning her head to her body. She made a fist, and the bones cracked. The whispers returned, but now, their names were known to her.

The first Queensblood Vittoria spoke in her mind, *"You're needed. You must protect our people. From the Darkling Prophecy. From kings and emperors. From gods. You must protect the people from the greatest threat they've ever known, avenge us, and then set our sisters on the right path before you're done."*

Three tasks. Rianne clung to them with everything she had. Protect the people. Avenge the queens. End the ascensions. So simple, and yet so difficult to accomplish.

Rianne's mother Charlotte spoke next, *"We'll stay with you. We'll give you the strength."*

Nataylia added, *"You'll never be alone again."*

Rianne's mind swam as the barrage of queens threatened to overwhelm her. So many names, emotions, memories—swallowing up all the pieces of her. She looked up to the sliver of light so far above.

And began to climb.

Her newly reawakened flesh strained against the effort, having lost the warmth and vigor of life. A part of her mind noted the effort, but she didn't feel the pain. Death had a way of turning off everything that was unnecessary. Pain, fear, and doubt were all needless—so they were gone.

The sun had risen again, and the crowds were assembling in the amphitheater around the pit, waiting for the sun to reach its zenith. Waiting for her to stay dead like all the other queens before, believing her blood would replenish the land and her death would protect them.

Rosalindt hissed, *"They were wrong."*

"Arise, our queen, arise," the executioner intoned.

Rianne climbed the sheer walls of the pit, one clawed grip at a time toward the blinding light. Her nails chipped and broke, her hair caught on the gnarled roots, and her grasp slipped more than once—but she climbed until she made her way out of hell.

Crowds cheered. Swords clanged. Queens screamed. Blood spilled to the ravenous stones.

"Arise, our queen, arise," he repeated.

She did.

The returned Queen Rianne pulled herself up from the pit and stepped out into the harsh light. Cold sun illuminated the deep red stains on the once-white dress. Her hair whipped in the wind filling the amphitheater. She caught a silver lock, rolling it through her pale fingers. Death had sucked the color from her body, and the queens that resurrected her filled her with silver essence.

The crowd was silent. They had cheered for her death, but now watched her resurrection still as ghosts.

Her glassy eyes cataloged the people in the courtyard. She burned each face into her memory. Taking a step forward, her own spilled blood from yesterday stuck to her bare feet.

"Your queen has returned," she said.

Silence.

If not for the steady beating of her own reanimated heart and the wind rustling the execution banners, she could be back in that emptiness of death. Their horrified stares roamed over her broken and bloody body. She raised her chin. Let them look at what she'd overcome.

When she died, she didn't understand what it meant to be married to her people. Now, it made sense. Everything made sense. Any emotions she once felt were gone. Any love she once had was gone. She felt neither happiness nor sadness, neither guilt nor shame. Rianne felt herself already slipping away. She was here for one purpose—to protect her people.

"My death will not protect you. I will," she said, voice rough and foreign.

The crowd gaped at the blood dripping from her dress and at the long, jagged scar across her throat. She lifted her chin to allow them the sight of their handiwork: skin parted to show blood and bone and sinew.

"Rianne?" Rhydian asked.

She turned. Rhydian and Jordyn waited near the swung open painted rock doorway to the secret passages. She glanced toward the crack in the wall where the other queens spilled out. Theo was next to them wearing an expression Rianne catalogued as disbelief. In the early hours of mourning, her friends plotted to save her family, and her family whispered about the sins of sacrificing their daughters. Their heroism meant nothing. She'd died all the same.

A flash of red caught her attention, a red fox creeping through the bloodrose vines beside the Queensblood. She spotted another figure holding a glowing sword near groaning, wounded soldiers.

Returned queen, Rebekkah, snarled, *"Grimfall."*

Samantah spat, *"What is that infernal elf doing here?"*

Morgana said, *"How did she find us so quickly?"*

"We'll deal with the elf later," Milah ordered. *"We must show them our strength. Get cleaned up so they remember they're dealing with a queen."*

So many voices all speaking at once, yet Rianne knew each one so well.

Milah whispered, *"Red is a better reminder of what you've become and how. You're the one who will avenge us and set us all free. You're the strongest of us, and you can afford to show no weakness in the days to come. You must be a pillar of strength."*

Rianne pointed to a fearful attendant, feeling Milah speaking through her. "You, bring me red to wear. I won't wear black like the other returned queens mourning their stolen lives. I mourn nothing."

King Cavendar came down the stairs huffing and wheezing. "You've returned!"

The bloodwitch, Whillow, said, *"That tired old king."*

Rianne turned her cold gaze upon him and strolled through the bloody mud toward him. If she—they—felt anything since dying, it was anger and was directed at the kings.

"How fortunate we are to have an ascended queen to advise us," he stammered.

Whillow's hate for the king threaded her icy tone. *"The fear in his voice... An old relic who's in our way."*

"Rianne?" Rhydian called from across the amphitheater.

A splinter of her snapped awake, searching, yearning to find Rhydian. Her eyes flicked in his direction. The desire was drowned by the numbness, and her focus settled back upon Cavendar.

The king, that old fool, continued to babble on. "We are so grateful of your sacrifice and honored at your return. Please tell me, what I, as your king, can do."

Nicollete's voice pushed to the forefront. *"He's trying to maintain his position as king. He would do anything to keep from losing his precious power. We've been back moments, and he plotted to keep Rianne from what was hers."*

Whispers grew from the crowds around them.

Whillow's bloodmagic pulsed in Rianne's veins. *"Forgiveness is weakness."*

The king's throat bobbed. "What can I do?"

Nicollete's bloodlust tanged copper in Rianne's mouth. *"Do it, Rianne. Put him down."*

Rianne's own memories sealed his fate. The smell of leather and hound filled Rianne's nostrils. The cinched strap on her face, pinching her skin. The blade driving into her thigh. His wine-drunk breath on her face. The flash of a dagger at Jordyn's ribs. The satisfied smile as she laid her head upon the block.

"You can die," Rianne said coldly.

The old king's mouth dropped open.

The souls of two bloodwitches, Safyrah and Noxanya, swirled through Rianne's arm and reached toward the ravine. Sharpened shards of bones flew to her in answer to their ancient magics.

The bones slammed into her hand, forming a terrible broadsword made from the bones of sacrificed queens.

Queen Vittoria studied it, swinging it once, then twice testing its perfect balance. Rianne might not have known how to wield a sword, but the warrior queens whispering in her mind certainly did.

They gave her the strength she lacked in life to avenge the things she'd had to endure. The endless parties parading around in front of the noblemen like prizes ripe for the taking. The scorn and glares and hungry gazes. Being beaten for speaking up, muzzled for refusing to be silenced. The dagger through her leg for trying to run. Every injustice she'd had to suffer. All those lives lost because alone, they could not break free. But now—together—they would right every last wrong.

"The land hungers for the blood you promised," she said. "Yours will do."

She swung. The bonesword sang through the air and freed the old king's head from his shoulders. Blood sprayed upward and pooled darkly upon the ground. Whillow kicked his head toward the ravine, where it disappeared into hell.

She raised her chin toward the amphitheater. "I give you my blood and my blade."

Rianne released the bonesword. Flying, it reformed into a skeletal bodice around her bloodied funeral lace, awaiting her summons.

To her people, she said, "I will protect you from the coming evils. I swear it to you on my life and on my death. Now, bow before your queen."

Blood magic of dead queens sparked in her fingertips. A burst of wind flung twirling bloodroses toward Rianne. Gilded bones from the ravine twined through the roses on her brow forming a harrowing rosebone crown.

As one, the crowd hit its knees. "Long live the risen queen!"

SHIFTING TRUTHS

CHAPTER NINE

Arise, our queen, arise.

— ASCENSION CEREMONY CALL TO RETURN.

1152 N.T.C. Castle Rodarr, Rodarri.

Death stilled the noise, the feelings, the sensations. Distantly, Rianne was aware of the sliding of freshly sewn fabric over her skin, of the bone corset snapping into place against her ribs, and the pinning of her now-silver hair into a long braid. Attendants fluttered around her, their faces a blur. She glanced toward the tall, thin windows letting in gray light—to where the darkness of the ravine called to her. The threads of the curse reached for her like crimson vines.

"Let me in." Rhydian's voice echoed in the halls outside her new office.

"Sir, the queen has given instructions not to be disturbed," a courtier said.

Rianne's gaze settled upon the door.

Milah's ruthless spirit flared within Rianne. *"You need to let him go now. It'll be easier for him that way."*

Rianne winced.

Nicollete's familiar coppery distrust slithered through her bones. *"Don't let him go. He's a powerful weapon to keep in your arsenal."*

"He's a good man and he deserves better," Rianne protested. *"I'm not using him. I'm going to dismiss him, to send him away."*

Rosalindt cut in. *"You have a duty. We brought you back for a reason, and he's just a distraction."*

Milah retorted, *"Not a distraction if he's useful."*

Rianne silenced them with a wave of willpower, *"I will do as I see fit."*

The queens hissed.

Rianne said aloud, *"You're not in control."*

As one, the queens replied, *"Not yet."*

A shudder ran down her spine, laced with fear.

I need to protect him from them.

Already she felt less herself. All emotions were dulled. All feelings smothered under a bubbling pit of rage. Keeping him around would only cause him pain. Would only risk his life and soul. Sending him away would break whatever was left of her.

Rhydian's tone was low and deep. "You don't want to stand in my way."

"Sir, please." The courtier's voice shook. "She will summon you when she is ready."

"I will see her."

"When she wants you to."

Theo's voice cut through the growing din in the hall. "Rhydian, she's alive. Give her a moment. Let's go for a walk."

Footsteps carried them away.

Rianne's sadness bled into the rage of the queens. The fading parts of her wanted nothing more than to run into his arms. She held onto those parts with everything she had as a reminder of who she was.

Her brain registered each bit of information and stored it for use later, but it was detached—like feeling it through a thick veil. Perhaps the veil of life and death separated her from the feelings of the living. The only sensation she felt sharply was the rage of the queens, and sometimes bites of sadness from the part of her that was still Rianne.

She straightened the leather panels of the black and red gown and traced her fingers over the stitched Rodarri roses and the smooth curves of the bone corset—seeking all the little sensations, holding them in her mind, and trying her hardest to remember them. Focusing on the little details grounded her against the thousand whispering queens in her bones.

Waving the attendants away, she stood before the mirror underneath the glass panels containing the glowing Vittoria's gift lichen. Her hair had been brown before with only a single lock of silver from where Rosalindt touched it. Now it was entirely silver. Her skin was pale, and blue eyes faded. Her gaze dipped lower. The gaping wound at her neck hadn't fully closed and white bone gleamed from within. She traced her fingers against the rough edges, wondering if it would ever heal.

"It'll distract the others," Milah said. *"Let them focus on the new queen you are."*

Rianne took a thick, black hair ribbon from her vanity and wrapped it over the wound. She'd commission some other necklace concealments to match her gowns, for *their* sake. She focused upon her tasks.

Protect the people.

Avenge the queens.

End the ascensions.

Now that she looked the part, to accomplish her goals she needed to hold conferences with the commanders, potential allies, and enemies. She needed to decide what to do about this invading emperor, and to do that, she needed more information. Speaking with Rhydian had to come first, as painful as it would be. It was for the best because nothing could distract her from her duty.

The frigid presence drifted away as the spirits stilled in her marrow. She placed her hand on the door and rested her forehead on the wood, summoning the strength to do what she must do. She knew if she pulled too much from the queens, she'd lose herself entirely.

Rhydian hurried toward Rianne's newly claimed office. She'd left the amphitheater without so much as a second glance his way, and he'd been trying to get to her for over an hour. Frantic energy danced through his blood. Only Theo kept him from bringing the castle down again before Rianne summoned him.

Why hadn't she wanted to see me immediately? Why delay?

He had to get to her.

Nesryn stepped out of an alcove, appearing in his path and planting her feet to block the hall. Her dark, too-wide elven eyes bored into his soul, and the tips of her sharpened canines pressed into her lips thoughtfully. Her platinum hair hung down her back in a long braid, swinging past her hips. Her skin was gray—as if all the color had been drained—and patterned in the camouflage of a predator.

He froze, breath catching and the hairs on the back of his neck stood up in the suffocating presence of the hunter.

"Congratulations," she said, with an edge to her tone that he never got used to. "You managed to not kill anyone and avoided awakening your curse, so I don't have to kill you *yet*."

"You don't need to—I'm going to fight it, for her. You don't need to follow me." He swallowed.

"I'm sure you will fight it, and you'll still fail. Nothing has changed," she murmured.

He swallowed and glanced over her shoulder toward Rianne's office doors, needing to see her, needing to talk to her, to hold her.

Nesryn sidestepped into his vision. "She's not the same person you knew."

Rhydian's gaze dropped to the elf, and despite his trepidation, he snapped, "She was just executed. Beheaded. She died. Her soul went beyond the veil and came back, of course she's different. She's traumatized, but she's still Rianne."

He tried to edge around her, but she grabbed his arm.

"She is not the person you knew," the elf repeated.

Irritation growing in his throat, he tried to wrench his arm from her grasp, but it was like iron shackles.

He swallowed an angry grunt. "You see the worst in everyone."

"I warned you." She released her grip.

He ripped his arm away, flexing his hand.

"Warbringer." Her tone stopped him cold in his tracks as icy fingers of unease caressed the bones of his spine. "I've given you leeway with your words so far out of mercy for your curse, but everyone is responsible for what they say, and I have a temper, too. Mind yourself."

As he inhaled, an unnatural weight settled upon his shoulders, but he shook it off and continued down the hall. Quiet footsteps told him that she trailed him. Theo came around the corner at the same time, Adonis behind him. Adonis flinched and averted his gaze from Rhydian, a large purple bruise coloring his face.

Guilt punched Rhydian in the stomach. "Adonis..."

The young sorcerer stared at the ground as he turned back around the corner and fled.

Theo pursed his lips. "You need to make that right, Rhydian."

Rhydian nodded mutely, grinding his jaw. Adonis fled Avyllon in the middle of the night to do ancient intricate magic with no preparation, and in thanks Rhydian struck him for trying his best.

And Theo had been a stalwart friend, facing danger and death without blinking an eye, without a moment's hesitation. All while Rhydian *presumed* his friend would give up his life for him and nearly brought the castle down on their heads. Rhydian didn't deserve either of their friendships, and there'd be a reckoning with the High Seer for striking her brother.

"Rhydian," Rianne called from inside the office.

Rhydian stepped inside and with a final look toward Nesryn and Theo, he closed the doors.

He hurried to where she sat on the couch beside the desk, kneeled, and took her hands in his. "I thought I'd lost you—Rianne, gods, what happened? How is this possible?"

"I returned." Her voice sounded like glass cracking, nothing at all like the soft lilt he knew.

He pushed a rogue lock of silver hair from her face. Her skin was cold, and paler than before. Light blue eyes were now transformed to a swirling silver eddy that flashed sharply. No emotions crossed her face that usually bared every secret thought. She sat straighter, stiffer, when she had always been graceful and fluid as water. The terrible wound on her delicate neck hidden by a choker of black lace, answered questions he dared not ask.

"How?" he whispered.

She answered, "Queens ascend and replenish their land with their blood, or they return and protect it with their blade. Rodarri needs protecting from the Darkling War, so that is what I will do."

"*How* did you return?" he asked.

"The spirits of the ascended queens brought me back."

His brows pulled together, not understanding. "Rianne... I saw..."

She cut him off, "There is power down there, in the death and blood and bones. It brought my body back together and kept my soul from departing. I cannot explain more than that." Her tone was curt, and she kept glancing at the clock.

He held his breath and traced his fingers across her cheeks, once so rosy. His gaze dipped to her lace necklace again, concealing the horrors she endured. He saw it again. Her kneeling, looking to the sky, and lowering her head. The ax coming down, and everything falling away behind a red veil of rage. Grief and relief clashed inside his throat.

"I am so glad you're back. I'll keep my promise, I'll take you all away from here." He leaned forward to kiss her, and she pulled away.

"I don't want to leave."

Rhydian's blood turned to ice.

"The throne is now mine," she said. "I can protect my people best by serving as their true queen."

"Don't you want the life we talked about?"

"That was only ever to escape the fate I already endured." She placed her hands on his chest gently, not pushing away, but keeping space between them. "It cannot be as it was. The girl you loved is dead. I am only here to protect our people."

He took her hands in his, panic coursing through his veins. "But you're here."

Her lips worked, as if searching for words. "I am... but in death your eyes are opened. I remember everything, but I am in fog."

"That will go away. You've been through hell."

"I hope you're right." Her voice sharpened.

"If you are to be queen, I will serve at your side."

Rianne glanced away. "I'm not sure how much time I have. I'm not here, not really."

Rhydian stiffened. "Don't say that."

"I died," she said. "I can feel the changes creeping into these bones. I hear the ascended queens whispering in my mind. I know each by name."

His heart hammered. "I'll remind you who you are. Just as you've done for me."

I won't ever leave you again.

"You must understand I'm not alive, and it's not just me," she said. "The other ascended queens are in my mind as well. I hear them, feel them. They brought me back for a purpose bigger than myself."

"I'll help you with it. Whatever you need."

"There's not much I can offer you in return," she said. "I won't be here long, and there are things I must do. Terrible things that must be done for our people, for the war, to right past wrongs. Not for me, but for them. I can make no promises to you. No commitments."

"You kept me sane and brought me back from the edge more times than I can count. And I still failed you. I didn't know that you needed me, and I left you alone to be brutalized and murdered. I will do whatever it takes to pay my debts to you. I fear I will do terrible things as part of the coming war, and I won't begrudge you doing the same."

"Know that I love you, but also that I'm barely here."

He nodded. "I won't leave you now. Just don't give up on us."

"I'll do my best to stay me."

"Let me serve you."

Her brow furrowed, and her lips twitched in unspoken conversations. Finally, she sighed.

"Then I appoint you General of the Queensguard and Armies," she said. "Please inform the former general and take up your duties. Prepare the armies for battle. I need to rest, but before I do, I need a word with the Grimfall."

Rhydian's throat was tight. Every bone in his body screamed not to leave her again, but he would obey her command. He grimaced but bowed and left the room. As he exited, his world crumbled around him once more and barely a flicker of hope remained.

Queen Rianne stood in the center of the room, clicking her silver capped fingernails against one another as she waited to face the wretched elf. Hidden knives, collected from forgotten vaults from queens long dead, were secreted into the folds of her black and red lace gown. Leather panels, like armor, lay underneath the corset made of queens' bones where her bonesword slumbered. She shifted, uncomfortable inside her own body as the smoky souls of the queens settled into her bones. They whispered to her.

Callysta's fractured soul chanted, *"Grimfall. Grimfall. Grimfall."*

"Grim falls on us all." Raechella's prophecies rang in Rianne's mind.

"Grimfall murderer," Rosalindt agreed.

Rianne used her will to force them into a muffled silence. As she did, the raging emotions faded away, leaving her with the numbness of death. Those were her options: feel too much or nothing at all.

The elf slammed open the door and swaggered inside. Her long white hair swung behind her, and her dark-water eyes narrowed. She grinned exposing her tipped fangs.

"Your Majesty," the elf said coolly.

Alive, Rianne may have pursed her lips or frowned or stuffed her shaking hands into the folds of her gown. She painted a smile on her face, forcing the muscles as best she could.

Nesryn snorted. "Drop the act."

The queens recalculated. Grimfall knew all their secrets, and, not having to pretend, Rianne dropped the mask.

"Grimfall," Rianne replied, expression flat.

Nesryn strolled across the room and plopped into a large circular couch, putting her boots on the table. "And who do I have the pleasure of speaking with? Rebekkah? Samantah? Rosalindt? Vittoria?"

Rianne said nothing, felt nothing.

Watching.

Waiting.

Grimfall smirked. "Maybe... You're not yet the one they fear to name, the one shrouded in darkness, in curses laid upon this land. The one who bound the Queensblood spirits to eternal torment. Could it be... Lexyra?"

A snarl erupted from Vittoria through Rianne's lips, and she bared her human teeth like a wolf protecting a meat-laden bone from a rival. Maybe her emotions weren't as dead as she'd told Rhydian; as dead as she'd hoped.

Nesryn let out a sound that could only be described as a triumphant chuckle overlaid atop a growl. Her eyes glimmered stormy gray.

Returned queen, Samantah, snarled, *"Summon the bonesword and drive it into her heart."*

Morgana's presence slithered through Rianne's collarbone. *"Kill the murderer."*

Rebekkah murmured, *"Destroy Grimfall."*

Nesryn cocked her head, and her gaze narrowed—as if she could hear the queens whispering inside Rianne's head. Her pupils contracted to feline slits, and she licked the points of her short fangs.

"We wish we could say it's a pleasure to see you again," Rianne rasped to the elf, several voices all fighting to emerge at once.

"You all *hate* seeing me."

Where Rhydian quieted all the lingering spirits, this godless elf woke every last one. Rianne could feel Nesryn's burning, soul-rending starlight sword driving through her heart, once for each returned queen the elf had slayed. She couldn't help but hate her too.

"We remember what you did." Rianne felt control slipping and gripped the edge of the desk to steady herself.

"You're going to have to stop talking in third person if you don't want everyone to realize you're not alone, Rianne. How much of you is left, anyways?"

Not enough.

Rianne refused to dignify the elf's words with the tears burning the corners of her eyes. She silenced the queens once more, trapping their emotions deep within her bones.

"Your attempts to rile us—me—are futile. Death burned away all emotion."

"You say that every time you return, and yet *each time* I manage to get a rise out of you."

Rianne felt one of the spirits, Morgana perhaps, muttering out her lips, "Maybe because you're so singularly annoying that even the dead hate you."

"I'm sure you remember my words, and I don't need to repeat myself. But I rather enjoy giving the warning." Nesryn put her hands behind her head. "I know what you are, you know my rule. Endanger this continent, fall to the darkness, and I'll kill you. Again."

"Try it." Rianne's fingers slid toward the bonesword around her waist.

Nesryn grinned. "This will be the... fourth time I've dealt with a returned queen?"

Rianne felt Rosalindt's hiss swirling around her tongue. "Go to hell."

"I'm already here."

Vittoria showed Rianne an image of a lonely gate forged in metal not of this world. *This is how you hurt her.*

Vittoria's cruel smile dragged across Rianne's pale lips. "If I recall, hell is in Etheria, now."

Nesryn's boots slammed against the ground, then she was across the room and standing a hairsbreadth from Rianne's face faster than she could blink. Darkness rippled under Nesryn's mottled color-changing skin like coiling serpents.

Nesryn whispered, "Say that word again, and I'll kill you, oaths be damned."

Rianne took a small step back, Vittoria now wearing her own triumphant grin. "We have a long memory too, and you're not the only one who collects secrets."

Any humor long fled the elf's face. Her too-large predator eyes narrowed to black slits and muscles in her jaw flexed.

"We'll have to keep each other's secrets, won't we?" Rosalindt purred inside Rianne. "I won't breathe a word about your greatest failure, and you take my secrets to your long-overdue grave."

Nesryn's steely gaze nearly frightened Rianne. The elf was preternaturally still, and judging by the darkness in her stormy eyes, battling demons in her skull. Prickles of adrenaline shot down Rianne's arms as she prepared herself to summon her bonesword if Grimfall lost the tenuous tether on the volcanic, world-rending temper Vittoria knew too well. Rianne's fingers twitched.

"All actions bear a cost, and ours is steeped in blood," Nesryn whispered.

Rianne's throat burned at those long-forgotten words. She wondered whether she pushed the monster slayer too far. Perhaps it would be prudent to remind the elf of her oaths.

Rianne said, "Your self-imposed rules will keep you from harming me, from anyone who doesn't meet your definition of sin, of monster."

Nesryn snarled. "You mention Etheria again and I'll make a hells-damned exception. At any rate, the corruption will eat away at you. It always does. And I'll be right there, waiting. Fourth time's the charm. Maybe this time you'll stay dead."

With a sweep of her long skirts, Rianne spun to lean against her polished desk. "It'll be different this time."

Nesryn angled her head.

Returned queen Morgana painted a smirk on Rianne's rose-stained lips, knowing it would infuriate the elf.

"This time I have a Warbringer," she thought.

Theo entered the gilded office, his mouth set in a thin line. noting Rodarri's new queen, sitting astride the gigantic wooden desk. Above her, pulsed the glowing Rodarri lichen that had nearly gotten him killed just weeks ago when Adonis had stolen it, reminding him that the beautiful things in Rodarri were deadly.

Nesryn had stormed out of Rianne's office, punching walls and muttering curses, and Rhydian's expression was dark and brooding.

On edge, Theo braced himself for what he assumed would be an unpleasant conversation.

"Your Majesty," Rianne crooned.

He stopped in the middle of a thick rug, woven with the scarlet roses of Rodarri, keeping ample space between them.

When Rianne emerged from the ravine, Rhydian hadn't noticed, but Theo sensed something was *wrong* with her. Her movements were shaky, almost convulsive. An unfocused look often crossed her face, but unlike Aurienne's where she was in another world, Rianne was... listening to something. Her blue eyes were swimming with silver, and her lips set into a cruel line. Every instinct and alarm bell in Theo's bones were ringing, and he watched her warily.

Theo gave her a nod, not bowing. She watched him hungrily, and long nights tending sheep taught him never to show weakness to a wolf. Mathis once told him that equals do not bow to one another, and as he would soon be King of Avyllon, they were equals. His heart twisted at the memory of the old sorcerer, drawing a grimace on his face.

Rianne tilted her head, studying him. Her eyes darted from his eyes to his mouth to his hands and back to his eyes—cataloguing him. She pursed her lips together a little too hard, as if she had forgotten how.

"Your Majesty, I am relieved to see you return," he said. "Rhydian...we thought you were lost."

"I was," she said. "Thank you for coming to rescue the queens. You risked much coming back here, and you did not have to."

Theo crossed his arms. "I made a promise to Rhydian."

She pushed back onto the desk and crossed her legs, leaning forward. "And what did he promise you in return?"

"Ask him."

"A kingly answer. How fortunate the High Seer was able to confirm your bloodline in the nick of time."

He stiffened. "I didn't want a crown."

"No, I suppose you didn't. Even the High Seer can't fake the

Sword of Souls responding to your blood. I remember when it was forged all those years ago... the things that sword has done..." She trailed off.

"What?"

She blinked and straightened her skirts. "Nothing. I suppose as two new monarchs we should discuss alliance."

"Our position against Emperor Rexil of Demorra holds, and we will ally with and defend those who stand against him. Aurienne said that your... predecessor made a deal with the emperor. Where do you stand?"

"I haven't decided. Perhaps I'll make a new deal with him," she crooned.

"The prophecy states he will destroy everything, including you," he said.

She leaned in. "It's Avyllon's prophecy. We're not convinced your seer always tells the full truth. We've known too many seers who shape their predictions to suit themselves. If there's a way to avoid war, we will consider it before forcing our people to fight unnecessarily."

Theo scowled. "Write me when you decide. I can see I'm no longer needed. Adonis and I will leave for Avyllon at once."

Rianne pushed off the desk and folded her arms, and he couldn't help but notice how her fingers lingered atop the bodice that had transformed into a magical bonesword. His instincts were screaming something was wrong. He took several deliberate steps back, and his hand rested on the hilt, ready to draw. Her eyes flickered to the Sword of Souls, and she stilled.

Aurienne had told him the Sword of Souls killed monsters and cleaved magic. It undid curses and sliced tethers. Rianne had a reason to be wary of it.

"I'll see you at your coronation," she said.

Theo backed toward the door, refusing to take his gaze off the queen. "Your Majesty."

As he stepped out of the office, Rianne snapped to an attendant.

"Bring my stationery. I have a letter to write to Emperor Rexil. It seems we have much to discuss."

Theo grimaced again.

Something is very wrong with her.

As he was about to close the door, Rianne hummed to herself in a strange, grating voice, "Oh, how the kings shall die."

SUN'S SHADOW
CHAPTER TEN

Brave warriors ventured into the woods, bartering our souls to save our families, becoming vampire. We risked everything, believing the love of our people would save us from eternal corruption. When we returned from defeating the Shadows, we were cast out by those we swore to protect—as the smiling demon knew we would be. The betrayal sealed our fate as monsters and can never be forgiven.

— Journal of Nico Rothbain, 1 N.T.C.

1152 N.T.C. The namesake capital city of Avyllon.

Blinding sunlit tattoos illuminated the small palace library Miella camped out in for the morning as the vampire hunter entered. Not even Marco's heavy leather coat and gloves could fully conceal the light from his magical tattoos. He took a wide stance in the center of the room, avoiding all flammable books and furniture.

"Where have you been?" she asked her several times removed uncle, flipping another page of the tome.

He grinned but instead asked, "What're you reading?"

"This is an old book of maps. I figure I should know where everything is," she said.

"You're smart," he said. "Just like your great-great-something grandmother."

She glanced up. "Stellan's daughter?"

Marco's grin faded. "Yes. I helped raise my niece for a while when they were all gone. I probably knew her better than he did at the end."

"What happened to her?"

"She became one of the greatest vampire hunters to walk the earth," he said. "For eighty years she was the bane of the bloodsuckers. It wasn't much longer after her eventual death that the vampires vanished."

"They imprisoned themselves," Miella corrected.

"That's what they claim. I saw how they loved the hunt. I don't believe they would have given that up."

A dust mote landed on the exposed tattoos of his neck and caught flame. Miella jumped. Scowling, he brushed the ashes from his shoulder.

"Let's take a walk," he said.

In a blink, he was already out of the room, and Miella scrambled to put her book down. He was nearly to one of the exterior doors before she caught him. She wrapped a wool cloak around herself as they exited the palace and wandered the chilly streets.

"How did you get those tattoos?"

"I told you."

"Not really."

He chuckled. "Fine. It was magic born from desperation. I was in love with a girl a few years older than I was. Elletra. I hadn't reached the age of manhood yet, and so when the battles came, I was not allowed to fight, even if I wanted to. I remained home with our family, with Stellan's family, protecting them. She was old enough to go with the others and went with the group that followed Stellan."

The words spilled out of Miella's lips, "She came back a vampire."

He nodded. "Yes. They defeated the Shadows, but she returned a vampire. At first, we didn't know what it meant. They didn't go out during the day anymore, and livestock were mysteriously going missing, but at first all seemed well. We knew something had happened to them, but we had no idea of what."

Miella held her breath, hanging off every word of the ancient story. The story of her people.

"By the time the war was over, I had become a man." A wistful calm settled over him. "Still in love with that same girl, I married her. On our wedding night, I learned the truth. Elletra told me their secret, of their human feedings. She promised she had it under control, that she could fight it. Madly in love with her, I told no one what I'd learned. I dug her a cellar in our house protected from all light. I'd spend time with her during the day, loving every moment. She'd leave for a while during the night, and I never knew where she went. Never asked. She always returned, glowing and happy. Those few lost hours were a small cost for the happiness we shared. Something was different, but I believed in her goodness."

Miella could almost see it. Young Marco in love, getting married, yearning for the fairy tale ending with his new bride. Overcoming all odds, all costs, they clung to each other for happiness.

His expression tightened. "One night, I caught her drinking from our neighbor. I grabbed her to pull her off him before she killed him, and she turned on me. Not recognizing me, she lost control and drank my blood. I had no idea how strong the vampires were. Even a little woman like Elletra could so easily overpower me. She bit my neck, held me down, and drank from me until I was nearly drained. I shouted for her, begged her to stop—but it was as if she couldn't hear me. Her fangs piercing my skin, I felt the life sucked out of my body as my soul began to slip through the veil."

"No," Miella breathed.

She closed her eyes, already guessing how this story ended in tragedy.

"As daylight rose, she realized what she'd done," he said. "She dragged my body into the cellar, and bit me again—differently. I felt poison coursing through my veins, along with her blood. I believe she was trying to turn me into one of those things."

Miella gasped.

Was it even possible to become one? They could make more? Were they making more now?

He grimaced as his face twisted in disgust. "I escaped her grasp and stumbled out into the sunlight. She watched me, panicked, from the cellar, unable to follow. She shouted for me to come back, but I'd rather die than become like her. I ran. All day I ran, and all night I hid buried in the earth in a grave I dug. I heard her searching for me, calling my name, flying overhead. I had no idea where I was headed; I just knew I had to run. Finally, I reached a place where the sun set over a waterfall deep in the Warden's Watch Mountains. It was as if the water sucked in the last drops of sunlight, and the entire falls were bathed in its glow."

Miella committed every word to memory, trying to guess how many days he'd run, what direction.

"I jumped into the golden sunlight falls just as the sun set over the mountains. The tattoos formed on my skin, soaking up the sunlight. It gave me the power to destroy them. One touch and they'd burn. I started with Elletra."

Miella's heart sank as the blood drained from her face. She nearly slipped on a frozen puddle of water between the cobblestones and caught herself on the edge of a pearly fountain.

"I let her find me. She was tired and hungry from searching. Blood-crazed, she didn't even realize my embrace would be fatal. I didn't let go until I burned her to ash."

"I'm so sorry," she whispered.

"Don't be," he said. "I tell you this so you remember that even the ones that claim to love you will turn on you. They always do eventually. Not even Stellan can control himself, nor can he keep the others under control. They're able to feed from criminals now, but it won't sate them forever. Their hunger will get the better of them, or you'll be in the wrong place at the wrong time, and you'll be next."

She shook her head. "I don't want to believe that."

"Neither did I."

They walked for some time, passing various merchants selling their wares and late breakfast items. Several fountains offered warm water—heated by the fires deep within the ground. They ended up in a crowded part of the city she didn't recognize. The buildings huddled close together, the roofs nearly touching. The streets became narrow, and fewer people were meandering around.

Miella remained lost in thought. Elletra sounded like she loved Marco. Even Marco described her as distraught over what she'd done, and that she wore herself ragged tracking him. She didn't even sense the danger when she found him, and she burned for it.

Gods—she had attacked him first though. He'd been helpless, unable to fight her off, and barely escaped with her life. If Miella was attacked now, she'd been in the same position or worse. There would be no fighting off their immense strength and speed, and now the vampires were a millennium older.

Her voice cracked. "What do I do if they do turn on me?"

"Do you really want to know?"

She nodded.

He studied her. "Come with me."

He turned down several narrow streets until they were at the far wall of the Avyllon. Slipping through an alley between two cramped buildings, they emerged in an open courtyard. Marco strode toward the center of the yard.

Miella slowed.

About a hundred people, mostly men, ambled around the spacious, protected yard. High city walls blocked them in at every side, and the only entrance appeared to be the narrow alley. The inhabitants all wore mismatched, repurposed armor. Crude straw training dummies were lined against one wall, weapons were piled inside an open doorway. It looked just like the war preparations in the barracks beside the palace, but less organized and sorrier stocked.

Horror prickled down her spine.

"What is this?"

Marco gestured around. "Every person here has lost a loved one to the vampires. Every day, more join our ranks. Every day, more people are slaughtered to sate the vampire's hunger."

Ranks.

She looked around again, really searching. The angry expressions, hushed whispers, and tense body language spoke volumes. These were not soldiers. They were only a few steps away from becoming a mob. Growing every day. Suspicious glares settled upon her from several groups nearby.

"You're training up an army of vampire hunters." Eyes wide, she took several steps back.

"I'm helping people learn to defend themselves."

She nearly laughed. "That is *not* what this is. Don't lie to me."

"You're right," he admitted. "I am gathering a force of people who want to stand up to the foul creatures. One day we're going to need it."

"You realize that the vampires have kept their oath to only kill *wicked* people. You've been following them; you know it's true."

He shifted and crossed his arms. "As far as we can tell."

"These people are the friends and kin of criminals," she whispered. "They might be bad people too, Marco. At the very least, they're angry. High emotions don't make rational decisions. This is a bad idea."

"They deserve only death."

Her mouth hung open. This was such a bad and dangerous idea; she had no words. This was exactly what happened last time. The vampires betrayed prematurely by those they sacrificed to help. A cold shiver raced down her spine.

Finally, she asked, "Why did you show me this?"

"Because I trust you not to reveal our secret."

Anger flashed in her eyes as her gaze narrowed. This put her in a terrible position, and he knew it. Marco simply didn't care. He'd do whatever it took to convince her of their treachery. Even as he did the exact same thing. Hellsdamned hypocrite.

"*This* is how we stand up to them," he said. "We train, learn their weaknesses. In groups, we can learn to defend ourselves."

She shook her head, scoffing. How could humans defend themselves against the might of the vampires? There was a reason Theo freed them. There was a reason the old stories warned children of them.

"Will you keep this secret?" he asked.

Miella threw her hands up. "I don't have much of a choice, do I? You've forced my hand at this point. If I tell them, they'll come here and kill you all."

Should she tell the vampires? They were fighting for her and keeping this from them felt wrong. But if she did, she knew she'd have blood on her hands. The smallest part of her wondered if she ever would have to protect herself from the vampires.

"Why're you doing this now?"

Marco said, "If they keep their word, I'll keep mine. I can't wait for them to decide to betray us. I have to be ready."

Someone across the courtyard stabbed a straw dummy while shouting, "Kill all vampires."

"Who will fight the Mooncursed if you attack the vampires?" Miella hissed.

His brow pulled together genuinely. "Vampires are more dangerous, more bloodthirsty, and more conniving than the Mooncursed."

"You haven't seen what the Mooncursed do to people."

"Have you seen what the vampires can do?"

She shifted her weight. "Just the aftermath."

He nodded, sunlight tattoos casting shadows on the uneven ground. "Let's hope you never have to see them feed. It may change your good opinion of them."

"They have only done what I asked," she countered. "They're fighting our enemies for us."

Scorn spread across his face. "It must've been such a hardship for them to be released from their prison to feed freely upon the world."

"The vampires imprisoned themselves," she said. "They didn't even want us to free them. They're only doing this because I asked."

"Or so they've led you to believe." He gently placed his gloved hand on her arm. "You cannot trust them."

Gods, she wished he'd never shown her any of this. Her heart twisted as she felt like the worst sort of two-faced traitor. There was no way this ended well for anyone.

"When do we get our special tattoos?" one of the trainees shouted to the hunter.

Marco replied, "One day you'll earn them."

Miella swallowed, torn between the betrayal in her head and the loyalty of her heart—unsure of which would win out.

RED FOG

CHAPTER ELEVEN

I promise our enemies will feel our rage at what they stole from us in every bite of the blade.

— *LEXYRA.*

1152 N.T.C. Castle Rodarr, Rodarri.

Blood. Everything was consumed by a crimson haze that drowned the castle walls. The bloodlust roared in his head, and Rhydian shook his head to escape the images. A maid passed, throat slit, blood pouring down her frock, and she stared at him with an odd expression. Except her throat was fine. A guard with furrowed brows passed, missing an arm at the shoulder, except he wasn't. None of it was real.

Rhydian leaned against the crimson-coated walls, clenching and unclenching his fists. He'd been far too close to losing himself to the curse, and somehow none of his victims had died. They'd been injured—broken arms, missing fingers, head wounds, and cracked ribs—but somehow, they'd all survived. The few who died, Theo had dispatched for him, and maybe the elf slayed a few. It was hard to remember. Most of the memories were foggy; all but those of Rianne. They were crystal clear.

Her corpse falling to the ravine. The castle crumbling around him and Theo. The way she'd crawled up from the depths with silver hair and pale skin. Worse—the stony expression carved into her face when she'd finally permitted him to see her. The sadness in her eyes when she said she was gone. The way her head tilted to the side as if listening to something he couldn't hear. The nightmare was an unending loop that haunted his waking hours.

The battle was long over, and yet his blood sang with fervor. Pacing the somber castle and organizing guard rotations did little to quench his appetites. His fingers itched toward his blades to make real the gory visions.

He started walking again, keeping his eyes fixed to the floor. Blood. He breathed in through his nose sharply, making his way out of the castle. If he could get away from others for just a few moments, maybe his heart would cease racing and his mind would quiet. He couldn't ask Rianne to help soothe his violent thoughts, not after what she'd been through. No, he had to be strong for her.

Even while fighting against the darkest impulses, he would do what he promised her.

Biting down on a snarl, he slammed his palms against the large doors to the throne room where the commanders, captains, and officers gathered. The men jerked at the noise, backing away from the doors and quickly clearing his path.

Rhydian paused in the center of the room, putting his hands on his hips and broadening his shoulders as he fought for control. His knuckles dug into the leather armor on his pants.

"Queen Rianne has ordered all regional armies be prepared to mobilize," he said. "All auxiliary units are to be called up, and recruiters will be sent to every village to bolster the numbers. Hopefully, we can avoid a draft—but that will be next."

No one moved. It was not the focus of soldiers memorizing

orders. Something else held back the expected nods of agreement. His curse flared—heating his blood as the tactical analysis flowed through his mind. The curse not only made him physically unstoppable, it unlocked the secrets of strategy. This was unrest. Uncertainty. Treachery.

The urge to cut down every man in this room to keep Rianne safe had Rhydian nearly reaching for his ax. But he couldn't serve her if he went mad. He had to keep it under control. There were other ways to bring them all to heel. It was just a game, and one he knew all the rules to.

He circled the room slowly, forcing each of them to make eye contact with him. Willing them to challenge him.

Rhydian allowed danger to lace his voice. "You have your orders. See to them."

Commander Brennin Tavish pushed through the crowd, his son Bram close on his heels. "Our king is dead."

Tavish narrowed his gaze, the unspoken questions heavy in the air. Where did Rhydian's loyalties lie? What changes would Rianne make? Would the commanders fall in line? It all boiled down to one question though. What was the future of Rodarri?

Rhydian allowed his hand to rest upon the top of the ax in the holster at his hip, thumb brushing against the honed metal. "Your *queen* has given her orders."

"What queen? I see a traitor who killed our king," Tavish said.

The commander glanced at the other eight commanders, their heirs, and the several dozen officers. He ran his hand through his thinning slicked-back hair while pursing his lips into a line. The gazes of the others darted amongst themselves.

Tavish couldn't be allowed to gain any support. Rhydian stepped forward, looking down on the older man.

"Rianne is your queen." Rhydian allowed some of the anger pulsing through his veins to echo in his words as he took another step forward. "She is the first to ascend and return in centuries. A returned Queensblood always leads us in times of need."

The men backed away as Rhydian advanced. His eyes felt like they were boiling, and his temples pounded.

"To defy this is to defy the gods," Rhydian continued. "And those who threaten Rianne face *me*. If she doesn't handle you herself."

Tavish lifted his chin in defiance, but said, "Fine."

Rhydian studied him, tracking every small tick in his expression. Every plot that crossed his mind.

"Prepare all troops to mobilize," Rhydian repeated. "I want a report by the end of the day as to your progress, numbers, and locations. Dismissed."

The commanders mumbled their assent before filing out of the throne room. Rhydian watched them go sensing the discord just beneath the tense surface. Shaking his head, he tried to focus on breathing through the growing urge to attack.

Theo and Adonis would be leaving soon. He'd promised to see them off. Gripping the top of his ax he headed that direction.

At the main entrance of the castle, Theo waved from the horses. "I've been looking for you."

Rhydian gritted his teeth, feeling a modicum of ease at his friend's presence. "Are you leaving so soon?"

Theo nodded. "Adonis is bringing the horses now. The coronation is soon, and they'll be missing me. Aurienne will need to know what happened, and we need to prepare for the emperor."

Rhydian's gut twisted at the mention of Adonis. He still owed the young sorcerer apprentice an apology, but he had been avoiding him.

Instead, Rhydian said, "Ah, I see."

"I hope to see you there," Theo continued.

Rhydian flinched. "Why wouldn't we be there? I mean, of course, we're coming. I wouldn't miss it."

He'd dragged Theo away from his new kingdom to help him save Rianne and had almost been responsible for the new king's early demise. Guilt gnawed at his chest.

"Your queen told me she hasn't decided whether to honor the alliance," Theo said.

Rhydian's blood cooled. "What do you mean?"

"She hasn't decided whether to take the emperor's offer or join us." There was a bite to Theo's voice. "She will inform us of her decision later."

That wasn't like Rianne. Why would she even consider siding with the emperor after all they'd seen? His head pounded. *Rianne* wouldn't.

Gods.

It all made sense though. She'd told him to prepare the army, but not what they were preparing it for. Why hadn't she trusted him with her plans?

Theo hesitated. "Rhydian, I just spoke with Rianne. Something is *wrong* with her. She's—"

Bile rushed up Rhydian's throat. He refused to hear it again. Nesryn's bitter words were bad enough, but he couldn't bear it if his friend shared those sentiments. They couldn't give up on her.

"Don't," Rhydian grated.

Theo exhaled.

"Just... don't." Rhydian cast a pleading, but firm glance toward Theo.

Theo opened his mouth but closed it. "Okay. I'm heading back. I hope to see you at the end of the month."

Adonis exited the castle with two horses, giving the Warbringer a wide berth, and refusing to meet his gaze. Theo cast a final wave back to Rhydian before they rode hard toward the nearest Way.

Rhydian didn't wait for them to go, stalking angrily into the forest. They were all wrong about Rianne. She'd endured hell. She *died*. Of course she was cautious. The other queens were whispering to her, but that didn't mean she'd changed. It meant she had a purpose. She was the same soft-hearted woman he'd fallen for, and he'd be damned if he didn't hold to that truth. Even if she forgot who she was, he knew.

He always knew.

Grunting, he sank his fist into a tree. They. Were. Wrong. He wouldn't give up on her. She needed him, and he would die before he let her down again. So, he would oblige as her general, protect her, and serve her. In time, he would prove his loyalty, and she would return to herself. Rianne was the strongest person he knew. She would overcome whatever battles raged in her head.

Bark exploded as he punched the tree again, savoring the release of energy. He struck it until it fell, before setting upon another and another. Most of the rage dwindled as sweat lined his brow. Chest easing, he felt like he could breathe. His knuckles were swollen and bleeding, but he could breathe.

"If your goal is to murder innocent trees, you're succeeding." Nesryn's harsh tone cut the clearing.

He spun to find her leaning against a tree with a bored expression.

"I'm just letting off steam," he snapped. "Better than taking it out on an unsuspecting person."

"That was your plan just hours ago."

He grimaced. "My targets weren't innocent."

The images of Rianne's head falling, her expression fixed in an eternal scream, brought a new layer of red haze. They weren't innocent at all.

"Rianne needs me," he said. "I won't fall to the curse while she's here."

The elf cocked her hip. "You came too close to back away now. It nearly had you in its grasp and it won't be letting you go. You got lucky, but you won't again."

"What's your plan?" He threw his hands up. "Follow me around until it's time to kill me?"

"More or less."

The answer tore his attention fast enough he nearly tripped on a fallen branch. The thought of her constantly stalking him, watching, waiting, brought chills to his damp skin.

"You are the greatest threat to humanity," she said. "Deep down, you know it too. You felt it digging its claws into you. You heard the poisoned promises and felt the strength pouring into your bones at every drop of blood spilled."

He did.

"The vampires have so far abided by their oaths to their young kin, and I'm killing all the Mooncursed I come across. You're the only one I have to worry about for now. Well, you and eventually Rianne." She strode forward until her breath was hot on his face. "I will follow you every waking and slumbering moment until the time comes. You will never be free of me. Even if you don't see me, I'll be there waiting."

Rhydian's blood froze.

"Not because I want to, but because I must." Her voice was almost sad. "And it'll happen any day now."

The elf pushed off the tree to stride into the forest.

"Tell me the truth," he said. "How do you really know that I am going to fail?"

She called over her shoulder. "Heroes only stay heroes for a short while. Those of us cursed with immense power always fall."

INKY TEARS & GOLDEN BLOOD

CHAPTER TWELVE

Tears possess unrivaled amplifying properties in therapies and workings. Tears gathered in laughter or happiness can significantly increase the power of healing works. General tears may be used in all remedies as a binding agent. Tears of discomfort, fear, or sadness should be cast out. Tears of true heartache or anger are potent and will ruin poultices and remedies. They should only be used in antidotes for poison—or dark curses.

— *BOOK OF WILDECRAFT.*

1152 N.T.C. The namesake capital city of Avyllon.

Flexing her broken hand, Aurienne nursed a steaming mug of lavendiir palm tea. She leaned forward to inhale the sweet berry fumes, careful not to drink too much of the powerful magic dampener. Drinking just enough to keep her brain from bleeding, yet not so much to lose her gift forever was a careful balance. Leaning back, she winced as her hand shot to her side. Her heavily bruised ribs still ached most of the time, but at least the stab wounds were healing. The injuries from the assassination attempt at the aqueduct, combined with the constant headaches, were a reminder of just how close to death she'd come. She took a small sip of the tea before setting down the mug and turning to her deck.

The rounded edges of Aurienne's divination cards brushed her fingertips as she shuffled absently. Shuffling was a habit, impossible to break, but she didn't intend to attempt a reading. Out of necessity, she was avoiding all magic. The visions leading up to the summit nearly weakened her beyond recovery. Her vision of Rianne was the first to come to her in days. After living so intensely beyond the veil for decades, for the visions to fully cease, she wondered for a few days whether she'd burned out her gift. She now knew that wasn't the case, but she still avoided drawing on that burning energy in her chest—avoiding the golden soulblood or crimson life blood.

Theo hadn't returned yet after racing to Rodarri to try and save Rianne from her long-fated sacrifice. Aurienne knew Rhydian had to go, knew Theo had to go with his friend. A month ago, she wouldn't have told either of them what was coming. They couldn't have stopped it, so why bother? However, after weeks of traveling with the golden-hearted blacksmith, she realized that taking away their ability to try would have been unforgivable. It wasn't her choice to make for them.

She curled up in a round chair on her balcony overlooking the thousands of fountains and pools in Avyllon. Below, the streets were busy with life and faint conversation that she could nearly make out. People laughing, bartering, arguing in groups—all experiences she rarely partook in. Even if she wanted to, she had no one to talk to. Their allies only sought her for advice, the other seers avoided her after what happened with Evani, and now that she prevented the visions—she realized just how much time she spent alone. And the one person she wanted to talk to was gone. Theo's absence was sharp and consuming.

"Ouch," she hissed.

The cards left a small paper cut. A crimson bead welled on her index finger before dribbling onto the card. Her eyes narrowed in annoyance. As she popped the cut into her mouth, she realized her mistake. The top card smiled and waved at her.

"You little bastards," she whispered to her cards as she fell head-long into one of the visions she'd been desperately trying to avoid.

Opening her eyes to the Second Sight, hordes of nightmarish enemies without faces surrounded her. In the distance, major cities crumbled to rubble in clouds of flame and dust. Around her ankles, golden crowns sank into the earth. She spun around to see a floating mirror, showing Aurienne her own reflection, crying golden tears. Everything was swallowed up by a crimson mist.

The mist cleared to reveal a stone temple atop a mountain. Four lonely pillars held up the carved stone roof. The absence of walls granted view toward each of the four cardinal directions. Wind swirled between the columns.

"The land will once again protect those that remember its ways," a voice whispered.

Golden threads of fate wrapped around each of the enormous columns, pulling it counterclockwise one quarter turn. The temple groaned but began to rotate beneath her feet. She nearly fell to her knees as the temple shook and moved. It came to halt, and now each column pointed to a cardinal direction.

The nearest column, east, burst into flames. The heat sent Auri-enne scrambling away as the hairs on her arms charred. The stone melted, twisting into a spiraling design.

Rain crashed at her back to the west, slashing numerous pockets and pools into the stone. She raised her arm to shield her face from the torrential streams. Water poured from inside the stone, down the cascading waterfalls and waterways. From the earth beneath her, the southern column reverted into a single boulder as wind carved the northern column into a flat square shape.

Each column tied to an element. Flame to the east. Sky to the north. Earth to the south. Water to the west. The clouds flew by as time raced on. Years. Decades. Centuries.

Mountains rose. Rivers changed. Forests grew and withered. The land transformed into something she recognized—the present.

"You will know what to do when the time comes," a voice whispered.

The vision faded away and Aurienne returned to the real world gasping for air. Her body shook despite her attempts to steady herself, and she crawled into the center of her room. Her hands clawed for purchase in the plush rugs. Golden soulblood dribbled down her chin from her gums and cracked lips.

She looked up and choked.

A dark shadow hovered in the center of her room. It was too dark, too murky, too aware. Aurienne immediately sensed the danger in it. The shape slithered back from the edges of the furniture, taking the form of a man.

She froze, recalling the assassination attempt in the dark room near the aqueduct and the floating shadow she'd seen there. Her fingers slid toward her golden athame on her thigh.

The shadow changed form, flickering between this world and another. The nameless one's face appeared in the outline of the shadow. Her spy. Aurienne's breath caught.

"It's me," he said.

Aurienne choked back a rush of emotion.

What had happened to him? He'd left Avyllon just weeks ago fully human and now...

The nameless one flickered between a shadowy outline, and a foggy image of who he used to be. He floated toward her. A formless wraith sank onto a bench, barely disturbing the cushions. Aurienne sat beside him.

"What happened?" she whispered.

What have you become?

"I fell between worlds, where I changed. Only by X'era's blessing was I able to survive," he said.

Her gaze roved over him, taking it in.

"On what I now know was the day of your summit, I had infiltrated the emperor's throne room," he said. "I watched him open the Way, send through those Mooncursed beasts, and return. He mentioned searching for an ancient map. I learned that he was looking for one marking the location of something that could allow him to invade. His powers are weak in Teridar, he's unable to hold Ways here or send over his Mooncursed for very long. Something is preventing him from invading. The map was found and brought to him, but I was able to destroy it before he learned the location of what he sought."

Aurienne swallowed.

"It was a matter of time before he found another, so I sought a means to destroy his twisted, mutant army," he continued. "With some help, I found a temple pyramid where they were creating and housing the beasts. I was unable to find the source that creates them but managed to destroy many of them. I did learn that the titan ore collars allow the Demorran wardens to control them. Without the collars, there are traces of humanity left in those poor souls."

Goddess.

She felt sick. "They're... people? People that they break apart and stitch back together with pieces of animals?"

The shadow's expression flickered solemnly. "Or beasts they attach human pieces to. Or pieces of other beasts. And there were other experiments. I fear there is no limit to the Mooncursed blight. We haven't seen the worst the empire will throw at us." His face flickered into view. "The bowels of that pyramid is an evil place that's infecting the entire city. I will never forget the look in that Mooncursed's eyes when it asked me to free it from the pain. I, myself, know the pain that titan ore can bring. It's like being cut off from your soul."

Aurienne ground her teeth, chewing on the reprisal she promised their foe, but waited for the spy to finish his tale.

"After that, the wardens took me to the emperor's dungeons and..." He stopped, looking faraway at the snow-capped mountains.

Aurienne placed a palm against her chest, the traitorous heart within throbbing with guilt. *Goddess.* She knew—the broad strokes—what they'd done. The same thing all kings did to spies. Just one more tally mark to add to her growing list of sins. Another failure. She closed her eyes, wishing she could take his pain from him. Wishing she could have endured the torture.

"You don't have to tell me anything you don't want to," she said. "But if you want to talk, I'm here."

Flickering in and out of sight, he shifted on the bench—hovering above the rugs and stone. "I'd like to talk about it. Just once, and then I can let it go. I need to. It's been gnawing at me. And I realized I don't have anyone, but you. The life of a spy is lonely. I'd never felt it until now, and I can't go home now." His voice broke.

Aurienne's gaze slid to the ground. She was all he had? She'd never thought about it before, but she supposed it was true. He cut all ties but to the one he spied for. It was the only lasting relationship he'd had, and she'd let him down. She hadn't even realized how much he needed her. Her nails dug into her palm.

"And I had a partner in Demorra," he said. "I used to pride myself on my ability to cut all ties and vanish. Now more often than not, I feel like I don't exist at all."

No.

Aurienne reached for his hand, but her hand passed through the shadows. The nameless one gave her a sad smile.

"See." He wiggled his fingers. "I'm not really here. I'm not sure what I am. Not a Shadow, not Mooncursed, no longer human. Best I can tell, I've become some manner of realm-traveling shade."

Aurienne scowled. *I won't accept that.*

There was one thing she could try. He'd become this after his body fell through the world between worlds. Her soul traveled there often for visions. Maybe...

She reached for her soul, for the burning magic in her core, and her spirit form stepped through the veil between worlds, finding the spy there. Her spirit settled into her body, inhabiting the space. She reached for his hand and found it.

It was cool beneath her touch, but it was there.

At her touch, he choked on a sob. He clasped her hand with both of his—clinging to it for life. Inky tears dripped down his face. Golden soulblood rolled down hers. Aurienne had been avoiding using her magic, but this was important. She was all he had; she'd sent him there. The least she could do was offer this comfort.

She turned her head so he wouldn't see the cost of her kindness. "I'll listen."

He told her, and she listened, absorbing every detail as the sun sank into the sky. She was in that damp dungeon with him, reliving every horrific moment as if she'd suffered it herself.

The titan ore they'd used on him cut him off from his new magic and escape. Stealing his hope. And then the screaming began.

Staked.

Cut.

Stabbed.

Burned.

Skinned.

Methodically, they broke him. Pieces of him were cut away until he didn't even remember the name he'd always fiercely protected. And the worst of it was that here in the world between worlds, she experienced glimpses of those memories. Glimpses she'd never forget and never forgive herself for. How he'd lasted so long, she had no idea.

When he finished, they sat in silence. He'd been tortured to the brink of death, and in his final moments recalled an adage about shadows. He stepped through a shadow and became one.

Her heart ached. "I am so sorry."

"I made this choice," he said. "I can't leave Demorra to him."

"If you help me protect Avyllon, I will do everything I can to help the people of Demorra."

The nameless one tilted his head, looking at her—through her. "I know. You couldn't stand by and do nothing. *You* never could." He studied her. "Are you okay? Your soul... I see—"

She released his hand and swallowed, drawing her dwindling magic back. "We all must make sacrifices."

CURSED HEARTS
CHAPTER THIRTEEN

There is no salvation for monsters or the heroes that slay them. Certainly none for those cursed to be both.

— JOURNAL OF NESRYN ASHWILDES, 93 B.T.C.

1152 N.T.C. The namesake capital city of Avyllon.

Three days of travel behind him, Theo pushed open the door to Aurienne's chambers, drained from the days of travel, sleepless nights, fighting, and being threatened by a queen who ought to be dead. Upon returning from Rodarri, he quickly bathed and though he was dead-exhausted, he went to find Aurienne. He closed the door behind him with a weary thud.

A smoldering fire crackled in the fireplace, and a hundred white candles reflected light off scrying crystals. Diaphanous veils separated her rooms and starlight reflected off a quiet fountain beside the glass balcony doors. White smoke spiraled upward from diffused reeds in a dreamy haze smelling of hellebore lily.

Aurienne rose from her wine-colored couch, wearing a dusky lace and satin dressing gown beneath a gold-threaded robe. "I've been waiting. I'm glad you're back safe."

Theo had spent too much time around Aurienne to ask how she knew. Whether her cards, the visions, or her spies—she always knew.

With a small smile, she gestured to the couch, and he sank into the plush cushions with a groan, rubbing his temples. She sat beside him, curled her legs underneath her, and leaned back.

He laid his head back. "Coldforges, what was that? This all seems like some horrible dream, and I just need to wake up."

She looked away, tracing her painted fingers along the cushions. "I'm sorry."

"It's not your fault everything went mad all at once."

"It feels like it," she murmured.

Theo reached and gently turned her chin to look at him. "It's not your fault, none of it."

His heart wondered if he meant it as he glanced as his Sword of Souls.

She reached up and placed her hand against his, pulling it to her cheek. They locked eyes for several seconds, the air filling with tension. Theo's heart hammered, wanting more than anything to kiss her. Since their kiss on the temple steps upon his return from gathering their allies, she had been painfully distant. And after she'd given him the Sword of Souls, he had no idea where they stood.

He'd kissed her before dashing off to Rodarri, but if he was honest, it was a consuming instinct that kept drawing them together. He hadn't meant to, but he had to stop. Fate had other plans for her.

Heart heavy, he finally swallowed, let his hand fall from her face, and leaned back. She placed her hands in her lap.

"What happened?" she asked.

A shudder slipped down his spine. "They cut off Rianne's head and tossed her head and body into that ravine. When we were trying to free the other queens, I watched her crawl out of the ravine covered in blood and summon a magical sword made from bones."

Aurienne tapped her fingernails on the back of the couch. "She's something else. The spirits of the queens, they've inhabited her or changed her. I can't quite See how."

"I *saw* them cut off her head, and now it's... back." He swallowed. "She wasn't acting like herself, and that bonesword? That's the stuff of legends and nightmares. I talked to her before I left, and she was humming something super creepy about 'oh how the kings shall die.' She said she's coming to the coronation."

Aurienne grimaced and chewed her lip. "Did she." Her voice was flat, irritated at something, and he was too tired to press.

Theo knew a little bit about being in denial, so he'd bit his tongue when Rhydian asked, but he'd seen the silver glints in Rianne's eyes and the strange mannerisms, heard the whispers.

"Something is wrong with her," he said quietly.

"The type of magic to bring a person back from the dead leaves a deep mark," Aurienne replied.

Theo leaned back again, rubbing his sore shoulder and arm. "I think we're going to lose Rhydian. Nesryn has been following incessantly, and his eyes are glowing red more often than not. Losing Rianne, or thinking he lost her, broke him."

"Nesryn will keep an eye on him."

Theo was about to reply, but tentative fingers found his shoulders and began to massage the knots.

By the mouth of the Goddess, that felt amazing.

Theo twisted to lean against her legs, as she banished the discomfort. She shifted, pulling her feet out from underneath her to press against his leg. He reached back and pressed his thumbs into the soles of her painted feet, summoning a happy sigh. Theo grinned, enjoying the reaction from his seer. No, not his, what was wrong with him?

Godsteeth. If she'd stop pushing him away, he could show her he was crazy about her.

Theo banished the thought. She made it clear she cared more for prophecies and wouldn't risk the ire of the Fates for him. His heart throbbed, but he continued pressing circles into her soles. The skin was smooth, aside from the scars of Foretelling Rites past—the horrors she endured to protect them that he wished he could take away. He pulled her leg straight beside him, rubbing her calf and tracing circles along the tattoos, hoping she didn't notice. Knowing he was setting himself up for heartache, he would take any time he could get. He was never as happy as when he was with her.

They were both quiet as the fire smoldered nearby, and the stars twinkled in the skies. A warm breeze lifted the veils separating the rooms and brought the aroma of flower petals from the temple gardens. The dark quiet summoned secrets from Theo.

Theo cleared his throat, broaching a subject they both avoided. "I'm afraid of the coronation and war. I can't lead an army or lead a nation. I can't outsmart kings and emperors to save everyone. I have no idea what I'm doing."

"I know," she said. "If there was any other path, I would have taken it."

"There's always another choice." The words were out before he could stop them.

Her hands went limp on his shoulders. "The other choice was slavery and death for everyone. The only path to survival is tied to you."

"I guess it wasn't much of a choice then."

"I wish I could take the burden from you." Her hands slipped from him into her lap. "I See what it costs you, all of you."

Theo turned on the couch to face her, finding her staring at her hands—as if she could see phantom blood on them.

Moonless sky.

She Saw it all. Everyone's pains. The deaths and loss, both possible and actual. In the Mooncursed and vampire attacks, he'd seen just a glimpse of the images that constantly haunted her. How could he be angry with her when she bore the weight of their futures more than any.

"You carry enough burden for the entire continent," he said gently.

She chuckled quietly, her voice fading away. Theo had traveled with her long enough to know exactly what that meant.

He leaned forward to catch her gaze. "Stay with me. Don't go into the visions."

Aurienne blinked, her cloudy iridescent eyes resting upon him. "Sorry."

Theo tentatively squeezed her hand. "Never apologize for who you are."

He felt her warm skin underneath the calluses on his hands. She was so close, his arm resting on the curve of her thigh, her hands on his knee. In these moments, it was so easy to be with her. Too easy to forget he needed to let her go. He gently released her hand.

"What did you See of my future?" he asked. "You never told me the whole vision. I thought I was only meant to gather the armies, but it appears fate has bigger plans for me."

She rubbed her hand with a wince, studying him. "Your blood showed me your past. Your futures. In your future, I Saw you making blades, living on a farm, and falling in love. You're meant to have a long, good life. If we survive this." She chuckled bitterly.

My past?

He blinked. "How much did you See?"

Her small smile was enough of an answer. "As to overcoming the Darkling Prophecy, I Saw all the nations of Teridar tied to you. I believed it meant you gathered the armies, but I know now you were meant to lead them."

"Did you See how we stop the emperor? Any hints?" he asked, heart sinking.

"Nothing yet. I need to let my soul heal before I can risk more visions." She gestured to the empty mug on the table beside the couch. "Lavendiir palm tea has been helping keep me sane."

He stared at the crackling fire, enjoying just sitting next to her. "We'll figure it out, together."

Abandoned Rooms
Chapter Fourteen

The trebuchet consisted of a long beam lever positioned off center on a forged pivot mechanism on a wheeled base that would support the entire apparatus (Fig. 3). The longer end of the beam held the projectile in a sling while the shorter end held a fixed counterweight, usually a boulder.

— Elderic's Treatise on War Machines from the Shadow War, 73 N.T.C.

1152 N.T.C. Castle Rodarr, Rodarri.

With a mind full of memories not her own, Rianne wandered abandoned rooms in the castle keep searching for her quarry. Closing her eyes, she drifted into the memory of a long dead queen. Centuries had passed since the last returned queen, Morgana, had entered the secret library, memories faded by time and death. So much had changed in those years since the knowledge was sealed away. In Rianne's fractured mind, the centuries turned back, walls moved, furniture disappeared, and rooms vanished.

Rianne's feet took her into an old storage room, and with the turn of a lichen lantern, she stepped into a once-brilliantly illuminated hall. Ragged tapestries returned to their former glory as she followed the memory deeper into the secrets of the castle.

Morgana whispered, *"I knew you would come. The final queen to return. The queen to free us from the curse, from the pain. I saved this knowledge for you."*

Rhydian shadowed her quietly, ever-present. He hardly let her out of his sight anymore, except when duty called him away. So many secrets; he could never learn any of the truths she carried.

"Lonely books and forgotten halls, darkened rooms and sliding walls." Raechella's fevered whispers echoed within Rianne's ribs.

"You should leave him to wait outside," Milah said. *"We can't trust him with our knowledge. He will betray us as they always do."*

Rianne said, *"I trust him with my life."*

Whillow's sadness caused Rianne's breath to catch. *"We once trusted as well."*

Callysta cackled. *"Shattered skulls. Poisoned blood. War comes. Cracked bones. Routed armies. War surely comes. Cities fall. Magic rises. War comes for us all."*

Rianne's silver-tipped fingers traced the stones, searching for a crack in the mortar until the metal claw slipped inside. She found it.

"Could you open this?" she asked Rhydian.

Rhydian stepped around her and pressed his shoulder against the wall. He heaved. Mortar cracked, dust sprinkled the floor, and the stones grated in their carved tracks, but the wall moved, and a doorway opened. Rhydian stepped out of her way, holding up the glowing lichen lantern for her.

She stepped inside. Spacious, it held ample room for six chairs tucked into alcoves. A band of glass circled the top near the ceiling with glowing lichen, pulsing with the heartbeat of Rodarri. Rhydian stepped inside and lowered the lantern.

"What is this place?" His careful gaze scanned every corner of the room for threats.

She skimmed the titles of the ancient tomes. "An ancient library for returned queens. They hid their knowledge away here so that the kings could not find it after Grimfall murdered them." Her tone grew icy.

"Nesryn killed the returned queens?"

"Eventually."

"Did they deserve it?" he asked softly, eyes haunted.

Rianne nearly lashed out at him, a reaction not her own, but stopped. The queens raged in her mind, some agreeing, some not. Others spouting nonsense. She pushed them down, realizing he spoke of himself.

Rianne stamped them all down. "The elf thought so."

"She killed my ancestors too," he said. "The Warbringers. She killed them all after they went mad. One day, I fear she'll kill me too."

"I won't let her take either of us," Rianne said, catching his gaze.

Rhydian smiled humorlessly. "I'm not sure she'll have much of a choice with me, losing you brought me too close to the edge. I don't know if I can keep it at bay."

Small pins of fear and worry pierced through the veil of numbness surrounding her heart. Since they met, she'd wanted to keep him from his curse. To be the cause of him finally succumbing nearly choked her.

"It was going to happen eventually. You always knew that," Marialynn murmured.

The numbness returned as a blanket, suffocating all emotions. She clung to the memories of holding his hands in the wildflowers. Who knew how long until both she and him were gone.

"We can't waste our second chances," she murmured.

She rifled through the hundreds of books lining the walls, searching for a few precious tomes. Hazy memories floated around her subconscious.

A tome bound in shiny black leather with a red strap around the outside, the pages crisp and new. The strap was lost. The leather lost its sheen. The pages yellowed.

She blinked. Another tome with soft brown leather, disguising the dark secrets inside. Another bound with leaves and flowers pressed between the pages. A scroll with carefully drawn engineering specs tucked inside a lichen glass.

Resting her hand on the shelf, she closed her eyes and steadied herself against the onslaught of memories.

Focus.

"One at a time, please," she thought.

Opening her eyes, Rianne searched for the first. She flipped through several books and looked in drawers of tables. Her hand paused on one volume with worn black leather and faded lettering.

"Here it is."

Time moved slowly as she searched the library for the hidden knowledge lurking in the shelves. She gathered a handful more into a growing pile on the short, circular table.

Ancient poison recipes.

Lost engineering schematics.

Primitive maps with magical waypoints noted.

Forgotten magics.

Satisfied, she stacked her terrible collection. Whether she accepted the emperor's demands or allied with the rest of Teridar, Rodarri would not fall. Perhaps Demorra and Teridar would tear each other apart and Rodarri would rise from their ashes. All she knew was that her people would be prepared for war.

"I'll take those." Rhydian reached for her.

Rianne handed them over, their fingers brushing—his blistering hot and hers frigid. He swallowed and kept his eyes on the books. A tiny starburst glimmered in her heart. Small, but there.

"Thank you," she said genuinely.

He glanced up and smiled, a smile that for once reached his eyes. She wanted to smile back, but that starburst was swallowed by darkness.

They departed the hidden library and shut the door, once more sealing the secrets to time.

The long, gray halls, peppered with rainbow flashes of stained-glass windows, led them back to Rianne's office. Her attention traced the ramparts back toward the high walls of the amphitheater, toward the ravine.

Rhydian's hand, laden with dusty tomes, hand brushed her arm. She tore her focus from the courtyard, and the smallest part of her nearly reached toward him.

"It will only hurt him," Milah warned.

Always so calculating, so emotionless, Rianne had quickly learned Milah was rarely wrong.

Rianne clasped her hands instead.

Rhydian pushed open the rose-studded door. Several dozen master engineers, sorcerers, and builders waited with uneasy expressions. Carefully selected, they'd been secreted here from all over Rodarri with no warning, and their apprehension tasted of overripe lemons. The knowledge was too precious to escape this room.

She rounded the desk, coming to stand before it with Rhydian stationed behind her holding her precious plans.

"Thank you for coming. I have tasks for you all," she said.

"Tasks, my queen? For what?" one of the most senior sorcerers asked, furrowing her brow.

"First, I must ask whether you are willing to keep confidential what I am about to show you." Her gaze lingered on each person. "On pain of death."

They exchanged glances.

"It is information you will never again discover in your lifetime. Ancient knowledge."

"For what?" a builder asked.

Rianne reminded herself to blink, to allow a knowing smile to cross her face—all the emotions they would expect from her.

"For war."

Rianne smoothed her skirts, allowing her nails to click against the gilded queensbone bodice. "I have written the emperor and invited him here to discuss alliance. If it is in Rodarri's best interests, we shall agree to terms. But if it is not, then we shall be prepared. Do you agree?"

They did. She knew they would. They'd been selected for their devotion to their crafts, and the promise of revealed secrets would be too much to refuse.

"You will be taken away from the city to conduct your research and complete this task," Rianne said. "You will not return until it is done."

Hushed murmurs offered no resistance.

Rianne opened the dusty pages of the tomes and spread them across the surface of her desk. The books opened with loud thunks.

"We build these," she gestured to the books.

Ballistas, giant crossbows firing steel arrows as tall as a man.

Trebuchets hurling boulders great distances.

Dragon's maw machines spraying flames across a battlefield.

Fang walls made from tree trunks sharpened to points.

The engineers, builders, and sorcerers packed in tightly studying the drawings and explanations of constructs long forgotten. Excitement filled the room.

"Holy hells," Rhydian murmured.

Her head engineer gaped. "What are those?"

Rianne allowed herself a smile, one that allowed happiness to brush against her dead heart. "War machines."

She gestured to one leather-bound book. "Metal Thrymr grizzly ankle traps, Shadow's Teeth spear pits, heartwood sapling spring traps, spiked barrier fang walls, lightning eel moats, and viper pits."

"Heart of the Queensblood." A builder kissed his thumbnail.

"Bentnails and coldforges," a blacksmith mumbled.

The senior sorceress leaned over a book, murmuring, "Dreamsmoke pressure traps, arrowhead... bombs?"

Rianne nodded. "Rig the oil to burst and it will launch poisoned arrowheads in every direction. They called them bombs."

The sorceress pushed her spectacles off her nose and gave Rianne a pointed look. "You want us to build *all* of these?"

Every face turned to their queen.

"Precise instructions of quantity shall be sent to each group with one copy of the plans. You have three turns of the moon before the first order must be complete."

She surveyed their wide gazes solving a hundred problems at once, the way they licked their lips with excitement at the challenge, the way they forgot to be afraid of her.

"We chose wisely," the warrior queen Whillow observed.

"Dismissed." Rianne waved her hand.

The group all filed out of her office, whispering to one another about plans for war. Several trusted guards would take them into the forest. After they all left, Rhydian shut her door.

Rianne glanced out a large window, watching the sun begin to set. Another task pressed at the edges of her mind in the dark pool of queens—something that was a long time coming. She needed the instruments of her revenge.

War Council

Chapter Fifteen

Cross my heart and hope to die.
We won't get out of this alive.

— *Mining song of the Titan Cliffs.*

1152 N.T.C. The namesake capital city of Avyllon.

Mortals and monsters from every corner of Teridar gathered in Avyllon's palatial war room. Library shelving and ceiling-height maps lined the walls, surrounding small groupings of chairs. A flat oval table with a carved map of Teridar filled the center of the room, wider than two men across. Faded paper maps, ancient battle strategy tomes, and current resource accounting documents were laid out across the main table and the smaller tables in the room. Windows carried inside gleaming sunlight from every direction.

Rubbing her hand, still concealed inside her sleeves, Aurienne surveyed the spacious room. Two dozen of their allies from every nation gathered at discussion tables, planning the war—Avyllon's leaders, the dwellers of the Seven Forests, People of Living Stone, and the adventurers who gathered their allies assembled in the room. Shimmering threads of fate tugged at them, and she knew they might never all be in the same room again.

One of the royal auditors and two members of the merchant's guild were talking in loud tones and animated hands over a stack of accounting documents. The dean of the sorcerer's university, Dean Chellaes, a short, stout woman, and willowy temple healer, Elianna, poured over stacks of magic tomes with Adonis. Aurienne circled the main table to join them.

Adonis tugged up the sleeves of his robes. "We need to find better shields to keep Rexil from opening Ways in the city."

"The walls were already warded," Dean Chellaes said, chewing the ends of her white-gray hair.

"Not well enough if he got in," Adonis muttered.

The nameless one's shade flickered as he answered, "His power was too strong. We need better wards."

All four of them started as the spy appeared from nowhere. Aurienne looked toward the shadowy outline of his head, giving him a welcoming smile. He deserved to feel included, but his appearing and disappearing made it difficult.

"And the real question is how he's able to open Ways wherever he pleases." Dean Chellaes wiped the sweat from her brow, causing her short bangs to stick up at odd angles. "Our only research on Ways is the portals doorways that are set in place with only specific destinations that require spells to open. Rexil can cut them open whenever he pleases and open them anywhere. We can't shield against them if we don't know how he's doing it. It's magic beyond our comprehension."

"Has anyone asked the elf?" Aurienne cut in.

"She was in Rodarri," Theo said.

"Where was she before she arrived in Rodarri?" Aurienne mused.

Aurienne excused herself from the table, frowning. If the emperor could open a Way at the summit, he could do it again. That type of immense magical working would be draining and couldn't be repeated too often, but it was only a matter of time.

His emissary had clearly been working with the Guild Masters, so the emperor might know where they were vulnerable. Where their barracks were. Their infrastructure. If they couldn't work out how to prevent him from opening another Way in the heart of the city, she needed to relocate them or bolster their defenses without altering anyone who might tip him off.

"Captain," she called to Captain Laurier. "I have a few things I need you to do. Discreetly."

Minutes later, he bowed and left the room. Aurienne sighed—hoping her secret plans would protect them from their enemies within.

She returned to the main table, watching their allies from other nations. Seven Forests elder, Dharek, conversed with Stone'ward and Ore'spike—the People of Living Stone. Dharek scratched the bark growing from the skin on his wrist, the cost of performing excessive forest magic. Stone'ward shifted, sprinkling dust on the crystalline quartzite floors, while Ore'spike perched on a wooden bench to avoid his metal spikes spearing the furniture. The tree giant, Allesan, sat cross-legged on the floor.

The Wildegrove witch, Kassia, and seer, Saryll, leaned over a book of wildecraft, murmuring about healing remedies and witchshields. Thaen, Dharek's son, skimmed a tome on various fauna species. His eyes darted to Kassia every so often, though she did not seem to notice.

Theo stepped into Aurienne's sights, setting down a steaming cup of elder rose honeyed tea, her favorite.

"Here you go." A roguish grin tugged at Theo's mouth, and mischief glimmered in his eyes.

A blush creeping up her cheeks. "Thank you."

Taking the ceramic mug from him, their fingers brushed, shooting bolts of heat through her chest. He sat beside her, nursing his own mug.

"We should have that checked for poison, High Seer." Sentinel Kolten leaned forward, catching Aurienne's gaze.

She swallowed.

A flash of annoyance crossed Theo's face. "I prepared the tea myself. There is no poison."

Kolten's mouth drew into a thin line. "That being true, after what happened at the aqueduct, we should check it."

Aurienne rubbed her arms to ward off the sudden chill. The dark room. The hands on her throat. The blade in her skin. The oily presence staring at her from the shadows, waiting.

Kolten reached for the tea. Theo snatched the porcelain cup before the sentinel grasped it, and without hesitating, downed a mouthful of the piping hot liquid.

He stared down the guard. "It's fine. No poison."

Aurienne's eyes widened. "Theo! You're going to be king; you can't take risks like that. What if the entire stash was poisoned! This is why we have testers."

"It's my job to protect you," Theo replied, choking on a cough.

Kolten bristled.

Aurienne stepped between them. "Everyone is here, waiting. Are you ready, Theo?"

He tensed and nodded.

"Now that we're all here, everyone, please gather," Aurienne announced. "Theo has news to share."

The room quieted.

"A week ago, Aurienne had a vision that King Cavendar would subject Rianne to an early Ascension," he said. "Rhydian and I traveled to Rodarri with Adonis but arrived too late to save Rianne. They killed her and tossed her body into the ravine. When we returned the next morning to free the remaining queens, Rianne... returned."

Expressions twisted from horror to anger to confusion.

"She climbed out of the pit and killed King Cavendar with a magical bonesword and took the throne."

Silence.

Aurienne waited for the chaos she could sense brewing.

Theo continued, "She has not decided whether to honor King Cavendar's commitment to the alliance but plans to attend the coronation."

"She came back to life!"

"Are you sure she was dead?"

Theo held up his hands. "It sounds unbelievable, I know. I saw them cut off her head with my own eyes. I'm *sure* she was dead. She came back up and her head was reattached."

Aurienne spoke up. "The coronation is scheduled for the Novahli festival of lights in two weeks. You are all welcome of course to stay here until after the coronation, and hopefully Queen Rianne will make her decision by then. I know you're eager to return home to fortify your own defenses."

Sentinel Kolten said, "In the meantime, we've received reports of the emperor's Mooncursed creatures prowling near Karme. They haven't attacked any villages yet."

"Do we know why?" Aurienne asked.

Kolten shook his head.

"They could be scouting, or testing defenses?" Seven Forest Elder, Dharek, said.

"They're looking for something," Aurienne whispered, glancing toward the nameless one. "Something that will ensure victory."

Everyone was quiet.

Aurienne frowned. The vampires were near the isthmus and should be returning soon with updates. Perhaps they had more information to share. Too much was unknown to make any real plans.

Adonis straightened. "Our parents live just outside of Karme in an outlying village. Should we warn them?"

Aurienne felt a wave of embarrassment. She'd forgotten about their family, having never truly been part of it. She sipped her tea, searching for words.

Her throat was tight, but she finally said, "Missives have been sent to every village in warning, but you can of course write them personally."

"I didn't know your family lived near Karme," Theo murmured.

His hometown. She inhaled. In another life, if she had not been bless with Sight and gone to the Triple Goddess's temple, he might have known her. They might have grown up near one another. Maybe even fallen in love. A wholly different fate.

"Is a coronation really the best use of our time and resources," one of the merchants sneered—banishing her thoughts.

Her eyes narrowed. "It cements the people's support in Theo as king. Morale is imperative before we send our soldiers off to fight. The alternatives are abysmal. We don't win unless we're united."

The merchant glowered but finally nodded.

Obermeister Gotrik entered the room, and Aurienne nearly dropped her tea. Her hands quivered around the delicate porcelain as the tall, lean man took a seat. The smell of sawdust emanated from him as he glared at her. The room spun of memories she'd tried to lock away. She flexed her broken hand, very aware of the injuries she endured.

Gotrik had never been implicated. The attackers died in the room that they'd meant to be her tomb, and no leads led directly to the Obermeister yet. She *knew* though. He was behind it all.

This is the man who tried to have me killed.

Theo glared at Sentinel Kolten, who pointedly glanced toward Obermeister Gotrik. Theo followed his gaze toward the smirking man lurking in the doorway. He glanced back at Aurienne, who felt the blood draining from her face.

Theo stood and leaned forward onto the enormous council table. "Obermeister. I don't recall inviting you here."

The Obermeister's gaze finally moved from Aurienne to Theo, and Aurienne felt a huge weight lifted. She swallowed, and Theo's knuckles turned white.

Gotrik's smirk was as thin as a snake's. "I'm sure a *blacksmith* hasn't had time to acquaint himself with the laws of Avyllon. I'll educate you. Along with the monarch and High Seer, the guilds' Obermeister, Head University Dean, merchant Trademaster, and bank Custodian attend all summits with foreign dignitaries or war councils."

"Not those under investigation of treason and murder," Kolten snapped before Theo could reply.

Aurienne's word fled as the room continued to spin. Theo glanced between her and Kolten, brows furrowing in confusion, before looking to the Obermeister.

"Unproven claims." The Obermeister smirked at Aurienne. "What happened to you was unfortunate, but I understand those responsible have been... eliminated." His expression soured.

I bet you hated that I lived, that your co-conspirators died. You never thought I would leave that room alive.

"What happened to you?" Theo asked under his breath.

She met his gaze, unable to explain, eyes pleading. Rubbing her hand, she pulled her arms closer to her body. Anger flared at the fear she felt, and she pressed her tongue against her teeth.

Theo straightened, shoving his shoulders back and jutting out his chin. "Until all doubts have been put to rest, you are not welcome here."

The Obermeister's head snapped toward Theo. "Excuse me?"

"Leave before I ask again." Theo's tone was dangerous. "My next request won't be so polite."

The Obermeister's cheeks reddened. "I wasn't aware I was under investigation."

Theo pressed his fists against the maps on the table, and the veins in his arms popped, though his face remained a mask of serenity. "I am handling the matter personally."

Gotrik stood stiffly before two sentinels escorted him from the room. Aurienne sent Theo an appreciative glance as Kolten retreated to the wall. The rest of the allies watched Aurienne with darting eyes. She reached down for the table as her legs wobbled.

"What is he talking about?" Adonis asked.

She hadn't told her brother about the assassination attempt; hadn't told Theo either, or anyone. Not even Saryll, who was probably her closest friend. She focused on Theo, studying every detail of his face. The tense lines of his stubbled jaw. The confusion in his forest green eyes. The fresh scar across his hair line. The bridge of his nose and curve of his lips. The details pushed the suffocating memories away long enough for her balance to return.

"We must be careful, enemies are everywhere," she said. "We'll wait for the vampires to report in and see what we can learn from Grimfall. After the coronation, we must prepare for war."

Turning from the war room, she strode out into the hall, forcing herself to take measured steps to not draw attention. Once out of sight, she began to hurry until she broke into a run toward her rooms in the temple.

"Aurienne?" Theo's voice echoed off the polished, white stone walls, but she didn't slow.

DAMNED SOULS
CHAPTER SIXTEEN

Fate be damned.

— *RALLYING CRY OF THE AVYLLON ARMIES.*

1152 N.T.C. The namesake capital city of Avyllon.

Storming after Aurienne, Theo glimpsed her ceremonial skirts turning the corner ahead. He'd tried to catch her after the war council meeting, but she'd fled the room.

Aurienne had never looked afraid before, and when the Obermeister entered the room—she was pale as the dead. Something had happened to her, and she'd kept it from him.

Darting inside, she disappeared into her room. Theo's palm caught the closing door with a thud. He pushed it open.

"Aurienne, what's going on?" he asked.

She was pacing, rubbing her hand.

"Aurienne," he said more gently. "Talk to me."

Shaking her head, she continued pacing. "It's fine."

He stepped into her path. "It's not fine. Tell me what's wrong."

Then he noticed the lace-covered bandage on her hand. His chest grew tight. He took her wrist, gently enough to not hurt her, but firmly enough to keep it in his grasp.

"What happened?" he asked, trying to keep his tone even.

She hesitated, refusing to meet his gaze. "It—it's fine. It's been taken care of—"

"What's been taken care of?"

She said nothing.

Someone hurt her. After all she'd endured with the Rites and everything she'd been through, her expression told him someone hurt her badly.

"What. Happened."

She looked up into his face. "There was an assassination attempt while you were away. They staged a few infrastructure attacks on the city, and I was foolish and let them get me alone." She glared toward the balcony. "I should've Seen it coming."

Theo couldn't breathe. He cradled her hand, imagining the small, cracked bones within. His pulse spiked, and his neck grew hot.

"Several guild members and a Guild Master planned to poison the water among other things," she continued. "After the sabotage on the aqueducts, I went to try and stop them. They were waiting. They meant to kill me but were unsuccessful."

Aurienne wrapped her arm around her ribs protectively. More than just her hand was injured. He released her hand to keep from harming her, as his quivering fists balled.

"What did they do?" he asked as softly as he could.

Slowly, she glided over to a wash basin. She collected a damp rag and returned. Her fingers paused at the hems of her gold-threaded gown before allowing it to slip to the floor, leaving her in a curve-hugging silk slip. Gently, she washed the paint from her face and neck, revealing layers of purple and green bruises. No longer covered in ceremonial designs, the swollen bumps on her cheek and jaw become prominent. She tilted her head to show the hand marks and rope patterns.

He could now see the stitches on her arm and rings of bruises on her wrists. The marks on her chest. The small cuts on her hands. Turning, she lifted her skirts to show him the dark bruises on her ribs and back.

Bloodsun.

His stomach churned.

"I saw this," he whispered. "When I was on the road, I had a nightmare you were in a dark room and three men were trying to kill you. It felt so real. I tried to save you, but I couldn't touch you."

"When I was nearly gone, I saw you there," she said. "You spoke to me, comforted me, saved me. I thought I was imagining it."

"It was bad enough to watch in a dream, but if this was real." He trailed off.

Theo's vision narrowed as rage overtook him. His hands were quivering with unspent bloodlust, and his lip pulled into a snarl.

"Who did this to you?" he demanded.

"They're dead," she said. "I killed them. I believe the Obermeister orchestrated it, but we have no proof yet."

The man who plotted to kill Aurienne was still alive. Believing he was safe. He walked the streets, free, believing he could hire someone to put hands on her and live. Not for long.

"I'll kill him," Theo growled.

He stood and stormed toward the door, hands itching for his Sword of Souls. He'd drive the blade deep into the man's chest after forcing him to name every single conspirator. Then he'd kill them as well and hang their corpses from the temple to serve as a warning to anyone who tried to harm her.

"Theo, wait!"

She circled around and placed both hands on his chest to stop him. He allowed himself to slow.

"You can't just go exact your revenge," she said. "We have laws. Trust me, I want to kill him too, but we can't. The war needs you. It's not worth it."

"*You're* worth it to me."

Their eyes locked, and Theo couldn't bear to break the connection. A hundred memories poured through his mind. Him saving her life at the Rite, and her being angry he interrupted her visions. Her wet-haired and barefoot in her chambers reading his fate, licking the blood from his hand. Long conversations on horseback. Sharing drinks in a tavern. Telling monster stories, laughing, and singing filthy shanties beside a campfire. Dancing underneath a midnight sky, surrounded by witches' magic. Kissing her as passionate sunfire exploded in his chest. Her remembering to sign his guild certificate and showing him the forge at Wyndsel—knowing him so well. All those little moments and so many more, and he'd nearly lost her.

"I can't let this stand," he whispered.

"Please."

His brow furrowed. She didn't understand why he had to do this. How could she not know?

Theo swallowed and took the risk of his life. "Aurienne, I..."

"Theo, we can't. I've told you," she interrupted and pulled away.

He said, "You've told me that a fate you don't understand says you can't fall in love, or it'll end in disaster. You don't know for sure what it means, whether it's changed."

"I..."

He gently grabbed her hands again. "You can't deny this. I can't stay away from you, and I don't think you can stay away from me."

"I can't stand the thought of harm coming to you," she murmured. "I can't let anything happen to you."

She cared.

Goddess, it was all the hope he needed.

"And I can't stand the thought of spending another day, another night without you, Aurienne. You're on my mind all the time. When I thought I was dying in that mountain cave, I thought of you. When the Mooncursed beasts were ripping us apart, I was thinking of you. I wanted you to be the last memory I had in this world. I will not lose you to a reading we don't understand."

"You could die," she said, sorrow crossing her brow.

"Then I die, but I want to be with you, and I know you want to be with me."

Aurienne's hands balled into fists, as though she was trying to keep from reaching for him. She glanced up and their gaze locked again, drawing him in. Theo could see past her seer armor, to the strong, selfless, and fierce woman he was falling for.

"My fate..." she whispered.

Her breathing hitched. She glanced first to his lips, then back to his eyes, fingers un-balling as she reached for him. At the last second, Aurienne paused. A war raged in her eyes between desire and hesitation.

Theo released a breath. He was willing to die for this. He wanted disaster if it meant having her.

"Fate be damned." He cradled her face in his hands and kissed her. She tasted like dark vanilla skies and honeyed heartbreak.

Aurienne wrapped her fingers into Theo's hair and kissed him with abandon.

Fate be damned.

She wanted him more than she had ever wanted anything in her life. Her heart surged as the dam on her emotions broke. Tired of giving all of herself away to those who cheered at her pain, who only saw the seer and the magic, she clung to the man who saw *her*.

With slow steps never breaking their kiss, she walked him back to the couch and pressed him back into the cushions. Aurienne slid her leg over him and straddled him on the couch, kissing him deeply. One hand roved down the curves of the muscles on his arms and over his solid chest. Their tongues met as the kiss was a salve on every hurt they suffered the past weeks.

If she could breathe him and only him, she would. His taste filled her senses, and the scent of his skin overwhelmed her with need.

His hands slipped under her thin nightdress and gripped her

hips, rolling them against the growing shaft in his pants. The silky fabric slid across her skin like delicious whispers. His calloused hands were hot against her flesh before they stilled against her still-healing scars, tracing them lightly, memorizing them. Her skin tingled and her breath came fast. She needed more.

She tugged his shirt over his head and tossed it to the floor, allowing her hands to rove over his shoulders, chest, and stomach. Drawing her name with her fingers across his chest, she claimed him. She wanted to own every inch of him. To claim him so thoroughly that he'd never be with anyone else without thinking of her. It would be her face in his mind if he took other lovers. Goddess—she wanted to ruin him because he'd already ruined her.

He traced kisses and bites down the side of her neck. His hot breath against her neck called forth a shiver as heat pooled between her legs.

Theo lifted her nightdress over her head, the soft silk sliding across her stomach. With an appreciative smirk, he studied every inch of her naked body straddling him. She reached down his stomach, into his pants, to find him hard and ready for her. With sure motions, she stroked his shaft from base to tip.

"Goddess' breath," he groaned.

Her body was on fire. It wasn't enough. Not nearly. She needed him, every delicious inch claiming her.

"I want you, now," she whispered against his ear.

"I've always wanted you," he murmured.

His fingers tightened against her hip as he bit his lip. She pushed upward from him and reached down to tug his pants off, needing more. He lifted his hips and kicked the pants off. Straddling him, she felt his erection against her entrance. The sensation of him so close to her core sent sparks through her.

Their lips met again, and her swollen lip cracked just enough for a little blood to coat his tongue. She felt it—the pull of her magic. Her Second Sight opened, and she entered the world between worlds, and for the first time, she could See Theo's soul too. It shouldn't be possible. Instinctively, she knew she could bring him with her, and her magic replenished as fast as it drained. Something about him strengthened her.

"I want to show you something I've never shown anyone, something I didn't know was possible," she said.

Theo's brow raised. Aurienne drew the ceremonial blade from her thigh. She sliced her thumb and reached for Theo's hand. Theo offered it to her, and she sliced his thumb before taking it into her mouth and licking the blood. The taste of fire jolted her tongue.

Theo's hardened shaft throbbed between her thighs against her core, slipping inside just a fraction, as he watched her slip his finger between her lips. She lifted her thumb to Theo's mouth, and he sucked it into his mouth and flicked his tongue against the small cut. She drew her hand from his mouth and pressed her forehead against his.

"Join me," she whispered.

Their blood shared, she retreated into her soul, bringing Theo's spirit with her. Reaching out with incorporeal hands, she parted the veil between worlds. With a breath of magic, she reached back for Theo's spirit. His spectral form grasped her hand before he followed her into the world of dreams.

They were in their world seeing another place drifting across their reality. Rays of golden sunshine shining between red trees appeared in her bathroom. A cool, mauve mountain stream bubbled over black stones ran across the carpets. Flowers as tall as people blossomed in a rainbow of colors on the balcony.

Flashes of memories appeared in her door frames, windows, and the painted artwork. Singing. Dancing. Kissing. Laughing. Theo's soul saving her life from assassins in a dream. Golden threads of fate wrapped around them both.

"Do you see it?" he whispered.

Eyes hooded, she nodded.

"We're meant to do this together."

Maybe he was right. He shouldn't be able to see her visions. For the first time in weeks, she used her magic without bleeding soulblood.

In both worlds, she slowly, inch by inch, lowered herself onto Theo until he was fully seated within her. He stretched her, touching the fiery nerves inside, and she tightened against him, stroking him with her inner muscles. Pain and pleasure danced as he stretched her to the core.

"You're a goddess," he murmured.

I'll be anything for you.

She lifted and lowered again, slowly at first, but picking up pace. She began to roll her hips, keeping eye contact. She gripped the back of the couch. Him staring into her eyes as she rode him nearly undid her.

His lips brushed against hers, and he traced his hands down her spine, causing gooseflesh to explode across her back. He leaned forward and dragged his tongue down the tattoos between her breasts.

"Theo," she moaned.

Her nipples, exposed to the cool air, hardened and ached. With purposeful licks, he circled her nipples before wrapping his mouth around one. He carried her toward the bed, and she continued to roll her hips against him.

Lowering her to the bed, he then stood, towering over her, eyes roving across her naked body as if memorizing her. Aurienne pushed onto her elbows and let herself enjoy her own view. Theo's body possessed scars over every hardened muscle—all the hallmarks of a man. Powerful. Determined. Hers. She felt herself grow even hotter.

Scenes of memories and visions danced around them, and stars covered the ceiling in the dreamy place between worlds. Sensations heightened, she could feel the furs tickling her spine and thighs, and the warmth emanating from the fireplace. Every sense was over-whelmed. She was so close.

Theo climbed onto the bed, kneeling between her legs. He

pushed her legs apart, devouring her with his eyes. Her breath hitched, as he positioned himself near her entrance.

"You're mine," he whispered in her ear.

It sent streaks of gooseflesh down her arms, this powerful, loyal man claiming her. Her insides clenched. She wanted him, needed him, now.

"Mine," he repeated.

She reached up and seized a fistful of blond hair, dragging her teeth across his bottom lip. She scoured her nails down the curves of his chest as he loomed over her.

She whispered into his mouth, "Mine."

"Forever."

Lifting her hips, he pushed inside of her, causing her to arch her back up to meet him, and he lowered his chest against hers. Her sensitive nipples dragged across his chest hair, sending spikes of pleasure through her. He pressed his tongue into her mouth and wrapped a hand into her hair, holding her down. Aurienne grinned through the kiss and dragged her long nails down his neck and spine.

The pace increased, and Aurienne felt herself tightening as they both raced to release. She pulled him tighter against her, unable to get close enough. She broke the kiss, locking eyes with him. Another thrust, and they came together, as pleasure ripped through her in waves that nearly caused her to black out and the visions of other worlds danced around them.

After, Theo kissed her again, slowly, passionately, and Aurienne returned the kiss—forgetting all else. They joined long into the night, crossing a line from which there was no return.

Faraway, in another world beyond veils of space and time, a golden thread of fate stretched until it nearly snapped.

GRAVEDIGGING
CHAPTER SEVENTEEN

Needle of bone, poison cursed.
Buried alone, now unearthed.

— HIGH SEER AURIENNE AZARRAH, PROPHETIC VISION.

1152 N.T.C. The royal cemetery, Castle Rodarr, Rodarri.

Under a starless sky, Rianne came to consciousness watching herself as though in a dream. She found herself crouched barefoot in a damp hole atop a forgotten grave, clawing at the packed cemetery dirt with her silver-plated fingernails. The gossamer skirts of her scarlet gown were weighed down by frozen mud, and she had long lost her silk slippers somewhere in the graveyard. The corset of ancient queen's bones—ready to answer her summons and forge her bonesword—dug into her ribs.

Rianne demanded, *"What am I doing out here?"*

"Let us show you," the queens all replied.

Fear and anger bubbled in Rianne's throat. She would not be

used, not even by them. She wouldn't be captive in her own body. Never again.

"Stop." Rianne's hand shook with effort but no longer dug into the earth.

Raechella hissed, the fractured pieces of her soul rattling Rianne's bones.

Rianne demanded, "What are you doing?"

She felt the spirits' tug on her fingers again, but she locked it down, struggling for control. They fought to wrest control away, but she held firm.

"Answer me," she said aloud.

The rose-scented fog of lost memories enveloped her. The thousand-year haze cleared, taking her within the freshly dug dungeons beneath the castle. Though in a memory, her wrists chafed against the polished edges of gold-flecked titan ore shackles. The magic warming Whillow's witch blood cooled against the dampening power. A king, whose name vanished in the pages of history, hauled her from the earthen pit to the Courtyard of Queens. She fought each step, digging her feet into the soil until she was brought to her knees and dragged along. The king wrapped the titan ore chain around her neck, forcing her gaze upon the row of queens beside the ravine.

"No," Rianne whispered the words in the present.

Whillow replied to her, *"Watch."*

The king yanked Whillow's head toward a small pile of grimoires. Rianne tasted the loss as commanders set the tomes ablaze. Years of hard work gone in a flash. The flames turned black as Whillow's blood ink burned.

The king of Avyllon emerged from the shadows of the bloodrose vines twisted around the door. Whillow's heart skipped. He was here! He would never let harm come to her. Her breath came fast as hope filled her chest. She stumbled forward, pulling against the chains. If she could just get to him.

His expression remained stone.

"Help," she pleaded.

"You've turned to the darkest magic. You've murdered innocents," he said tightly.

Whillow froze. That was not the voice of the man with whom she'd shared pillow whispers, who held her close in the quiet of night. This wasn't the man who'd touched her, worshipped her.

Her lips struggled on the words. "I told you it's not dark magic."

"How did you use it?" He clenched his fists.

Broken, contorted bodies. Sallow faces. Screams frozen in death. Shriveled veins. The dead commanders flashed before her.

"I did it to stop the ascensions," she said. "You've even said they're wrong."

He glanced to the Rodarri king uneasily.

"Now you understand us," the Rodarri king said.

Tears trickled down Rianne-Whillow's cheeks.

"This is the price of your rebellion," the Rodarri king whispered in her ear.

"Please," Whillow looked to the Avyllonian king, eyes pleading.

He didn't move.

Guards pushed the shackled queens into the ravine.

A scream erupted from Whillow's bleeding mouth, joining the falling queens. Their screams ended long before hers did.

Rianne stared into the cemetery's mist as Whillow's memory faded.

"They always betray us," Whillow said. *"The kings are from tainted lineage. The sins remain in their blood, a cycle repeating through time. All the kings must die. They must suffer what we have. The instrument of our vengeance is below."*

"Fine. Do not take control like that again," Rianne whispered.

Cool pulsing energy was their only reply.

Her hand relaxed, allowing the queens to guide her.

"Dig and dig and dig it up. Buried alone, now unearthed. Needle of bone, poison cursed. Dig it up, deadly cuts," Callysta muttered.

Rianne crouched again, digging deeper to reach the crypt, where the bloodwitches within her sensed the dark object was buried. From the moment she returned, she had been unknowingly drawn to it, craving the symmetry of ending that story with its beginning. Innocent bones cut down by royal blood, now ancient bones would destroy their condemned bloodline.

Poetry.

Rianne shook her head, unable to discern her own hazy thoughts from those of the incensed queens. She allowed them to guide her, watching in dread.

"Queens fall one by one by darkened hand. Darkened bone returns king's blood to sand," Callysta cackled.

An emerald serpent slithered by, and Raechella hissed at it eliciting a retreat from the scaled beast.

"You can't kill what's already dead," Rianne sang quietly as Callysta's presence pushed forward.

Her claws raked against the granite crypt stone. Carefully, she cleared the dirt off, revealing a small flat square door hiding in the earth, sealed by time and clay. She dragged her silver claws down the seam before wedging a long, pressed iron rod between the stones. Using the side of the pit as leverage, she pressed her weight against the rod.

"Useless frail body," Whillow said.

With precise motions, Rianne wrenched it back and forth, loosening the crypt stone. She gripped her lever with pale, nearly bony hands and heaved a final time. Grinding stone scraped against stone, and finally the small capstone shifted from the depression. Dropping her lever, she slid the stone open, revealing the steep staircase within.

Rianne crept down the ancient stairs, smelling the tang of stale air and utter darkness. Mice skittered across the floor, and spiderwebs spanned every corner. Her feet crunched a small vermin skull, causing her foot to bleed. She mentally noted the need to cleanse and wrap her foot later to keep it from festering. Her nails dragged against the rough granite walls with a series of clicks, until she reached the sealed vault. Silver spirits whirled out of her mouth to circle the door like a sterling whirlpool. Metal gears and locks inside the vault clunked and turned, and the door swung open. The frigid spirits seeped back into Rianne's skin, finding purchase in her bones, taking her breath away as though she'd been doused in a winter river.

Muddy skirts brushing against dusty stones, she entered the vault. Three raised stone coffins filled the room, covered in remnants of flowers and scraps of silk. She brushed the small tokens away from the center coffin. Only the oldest whispering spirits remembered who was buried there, even remembered this crypt existed at all.

This final resting place of Kairya, the bloodwitch, and her coven of Rodarri witches had remained undisturbed since the Shadow War a millennia ago. King Cavendar, the first Rodarri king, kidnapped Kairya's coven and sacrificed the Safyrah and Noxanya as Queensblood. In reply, she attacked, slaying a regiment of his army and nearly killing him. That night, she cursed the bloodlines of all the kings of Teridar, a promise that her departed sisters remembered these centuries later. A promise Rianne would keep for them.

Kairya's soul lingered within Rianne beside her covenmates Noxanya and Safyrah. She'd never ascended, but so great was their bond, she'd found them in death.

"King Cavendar is dead," Raechella crooned. *"Dead. Dead. The kings of Thrymr and Titan Cliffs are dust, their lines ended. Two remain. King Jaekob Juri, and King-apparent Atheodoren Aradey."*

Rianne swallowed.

Kairya's emotions bloomed sharply in Rianne's chest. Loss. Anger. Grief. Devastation. The promises made and broken.

"Now do you see?" Vittoria asked.

Rianne pressed a kiss to the coffin lid with her fingers, feeling Kairya's presence. "Our time has come, sisters."

Rianne slowly rolled the lid open, exposing the veiled face of the bloodwitch, Kairya. She reached inside, finding the witch's skeletal hand.

Crack.

She snapped the left index finger, separating it from the corpse.

Carefully, she lifted it. The fingertip was pointed and sharp, like a needle, Kairya's favorite weapon. The bone was black to the marrow, a remnant of the dark magic once coursing through the witch's blood.

"Perfect," Nicollete crooned.

With a final look upon the veiled face, she rolled the lid back in place and set her hand atop the smooth stone. The spirits rattled in her bones, and she shed a single silver tear, one long owed to the witch.

A quiet voice whispered, *"A thousand queens dead for nothing, and not one more shall die. Our revenge is long overdue, and I shall have what is mine."*

She slipped a ruby ring from her finger and placed it atop the coffin. Then she left the vault and sealed the door. She glided through the dusty passage and back to the steep stairwell. With light steps, she climbed the stairs to the world above.

"Oh, how the kings shall die," Rianne found herself murmuring.

Rianne crawled out of the crypt and, feeling eyes on her, glanced up—palming the cursed bone needle in her long lace sleeves.

Above, Rhydian stood in the desolate cemetery staring down into the hole where she was covered in grave dirt. His brows furrowed deeply. She tilted her head, trying to read him better, and it only served to deepen his scowl.

Milah said quietly, *"He can't learn the truth."*

"He will foil our plans," Whillow agreed.

"Kill him!" Morgana shouted.

Rianne came screaming to the surface of their mind, fighting back all the queens with silver claws.

Rianne snarled, *"Not him!"*

Shrieking, they fled into her bones and blood.

Having searched half the night for his queen before finding the small footprints leading to nowhere, Rhydian never expected what awaited in the abandoned corner of the royal cemetery. He froze at the nightmarish sight of Rianne standing in a dug-up crypt, covered in the dirt of the dead, singing riddles to herself. She slid the crypt stone closed, and it fell into place with a boom.

She cocked her head unnaturally, silver eyes glistening, and for a moment Rhydian forgot it was Rianne staring up at him. His Warbringer blood woke in the face of danger, softly humming for violence. As frozen needles burst inside his veins, he instinctively gripped his sword hilt, and her shimmering silver eyes darted to his hand.

Her gaze narrowed for a half second before she shook her head until her expression softened. The familiar dazzling smile he knew bloomed across her face.

"Why are you out here alone—what are you doing?" he stammered.

With wide eyes, she reached and said just a little too sweetly, "There was an artifact I was searching for, something I saw when I was... when... well *they* showed me something, and I thought it could help us."

He scowled but leaned down and helped her out of the hole. Her skin was cold against his. Her skin never used to be cold.

"Did you find it?" he asked.

She shook her head, but her sharp gaze flicked to his face, just for a moment as if studying him. *A lie.* Rianne never lied before.

Rhydian took a step back, tugging his hand out of hers. Maybe she had changed more than he realized. He watched her warily, wondering whether it was really Ria—

"I'm cold," she shivered. "Can we go inside now?"

She looked up at him, the color of her eyes bleeding into a sky blue.

Rhydian's heart twinged, and he immediately pulled off his fur-lined cloak. "Here, take this. It's too cold for you to be out here alone."

Eyes watering, she nodded. "I don't remember coming out here. It was like being in a dream, but real."

"I'll remind you who you are, just as you've done for me."

She tripped, and he noticed her shoes were gone and her gown was coated in mud. With another shiver, she pulled the cloak around herself and struggled against her skirts.

He stopped and held his arms out. "Let me carry you."

She wrapped her arms around his neck and pressed a cool kiss to his jaw. "Thank you."

So many moments now, he hardly recognized her. He could see the spirits of the queens taking control, wearing Rianne's face like a mask. But in these tender glimpses she was Rianne. Relief flooded through him, and he pressed a gentle kiss against her hair and held her tightly as he trudged back to the castle.

ANCIENT PACTS
CHAPTER EIGHTEEN

Wolf's tooth and shadow's maw
Ancient curse and blackened claw.

— *High Seer Aurienne Azarrah, prophetic*
vision.

1152 N.T.C. The Hunger's Teeth Mountains, near the Terre Isthmus.

That night, Stellan did not hunt. He watched, and he waited. Chilled winds blew through his perch in the lonely mountaintops. Again, the cursed creatures crossed from Demorra into Teridar across the isthmus. As night bled into day, the beasts ran back across—avoiding his vampires as much as possible. He couldn't be sure if they were the same Mooncursed leaving each night, but it seemed they didn't remain long. How long could the beasts remain? And where were the emperor's armies? They should be here.

What are you looking for? Why?

Questions he pondered all through the sunlit hours.

Tonight, Stellan would have his answers. Crouching on all four clawed hands and feet, he waited for the last dregs of sunlight to expire. Then he flew. He took to the skies with several dozen of his creations. Drifting from one wind stream to another, he caught flashes of fur between the trees. Tucking his leathery wings tightly against his back, he descended upon the small pack like a whirlwind. Stellan landed in the midst of the deformed creatures with a crack that split the earth beneath his feet. His limbs and fangs were a blur hurling fur and flesh flying through the trees.

A large Mooncursed lunged at him, swiping its massive paws toward his head. This one had been sewn together with pieces of man, wolf, and a bear. It lumbered toward him with a slack jaw and unblinking eyes. Stellan's keen senses caught the tiniest tensing movement in the creature's neck, and he dodged sideways. Not a second later, the Mooncursed's bear-like jaw closed where Stellan had just been, the rows of teeth snapping.

Stellan punched through the bear's chest bones, grinding against the titan ore plates beneath the skin. Hissing, he yanked his fist backwards, but it caught against the plates. The Mooncursed roared and slashed at the vampire. Stellan leapt backward, but the bear's claws raked his shoulder. Dark blood oozed from the ripped flesh, and his weakened arm burned.

Another Mooncursed—this one a wolf and a mountain lion— dove at Stellan. He wheeled the bear around, blocking the attack. The mountain lion sprang again, but Stellan kicked it in the head, and it went sprawling into the trees.

Stellan narrowed his eyes. He took a large step forward and punched harder through the chest plate. His fist met the beast's heart. Claws wrapping around the organ, he ripped backward— freeing the heart and plate together. The Mooncursed bear roared, and Stellan took a large bite out of its heart.

Shooting forward, he sank his teeth into its neck, and drained what blood remained in its veins. Stellan watched as the fresh blood mended the slash marks in his skin.

Nearby, Mooncursed howls and vampire hisses signaled conflicts throughout the woods. He could smell the spilled blood even miles away.

The mountain lion soared out of the undergrowth. Stellan caught it by the throat. It struggled in his grasp, snarling and kicking. Its back claws caught him in the forearm, slashing him open to the bone, and the front claws tore into his hand. With a flick of his wrist, Stellan snapped the creature's neck, and it hung limply from his grip. He drank from the beast, and his injuries vanished again. The corpse landed on the ground with a squelch.

A massive form slammed into Stellan's back and sent him tumbling against a tree. Whirling around, a two-headed wolf lunged for him. He caught a thick neck in one claw, but the other head snapped and snarled a hairsbreadth from his face. Spittle coated his cheek, and he kneed the beast in the chest to create space. Kicking both feet out, Stellan launched past the tree and into the air. The wolf lunged at the tree, all six limbs scraping against the bark and branches as it climbed. The tree groaned under the wolf's immense weight. Stellan flapped his wings, but the canopy left little room for him to gain altitude.

The wolf launched off the tree. Stellan beat his wings until his back muscles screamed, but the Mooncursed caught him by the ankle. It dragged him back down to the earth.

"Stellan!" Julietta cried.

Julietta launched for the wolf, who slashed her stomach open, sending her to her knees. She screamed and hissed, pressing her claws into her innards. Another smaller Mooncursed tackled her, and the two rolled into nearby evergreen saplings.

The two-headed wolf circled Stellan. Julietta's enraged howls tore his attention away from his foe. A low rumbling emerged from the large wolf, as six paws padded the soil. Its muscles bunched.

"I won't lose another," Stellan growled.

The wolf launched again. At the last moment, Stellan clawed at the wolves' throats, but his long claws screeched off the titan ore collar. He sent his elbow into its ribs, and it howled.

Slash.

Punch.

Swipe.

Knee.

Slash.

Bite.

Stellan descended on the wolf in a fury. He sank his fangs into one of its limbs. The fresh blood mended the wounds he earned from his efforts before it shook him off. He licked his lips, savoring each drop.

Wrathful screams arose from Julietta somewhere nearby, and he knew he had to get to her. He heard the breaking of saplings, the churning of soil, and the falling of pine needles. From the smell, both the vampire and wolf were bleeding heavily.

The beating of wings signaled Nico's arrival. His nephew landed on the wolf's back from the skies, biting down into the back of its neck. It howled, shaking and slashing for the vampire. Stellan shot forward, fangs piercing into its throat. The beast stumbled and fell to its stomach. It shuddered as the fight finally went out. Eyes wild, the beast stilled.

Stellan released the wolf and half-flew into the saplings where Julietta had wrapped her claws around the wolf's throat and was squeezing.

"Are you alright?" he asked.

Covered in a litany of scratches, she nodded.

"Hold it," he ordered Julietta.

Wiping his crimson stains on his mouth across the back of his hand, he approached the snarling beast caught in her claws. It struggled against her firm grip, but it was one of the smaller beasts he'd seen, and it would not escape her now.

Nico stepped into the grove, eyes black from the hunt.

"Collect the titan ore from the others. And stake this one to the ground," Stellan ordered as the Mooncursed struggled beneath his claws.

Nico disappeared, returning soon after with bloodstained titan ore collars, plates, screws, and stakes.

Stellan selected a few pieces. "If there's any part of you not gone to the curse, I am sorry for this," he said, before driving a long stake through the beast's chest and into the ground.

It screamed, a sound entirely too human.

Nico wrapped chains around it, locking up its limbs and securing it to a tree. The beast wouldn't be escaping. It hissed and snarled.

"Did you find the warden?" Stellan asked.

Nico grinned. "She was delicious."

"Good," Stellan said. "Then hopefully no one will come looking for this one."

Licking his fangs, he glanced at the lightening skies and then back at his female companion. She was dripping blood from a dozen wounds, and a large, jagged wound in her belly threatened to spill her insides.

"Heal your wounds," he said to Julietta. "Dawn approaches."

"As much as I enjoy the thrill of the hunt and agitated blood, we will tire of this," she replied, sticking her claws through the holes in her silken shirt. "We lived in the dirt and filth for centuries. I, for one, crave the luxuries we were deprived. Fine cloths. Baths. Beds. Palaces. Royal blood."

"We aren't having this conversation again." He bristled. "I have spoken on the matter. We swore an oath to our families, and it lives on in the girl. Until the enemies seeking to destroy her home are gone, we will fight."

Julietta rolled her eyes and tussled her thick, dark hair. "You could just grab her and fly her to another continent. She'd be safe then. And we could follow our true desires."

"Julietta," he hissed. "You forget we agreed to only kill those with the darkest of sins or the enemies of Miella. That was the deal for our release. We are not oath breakers."

"We've given enough," she shot back. "I bore of this. I want to play."

Nico's dark eyes gleamed, and Stellan could sense the hungry anticipation in the air surrounding the others.

"The matter is closed," he said firmly. "Our oath holds."

Julietta hissed under her breath, and Stellan snarled at her until she pursed her blood-stained lips. A pop of air and dark shadow in the skies was all she left in her wake. Stellan licked the black blood from his fangs.

"Let's find shelter nearby. I want to see what happens to this beast," Stellan said.

"There are no caves for miles," Nico replied.

"The earth it is," Stellan said.

Stellan dug deeply into the earth, settling himself in the musty embrace, waiting. He listened to the screams of the captured Mooncursed. Dawn broke and memories came rushing back. He nearly wanted to go free the creature from its misery, but the self-preservation of the curse would not let him go into the sun. Instead, he shed tears as he listened to it suffer.

The next night, the beast was still alive. Stellan left it food and water, and eventually it succumbed and partook. The injuries were not severe enough to kill it, yet it was already substantially weakened. As he suspected—something magical was at play.

Stellan waited another day, listening to the mournful howls of the beast. As dusk fell, the Mooncursed quieted. Stellan pushed out of the ground, shaking the dirt free. He stood over it quietly. It had wasted away to nearly nothing in a day, even with ample food and water nearby. It had not lost enough blood to have died naturally.

Two days.

That's all the Mooncursed could remain inside Teridar's borders. But why? Why were they forced to flee the continent? Understanding tickled the back of his mind but eluded him.

What is the emperor doing?

Stellan turned over the strange behavior in his mind. Wolves running in and out, unable to stay very long. As if something was keeping them out—the thing they were looking for. He straightened as realization clicked.

They're looking for a way in, to stay in.

Maybe the magic of those ancient pacts still held from all those centuries ago and still kept the Shadows out, for now. And maybe the Mooncursed were searching for it to tear the protection down.

Taking to the skies, Stellan flew as fast as his wings would carry him. Julietta and Nico raced behind him. Stellan followed the winds, each beat of his wings booming in the skies with thunder. Toward the isthmus, he flew.

As he reached the borders of Teridar, he felt a strange resistance in the air. Pushing through, he sensed a pop. He slowed his advance, going back and forth through the invisible barrier. It was a definite and clear demarcation.

On the other side, the air felt murky, heavy, and wrong. Corrupted magic walked these lands. Teridar's protection only extended so far.

And beyond that, he could sense the gathering power of the Shadows of old. They were there, waiting to attack. Waiting for the protection to fall. And once they did, even the terrible Mooncursed would look like child's play. Gods save them all.

"What is this?" Julietta whispered.

"It feels like—" Nico began.

"It is," Stellan answered.

Without another word, Stellan turned and raced for Avyllon to warn Miella and her allies. All their questions had been answered. Ancient pacts remained, though they were now in danger. If the emperor got his hands on what he sought, then the Shadow Wars had been for nothing. The protections would fall and beings worse than the Mooncursed would come for them.

I know what the emperor has been searching for, and why he hasn't found it.

Hangman's Noose

Chapter Nineteen

You have not seen their hearts as I have.

— Grimfall.

1152 N.T.C. Castle Rodarr, Rodarri.

A letter stamped with the seals of the nine commanders of Rodarri taunted Rianne. She skimmed the relevant portions again.

We do not recognize the authority of Queen Rianne...

In three days' time, the commanders shall convene a council to select the next king...

Your sacrifice is praised and appreciated but...

Our armies march to the capital for the selection of a new king.

Face frozen into a mask devoid of emotion, Rianne tapped her silver-plated nails against the letter on her polished desk in a slow rhythmic pulse.

Milah muttered, *"Unexpected."*

Of all the actions they'd anticipated the commanders might take, this was not one of those deemed likely. Not this quickly. The queens expected pressuring, scheming, bargaining. Not outright treason. Perhaps they should have seen it coming though.

"Those entitled, foolish old men would never see our claim to the throne as valid." Whillow's rage simmered.

Nicollete's coppery distrust crawled up Rianne's throat. *"A mistake easily rectified."*

"Bold of them to attempt a coup so soon," Morgana said. *"Perhaps they recognized this as their only opportunity."*

Rianne said, *"If I was able to stabilize my power, they would never wrest it from me, and they knew it."*

Samantah said, *"They're foolish."*

They witnessed her return, the king's execution, her magic—and still they believed she would give up her throne?

Rhydian stepped into her office and gave her a shallow bow. "My queen."

"Summon the commanders to the Courtyard of Queens in two hours. Bring their families as well. Tell them I plan to respond to their letter." Her eyes studied each waxen seal pressed into the bottom of the paper.

She could have cut them all down that bloody day of her return but instead spared them, and they repaid her with treason. No one could say she did not first give them a chance to obey. What came next was of their making.

Rhydian's gaze darted to the letter. "As you command."

He strode out of the office, and Rianne could sense Nesryn somewhere nearby, always tracking him. That elf was a complication she had not accounted for and was not yet equipped to handle. Three queens demanded justice from their residence in her bones but facing the elf now would end in certain death.

Turning her thoughts to the commanders, she listened to the spirits. They calculated the responses—seeing the strengths and weaknesses and potential consequences.

Milah said, *"They'll never stop plotting to take your throne."*

"Mercy today will bring death upon wings of betrayal. The seed of treachery will grow vines that snuff you out." Callysta's voice rang with prophecy.

Milah finished, *"They've made their choice, let them see it through."*

"What of those loyal to them? They'll hate me more," Rianne whispered.

Vittoria murmured, *"The people will never love you, but they can fear you."*

Whillow agreed, *"Show them your strength. Teach them to obey."*

"Cleanse the land." Nicollete's rageful laugh joined.

Rianne stammered, *"I can't..."*

"You must," Milah said. *"Or they take control, and the ascensions begin again."*

"We'll be no better than they are." Rianne swallowed.

Milah said, *"Swift and ruthless acts are required to pave the way for change."*

Rianne's heart fell. They were right. She'd seen history repeat in an unending cycle. If she didn't stop them now, it would repeat once more. With shaking hands, she scribbled a note and rang a bell for her courtier.

The young man entered the room, chin high, refusing to look her in the eye.

She handed a small slip of paper to her courtier. "I want this done immediately. Within the hour."

The attendant's mouth went slack, and her eyes widened into saucers.

"A problem?" Rianne crooned.

"Right away, Your Majesty." The attendant bowed low and scurried out of her office.

"And send my sister to me," Rianne called.

Soon after, Jordyn slipped inside, avoiding eye contact with Rianne, playing with her skirts. A small voice among a thousand was hurt, but the rest expected this. The other returned queens remembered the responses to their own silver eyes, the glances darting to the never-healing neck scar. The whispers in dark passageways. The fear.

"You asked for me?" Jordyn mumbled.

"Things will change around here."

"Like what?" Jordyn asked.

Rianne gazed out the stained-glass windows to the surrounding castle town. "Everything."

"You never told me... what happened."

Rianne gritted her teeth. "You'll never have to find out. I'll make sure of that."

Protecting the Queensblood was why she was willing to do as the queens suggested. Why she would allow her hands to be stained crimson.

"But what happened?" Jordyn asked.

"I don't wish to relive my own death if you don't mind." Rianne's tone was level, stripped of emotion. "It was terrible and while there may be peace in death for some, there was not for me."

Jordyn's gaze slipped to the floor. Rianne studied her sister. Fifteen. So full of hopes and dreams. Believing she had all the answers, and yet knew nothing. Beautiful enough to have whatever she wanted, but too weak to have escaped her fate on her own. Just as Rianne had been.

The attendant stepped into Rianne's office with a deep bow. "It's ready, and they're waiting."

"Come see the beginning of this change," Rianne said to Jordyn.

Rianne gestured for Jordyn to follow, walking the long stone castle halls. She stepped into the waning afternoon light to find the cursed courtyard full of commanders, their families, and a hundred courtiers and castle staff, all casting furtive glances at the large, covered object beside the ravine. Around the high amphitheater walls, dozens of Rodarri guards were posted.

"I received your letter," Rianne announced to the waiting commanders.

They glared at her, expressions dripping with malice.

Rianne folded her hands. "You wrote that you do not observe my authority as queen, though I bested the king in combat. I returned from the dead to protect Rodarri, yet you plan to select another to rule? Do you deny it?"

"Queens do not rule Rodarri, certainly not Queensblood," a commander hissed.

"Do any of you deny it?" Rianne surveyed the gathered.

Silence.

"You have admitted to your crime: treason."

Dozens more guards filed out of the doorways, weapons drawn toward the commanders.

The commanders glanced at one another, faces twisted into what Rianne identified as confusion. She blinked. Why were emotions so hard to distinguish now? Many guards glanced to Rhydian, who hadn't moved. Several queens crept out into the courtyard. Maids and butlers watched from doorways.

"You shouldn't have tipped your hand," she said. "Your pride and egos will be your downfall."

The commanders exchanged wry glances.

"I do not accept your terms. Your heirs will lose their titles and armies disbanded and reformed into a single royal army—who will answer to my Warbringer. As for you..." Her silver eyes darkened. "The punishment for treason is hanging."

Gasps erupted from the small crowd as attendants pulled the covers draped over the structure to the dirt. Color drained from every face.

Nine nooses swung in the breeze on the executioner's platform.

The musty wood smelled of stale water from the dungeons, but it would do.

Jordyn's face paled when her eyes locked on to the platform, and she glanced to her sister, eyes wide. "No."

Rianne motioned to the guards who grabbed the commanders and dragged them to the executioner's platform. The men fought feebly, unable to free themselves from the overwhelming force.

"No!" a wife cried out.

"Unhand me! I command you!" Commander Tavish shouted at the guards.

Bram Tavish, recently twenty-three years old, drew his blade to defend his father, but four guards arrested him.

One wife, carrying a new infant, dropped to her knees, pleading, "Please no, he did not understand, please."

The guards dragged the commanders to the top of the platform, holding them in place behind the swaying nooses.

Sobs and wails echoed in the amphitheater.

"You cheer when I lose my head, but cry for them?" Rianne-Nicollete snarled at the crowd.

"Rianne," Rhydian whispered, but she waved him off.

"The death of innocent Queensblood has always been met with banners and cheering," she said. "Yet the fate of your treasonous commanders is met with tears?"

"Please spare my husband. We have children," a woman cried, gesturing to her young children.

"I take it back. We recognize your reign," a commander begged, tears streaming down his bloated face.

"Have mercy," another said.

Rianne surveyed them coolly, expression still as stone. "Mercy? A thousand queens died without *mercy*. You had your chance to submit and answered with treason."

The hooded executioner stood waiting beside a long lever. Rianne gestured to the guards. One by one, the guards looped the nooses around the commander's necks. More guards held screaming wives and shouting children back. Rianne blocked out the screaming, for it did not matter.

The sons of the commanders looked only at Rianne. Bram Tavish wore a promise in his unblinking glare. She knew their hate. It was the same she felt at every ascension of her family.

"Rianne," Rhydian whispered. "Are you sure you want to do this?"

Rianne gazed toward Rhydian's pleading eyes. A few voices inside her head begged her to stop, but they were too quiet among so many vengeful voices. There was no other viable option. Once a dog turned on its master and drew blood, it could never be trusted again. Nothing could sway her. Her withered heart held no mercy.

Nooses tightened around nine necks, and the executioner looked to Rianne.

"Give them what they deserve."

The platform dropped, and families screamed.

"A thousand queens, dead for nothing. A thousand more to die. A thousand queens, dead for nothing, and not one more shall die," Rianne murmured.

Boots twitched until they all fell still.

Rhydian's limbs were as frozen as his expression, watching the commanders swing from ropes in the cursed amphitheater with its insatiable appetite that he now feared would consume them all before the war was done. The cries of wailing families sliced the air like shattering glass. Disbelief and anger etched into every face. Unending cycles of hate continuing through generations.

There had to be a better way.

Nesryn appeared beside him, a shadow materializing from the mists. She watched the swaying corpses speculatively. "Hell reigns when gods and monsters go to war, and mortals are caught in the middle."

"Are you going to kill Rianne?" he whispered.

She gazed at him unblinking. "For what?"

He glanced to the horror behind her.

"For killing a few bad men?" Nesryn shook her head and strolled into the castle, leaving him all alone. "She'll have to do worse than that."

Rhydian was quiet for long moments. His mind refusing to make sense of what he saw. Of the choices Rianne could never take back, and he wondered if he ever knew her at all.

Rianne waited at the top of the grand staircase in the royal ballroom, watching the assembled Queensblood gather at the foot of the stairs. Dozens of queens watched her warily.

Rianne smoothed her long black gown, fighting the urge to trace the lattice designs weaving up her throat, concealing her wound. Long scarlet panels hung from her shoulders and draped the floor with five fist-sized gold discs spanning each panel. The top discs connected with a doubled gold chain crossing her bosom. Her long, tight sleeves were velvet, matching the velvet roses on her skirts. The bodice of gilded bones peeked out from underneath the draped panels.

Milah reassured Rianne, *"This is necessary too. They must be made strong if they are to ever truly be free."*

Rianne whispered, "I know."

Bit by bit, these crucial acts chipped away her soul. By the end, would anything be left?

"I should have addressed you earlier, but there was much to do. I had to secure my power to ensure the promises I make to you all," Rianne announced.

She eyed the queens below, and beside them glimmered a thousand more spectral faces of queens she was too late to save. The living queens stared up at her, expectant and afraid. Huddling like sheep cornered in a pasture with a wolf. Feeling Whillow's presence, Rianne's red rage tinged with the green of disgust. No wonder they were treated like victims and sacrificial lambs—they acted like it.

"Mine was the last ascension. Never again shall Queensblood ascend. I shall destroy the practice root and stem. You are all free. You are welcome to remain in the palace, or you may leave. No one is stopping you. The days of the Queensblood died with me."

Tears sprang from every eye.

"Really? We won't ascend?"

"How will we protect Rodarri?"

"What happens once you're gone?"

So many questions, and none of them mattered, so Rianne ignored them. "Who intends to leave?"

Silence met her, as she suspected. There was nowhere else to go.

"The commanders committed treason, signed with their seals. They did not recognize my authority and paid for their transgressions. It leaves open nine commander positions," Rianne said.

"In a world coddling such darkness, if you want power you must reach out and rip it from those who hoarded it," Vittoria said. *"The weak will be caged, walked on, beaten, and tossed into a bottomless ravine of death."*

"I will fill the positions with former queens," Rianne continued. "Once you've earned it."

Silence met her. Blinking eyes. A mewling babe. Slack faces.

"Aunt Yllicea for region one, Aunt Tamiira for region two, Cousin Marta for region three..." she listed off the names and finished with, "and my sister Jordyn for region nine. The rest of you will be given administrative positions, unless you select otherwise."

Jordyn squeaked, "I don't know anything about running a region, or leading a battalion—and not into war!"

The other women nodded fearfully.

Gritting her teeth, Rianne said, "Rhydian and I will help you learn what you need to know. You'll shadow us until you're ready."

"But..." Jordyn continued.

Rianne's mind was flooded with images of the queens before them falling to the same fate. She could imagine her sister's broken body crunching against the bleached bones. She would never allow it.

Nicollete and Whillow's rage bursting inside her, Rianne flew down the staircase, boots hardly touching the stairs. Jordyn recoiled but Rianne grabbed her by the arms and shook her, silver plated fingernails digging into her sister's skin leaving ten bloodied marks.

Rianne and Whillow snapped, "If you don't want to be some weak helpless little victim again, you'll learn and you'll take the opportunity offered to you. You should be jumping at the chance to be something more than useless, with your only value in your death. You should be ashamed."

Tears streamed down Jordyn's cheeks as betrayal lurked in the corners of her expression. The others edged away from the pair, holding their breath. Rianne clutched Jordyn's wrist and dragged her to the main library, four-dozen-some queens stumbling behind them to keep up.

Rianne shoved Jordyn into the library and snapped her fingers at the other queens to filter inside. The anger boiling inside her at the thought of losing her family unleashed all the emotions of the queens.

Pointing to the books, Rianne hissed, "All of you nearly died. You accepted your fate and it's pitiful. At least I tried to escape, to help you all to escape. You *will* be the new commanders, and you will fill your heads with enough knowledge that others will respect you. Each of you will be expected to take up a job in the castle to pull your dead weight. And before that, your training begins at dawn." Rianne paused and dragged her gaze across the pale, tear-stained faces, feeling the influence of the queens in her brain. "If you want to be treated like you matter, then stop acting like you don't."

Choking on a silent sob, Rianne stormed out, leaving the queens in the library to decide futures they never thought they would be offered all while hating her for it.

Vittoria whispered to Rianne, *"Let them hate us. At least they would be strong."*

Faces of the Goddesses

Chapter Twenty

The Goddess knows all.

*— Book of the Triple Goddess, article I,
verse 1.*

1152 N.T.C. The namesake capital city of Avyllon.

Wool dust covers slipped to the floor, revealing life-sized golden griffin statues with sparkling amethyst eyes. Master carpenters hoisted beams upward on pulleys as newly hired palace staff shook out dusty tapestries and masons examined the stones for damage. The royal palace of Avyllon descended into a frenzy as Aurienne directed the preparations for Theo's coronation and planned every meticulous detail to endear him to the people.

"Protect the tree throne from the construction," she gestured to a handful of workers surrounding the throne in metal forged scaffolding with floor-length dust sheets.

"We've finished hanging the stars, High Seer," a glassworker said.

She glanced up. "We need twice as many stars to reflect the sun."

The glassworker's eyes widened but the woman bowed and scurried away.

The coronation was more important than any of the allies realized, than even Theo realized. It was the beacon of his legitimacy; one he would need when leading their people to war. More than one voice questioned the need for a party in the face of impending war—but she'd seen the outcomes without it. The Guild Masters, merchants, and other powers in Avyllon needed to see the people's support of Theo. They needed to see the people love him, and of course they would. How could they not? She smiled to herself before re-focusing on the task. Everything must be perfect.

Pacing the room, Aurienne scrutinized every detail. Sentinel Kolten tracked her every step from his position near the wall.

Adonis entered the throne room and barely sidestepped one of the dozen workers hurrying about their work. His sorcerer's apprentice robes swished against the newly polished tiles, and the leather satchel looped over his shoulder contained a handful of tomes. He danced around another worker carting window cleaning products and tools. Finally, her brother reached her.

"Have you and the others at the university identified any magical sites that the Mooncursed might be searching for?" she asked, still studying the preparation schedule in her hands.

Adonis shook his head. "So far, the Mooncursed have only been reported in southeast Avyllon around Karme and south toward Riverlim, nearly to Heartspring. They're staying close to the coast. There are no Ways nearby. Even on the oldest maps we've found, there are no magical monuments in that area. The king's catacombs of Wynds are also too far. They're not straying inland far enough to be interested in the Courtyard of Queens, any of the original cities before the Shadow War, or the fabled Warrior's Weald. There are no religious sites or old god temples there. There's... nothing."

Aurienne grimaced and continued to review her list.

Adonis followed her through the throne room. "Even the

ancient walking forests were farther south, while the golden winged warriors of the Lost Pass were farther north. There are no sinkholes, dancing lakes, wind vortexes, shifting earth, or hellholes nearby. Even the water sprites, dark water reaching streams, fire beasts, gargoyles, and sirens were never reported there."

She pinched the bridge of her nose as her heart sank.

Another dead end.

"Thank you. Keep searching," she said.

Adonis cleared his throat. "My final test to earn my Sorcerer Journeyman guild certificate is in just a few weeks. I need your signature."

"Of course," she said. "Hold the question in your mind."

She drew her divination cards from a velvet bag in a hidden pocket of her gown. Quick fluid motions, she shuffled them, whispering to them, until they grew warm.

"Do I have approval to take the test?" he asked.

She flipped the first card. The Magician figure on the card grinned at her before slamming his fist into a tome and disappearing into an eruption of papers.

Rude.

Flipping the second card, she revealed The Night, signifying nightmares, anxiety, grief, depression. She glanced up at Adonis, noting the bags under his haunted eyes. The fading yellow bruise on his cheek from the Warbringer. The firm set of his jaw. The carefree brother was gone and in his place was a survivor.

The third card turned to reveal The Sea—change, rebirth, transformation.

"Well?"

None of these were good omens, but The Sea signified transformation, and Aurienne did not want to stand in the way of her brother's evolution.

"Hand it to me," she said.

With a looping scrawl, she signed her name to the approval form

—similar to the one she signed for Theo what felt like an eternity ago.

"Adonis—" she began.

"I'd like a word," Obermeister Gotrik interrupted, pushing his way into the throne room.

"Thanks," Adonis gave her a two-finger salute and slipped out.

Aurienne steeled herself, fighting the tremors in her body. Impatience, anger, and a thin sliver of fear thrashed inside her mind. She crossed her hands in front of her, fingers brushing against the ceremonial blade she concealed in her skirts.

"High Seer," the Obermeister's voice was scales on stone.

Sentinel Kolten pushed off the wall and came to stand beside her, hand on his sword.

"I'm glad I caught you," Gotrik said in a clipped tone.

"I'm quite busy with the coronation preparations," she retorted.

"You look tired. *Beaten* down, perhaps. I do hope you're staying in good health?" he replied.

She glared. So far, the sentinels had turned up no evidence that he was involved in the assassination attempt, but they both knew he was behind it.

"My requests are related to the coronation. Could we speak in private?" he asked.

"And give you a second chance to kill me?" she snapped. "No. We'll speak here."

His jaw ticked. "That was an unfortunate event, but I hear the perpetrators have been dealt with. I do need to speak with you about the coronation before it is too late to remedy the situation."

Her gaze narrowed and she wrapped her fingers around her blade. In a vision, one not terribly unlikely, she watched herself slam her blade into his chest here in front of all these people. She blinked the vision away, smelling the coppery promise of blood.

"There is nothing to remedy," she said "In fact, the coronation has nothing to do with the Guilds or you. The Sword of Souls identified royal blood, and we must honor it. It is the law."

He stepped forward, and she had to force her feet to remain still. She buried the fear from that horrid night in her throat. This was not one of the men who strangled her, stabbed her, tried to drown her, but his association blurred the distinction.

"We can gather the signatures to force him to step down," he jeered. "No one believes your act. You've used your sorcerer brother to whip up some trickery. If you agree to talks now, it can save you and *the blacksmith* embarrassment."

"Theo is the rightful heir to the throne and will be crowned on Novahli day," she said. "The people love him. He survived the Moon-cursed attack, stood up to Emperor Rexil, and brought the nations of Teridar together. He's a hero, and this is a pathetic final grasp at power that was never meant to be yours."

"Everyone knows what you are. A power-hungry harlot who wants her newest bedwarmer to become king," he hissed.

"Aurienne," Theo said, striding across the throne room.

The workers and new staff scurried out of his way, clearing a wide path. His hand rest upon the hilt of the Sword of Souls as he came to stand between the Obermeister and her.

Gotrik glared at Theo, while Aurienne exhaled tension. Theo's arrival quieted the fear coursing through her where even the sentinel at her side could not.

"Obermeister. I'll be the king of Avyllon in several days, and you may call me Your Majesty," Theo said tersely.

"I don't recognize your rule." Gotrik smirked.

"I see."

In a fluid motion, Theo drew the Sword of Souls from its sheath. An inky light erupted from the blade and filled every surface of the colossal room. It was a moonless sky, dark waters on a cloudy night, a gaping maw. The staff turned to stare at Theo with awe in their eyes.

"Don't forget who you're talking to." Theo sheathed the sword, glaring at the man.

The Obermeister stiffened and peered over Theo's shoulder at

Aurienne. "I hope the magic between your legs rivals the magic in your eyes, or you'll lose your hold on him."

"Don't speak to her that way," Theo advanced, his tone cool as melting ice.

In the blink of her clouded eyes, Aurienne felt a boiling weight fall upon her shoulders and a growl escaped her lips. Foreign darkness bloomed in her eyes, shadows overtaking her vision. She knew without looking her eyes bled midnight black instead of their starry white. In the reflection of the polished glass, the writhing shadows made it appear as though three other women occupied the same space—too many limbs and eyes and faces. Her chin lowered and her shoulders straightened, feeling her head tilt to the side.

Words spilled from her lips that were not her own. "You dare scorn the Triple Goddess and her human vessel? Have you not seen how the Goddess punishes those who do not obey Her will?"

Gotrik stumbled backward as Aurienne stepped around Theo and advanced.

"Aurienne," Theo called.

A cackle erupted from her throat as Gotrik's face twisted in blind terror. He stammered and backed away.

"I have Seen all your futures, your deaths, your hells. Would you like a glimpse?" she whispered, feeling so far away from her own body.

Fast as a viper, she pressed her painted fingertips to his forehead. His eyes rolled back into his head as he writhed. Then he screamed.

The unnatural weight left her, and she could breathe normally. Her thoughts and control returned. Then she realized what she had done. She showed someone else their futures, a feat she had never been able to do. Magic *she* should not be able to do. Magic that should not be possible, except...

Blood streaming down her face, Aurienne ran.

"Aurienne!" Theo called.

"High Seer?" Sentinel Kolten shouted.

Both men chased her through the palatial halls, outside, and to the adjacent temple. She did not stop running until she reached her room. She unlocked, opened, and locked the door behind her.

Sliding in front of her mirror, she studied her reflection. Her eyes were white and cloudy. Her face her was own; the tattoos on her body were unchanged. She reached out and touched the mirror.

The face of the Triple Goddess slammed into the other side of the glass, and Aurienne shrieked and scrambled backward. The seer quickly knelt in the presence of divinity.

"Goddess, tell me your will," she prayed.

The reflection threw her head back and laughed before she faded, leaving the seer alone once more. Trembling, Aurienne pressed her hands to the glass.

Her enchanted divination cards flew from their spelled box, assailing her from all sides, the ink changing to form images. Four tall columns held up the clouds and stars in the sky, before they came crashing down. A fifth, quiet tomb, sank into the earth.

Behind her in the reflection, a dark shadow appeared—taking the shape of a woman Aurienne didn't recognize, but she sensed the oily quality of the air and knew it was the same malevolent presence she'd sensed in the Way. Veiled in shadows, with glowing purple eyes and glowing purple runes, it reached for her with wicked silver claws.

Aurienne backed away from the mirror, terror racing through her veins.

"Aurienne!" Theo pounded on her door.

She opened the door, unshed tears welling in her eyes, and threw herself into his waiting arms.

He pulled her to his chest. "What happened?"

"I'm losing control. The Goddess... she's taking over." She glanced at the mirror. "They both are."

Before vanishing, the dark entity whispered, "I have such plans for you."

Dead of Night

Chapter Twenty-One

Don't underestimate what I will do for revenge.

— Journal of Queen Samantah Julietta Lenore, Returned Queen of Rodarri, 349 N.T.C.

1152 N.T.C. Castle Rodarr, Rodarri.

Clasping her hands, Rianne circled the crowded training rings. She'd thought that death dulled the emotions of life, but the embarrassment she felt made her question that truth. In the large ring, five rows of Queensblood tried to follow the simple pattern the grizzled trainer demonstrated.

"Advance, one, two, three, advance four, five, six. Reset." The trainer swung his sword in smooth, small motions.

Wooden training swords pointed awkwardly in every direction. Marta stepped the wrong way, bumping into Atley, and they both went down. A dozen queens in cotton training pants and tunics jogged around the outside of the training rings, drenched in sweat despite the winter breeze.

Rianne glanced toward the smaller ring where Rhydian coached each queen one at a time. Across from him, Jordyn's arm quivered and the dagger wobbled as she attempted to copy the simple combination. The wooden hilt caught on her pants as she struggled to raise it. She stumbled and fell to her rear as her dagger skidded away through the sand.

"It's been hours, can we take a break?" Jordyn asked.

A blunted arrow landed just beside Jordyn's leg, eliciting a scream. Several rings away, Elayhna threw her bow and shouted apologies.

Rhydian glanced toward Rianne, and she shrugged. They'd never be warriors, but that wasn't the point. Perhaps they'd recognize their self-worth, they'd learn discipline, and maybe they'd eventually become as self-reliant as the villagers that worked to fund their pampered lifestyles these long years. At the least, it gave them something to do all day and get them used to working instead of wallowing in their gilded opulence. They'd been kept weak too long.

Rhydian glanced back to Jordyn. "Up, again. It's the same with the swords as the daggers, it's just a smaller circle."

Jordyn stood and collected her training daggers. "This is pointless."

"How can you ever escape the mental prison we've been born to if you can't rely on your own body? On your mind? This is the first step in breaking free." Rebekkah-Rianne snapped.

Inwardly, Rianne chided, *"You don't have to be so hard on them. They're trying."*

Samantah retorted, *"If someone had been harder on all of us, maybe we wouldn't be dead. If we're going to break this cycle, we start with them."*

"We have to make it so they won't allow themselves to be enslaved for ascensions again," Rosalindt agreed.

"Crushing their spirits won't give them the strength or hope they need either," Rianne argued.

Jordyn scowled but took a deep breath and began the sequence again. She managed to complete it this time without falling over.

"Good, go ahead and grab some water before you rotate to the next station," Rhydian said gently.

Wiping the sweat from her brow, Jordyn dropped the daggers on the table and trudged toward the ring with the ranged weapons. She cast more than one glare back toward her sister.

Rhydian leaned on the ring railing beside Rianne. "You're working them hard."

"Just half the day," she said. "The other half is indoors studying, and they get to pick their subjects. They're fine. It's a fraction of what the farmers are expected to do."

"It's a big change from selecting dresses and sitting beside crystal pools," he observed.

"A big change is necessary if we're to rewrite history for a new future." The frosty words tasted like Milah's.

He grinned. "You're already changing the future."

They caught each other's gaze and held it.

Guilt twisted in her heart. "You'll need to leave for Avyllon today if you're to make it there on time. I need to know that it's safe for the arrival of our caravan."

"You're sure you don't want me going with you?" His brow furrowed. "With Mooncursed scouts hunting, I'd feel more comfortable at your side."

It made sense. But she had a stop to make along the way, and she didn't need him knowing every detail of her plans with the emperor.

"We don't know how we will be received. You go on ahead, check the roads for Mooncursed and ensure that Avyllon is safe."

He nodded slowly, staring at her for far too long. "If you need anything, just say. You can tell me. Let me help you."

Her heart ached to tell him the truth. Her lips parted, the admissions nearly spilling out.

Three young Queensblood under the age of ten, pushed their heads through the fencing. "We want to train too, Rhydian!"

Rhydian laughed. "Well then grab some daggers and let's practice!"

They squealed and tumbled inside the ring, eagerly scrambling for the wooden daggers. Rhydian began leading them through the same moves. Their faces were all smiles, easily mastering the moves and begging for more.

Rianne whispered, "If we can save the next generation from our misery, it'll all be worth it."

Nine hundred and ninety-eight queens murmured their agreement.

Rianne sighed.

What would it cost?

Rianne watched the queens training under the winter sun, feeling herself slip elsewhere. She sank into the memories, fading to a time she'd watched queens train in the dead of night and spell blades with curses.

An unknown voice whispered, *"When she wakes... destruction will follow."*

Under a midnight moon in a forgotten memory, Rianne watched three dozen stony-faced women silently train in a field of crushed grass. There were no training rings, no coaches, and the swords were made of steel. Their movements were fluid, practiced, and precise. Not a single strike was out of place. Unlike the Queensblood of the present, these women were warriors. She slid into the body of the woman with shorn, dark hair at the front, feeling the weight of the sword in her hand, the sweat beading on her brow, and the strain of her shoulders.

A memory, but not one of the queens she recognized in her

bones. So, whose? What unknown queen had she stumbled upon? And why wasn't she with the others inside Rianne?

Hours passed and still the queens trained. Slice, block, stab, slice, slice, block, stab. Each strike packed as much power as Rianne could manage, leveraging her entire body weight behind it. The sword was heavy, threatening to drag her slender frame off-balance, but her muscles drove the blade into the next strike and the next. Rianne felt the shake of her arms and found herself fighting for breath.

Dawn broke, and finally the woman silently sheathed her sword and the others followed. With a quick flick of her hand, she pointed back to the castle.

Soon, their blood will coat our blades, the woman thought.

The commanders didn't know that the demure trophies spent their evenings training for the rebellion to come. They didn't know their precious new Queensblood had it in them to fight back.

Rianne felt the woman's lip pull into a snarl.

Not long now.

Something foreign coiled in the woman's heart, and Rianne felt it writhing in their shared chest like a serpent.

Time raced forward, dragging Rianne with it.

A wooden table was set with bleached bones, bubbling potions, bleeding grimoires, and a large stone bowl full of blood. Foggily, Rianne slipped into the same queen from before sitting behind it, looking out her eyes as she poured bloodrose thorns into a pestle. With bandaged hands, she began to grind. When they were a fine dust, she set it aside and began to crush bloodroses over a small stone cauldron.

She whispered ancient words as the petals fell into what must be Moonwater. Next, she added the bloodrose thorn dust pinch by pinch in a series of tiny bursts of light. Nightshade berries and a dark liquid with rare, floating nightflame flowers joined the mix, causing it to boil and crack. Finally, she added a sprinkle of dried corpseroot. The woman leaned forward and whispered over the bubbling liquid before slicing her finger and adding her blood. The mixture stilled at once.

"It worked," she whispered.

Rianne stiffened. What was the women doing with that kind of poison? The tiniest sip would mean certain death for any who took it, and there was no cure. Even the darkest of poisoners refused such potions.

Carefully, the woman poured the concoction into tiny glass vials and sealed them with wax.

Another woman burst in. "The commanders have been tipped off. They're searching our quarters."

"Kingshit," the first woman cursed.

"I'll distract them." The other woman darted away, closing the door.

The queen hurried to a stone slab wall and dug her fingernails into a long crack. She pulled back a hidden panel and began to stack the vials inside carefully.

"Where is she?" a man's voice demanded outside.

Muffled voices came next.

"Hellsdamn it." The unknown queen slipped the last of the vials into the secret compartment and closed the door.

With a sweep of her arms, she gathered up the bone runes and the cauldron and tucked them away. She looked around and gasped, one of the vials sat on the edge of the table. She reached for it, but her hand knocked it onto the floor where it shattered. The blood drained from her face.

The doorknob turned. "What're you doing in here?"

The queen stepped onto the crushed glass of the vial leaning against the table. "Praying."

Several guards circled the room, studying the table, the shelves, and the walls. Rianne felt the queen forcing herself to keep eye contact with the commander to not give away any secrets. One stopped directly near the wall with the false stonework.

Please no, the queen thought.

"Back to your chambers," the Commander hissed.

The queen cast a glance back at the room.

Time jumped again.

A bleeding eclipse painted the sky, promising dark deeds that night. All the Queensblood were dressed for war. Daggers and swords filled every palm. The younger girls held cursed vials. The older women carried burning torches. The queen sliced her palm and pressed a handprint of blood upon each of the gathered women.

"The magic of our blood will protect us this night. Not one of us shall fall until dawn," she promised.

Rianne sensed the power behind the words. Bloodmagic.

"If we fail tonight, they won't stop," the queen said. "They will sacrifice us for generations, and we won't be strong enough to stand against them. We've been preparing for this for years."

Determined gazes met her. Even the youngest children wore somber expressions.

"They are many, but we are powerful." Her tone was sharp as a blade's edge. "Let's make them regret creating this wretched practice. Tonight, *their* bodies shall litter the castle."

Through secret tunnels, through the darkness, they descended upon the unsuspecting castle. Flames rose in locked sleeping quarters and the smoke filled the skies. A man ran past Rianne, choking on blood as it streamed down his face. The queen cut him down with a practiced slice. Several guards dropped their wine glasses, clawing at their throats while their bloated, panicked eyes set upon the grinning children.

Half-dressed commanders were cornered in the same hallways they'd preyed upon the Queensblood. The queens sliced them from shaft to chin, and their entrails spilled onto the floor. Commanders shouted the alarm, stumbling for their weapons, but the queens stepped out of the passages, out of the shadows, to drive daggers into their hearts and across their throats.

"Revenge shall be ours!" the queen shouted. "Find the king!"

Rianne was no stranger to death, to horrific images, yet the darkness filling the castle that night was beyond her imagination.

The memory faded into bleary screams, and Rianne found herself in another memory.

The same unnamed queen thrashed against the ropes lashing her to the stake. Other queens kneeled before wooden blocks beside the ravine. The rest were bound and kneeling near the castle walls. Tears wet several faces, but their determined gazes from the night of the revolt remained.

Rianne glanced around. Avyllonian and Wyndsel soldiers stood beside the meager Rodarri forces. The three kings of the nations gathered in the Courtyard of Queens wearing hateful expressions.

"The Queensblood have betrayed their country, their sacred duty, and turned to bloodmagic," someone announced. "They bloodwitches attacked their own people and now must pay the price."

Rianne felt the queen rolling her eyes at the words "sacred duty." The first ascension only happened thirty-one years ago, and it was never intended to continue.

The king wearing the Rodarri rose crown approached. "Do you have anything to say for yourself?"

"I only wish I'd killed you first," she snarled.

"You vile witch," the king hissed in the queen's face. "Do you know how many died in your siege? In the month you held the castle, you cut our army by half. You're a murderer."

"How is it any different from what you've been doing to us? You've been murdering us year after year. You've killed us and now we've killed you. If you'd only just let us go, this all could have been avoided."

His jaw worked. "You killed thousands."

She grinned wildly. "Perhaps we're just better at killing."

He balled his fist and struck her. "And now you'll be better at dying."

The queen spat blood into his face. "You bear the consequences of this. These are your sins."

Rianne sensed the blood on his face sinking into his skin. The bloodmagic already sought his soul, though he did not know it.

"Light the stake."

A commander touched a torch to the hay at the queen's feet. Rianne felt the heat already blistering her skin. Her flesh boiled and bubbled, but the queen gritted her teeth.

"And send the rest to hell."

One by one, the guards holding the queens before the blocks lifted their swords. Their bodies fell to the ravine. The heartache that tore through the queen broke Rianne. Feeling herself weaken, she willed the boiling blood in her veins to fuel one final act. She glared at the kings.

A snarl escaped the queen's lips, "With spilled blood and eternal magic, I damn you. I lay a curse on this wretched place that will last a thousand years and a thousand deaths. Every pain we suffer shall be cast upon our enemies one-hundred-fold, and you will drown in the blood of the slaughtered. Death will consume your soul, and vengeance will be ours."

Rianne tasted the vile bloodmagic laced into each word. Dark tendrils of magic erupted from her throat and swirled across the Courtyard of Queens to circle each Queensblood corpse—binding their souls to remain in that wretched ravine. Struggling to breathe, Rianne choked on the coppery, earthen taste. The magic speared the ground, sinking into the roots of the Queen's Root tree and the connected Vittoria's Gift lichen. The curse sank deeply into the bedrock, awaiting its chance to keep the queen's promise to return.

Death came quickly for the queen. The flames overtook her body, but her soul lingered. They threw her smoldering bones into the ravine with the others, and the souls of the queens blinked at her with silver eyes. Her magic bound them all together, and she sank into a deep sleep as she waited.

One day, one of us won't fail. One day they'll remember my name. Lexyra.

Strategies and Secrets

Chapter Twenty-Two

Four ancient sites rest at the four cardinal directions, one for each element. The colossal towers embody the element of their naming (Earth, Sky, Flame, Water) of unknown construction and origins, which are theorized to protect the continent from dark magic dating back to the Shadow War. North and south, and east and west, respectively sit equidistant from one another. Long have rumors circulated of a fifth, centrally located somewhere deep in the Warrior's Weald, one formed from an unknown power.

— A Study of Elemental Magical Artifacts by Master Sorcerer Kalistera Blackstone, 244 N.T.C.

1152 N.T.C. The namesake capital city of Avyllon.

Leather wings flapping and pops of displaced air in the courtyard jolted Theo to his feet. He'd been drowsily reviewing battle plans but knew those sounds anywhere. Vampires. Skin prickling, he gave Aurienne a quick, reassuring kiss and stormed into the main hall. Not even the heavy metal doors slowed his advance, and he shoved them open with a boom.

Stellan, Julietta, and a handful of others waited—wearing all black finery. Dressed impeccably, the vampires reeked of damp soil, singed fur, and old blood. Theo's stomach churned. Every instinct in his body screamed for him to run from what was certain death, yet he found himself strangely unable to tear his eyes from their lithe movements, glimmering black eyes, and exposed fangs. Terrifyingly beautiful was the only way to describe such creatures. He gripped his Sword of Souls until his knuckles cracked, feeling the heavy mantle of his decisions.

"We have news to share," Stellan stated. "It's vital to our defenses. Everyone should hear this."

The first vampire's eyes were dead, cold, and devoid of emotion.

Theo hated how much they needed them, and the rising cost of blood that metaphorically stained his hands.

"This way," Theo said, gesturing in the direction of the war room.

The vampires took measured steps behind Theo. He knew the vampires could have arrived in a blink with their supernatural speed, but they remained moving slowly with their claws clasped and wings furled tightly behind them. All efforts to appear more civilized than they were—but Theo wouldn't be fooled.

He signaled an attendant to gather the allies, who all soon arrived. Dharek and Thaen came first with the forest giant Allesan. Kassia, Saryll, and Adonis were not far behind. Miella followed Marco into the room, face pale and eyes wide, casting furtive looks between the vampires and vampire hunter.

Scratching his chin, Theo wondered why she was acting so strangely. She'd never acted that way before.

Stellan immediately went to her, bowing low and taking her slender hand delicately in his razor-sharp claws before planting a fatherly kiss on it.

"My heart, have you been well?" he asked.

Miella swallowed, glancing at Marco. "I have. Not much has happened here yet. Just planning."

"Good." He released her hand. "I am glad your allies are taking care of you."

To Theo's surprise, Rhydian arrived next.

"I wasn't sure you'd come," Theo said to his friend.

Rhydian's grin was half-hearted. "I'm glad to be here."

Theo glanced behind him, but no one else entered. No royal delegation, no guards, no one.

"Where's Rianne?" Theo asked.

"She sent us ahead," Rhydian said. "She should be here soon."

Her absence didn't bode well for the alliance, but Theo forced himself to nod. Nothing could be done about it yet.

Aurienne entered last, wearing the gown of the High Seer, looking pale. She took forcibly measured breaths, and her shaking hands cupped a clay mug of steaming lavendiir palm tea. The recent brush with her goddess left her weak. Theo grimaced. Her magic was part of her very soul, and he knew that cutting it off would have dire consequences, but her body couldn't withstand much more.

Theo gestured to the vampires. "Everyone is here."

Eyes black as a moonless night, the vampire glanced toward Rhydian. "Do you want to share this information with one not allied with us?"

Theo tensed. "I trust Rhydian."

Stellan crept to the head of the table, movements silent as the dead. "We have discovered the emperor's plans."

A shadow detached from the wall and the nameless spy said, "You found the monument or artifact he's been searching for?"

Stinging needles of surprise flooded Theo, but he forced himself not to react. Aurienne had told him that the spy had returned changed. He'd seen him several times in the palace, but the sight never ceased to unnerve him. The vampires, if surprised, however, did not show it. Perhaps nothing affected them anymore.

"What do you know about the Pillars?" Stellan asked.

Adonis raised his head. "There are old journals from around the time of the Shadow Wars discussing the four Pillars of Teridar. The accounts about the Pillars' origins are ancient and scattered."

"They were erected by the warriors of the Shadow War to form a magical protection shield around the entire continent," Stellan said. "Each pillar represents and was imbued with one of the four elements. If the pillars fell…"

Theo inhaled sharply. "The protection shield might fall."

"The question is whether the shield is keeping something out, or protecting the world from what's inside," Aurienne murmured beside him. "Four pillars lost and the fifth lost by Fate. Darkened skies fill with howling hate."

He recognized the lines from her birth prophecy.

"Four pillars lost," she said. "I always assumed it to be symbolic or to refer to the Foretelling Rites, but what if it was literal. What about the fifth pillar?"

"There's one tome discussing the lore surrounding a fifth pillar," Adonis said. "One scholar claims to have found a fifth, but the tome was discredited. It's said to be in the Warrior's Weald, north of Rodarri. But there are claims of all sorts of fantastical items and creatures there."

Theo's mind swam with possibilities.

"The pillars are myths," Adonis said. "No one has seen them in centuries. They're little more than fairy tales."

"They're very real." Nesryn's voice cut through the crowded room.

Theo glanced toward where she leaned against the wall, hip cocked, silver hair flowing. She winked at him, almost knowing the questions in his head. When had she arrived? How had she gotten in without anyone seeing her?

"The Pillars keep the Shadows out," Nesryn said. "If the emperor somehow learned of this and is searching for them… he wants to use the Shadows in his war. You think the Mooncursed are bad? They're nothing compared to the Shadows. Mooncursed were created from just a touch of the Shadows' magic."

"If the Pillars are keeping out the Shadows, we must protect them," Theo said.

"No one knows where they are," Adonis said.

Theo glanced at the vampires. "Do you?"

Stellan tilted his chin. "I am not entirely sure where they are anymore. Much has changed in the land. They were also hidden."

The room fell quiet.

Nesryn joined them at the table, splaying her hands across the wood. "I know where they put them."

Theo's gaze remained on her, trying not to think about how she knew. What that might mean.

"If they're only around isthmus, they're looking for the Pillar of Flame." She pointed to the map. "But they're on the wrong side of the mountains. It's why they haven't found it yet."

Stellan pointed to the map. "The emperor's army posted is just beyond the isthmus. They have our forces outnumbered six to one. He must be waiting to bring them in until he has the Shadows at his command."

Silence filled the room like floodwaters.

"Thankfully, we have time," Stellan said. "They aren't marching. Not yet. I also see no major forces of Mooncursed with them."

The nameless one said, "I destroyed many of their Mooncursed before I was cast out of the city. It will take them time to replenish their ranks."

Theo looked for Nesryn, about to ask how the Pillars might be protected. The elf was now standing near an open window, whispering to the red fox in hushed tones. Theo glanced at Aurienne who was watching the interaction as well.

Nesryn caught them looking and grinned. The fox brandished its tail, golden eyes dancing with amusement.

Rhydian bristled when he saw them. "Why didn't you tell us this before?" he demanded. "We could have used your insights weeks ago."

"I was a bit busy trying to assassinate the emperor." She licked the points of her teeth.

Theo blinked.

Nesryn said, "I tried to kill the emperor, but the entire city is warded. I've spent time searching for a way in, but the defenses are impregnable."

The nameless one said, "I too can no longer return. After I destroyed one of their magical laboratories, they pushed me out with strong wards."

Rhydian stepped forward, staring the elf down. "You didn't say how you got there so quickly."

"A Way." She winked at the Warbringer.

More silence.

Adonis looked up from his tome. "There are no known Way gates in that area."

The elf threw her head back and laughed. "Who do you think created the Ways in the first place?"

Quiet gasps filled the room. Even Theo felt the floor spinning beneath him. Everything they'd thought about the Ways was wrong. Their histories were woefully incomplete.

"My people left the Way gates behind for you all during the last war, but we can create them at will," she said. "The emperor opened one such Way at the summit, without using a gate. It shouldn't be possible. He's using ancient elvish magic. I don't know how; but I'm going to find out."

The elf waved him off. "If the emperor is looking for the Pillars, we will need to ward them. And the city too." She looked to the University's Head Dean, Chellaes. "I will give your people the wards to protect the city walls. It will take me some time to prepare them. I will let you know when I have finished."

Theo stared. What other magic did Nesryn possess? Ways? Wards? Her starlight sword. What other secrets was she protecting?

Dean Chellaes bowed.

"We need to send a small force to guard the pillar, and the rest draw out by going to a decoy location," Kolten said. "I'll select sentinels for the task."

"After the coronation," Aurienne cut in. "Every reading demands we crown Theo first."

Nesryn was now standing between Theo and Aurienne, slipping soundlessly across the room.

"What else do your cards say, seer?" The elf's eyes bored into Aurienne's.

After a moment's hesitation, Aurienne took the deck from a pocket in her gowns. She shuffled carefully, and Theo noticed the ink on the cards changing mid-shuffle.

Before Aurienne could lay out a spread, the entire deck shot into the air above their heads.

The Goddess card had three gouged out eyes bleeding gold.
The King wielded a broken sword under a full moon.
The Dead Queen held a bonesword, bleeding from a neck wound.
The Warbringer and Grimfall cards spun around, locked in battle.
The Vampire stood under a burning sun.
The Hunter wore chains of darkness.
The Heart was ripped in half by clawed hands.
The Witch choked within tightly wound thorned vines.
The Magician disappeared under golden book pages beating like wings.
The Living Flame danced on hot coals.
The Shadow sat on a throne, screaming silently.
The Siren curled her finger seductively at a castle.
The Living Stone was crushed by a mountain.

*The Seventh Tree watched a falling star burn the
forests.*

Everyone was transfixed by the cards, watching the ink shift into these terrible images. Few dared breathe. The cards burst into flames and disappeared entirely.

Theo glanced at Aurienne in concern.

"Those dramatic fuckers," she breathed.

"Are they—"

"They'll be back in their spelled box soon," she said.

Theo glanced toward the window, but the fox and Nesryn had both disappeared. He swallowed.

No one would mistake the bad omens they'd just seen.

Wayward Hearts

Chapter Twenty-Three

Wayward hearts at lost crossroads,
Make darkling deals to devils owed.
Gleaming bones and bleeding crowns,
What is lost shall never be found.

— Song of the wayward hearts.

1152 N.T.C. Outside the namesake capital city of Avyllon.

Nestled within a heavy fog, Rianne waited in a forest thicket beside a river just south of Avyllon. She watched through the silver veils in her mind as she allowed the queens to momentarily take control. A biting chill cut the air, but she needed no shawl. The more time passed from her death, the less worldly concerns bothered her.

The emperor should arrive any moment.

She glanced around the empty clearing for signs of his arrival. Silence echoed through the thick-trunked trees and spongy moss.

Her own escort was a mile away, and she felt exposed in the falling dusk.

Rianne murmured to the others, *"I'm not so sure about this. Maybe I shouldn't have sent Rhydian ahead."*

"That hellsdamned elf won't stray far from him, and the emperor won't negotiate if he senses her nearby," Rebekkah said. *"She'd attack or he would, and we'll get nowhere."*

Rianne mused, *"And what if she killed him and ended it all?"*

"After watching their skirmish at the summit, it's unlikely," Milah said. *"We don't know enough about his magic yet. We need to learn more."*

Rianne glanced at the shadows between the trees again. *"He's declared war on the continent. Meeting him alone seems like a bad idea."*

"We brought him here for a reason," Milah shifted from Rianne's shoulder into her chestbone. *"There's power in these woods he won't be expecting. Places we can disappear if need be. He may have magic, but so do we. And we have our needle and the bonesword."*

Samantah cut in, *"We are not convinced of the seer's prophecies. It's worth hearing him out in any case. We ought to make our own decision when war is at stake."*

"War is to be avoided at nearly any cost," Elisabel murmured.

Rianne replied, *"I don't feel good about betraying my allies. My friends."*

Rosalindt scoffed. *"Your friends? The ones that allowed you to die."*

Rianne said, *"They didn't know."*

"Or care," Rosalindt replied.

Whillow said, *"Your kind heart was not made for the demands of politics. It takes time to get used to."*

"The burden of leadership is heavy." Vittoria's calming presence and weighty words decided the matter

Rianne swallowed. *"We'll hear him out, but I make no promises beyond that."*

A twig snapped as Emperor Rexil stepped into the clearing alone carrying a glowing, purple-flamed lantern. His straight black hair was tied back, highlighting his striking dark eyes and cheekbones. He walked with the easy gait and regal posture of a warrior-emperor. A smirk tugged at the corners of his mouth. He stopped before her, looking down.

Rianne's skin warmed. He was one of the most handsome men she'd seen, and he walked like he knew it.

"It's nice to meet you, your Imperial Majesty," Rianne inclined her head respectfully, feeling her sluggish heart flutter in his presence.

His eyes roved over her. "We met at the summit."

A lifetime ago.

A small smile escaped Rianne's control. "Did we?"

The silver, unblinking gazes of the spirits within her peered out of her eyes. He was close enough she could see a flash of silver in her eyes reflected in his.

He leaned in. "Perhaps not."

The bloodwitch, Noxanya, said, *"Do you sense it? His energy reminds me of the Grimfall. A dark mirror, exactly opposite to her magics. Ancient and corrupted."*

"Queen Rianne Lenore, Queensblood of Rodarri." Rianne offered him her hand.

He bent low to kiss it. A shiver raced across her usually numb skin at the brush of his lips.

"I didn't know if you'd come," she said, slowly pulling her hand away. "You're bold or reckless to come alone."

He chuckled. "As are you. I sent men here hours ago to pick apart these woods looking for traps, ambush, or treachery. You can imagine my surprise and delight in finding none. You're here, alone, unarmed as promised."

Unarmed.

The queens all laughed.

"King Cavendar is dead. I rule Rodarri now, and I haven't yet made my decision about alliances in this war. I'd like to know your offer."

Emperor Rexil scratched his chin thoughtfully. "He's dead? So soon? How?"

"He broke our sacred laws regarding ascensions," she said.

"I see. I had sent my offer to him. Along with—"

Rianne waved her hand. "I saw your original offer and the bribe that went with it. I'm not interested in either. Knowing I might be your only ally on the continent you're at war with, I want to know what your new offer will be. I believe my value has increased beyond the old king's."

A wide smile settled on his handsome face. "To the point. Discerning. A refreshing surprise. I thought there was more to you than the sweet young queen you seemed at the summit, or perhaps you've changed since. I'm looking forward to getting to know all these intriguing layers."

Rianne shrugged. "I don't suspect you're exactly what you seem, either."

He laughed. "I've come a long way from my roots. You want a new offer fitting of the queen? Here it is."

Emperor Rexil laid out the new terms, approximately half of what had been demanded originally.

Kindhearted Elisabel said, *"These are good terms."*

Rianne replied, "The gold, resources, and soldiers can be negotiated further but are within the realm of what I might accept. But your terms regarding those with magical gifts... Do they include the other Queensblood? For centuries, it was believed that our blood was the only blood that would protect Rodarri as you likely know. That has been recently disproven. I shall not be sending my kin to Demorra."

The emperor narrowed his eyes. "Perhaps just a small sampling for research purposes."

"No."

"One then?"

The queens began whispering, but Rianne silenced them with a wave of willpower. "Not one. I vowed to them and to my people that they would not be lambs to the slaughter, and I won't instead promise them as test subjects. We can send some of the sorcerers we have, perhaps a few witches from the villages, but the Queensblood are not part of this."

He looked her up and down, assessing. "If the myth has been disproven, then the need to study further evaporates. Perhaps I could verify some of these rumors on my own with you, privately."

Rianne's face grew hot. "Perhaps."

He wasn't at all what she expected. He wasn't lying or hiding anything that she could tell. Determined. Powerful. What secrets of his did Aurienne know? Was she right?

He grinned wolfishly. "It seems as though a deal could be struck then."

Milah said, *"We need to know more about his armies, especially the Mooncursed."*

"Tell me more about your pets," Rianne said. "I've heard of the aftermath of the Mooncursed attack. They're not like any were-wolves or Mooncursed from the stories."

"How about you first tell me how *Theo* and the others survived?" he countered. "There shouldn't have been any aftermath. If I'm to share my secrets, I expect the same in return."

Milah-Rianne asked, "You use titan ore to bind the Shadows to the Mooncursed, but they still infect with scratch or bite?"

He stepped closer. "I'm surprised you noticed."

Rianne shrugged. In their many lives, the queens had seen were-wolves, Mooncursed, Shadows, and whatever these new Mooncursed were.

"You're right," he said. "I've improved the original Mooncursed, using werewolves, shifters, and other beasts from the farthest reaches of Demorra and Shadows and they do still infect—but you already knew that. Now how did Theo escape?"

"He didn't exactly," she said. "I heard that a sorcerer defeated your beasts. I don't know what he used, but I overheard talks of his death."

His gaze narrowed. "I see."

"What else do you have?"

He smiled and said nothing.

That's ominous.

"Accept my offer to join the empire and you'll never have to find out," he countered.

Nicollete sent him a cunning grin in return. "I've been talking about an alliance, not an offer of submission."

He stepped close enough his knees brushed her skirts, and he traced his fingers down her arm. "Why not both? Sometimes the best alliances are ones of mutual *submission*."

Rianne backed away. "Your offer seems reasonable. I'll let you know what I decide."

He called after her, "Don't wait too long. My war waits for no one."

"The wait makes the reward sweeter," she said.

"Where are you going?" He raised his hands.

"To settle debts centuries in the making," Vittoria whispered.

Whillow called back to him, "I have a party to attend. And I wouldn't miss it for the world."

PART TWO

INTERLUDE

I vow to be true and weather all storms. I vow for my love to be as constant as these never-ending waves pooling beneath our feet, flowing endlessly from the depths of the sea. In life, may our love sustain us both as long as we both live. In death, may we find one another again in dark water's embrace.

— *ANCIENT SEAFARING WEDDING VOWS.*

1152 N.T.C. Wynds city, Wyndsel.

Princess Arissabett adjusted the strands of pearls adorning the waves of dark hair piled atop her head. Her white and cerulean wedding gown was fitted around her hips and fanned out by her feet like a mermaid's tail. The gown was covered in intricate patterns of tiny turquoise and aquamarine seaglass beads polished into starbursts so small they caught the sunlight like diamonds. She brushed her hands over the intricate star chart designs —the ones she'd sewn herself these past months.

"You are the most beautiful woman in the entire country," one of her bridesmaids gushed.

I hope he thinks so.

"And you get to marry Prince Donovan," a red-haired bridesmaid murmured dreamily.

A blush climbed the princess's cheeks as she bit her rose-stained lip. Donovan's tanned skin and dark hair, that roguish smirk he wore, and the way his lips felt on her skin stole her breath. Watching the sweat trickle down his chest and arms while he trained with the guards inspired indecent fantasies. She sighed happily.

As if reading her mind, another dark-haired bridesmaid said with a wink, "And it's your wedding night."

Having enjoyed his company in every other way, Arissabett refused to let their trysts cross that line before now. Today she would consummate her marriage to the Arryn-born prince and give herself to him fully. The thought sent shivers crawling down her spine. She couldn't wait.

She tucked a white shell hair comb into her curls and admired herself in the mirror. The spectrum of bright blues in her gown complimented her dark skin. Her hair was pulled up, exposing her pearl-clad shoulders and neck. She leaned forward to dab pink powder to her cheeks, hoping Donovan found her to be as beautiful as she found him achingly handsome.

"I can't believe this day is finally here. We've been engaged for two years, and I can't wait to be his wife," Arissabett said dreamily.

Biting her fist, she suppressed a squeal of excitement as her bridesmaids exchanged knowing looks. She wanted nothing more than to make that man her husband. Today, she would marry her charming prince and live happily ever after. The so-called Darkling War loomed across the continent, but Donovan would lead their armies to battle and return victorious—of that she had no doubt. A trivial distraction in their lifetime of bliss.

She paused, recalling the High Seer's reading for her. "*You will get your heart's desire, but the road to your fate is lined with pain, death, and betrayal."*

"Your Highness, it's time," a maid announced.

With another giggle, the bridesmaids collected their orange and white bouquets and headed to the beach. Arissabett gave herself a final glance in the mirror before she joined the bridal procession.

Down at the beach, Arissabett watched her bridesmaids and the groomsmen take their places beside the waiting witnesses. She took a deep breath, steadying the excitement running down her arms. So happy, she thought it might burst out of her.

Beaming, she took her parents' arms and walked down an aisle of sunset-colored poppies and orange tree blossoms. The sand was warm beneath her bare feet, and the petals soft in contrast to the grainy shore. A soft sea breeze kissed her tanned skin. At the other end, Prince Donovan waited with the priest. They approached the hexagonal beach arbor wound with white and orange flowers, smelling of clementines and seafoam. The beads of her dress clinked as a harp played over the sound of crashing waves. She stepped under the shade of the arbor, protecting her from the midday sun. Her parents released her with a kiss and retreated to where the other nobles stood waiting.

Prince Donovan's family, freshly arrived from the nation across the sea, Arryn, stood apart from the others in dark blue tunics. She chanced a glance at them, hoping her new family would love her.

Donovan smiled and reached for her. They clasped hands in front of the priest.

"You are stunning," Prince Donovan whispered.

Her heart leapt.

The priest of their god, Neriwyn, commenced, "We are here to recognize the union of Crown Princess Arissabett of Wyndsel and Prince Donovan of Arryn."

Arissabett's gaze locked onto Donovan. She wanted to marry him, kiss him, love him. Two years of courtship was far too long, and at nineteen years old, she was not a young bride. She had been dreaming of her wedding since she was a girl and waiting to marry Donovan for what felt like eternity.

The priest asked Donovan to say his vows. They stared into each other's eyes as he spoke the words she had been dying to hear. Arissabett repeated the vows.

The priest wrapped a rope from an Arryn ship around their wrists and sprinkled seawater atop their hands. "In the eyes of Neriwyn and these witnesses, you are hereby married. Kiss and seal the vows."

Donovan bowed before her, pressing his lips to their bound hands. He straightened, and Arissabett bowed forward kissing his hand. Then Donovan shook off the nuptial rope, took her into his arms, and pressed a passionate kiss against her lips.

She kissed him back, breathing in the smell of him and twirling her fingers into his curls. His strong arms held her tightly, and his skin was warm against hers. This man was now hers.

The crowd erupted into hoots and cheers, showering the newly-weds with petals. Arissabett leaned into Donovan's chest primly, slightly embarrassed at kissing in public. He wrapped a possessive arm around her waist and her heart soared brighter than the sunny skies beside the striped gulls.

"Prince Donovan of Arryn joins the Juri family and now becomes Crown Prince Donovan of Wyndsel, heir to the throne of Wynds." A small, satisfied smile parted King Jaekob's lips, and he placed a crown atop the prince's head.

Donovan straightened and puffed out his chest. The crowd cheered and shouted his name until it became a chant.

"Long live the future king!" they cheered.

Arissabett swallowed, confusion filling her chest. This was all wrong. It sounded like Donovan was now heir to the throne, and she his property. She expected far more fanfare over the bride on her wedding day, but instead, she already faded into obscurity. She forced herself to smile, telling herself she was being silly.

"And now the groom shall prove his worth by rowing them past the break, and they shall seal their love on Neriwyn's Island," the priest announced.

She nearly squealed. The time had come.

They sauntered down an aisle of petals lined by seashells toward the breaking waves. A bridal skiff waited on the beach. Donovan offered her a hand and helped her inside. She sat, surrounded by flowers, sparkling wine, and soft white blankets. As she smoothed her skirts, Donovan rolled up his pants and pushed them out to sea. He took up the oars and began to row, while the wedding party watched from up on the beach. Back and arms straining, he rowed them to the small island past the breaking surf.

"Don't worry my love, I will get us there safely," he promised.

She leaned forward, exposing a hint of cleavage in her turquoise beaded gown. "I have no doubts, my prince."

He grinned and rowed harder to the place where they would consummate their marriage under the watchful eyes of the sea god. They reached the island soon, and he dragged the skiff up onto the beach. He helped her out, and she looked around. White sand beaches shaded by palm trees met her gaze. Only the sounds of the waves and gulls surrounded them.

"It's beautiful," she said, feeling her eyes glisten.

"Just like you," he said tenderly.

He took her hand and spun her around to the music of the sea. Bringing her close, his hands traced down her back at the laces while he kissed her. He pulled her against his chest, and she felt his erection pressing into her. He reached a hand down the front of her gown, cupping her breast and sending waves of heat between her legs.

"I've been waiting for this for so long," he groaned.

"Me too," she whispered.

He reached down toward the sand, under her gown and rose slowly—tracing his fingers up her leg and to her center. He stopped between her legs and brushed his fingers against her. She continued kissing him, allowing her hands to rove his chest. With his free hand, he guided her hand into his pants. Though feeling trepidation at the pace they were moving, she obliged and stroked him. It wasn't the first time she'd felt him, so she wasn't sure why she was hesitant.

Suddenly, he slipped his finger inside of her and she gasped. He pressed his lips to hers, whispering into her mouth and pulling her against him.

"Do you like that?" he asked, pressing his finger to the knuckle.

She moaned, enjoying the sliver of pain with the pleasure.

"By Neriwyn, you're ready for me now."

"Should we lay a blanket out?" She gestured to the waiting blankets and flowers.

"I need you now," he replied. "We need to take this gown off."

She gasped as he spun her around. He worked at the laces while she squirmed. Then he took her gown in his hands and ripped it open in the back. Her heart plummeted as her destroyed gown slipped to her ankles. Several hundred hours of work ruined.

He turned her around. "There we go."

Before she could reply, he took her breast into his mouth and her knees buckled at the wonderful sensation. His skin smelled of wine, sweat, and brine—delicious and repulsive at the same time. He pulled her closer and she relished the affection. He kissed her hard enough her lips bruised as he slipped his tongue between her teeth.

The prince spun her around, pulling her tight against him.

She looked over her shoulder. "Wait, what are you—"

He held her in place. "Shhhh, my love."

He reached forward and rubbed her most sensitive place and followed as she sank to her knees, and his hand pressed against the back of her neck, pushing her forward onto her elbows in the sand. Arousal, apprehension, and excitement whirled through her mind.

She felt his erection at her entrance, and she squirmed in anticipation. Her mind swirled with pleasure, and she ached to be filled. In a single stroke he thrust into her halfway, another stroke nearly to the hilt, and the third stroke filled her entirely, eliciting a gasp from her lips. His efforts were rough, drunk, and frenzied—pleasure and pain knotted together.

"Donovan!" she cried out, trying to catch her breath.

"Arissa, love, you feel amazing."

One hand gripped her hips, the other wound into the pearl strands in her hair. Coarse sand rubbed against her elbows, but she found herself pressing her back against him in rhythm. Her pleasure built and built nearly to the point of climax, but then he finished.

Pulling out, he lay back on the beach. She pushed up out of the sand, no longer a virgin and not quite sated.

"That's..."

"Was amazing, wife," he said. "Can you pour us some sparkling wine?"

"Yes, thank you, *husband*." The word was delicious on her swollen tongue.

The princess pulled on her destroyed dress, watching the seaglass beads raining to the sands.

Forcing herself to smile, she handed him a drink. "It's torn."

"I'll buy you another." He tilted her chin up. "We only have one wedding day."

She smiled, banishing the sadness. He was right of course. There was no way he could have known that such a dress couldn't be bought, and she wouldn't tell him because it might hurt him to know what he'd mistakenly done.

Drinking wine and sampling the cut fruits and fresh fish, she watched waves crash into the continent. Hours passed as the prince claimed his bride under the eyes of Neriwyn.

Her thoughts circled upon her people chanting his name, forgetting all about their true born princess. Fleeing her doubts, she drank more and more, telling herself everything was fine. Her wedding night ended with her feeling weary and drunk. She felt her crown slipping from her fingers into the hands of the man who now owned her.

The happiest day of her life.

THE GRIFFIN KING
CHAPTER TWENTY-FOUR

*All hail the coronation of King Atheodoren Willem Thatcher Aradey,
long may he reign.*

*— Coronation proclamation, Novahli, the
festival of lights, 28 Nova 1152 N.T.C.*

1152 N.T.C. The namesake capital city of Avyllon.

The coronation of King Atheodoren Willem Thatcher Aradey would be remembered long after the bones of those in attendance crumbled to dust. Aurienne didn't need to use her gift to know that it was a pivotal day. A long-lost descendent of the first king of Avyllon rising from the simple, working life to take the throne would be a tale people clung to. It would inspire the hope and unity necessary in the face of the coming war as they warded their pillars against the emperor's looming invasion.

In full regalia, Aurienne waited for Theo's grand arrival on the front steps of the royal palace. The enormous doors had been freed from decades of rust and thrown open to reveal the throne room, and a crowd was packed inside. The growing cheers of the throngs lining the streets told her that he'd arrive soon.

The royal processional traveled around the city walls then spiraled deeper in the heart of the capital before arriving at the royal palace. Often, the monarch-apparent rode in the gilded carriages, but Theo had opted to ride horseback, a show of strength. Aurienne smiled to herself. Already, Theo's instincts on winning over the people were perfectly suited to the position—whether he knew it or not. There was no one better to lead them, and the fact that he wanted it so very little made him even more perfect for it. Perhaps one day he'd forgive her for asking this of him.

The clacking of hooves on the pearly cobblestones signaled his arrival. Theo's gray-speckled, royal war stallion drew up at the bottom of the steps, stamping and snorting. Goddess—he was handsome. Every inch the king, Theo dismounted, as the procession of several hundred cavalry and sentinels trailed. The golden, royal vestments fitted as though he was born to them. Chin raised and shoulders back, he climbed the stairs to stand before her. Her pulse leapt, and she had to ignore the urge to reach out and squeeze his hand. He tried to whisper something, but the roars of the crowd drowned it out. A grin tugged at the corners of his mouth.

Aurienne bowed low, glancing up to catch his gaze. Not so long ago, he'd been looking up at her for the Foretelling Rite. How things had changed so quickly. He offered her his hand and gestured for her to rise. Taking the hand, she straightened, noticing his fingers brush her knuckles. She followed him into the throne room on the narrow path left clear by those inside.

Confident strides carried Theo through the grand hall, the Sword of Souls at his back. She caught him glancing upward as the glistening glass stars hung from the ceiling reflecting the sunlight into millions of starbursts across the windows. He took his place before the metal-wrought tree throne tucked between life-size golden griffin statutes with sparkling amethyst eyes. Five nooks on the base and back of the throne flickered with candlelight.

Theo grinned at his parents standing beside the other royal guests of honor. Rhydian stepped away from the guests to stand beside the throne, waiting.

Straightening, she focused her clouded gaze upon the assembled. "As your Goddess-sworn High Seer, I have read his Fate. He is the only one who gave stand before the waves of darkness. He is fated to assemble and lead the armies in the coming Darkling War. The gods have sent us our salvation. He is the blood of the crown returned."

The crowd roared.

Aurienne took her place beside Theo. "The branch, the scepter, the mantle, the book, and the crown. Each of the five are a worldly symbol of the divine duty and responsibility of the sovereign."

She took the first two symbols from their sapling-shaped book stand beside the throne and held them up. "The gilded branch represents the deep roots of Avyllon and the magic found in our land. The lunar scepter represents the dedication of the monarch to the pursuit of wisdom."

Theo's warm hands brushed hers as he accepted the regalia. He faced the throne and placed them into the carved nooks.

"The mantle of the wolf, a promise of protection from the gods," she said.

Rhydian, his selected second for the ritual, placed the mantle upon Theo's shoulders.

"The book symbolizes the blood of the royal line," she said, "and the crown is the symbol of the unbreakable oaths sworn."

Aurienne took the Book of Crowns from the stand. Theo placed his left hand upon the book, keeping his right hand upon the hilt of the Sword of Souls.

"Do you, Atheodoren Willem Thatcher, last remaining descendent of the Aradey line, accept this duty?"

"I do."

A glistening, golden thread of Fate, visible only to Aurienne, wove around Theo's chest.

"Do you solemnly swear to lead, govern, and protect the people of Avyllon to the best of your ability?"

"I do."

Another thread sprouted from the throne and wrapped itself around his brow, a crown of fate. He stiffened and tilted his chin upward, as though he could sense the weight resting upon him.

"Will you cause law and justice to be executed in all your judgements?"

"I will."

A thread enveloped his sword arm. He'd already made an unbreakable oath when she'd first handed him the Sword of Souls, but now his duty grew. She held his stony, knowing gaze. His eyes remained fixed upon her as though she was his only lifeline.

"Do you swear to stand as a light against the darkness and keep these oaths for as long as you shall live?" she asked.

His voice never wavered. "In the presence of all the old and new gods, I will keep these oaths for as long as fate permits me to live."

Aurienne returned the tome to the book stand and opened it to a black page. She offered her golden athame from her thigh, and Theo pricked his finger. With the ancient quill of a griffin, he signed his name to the book in blood.

Turning, she carefully took the Avyllonian crown from its royal cushion. With a flourish of his royal fur cloak, Theo knelt before her. His elbow pressed against his knee, and he bowed his head. The crown was heavy in her hands, and not just from the weight of the metal. Her heart hammered.

"May the gods and Fates protect you," she whispered to only him.

His gaze shifted, showing he heard her. She placed the crown on his head, allowing her fingers to linger for the barest second.

"All hail King Atheodoren Willem Thatcher Aradey, the griffin king, long may he reign," she announced.

As he stood, Theo drew the Sword of Souls from the black rune-scrawled scabbard and held it high above his head. At his touch, it exploded in the blinding light, confirming his ancient heritage. For a shining moment, the crowd's roars erupted into a deafening thunder that shook the city walls.

Garbed in stifling full regalia beside his guests of honor, Theo oversaw the Festival of Kings from a stout wooden throne behind a mountainous feast. The outdoor dais overlooked the royal courtyard that was packed full of booths and patrons. Beside him, the royal guests from all nations dined on the mountain of food. The crown dug into his brow, the itchy fur mantle was heavy, his shiny black boots pinched his feet, and he wore so many layers of vests and sashes and shirts that he'd lost count. The warm winter sun beat down upon him as he was forced to sit stiffly on the hard, wooden seat.

Aurienne's hand touched his arm as she whispered, "You did well today."

Glancing back at her, his breath caught. Her clouded eyes studied him cautiously, as though trying to read his innermost thoughts. A reassuring smile painted her lips. Gods—she was beautiful. He covered her hand with his and squeezed, feeling his skin heat at the contact.

Her long hair was adorned with tiny gold chains and beads that matched those upon her gown. Tattoos covered her skin along with the ceremonial paint and jewelry. Every eye in the square lingered upon her, seeing the Goddess instead. Yet, she needed no adornment for her true beauty to shine through.

"Thanks. Perhaps we can celebrate a bit more tonight." He winked.

She blushed and the edges of her mouth pulled into a grin. "I should pay my respects and show fealty to our new king." She traced her fingers along his forearm.

He chuckled, idly surveying the laughing, shouting crowds. He should have been more excited about being crowned king. Who wouldn't be? He'd no longer want for anything, and neither would his family. He'd once asked Aurienne what freedom felt like, the ability to travel anywhere and buy anything. She said she was a slave to fate, and he understood now. While nothing was out of reach anymore, he was burdened by the responsibilities. The only thing that made it all worth it was this remarkable woman sitting beside him.

"I mean it," she said. "Today was important, and you don't realize how perfect you are for this. You are exactly what they need."

"I'm just glad it's over." He gestured to their raised dais and the heaping portions of food. "None of this is really me."

A thoughtful expression settled on her brow.

He was singularly aware of the fact that her hand remained in his. His pulse hammered in his palm, but he remained still as he watched the festivities.

A large group of men and women gathered around a fenced-off series of wooden targets, taking wagers and hurdling axes. Another table boasted dozens of varieties of ale. Artists painted children's faces with swords, stars, and trees. Blacksmiths and wood carvers boasted their creations, as weavers and merchants unfurled bolts of colored fabric.

Theo breathed in deeply, trying to catch a whiff of mist from Avyllon's famed fountains and pools framing the city-wide celebration.

The people watched him, and more than one child unabashedly stared at him. He lifted his hand just enough to wave at a child holding a wooden sword who kept eyeing him from the corner of the courtyard. The boy pretended not to see, but a wide grin split his face.

"What would be *you*?" Aurienne asked.

"What do you mean?"

"You said *this* isn't you. What is?"

He leaned back, considering her words.

"During the Festival of Fates, I just lost myself in the crowd. I wanted to see, smell, hear, taste, experience everything. I planned to see more of the city before I was hauled away." His tone was light, and he squeezed her hand again before letting go.

She laughed softly. "So do it."

"What?"

"No one can tell you what kind of king you have to be," she said. "Trust your instincts."

Theo tapped his fingers on the edge of the armrest. What kind of king did he want to be? Certainly not one who sat up here isolated all day, looking down over his subjects with more food than several dozen people could ever finish, and on the brink of war. They'd given him a great trust and it was his job to earn it now.

With a loud scraping screech, he pushed back his chair and brushed off the fur mantle. Several nearby citizens glanced his way as he handed Aurienne the crown and stripped several layers of vests and royal sashes. A few people held up their ale mugs and cheered. He rolled up his sleeves and pressed a kiss to Aurienne's forehead.

Her eyes widened in amusement.

Theo gestured toward a handful of sentinels guarding the dais. "Let's bring this table down. No sense in letting the food go to waste."

Crown Prince Donovan mumbled something to King Jaekob, as the newly arrived Wyndsel delegation rose. They all shot dark looks Theo's way as they retreated inside the palace. Rianne remained perched in her own chair, watching the crowd with a narrowed silver gaze. Dharek, Thaen, Allesan, Stone'ward, and Ore'spike helped twenty sentinels bring down the royal feast to be shared.

Theo jumped off edge of the dais and leaned back to pull off his heavily shined boots. "Does anyone have some regular leather boots? These things are awful."

Seven vendors scrambled forward, holding up their wares.

"Perfect." He selected a soft brown pair and handed the vendor a gold coin—about five times what the boots were worth. "I'll need to be comfortable if I'm to prove my worth in the ax throwing."

The courtyard erupted in delight as he tugged on the new boots and strode toward the small ring.

A man handed him an ax with a sly grin. "Your Majesty. Just because you're a king doesn't mean we're going to let you win."

Theo gripped the ax, finally feeling himself for the first time all day. "I would expect nothing less."

He lined up before the first target and let the ax fly. It struck the second-most center ring, just off the bullseye. The crowd cheered, sounding surprised.

The booth organizer grinned. "Not too bad."

Theo stretched and rolled his shoulders. "Let's go again."

About a hundred people now gathered, straining to watch their new king prove himself. He took a deep breath, steadied himself, sighted the target and let the ax fly.

The next throw hit the edge of the bullseye.

"I'm not sure I'll get any closer than that!" Theo announced.

A woman yelled, "Anyone who beats the king's throw gets a free ale!"

Rhydian entered the booth with a sly smile, selecting four axes. "Anyone want to make a bet? Four bullseyes at once?"

Theo excused himself as the booth filled with eager onlookers. He stopped by the ale table, selecting a golden winter blend and paying for two mugs.

Striding toward Aurienne, who was now leaning against the steps of the dais, Theo handed her a mug.

"Can the High Seer hold her ale?"

"I suppose we'll see." Her eyes danced as she tilted her head back.

Citizens crept closer, cautiously eager to be near their High Seer and new king.

Theo waved them over. "Try the food!"

Theo grabbed Aurienne's hand. "You ready to enjoy a festival?"

She smiled. "Show the way, Your Majesty."

"What do you want to see?"

"Everything."

He bowed. "As you command."

They wound their way several streets over to the blacksmith and goldsmith block. After walking past several vendors, he spied a small golden dagger.

He pointed, "Is that bog-iron steel?"

The master blacksmith's words tumbled out. "Bog-iron steel forged with gold, perfect for your royal use."

Theo inspected the edge, running his thumb against the edge. The blade was well-made, covered in star maps with the phases of the moon.

Theo handed the vendor a few shiny gold coins and presented it to Aurienne. "I know how you love to stab things."

"Thank you." She grinned. "What're you going to buy for yourself?"

He pressed a kiss to her hand. "I have everything I want."

The rest of the day, Theo and Aurienne, accompanied by various allies and friends, explored the city to the awe of their citizens.

Theo bought Aurienne several golden necklaces and ceremonial crystals, a few tomes for Adonis, and a leather cloak for Rhydian. He sampled nearly every variety of food—to avoid offending the chefs—and strolled arm in arm with Aurienne under the waning sunlight.

"We should head back to the courtyard," she said. "There's a final surprise."

They finally returned to the courtyard, finding Rhydian, Rianne, Adonis, Saryll, Kassia, and the other honored guests sitting on plump cushions.

Sorcerers' alchemical fireworks burst to life, painting the dusky sky with rainbows. The fiery glow reflected off the countless fountains and hardened glass tiles atop the underground rivers. Crushed colored glass glimmered from the stone walls, and crystals and mirrors reflected dancing motes of light from the paper lanterns. Candles floated in quiet pools of crystalline water.

Theo slipped his hand into Aurienne's, breathing a sigh of relief at the end of the longest day of his life.

Just before screams and wolf howls ripped through the night.

HEART OF AVYLLON
CHAPTER TWENTY-FIVE

Centuries-old oral traditions of hereditary shapeshifting wolves, known as Lycanthrope, are found across Lythea. Werewolves, however, were said to be cursed by the moon when hunters murdered her favorite child, the wolf, and can infect others with scratch or bite on the night of a full moon. Both tales predate the emergence of the Moon-cursed, which are Shadow-corrupted creatures. Neither man nor beast, they are akin to waking nightmares.

— ON WOLVES BY PROFESSOR LI HUANG, 531 N.T.C.

1152 N.T.C. The namesake capital city of Avyllon.

Crackling energy sent up the hairs on the back of Nesryn's neck just moments before the blinding light of a Way cut the night air. She was already sprinting toward the royal palace with A'estell'ia drawn when the flood of Mooncursed poured into the heart of Avyllon. Gelatinous, pitch-black blood sprayed the polished white sandstone courtyard walls with every precise swing.

Screams rang through the defenseless crowd as the wolf-like beasts tore forward. The crowd dispersed behind her as Nesryn swung her glowing sword in large defensive arcs that rent flesh and shattered bone.

Shrill warning bells cut the air with sentinels' thundering boots, but by the time help arrived, the gutters would run with Avyllonian blood. Rage prickled her blood as defenseless people fell. This was why all monsters needed to be destroyed. It always ended like this. Screaming victims sent shockwaves through her skull, and she planted her feet with a snarl as families huddled together. She would be their shield and their sword, and the emperor would regret attacking here today. He better pray to the gods she didn't find him.

Nesryn advanced through mounds of hairy corpses. Deformed wolf claws slashed at her, but she sidestepped and flicked a dagger into its skull. Teeth from another snapped a hairsbreadth from her shoulder, barely illuminated by torchlight. She rammed her elbow into its jaw, cracking its teeth before her sword slashed through its neck. She stepped over the corpse and danced under the blazing starlight magic of her sword that never slowed.

Her sword clanged off a Mooncursed, sending painful reverberations through her sword arm. With a twirl, she absorbed the rest of the shock and continued the motion into a deep thrust through its chest. She kicked it in the chest, using her boot to free her sword. Black metal, fused into the skeleton of the beast and crackling with energy, caught her eye. Flecks of clear diamond and gold reflected the waning sun.

Titan ore.

It bound the Shadow magic to the hybrids and allowed the sorcerer wardens to control them. She bared her fangs and searched for the wardens—and found one. A mostly human mutant wearing titan ore armor urged the creatures on. Her sword found him. His head bounced off the white walls and rolled down the street. The Mooncursed nearby howled in delight as it shook free of the compulsion. With a hateful growl, it began ripping off the warden's armor and devouring him. Two wardens stepped through the Way to take the place of the first. Just as at the summit, wading through the army of pawns wouldn't stop this onslaught. She had to crush their leader. With another spin, she decapitated two more Mooncursed.

Nesryn snapped her head toward a distinct roar and backpedaled as a giant hybrid bear slashed its metal claws at her. She brought her sword up just in time. *Slash. Slash. Slash.* And the bear fell. She gritted her teeth as she spotted more hybrid monsters pouring out of the Way.

The emperor had infected more than just werewolves with Shadow magic. Mooncursed monsters of all forms—hybrids of lions, bears, buffalo, and elephants—emerged. Those other forms were more difficult to combine with the shadows as they were creatures of the day. The emperor was growing in power, using elven magic that should have long faded from memory and remained buried. She tightened her grip on A'estell'ia, Starlight Justice. Rexil was a threat that needed to be put down.

A few more seconds and she'd be at the purple Way with the ragged, torn edges. She could see through the portal to the dark dungeon on the other side and the glimpse of golden and purple imperial robes. She'd slip through the portal and drive her sword into the emperor's heart.

Robed sorcerers emerged with eyes glowing purple behind titan ore masks. They raised their fists, and green flames erupted, aimed right for her. Nesryn skidded to a stop and ducked to avoid a fireball singeing the top of her head. She rolled into an alley as another fireball exploded where she'd been standing. Fireballs flew overhead and crashed into the nearby buildings.

Avyllonian sentinels thundered down the alley behind her. She raised her hand, and they ducked behind the wall.

"Use archers to target the sorcerers," she ordered. "You won't be able to seize the Way until they're gone. Swordsmen, protect the people from the Mooncursed."

The soldiers hesitated, not recognizing the stranger who now gave them orders.

"That's a…" a man trailed off, staring at a deformed Mooncursed.

These soldiers had never seen a Mooncursed.

She nearly groaned. "Yes. They're real. And they're killing your citizens. Now go!"

Without hesitation, Nesryn stepped out of the alley and hurled a dagger straight for the flash of golden robes through the Way. Her dagger bounced off the empty air. She hissed, searching for the source of the wards.

Hellsdamn them.

She'd have to find a way to break through the wards. More concerning was how Rexil knew those spells. More elven magic that no humans should have uncovered, much less mastered.

Priestesses with glowing rings burned into their foreheads fanned out, standing shoulder-to-shoulder beyond the Way.

Glancing down, Nesryn watched the sentinels pairing off to fight the Mooncursed while archers fired on the sorcerers. More sentinels arrived, along with soldiers and cavalry. From the Way, human Demorran soldiers flooded the streets. The emperor must have run out of Mooncursed. Or he was saving them for something else.

Needing to organize their reinforcements, she glanced toward the royal courtyard.

Theo drew his radiant Sword of Souls and settled into an awkward fighting stance. Beside him, the Warbringer drew his own steel sword.

Fucking hells.

The last thing they needed was for a deranged Warbringer to start attacking everything and everyone in sight without. He'd do more damage to the people running for their lives or huddling in the buildings than to their enemies. She'd seen it before too many times.

Unable to breach the Way, and now far more concerned with the idiotic Warbringer, Nesryn slipped through the alleyways and stomped toward the pair. Demorrans and Mooncursed alike fell beneath her ravenous blade.

Then, the Queensblood touched the Warbringer's shoulder and whispered, "It's too risky. Come protect us inside."

Nesryn's pointed ears twitched, her heightened senses picking out the words from across the courtyard.

White-knuckled, the Warbringer nodded and sheathed his sword. The pair stepped inside. Nesryn's eyes narrowed suspiciously. Those vengeful, wicked spirits puppeteering Rianne's body didn't have his interests at heart, so what was their game?

No time. Focus on the young man with the magical monster-killing sword that he apparently didn't know how to use.

A formless shadow appeared next to her as she approached the confused group.

The nameless spy said, "Target the wardens. They control the Mooncursed."

"I'm aware." Her tone was clipped. "Can you get through?"

"I can't get through the wards," the shadow man replied.

"Neither can I. They're around the entire city and those priestesses are holding them before the Way. See if you can slip through, and in the meantime..." Rumbling earth sent her head snapping the other direction. "...kill something."

The source of the reverberating booms stepped through the shimmering Way. Twenty paces tall, stone constructs with glowing purple eyes emerged. Seven of them. Purple light emanated from the seams between the boulders.

Impossible.

This was magic from her home. Lost magic. A stone giant swung its massive, balled fist and the second level of a nearby building exploded in a cloud of dust and debris. Slowly, the construct turned and smashed its fist into another building. The ground rumbled as the building collapsed.

Her blood ran cold as the stone giants lumbered through the royal courtyard. She glanced around at the gathered, mind working on the chess pieces available. The High Seer, Theo, and the young sorcerer gathered with their newfound allies. Her sights settled on two.

"Stone'ward, Ore'spike—focus on the stone giants," Nesryn ordered.

The People of Living Stone advanced with hands outstretched. A giant began to quiver as small avalanches of rubble smashed against the ground. The gaps revealed glimpses of the glowing purple shadow magic. The outer stones would be impenetrable, but the core could be destroyed.

Good. Now for the Mooncursed.

She glanced toward the young king, Theo. His sword was glowing, but she sensed the soul-rending energies were all but slumbering. He wasn't tapping into the magic.

Hells.

If he couldn't use the magic, he'd have to best them with his skill and he was still new to the blade.

Spinning on him, she said, "Your sword damages the spirits of those with magic. Focus your energies on those that are harder for your soldiers to kill—first giants, then the Mooncursed and their wardens. Let the sentinels take care of the Demorran human soldiers."

Theo nodded, casting a firm gaze on the charging wave of giants. To his credit—his hands did not shake, though sweat poured off his brow and demons haunted his eyes.

"How do we kill stone?" Theo swallowed but clenched his jaw.

"You can't," she said. "But your sword cuts through the magic for you. Just don't get crushed."

"How do I use the magic?"

"It responds to your will," she said. "You have to want the beast dead."

Theo followed Nesryn toward the monstrosities.

"We can delay their progress," Seven Forest Elder Dharek said from his place beside the courtyard gates.

"Father, let me help." Thaen grabbed Dharek's arm.

Nesryn glanced between father and son, sensing Dharek's hesitance. Watching how he glanced toward his own arm, the one covered in painful bark. An impossible position. Save the son and risk everyone, or allow your son to become a leader and risk his life.

Dharek's brow furrowed, but he finally relented. "We will go together."

Vines erupted from the white stone roadways, lashing two of the stone giants down. With every turn, the giants snapped vines, but more and more sprung from the earth.

Good. The giants' focus turned toward the naturalists and elementals, halting their path of destruction.

Nesryn's blade whirred in a tight circle, slashing and spearing Mooncursed beasts who darted for her from every direction, their oily blood soaking into the pearly cobblestones. She studied the city whilst keeping an eye on the enemy at hand—searching for any potential advantage. Sorcerers threw fireballs at the glass street panels while human Demorrans slammed hammers against them. Underneath her boots, underground rivers thundered through the city.

Aurienne gasped, drawing Nesryn's attention.

"I'm going to engage our defenses," the seer murmured before she slipped away.

At least someone was doing something helpful.

"Aurienne—" Theo started.

"With that Sight of hers, she'll be fine," Nesryn interjected. "You focus on your people. Let's go."

Stone giants continued to break apart at the hands of Stone'ward and Ore'spike, revealing more of their inner core. They struggled against the vines, unable to wreck the destruction they sought. Grinning, Nesryn charged a lashed giant, leaping off its wide leg and driving her sword into the heart of it. Her sword pierced the Shadow magic, evoking a throaty bellow as she landed. Though the giant moved slower, it had not come apart.

"Theo, now!" she ordered.

Theo dodged massive swings of the giant's arms. The giant lifted its leg, and it clipped Theo and sent him sprawling. Coughing, he struggled to his feet and staggered toward the giant again. If he was using his magic correctly, one cut and the creature would go down—but he wasn't tapping into it yet.

Nesryn danced forward and managed to sink her blade into the giant's core again. It writhed and threatened to tear her sword from her hand, but she quickly launched back and avoided its thunderous fist.

Dharek and Thaen shouted at the effort as vines tore through the cobblestones, whipping against the giants and pulling them down.

Theo launched forward again and this time the Sword of Souls drove deeply into the core. Though the magic didn't awaken, the giant shuddered and exploded into a storm of boulders and dust. Theo froze, watching the chunks of earth falling toward his head. He'd be crushed.

No!

Nesryn dove forward and tackled him out of the way of the falling rubble. He slammed the ground under her and choked as the wind was driven out of his lungs. Relief coursed through her. They couldn't afford to lose him yet.

The six remaining giants broke free of the vines and lumbered away, destroying everything in their paths. Nesryn jumped up.

Behind them, the young sorcerer, Adonis, drew shaking, clinking bottles from his bag. He ran forward and hurled a handful of the bottles at a giant. It seized and fell to its approximations of knees. The light went from its eyes and the boulders crumbled.

Her pointed ears perked up. That would be helpful.

"Do you have any more of that?" Nesryn asked.

The boy's breaths were coming fast, and his hands shook violently. "It took me weeks of work to make just those."

"Good work," she said, shoving down her disappointment; his wide eyes telling her he needed the praise.

Screams and growls echoed through the city. The Mooncursed

were tearing through their people, but if the giants weren't put down, they'd destroy far more.

The sun dipped below the horizon and immediately the skies darkened with the beating of a thousand wings—the vampires.

Nesryn glanced from the Way to the vampires and then to the palace where Rhydian had retreated—unsure of which was the greater threat.

Fuuucking hells.

Dodging falling rubble and avoiding packs of howling Mooncursed, Aurienne sprinted toward the palace with her sentinels following. Her thoughts raced. How did the emperor hide this attack from her? Why hadn't she Seen it coming?

The first defense that came to her mind when the Way opened was the scorpion crossbows mounted on the city walls, but they were aimed outward toward invaders and too far to reach the center of the city. The next defensive measure in their emergency plans was to protect their water, and it was several miles away through enemy beasts and sorcerers. But she had an idea.

"High Seer!" Sentinel Kolten called from behind.

She slowed just enough to let him catch up. "Are the archers defending our people?"

"The... elf organized them already," he said. "They're targeting Mooncursed and their wardens."

Aurienne panted, holding her cracked ribs. "Good. Sentinel Edran, gather the seers to assist with the battle. Saryll will know what to do. Then alert our sorcerers."

As Edran raced away, she turned to Kolten. "We can't let them poison our water. They've already tried once, and this attack is the perfect opportunity for it if it occurs to them. The main diversion can save most of our water."

He cocked his head. "The diversion is in the main testing access point."

Aurienne stopped near a wooden crate just outside the temple and lifted out several of the fireworks they'd planned to use for the coronation. "It'll help clear our path."

His eyes widened as she tore the bottom of her skirt off and tied it into a makeshift satchel before loading it with all the contents of the crate. She reached up and took a torch from the temple wall. Without a pause, she hurried into the fray holding up a firework like a hand canon.

Together, they raced down the streets. A Mooncursed with a lion's mane and a wolf's body darted out in front of her, saliva and blood dripping from its jagged fangs. Its green and purple eyes narrowed on her. With a dark smile, she aimed the firework at it and lit the fuse near the base. It exploded, launching her unexpectedly backward into Kolten as it blistered her skin, and she nearly fell. The firework struck the Mooncursed in the chest with a boom that sent pieces of the beast flying.

"Hagsteeth," Kolten stammered.

Aurienne pushed off Kolten and raced forward, digging another firework out of her satchel. They passed an intersecting road leading toward the Way and the sorcerers stationed nearby. Aurienne aimed the firework and lit the fuse. It hurled into a group of three sorcerers who turned toward her at the last second. Surprise twisted their expressions as the firework tore them apart.

The next mile was a blur to Aurienne. Rainbow lights and burning orbs mixed with blood and souls of her targets—an equally beautiful and terrible sight. She wasn't sure how many she'd killed when they reached the large square building, but her empty satchel was an answer.

Kolten pushed open the door to the access point, and Aurienne froze. Memories of that dark night where she'd nearly lost her life hit her in a barrage. The same as every nightmare she'd suffered every night since the attack. The sound of iron doors slamming shut and caging her in with her captors rang in her ears. Three men wielding clubs and knives, grinning at her fear. Their fists upon her body and hands at her throat. The burn of the water at the back of her throat and her flesh under their blade.

She backed away, cradling her broken hand as she heard the crunch replay in her mind and could feel the bones shatter under the Guild Master's strike.

"High Seer? Aurienne? You don't have to go in. I can do it." Kolten's voice was so very far away.

She shook her head and pushed open the door. Inside, she froze again. Kolten stepped around her and began turning the wheel to divert water from the city into the ancient emergency spillways she'd ordered unearthed after the aqueduct sabotage.

Unable to move, she stared at the floor where she'd nearly lost her life. At the wall they'd pinned her against to choke the life from her. She could feel her blade slide beneath their skin and the crunch of the man's skull. Acutely, she remembered the thrashing of the Guild Master as she wrapped the rope around his neck until he stopped moving.

She backed against the door, feeling her breaths come fast.

"It's done. We can go," Kolten was saying.

She nodded numbly, following him back onto the streets and toward the temple. Everything was a blur, and she remembered none of the trip.

Somehow, they made it back to the temple, and she climbed atop the roof.

Away from that horrible dark room, she shook off the nightmares and focused back on the battle. Saryll and the others turned to their runes and cards, shouting orders to the captains below.

Aurienne strode to the edge of the roof, watching her city burning and crumbling. She leaned weakly against the wall. She reached for her magic, but only embers remained. It was still depleted. She swallowed.

Could I help them if I Saw more? Would it matter?

Using it risked death. If she died now, she wouldn't be able to help win the war. Heart heavy, she watched her city fall.

With the stone giants finally downed and vampires tearing through the remaining Mooncursed, Nesryn strode toward the Way, determined to break through the wards. This would end now.

A loud horn blared from inside the Way, and soldiers and sorcerers began pushing back through the wavering portal.

The fox darted into her path, blinking with large golden eyes as it spoke into her mind, "*The wards on the titan ore armor allow them to pass through the Way. If they can pass through...*"

She grinned. "Then I can send them back through."

The fox swished its tail. "*He warded them against you specifically.*"

"But not his own forces," she finished.

The fox bared its teeth at her in something resembling a smile. It darted away, clawing and snapping at howling Mooncursed with golden bursts of magic.

Nesryn climbed the smooth sandstone walls until she reached a fountain balcony. She stepped out into plain view, brandishing her sword. A sorcerer aimed green fire at her and released it. It hurled toward her.

Not yet.

Not yet.

She caught the flame on her sword and ricocheted it back toward him. The magic of her enchanted blade sent the fireball straight into the sorcerer's heart and knocked him back through the Way. From the other side, a smoking corpse was all that remained. Emperor Rexil stared at the mangled body at his feet before glancing up to meet her eyes.

She grinned, baring her fangs, as several other sorcerers took aim not realizing their mistake.

Perfect.

"Cease your fire!" the emperor shouted.

It was too late.

Three green fireballs hurled toward her. She caught them on the side of her sword and flicked them back at the emperor. Her aim was true. Three sizzling fireballs flew through the wards and caught the emperor in the upper chest and shoulder. He fell.

The Way flickered. Sorcerers, wardens, and soldiers shouted and scrambled to flee back through the portal. The emperor raised his shaking hands as blood dripped down his face, fighting to keep it open. His breaths became labored, and finally his hands dropped.

The Way collapsed, leaving crimson stains in its wake.

MERCY
CHAPTER TWENTY-SIX

*Water blessed by the gods in the light of the moon can heal maladies
and certain curses. While crushed nightflame cures curses and corrup-
tions, it may also be used in dark ceremonies to seal curses that cannot
be undone.*

— BOOK OF WILDECRAFT.

1152 N.T.C. The namesake capital city of Avyllon.

Sorcerers' fires smoldered in the bleeding city under Theo's somber gaze. The attack had been quick but brutal. It highlighted just how unprepared they were, even after all their plans and schemes. Nesryn managed to injure the emperor and push them back, but in the aftermath of the destruction, it was a hollow victory if it could even be called that. When the full invasion came, they'd be in trouble.

The questions immediately came pouring in for the new king.

An administrator ran up to him, waving her arms, "Your Majesty, the hospital is over capacity, where should we bring the injured?"

Theo stammered, shaking his head.

"Your Majesty," a man pushed forward, "there are fires burning in the southern parts of the city that need to be put out."

"Go, take who you need to douse them," he said.

"We're stretched too thin digging people out of the rubble," the man protested.

Coldforges.

Now that the heat of battle had stilled, his mind moved too slow. The shock paralyzed him. His vision blurred at the edges.

"Your Majesty, we have no more housing for those displaced by the damage."

"I—uh..."

"Your Majesty, there are still sorcerers in the city who failed to retreat. We need help dealing with them."

"Your Majesty, what do you want us to do with the soldiers who surrendered? The dungeons are full."

He felt a hand in his, squeezing. Looking up, he found Aurienne's translucent gaze meeting his, encouragement thick in her expression. He straightened. He'd made a promise to do this.

"Take whoever isn't injured to tend to the fires. Recruit any civilians you see. Take all the additional injured to the temple or the palace, Aurienne will ensure you have what you need. And take the enemy troops to the barracks. We'll house them there until we find a more permanent location." He forced himself to keep moving, keep doing, because he was afraid that if he stopped, he might not start again. "I'll deal with the sorcerers."

He quickly found the remaining skirmish. His sentinels had pinned down the masked Demorran sorcerers, but by the time Theo arrived the Avyllonian sorcerers were making quick work of those who remained. All he remembered of the next moments was blood and green fire. The Demorrans never offered surrender, and he wasn't sure he'd have accepted.

Finally, the allies regrouped in the palace courtyard. Theo rubbed his temples and leaned against the wall seeing stone giants and sorcerers, and new hellish forms of Mooncursed.

What were those things?

"Here." Aurienne held out a large mug of water to him.

He cast her a tired smile. "Thanks."

"I should've Seen this coming," she said quietly.

"We'll be ready next time." He glanced around. "Where's Nesryn gotten to?"

Nesryn, as usual, appeared from thin air with perfect timing. "I've instructed your sorcerers on how to create wards that will prevent the emperor from opening a Way in your city again. I should've done so before I left, but I believed I could kill the emperor myself. I didn't yet know the depth of the magics he accessed." She cast a glance toward the palace. "And then I had a rampaging Warbringer to deal with."

"What type of magic is the emperor using?" Aurienne asked.

Nesryn's expression was tight. "He's found magic that should never have existed. The Mooncursed are not even the worst of what Rexil will bring."

The vampire, Stellan, landed, hands and face coated in blood. "With the Pillars up, even the hybrids can't remain on the continent very long. Only a few days at most."

Theo scrubbed his jaw. They'd buy some time with Nesryn's new wards, but the costs of the war that came would be even greater. The emperor's forces were held at bay by the protective Pillars. If the Pillars ever fell...

Nesryn tapped her scabbard thoughtfully. "As long as the Pillars are up, he can't bring the Shadows here. Once the Pillars are down, he will send the Shadows and worse. What you just faced will look like a children's bedtime story next to that nightmare that comes."

Something was nagging at Theo about the timing of this attack. He'd been going over the previous attack on the caravan over and over to figure out what he'd missed.

"What happens if the Flame Pillar falls but the rest remain intact?" Aurienne asked, cutting into his thoughts.

"Likely, they will be able to come halfway into the continent, up to where the remaining three Pillars protect," Nesryn said.

Aurienne glanced at Rhydian and Rianne emerging from the palace and whispered, "Unfortunately, Rianne hasn't honored the alliance yet, and the Pillar is near Rodarri."

Others were whispering, but Theo knew something was wrong. Something they'd missed. What happened at the last attack? They buried the dead. Planted the flowers. Collected the titan ore. What was he forgetting?

"We need to get to the Pillar and protect it," Aurienne said. "Immediately. Or the Shadows will overrun Avyllon."

What was different? Theo looked up toward the moon, realizing. After the caravan attack, they'd cleansed with moonwater. Theo inhaled sharply as his water mug clattered against the stones. It dawned on him what he'd been too thoughtless to realize.

The group turned toward him.

Theo's face drained of blood. "It's a full moon tonight. The stories say that you must cleanse before the moon's rise. The moon has risen. Anyone scratched in the attack can't be cleansed. It's too late."

Everyone froze. Even Nesryn's expression tightened.

His gaze fell from the angry white moon toward the hospital and healer's tents. "The infected are going to change soon."

"How are the infected different from the emperor's Moon-cursed?" Kassia asked.

"Without the titan ore collars and plates they won't attack on command, but they're dangerous and feral all the same," Nesryn spoke. "They won't have the blood and parts from other beasts, so they'll contort in unpredictable ways, but they'll change all the same."

The color drained from Aurienne's face. "We have to get them away from the others, they'll start infecting more and more."

"How many are wounded?" Theo asked.

"Over two thousand injured tonight at last check," Aurienne murmured.

Theo clenched his fists. "How many were injured by the Mooncursed?"

"Half," she answered.

He met Aurienne's eyes. A thousand potentially infected victims. There was no way they could triage them in the unsecured hospital rooms. They didn't have the time, the people, or the resources to do it there.

Theo took off toward the hospital with Aurienne, Nesryn, and Rhydian matching his pace.

"Where can we take them?" Theo asked, never stopping his hurried steps.

Fires burned around them, orange and green and purple. Rubble blocked the streets, and blood stained the cobblestones. People were pale and dirty, watching him with listless gazes.

"The Eyrand Arena has high walls and can be secured," Aurienne said. "It's less than a mile that way and the only place big enough."

The hospital doors slammed open, and Saryll met them.

"What's going on?" Saryll asked.

"Mooncursed infection," Aurienne whispered.

Theo tried to keep his voice down to avoid inciting panic. "Any wounded by the Mooncursed must be moved."

Saryll gasped, looking to the sky. "I'd forgotten it was a full moon. Goddess' breath. More injured are trickling in by the minute. And some might not have even come."

Aurienne pushed through another set of doors to rows and rows of beds. Theo stepped inside, feeling his insides knot.

To the entire room, Aurienne announced, "Everyone, if you were wounded by a Mooncursed, if you were bitten or scratched, we need to get you to the arena. Those wounds must be cleansed."

Theo glanced at her to find her mouth pursed. Not quite a lie, she neither told the truth. For half a second, his stomach sank—

wondering whether she'd used the same tricks on him. He shook it off.

"Let's go. This way." Theo started guiding the injured toward the doors.

Several patients were already beginning to sweat, and their eyes were red and blotchy. Others held their stomachs in pain. They were already turning.

"Let's go quickly," he said loudly. "We don't want the infection to spread before we get there."

Aurienne disappeared into another wing to gather more wounded. Kassia arrived, and after a few quiet words with Saryll, slipped out into the tents to send the rest toward the arena. Theo continued to usher potential infected outside.

Glancing back through the hospital doors, he saw husbands and wives kissing and friends hugging friends. None knew the truth.

Theo leaned toward Saryll. "Put any who came into contact with the infected into a separate wing to be monitored. Give them moon-water and pray they weren't scratched... or they were scratched after midnight. Try to keep them as separate as possible. Hopefully we can stop the spread here."

"Goddess willing," Saryll said.

"Let's go," he called loudly. "We must hurry."

Hundreds had joined the long procession toward the arena, but more and more began showing signs of the change.

"My scratch burns," a man said, holding up the red, swollen wound.

"Get to the arena as fast as you can," Theo said.

At Aurienne's command, soldiers lined the street to guide people.

Another man held his head. "My head is pounding. I can't see."

Theo swallowed and motioned to a sentinel. "Make sure he gets there immediately."

"Healers will meet you at the arena!" Saryll called over the din.

"Sir, you've not been injured," one of the healers was calling to two men.

"I'm going to help my brother get to the arena for cleansing," one man said.

"We can help him, you should stay here," the healer said.

"He's my brother. I won't leave him," the man said with a tight tone. "I won't."

The man looked to Theo as he passed, giving no quarter. Theo watched them go, knowing that the man's devotion to his brother was putting him at great risk. It might even kill him.

"Mommy, I want to go with you," a girl of no more than eight said.

The girl's mother looked to Theo. "Can she come too?"

Theo's stomach clenched and threatened to come up. "Was she injured by Mooncursed?"

"No. I hid her in a closet when they came. But they reached through a window and scratched me." She showed him an oozing bright red wound on her shoulder.

The small relief he felt immediately turned to sorrow.

"Then no, she should remain here," he said. "Is there anyone she can stay with?"

"My sister can watch her."

"Mommy, I want to go with you," the girl said.

Theo knelt beside her and took her hands. "Your mommy needs to go with the healers. Can you be very brave and stay here?"

Tearfully, she nodded.

Theo tried to give a smile. "Tell her goodbye."

Her mother watched Theo carefully, reading something into his features he tried to hide.

"I love you, baby," the mother said.

The girl sniffled as her mother walked out the doors.

The mother stopped beside Theo and asked, "Is something wrong?"

Her genuine expression turned the lies to ash in his mouth.

"The Mooncursed infected their victims," he said.

"And there's no cure?" she asked.

Theo gritted his teeth. "We will try."

"I see. I would be a danger to her if I stayed?" the mother asked.

He nodded.

Tears rolled down her face. "Then let's pray your cure works."

Theo watched the mother solemnly walked toward the arena. She looked back several times, waving to her daughter, before she faded into the distance.

Please let this work.

Theo stopped a sentinel at the hospital doors. "In case there are any we've missed, keep the injured as far from one another as possible. And watch for any signs of infection. Fever. Sweating. Spontaneous sharp pains. Get them to Eyrand or lock them away somewhere, and don't let any scratch you."

The sentinel nodded gravely.

Anger bubbled in Theo's throat. The emperor deserved to pay for this. So many innocents they couldn't save. What sort of monster unleashed this on the world? Even on his enemies? Theo swallowed as his thoughts turned to the vampires.

"Blacksmith." Obermeister Gotrik's voice was scratchy dry grass on Theo's growing rage. "What is the meaning of this?"

"The injured are exceeding the hospital's capacity." The words were a bitter draught on Theo's tongue. "Those injured by the Mooncursed require special cleaning and treatment."

"Special treatment?"

"To ensure speedy recovery." Theo glanced toward the lean man. "Were you injured?"

Gotrik puffed up his chest. "No."

Theo opened his mouth to tell the man to remain at the hospital, that the cleansing wasn't required.

Obermeister Gotrik pushed past Theo toward the procession. "But if special cleansing is being offered you should've informed us officials. We deserve priority treatment."

All Theo could see were the bruises and injuries on Aurienne's body. The wince on her face when she moved too fast. The haunted look that sometimes crossed her eyes. Gotrik had orchestrated that assassination attempt that'd broken Aurienne's hand and ribs and left her covered in stitches and bandages. He recalled his nightmare come to life where he'd watched them try to squeeze the life from her throat, where he watched from miles away as she fought for her life in that small, dark room. How she woke screaming.

The protest died on Theo's lips.

Theo watched Gotrik join the crowd heading toward the arena that would be their tomb. If the Obermeister entered the arena, he would likely never leave. Theo didn't stop him.

"It is what you deserve," Theo whispered—feeling not an ounce of guilt.

Theo took up the rear and followed the stragglers. Some rode in small carts, others were carried by friends, more yet limped their way toward the destination.

The last of the Mooncurseds' injured entered the arena. None had changed yet, so they'd made it in time. He'd have to send out sentinels to patrol the city that night for any other infected who hadn't gone to the hospital.

Gods—it's going to be a long night.

Nesryn appeared from nowhere, while Rhydian, Aurienne, Saryll, and Kassia gathered outside with the sentinels. Nesryn placed her hand upon the outer stones of the arena and closed her eyes.

"What do we do now?" Kassia asked.

"We could go bless water from the nearby pools and deliver barrels of moonwater inside," Aurienne said.

Kassia rubbed her palms against her green floral dress. "We can add cleansing remedies to the water to increase its strength."

"I'll go summon more seers to help us bless the water," Saryll said.

"Go," Aurienne commanded.

Nesryn opened her eyes. "The cleansing will only work on those turned after midnight. Bring the water but know it won't help most. The emperor's Mooncursed are creations tainted with Shadow magic that corrupts the werewolf curse. Those inside who've been infected with both will remain in their shifted forms unable to change back to human even after the full moon. True werewolves only change at the full moon, but the emperor's Shadow magic forces them into a state of permanent transformation."

"Can we help them?" Theo demanded.

The nameless one appeared from a nearby shadow. "The Mooncursed exist in a state of unending agony. It's the cruelest existence. A living hell."

"There's no cure to Shadow magic?" Aurienne asked Nesryn.

The elf shook her head. "None while the bridges to my world remain closed, and we do not have the power to open them again."

"What can we do?" Saryll asked.

Theo was slowly piecing together what the others were saying. Nothing could be done now. The corrupted and fused curses ensured such. It's why the emperor attacked on a full moon. He might've wanted to disrupt the coronation, but more than that he wanted to weaken Avyllon by causing as much damage as possible. And now, there was only one thing left to do.

"Bless all with what you can. Perhaps, they'll get lucky and the cleansing will work. The rest, we'll give them the only thing we have to offer. A merciful death," Theo said tightly.

Silence.

Downcast faces came to the same realization. They'd save any who didn't change, but the rest... would have to be put down. They couldn't keep them in the arena forever, couldn't risk them in the city.

"I'll do it," Theo said.

Nesryn drew near. "I will go with you."

At least I won't be alone, won't have to bear this alone.

"Thank you." He nearly choked on the words.

Rhydian stepped forward, but Theo shook his head. "I appreciate the offer, but it's a night for death, Rhydian."

Goddess—will my soul ever be clean?

His sins grew and grew with no end in sight. What horrible acts would he commit before the war was won? Would he even recognize himself when it was over, or would he be something entirely different?

Theo paused before the group of sentinels who'd helped bring the injured there. "I need all the exits well-guarded and a few volunteers to enter."

Sentinel Kolten stiffened and glanced at Aurienne before he stepped forward. "I'll go in with you. How many do you need?"

Nesryn answered, "Twenty of your best to enter the arena. Two hundred to guard the gates."

Kolten walked away as he began calling out names and assignments.

Theo stared at the arena, hearing the shouts and cries inside. It soon turned to screaming. The sentinels raced toward the gates.

Theo drew his Sword of Souls. With a heavy heart, he approached the Eyrand arena.

"Theo," Aurienne caught his arm as he passed.

"It's the king's duty." He pulled his hand away before leaving her in the street.

The duty she'd given him even when he'd begged her not to. This was the cost, and he'd have to bear it now.

"What if we get scratched?" Theo asked Nesryn.

"It's after the full moon's rise, if you're cleansed before tomorrow's full moon, you'll be fine," Nesryn said. "But that is not the greatest danger inside."

Growls and shouts echoed against the walls.

Fuck.

"Are you ready?" Nesryn asked.

I'll never be ready for this.

Theo nodded.

Theo, Nesryn and the small group of sentinels slipped through the gate to enter the arena. Immediately half-turned beasts attacked. Theo's sword sparkled like a midnight sky while Nesryn's glimmered with the light of a star, and blood sprayed the walls from both.

People cowered in groups against the walls as their friends, neighbors, and family turned to beasts before their eyes.

"Help us!"

"Please help us!"

Swinging his sword, Theo shouted, "We can't cleanse those who've been infected, but those who do not turn tonight shall live. We'll defend those who do not change."

The arena descended into chaos. People clamored against the gates, screaming and begging for escape while the infected transformed alongside them—growing fur and fang with breaking bones and shattering souls. They writhed as the Shadow magic of the Mooncursed ravaged their bodies.

Nesryn herded the Mooncursed together, while the others huddled behind them. Theo took a stance between the screaming group of people and those changing. He swung and swung, his magical blade cutting through the attackers. At his side Nesryn, twirled and spun in a fury of blade's edge. Behind them, the sentinels guarded those yet to change, and at the sign of the change—cut them down.

Bodies piled up.

At Theo's side, a man began to moan loudly and hold his head. His fingernails had already turned black.

"What's going on!" Gotrik grabbed Theo's shoulder.

The transforming man snarled and lunged. Theo stepped away, leaving Gotrik in his path. The man's emerging claws raked Gotrik's gut, and the Obermeister's innards fell out. The surprise froze on Gotrik's face as he fell, but Theo felt no remorse. The Mooncursed lunged toward Theo, and he lobbed its head from its shoulders.

"No!" someone was screaming.

A Mooncursed clawed Theo, raking his shoulder and arm.

Nesryn drove her blade through its chest. His arm now hung at his side, thankfully it wasn't his sword arm. He tucked it against his ribs.

"More are changing!" a sentinel shouted.

Nesryn held off the fully changed, while Theo turned on the group yet to change. He tasted bile as he noticed most of the group beginning to show signs or thrash around.

"Move the healthy over there!" Theo shouted.

He descended upon those in the middle of transforming, cutting them down before they were taken by the agony of the Shadows.

"Please not me!" a woman sobbed before his blade found her heart.

"No! No! You said you'd cleanse us! You promised to help!" a man shouted, protecting his changing wife with his own body.

He didn't even notice that her teeth had been pushed out of her skull by newly formed fangs that sank deeply into the man's throat. Theo freed her head from her shoulders.

Screams.

Theo spun. The uninjured man who'd accompanied his brother into the arena was holding his brother's shoulders as he was caught in the throes of transformation. Bones breaking. Skin stretching. All that was missing was the cruel titan ore plates the Demorrans adhered to their creations. The man cried out, holding a wound on his arm from his brother's claw. The brother turned, consumed by the madness, and attacked. With a swing of Theo's blade, they died together.

As the moon rose, the mother who'd sacrificed herself to save her daughter cowered against the wall, shaking with fear. She hadn't changed. Theo stood in front of her, willing to die to ensure she went back to her child again. He struck wounded Mooncursed. Claws raked him. A Mooncursed slammed him against the wall, and he coughed up blood but refused to move from his position guarding the unchanged.

Theo raised his sword and continued to cut through those the change overtook. Nesryn remained beside him, fending off the beasts' ferocity. The vampires arrived and began attacking and feasting. The end came quickly after that.

At some point, Theo reached up to find his cheeks wet with tears he didn't even know he'd shed. He'd said it would be mercy, but this was the vilest of acts. Over a thousand innocents died that night in the Eyrand arena walls, and Theo knew his soul would never be clean.

WITCH'S NEEDLE
CHAPTER TWENTY-SEVEN

The kings will die. The kings, they will all die! The kings shall die by blood and flame and claw, the kings of old shall die! Oh, how the kings shall die.

— FOLKSONG OF RODARRI.

1152 N.T.C. The namesake capital city of Avyllon.

Rianne tapped her silver-plated fingernails against the vines inset on the polished wood table in Avyllon's war room. While the room brimmed with vampires, naturalists, seers, witches, kings, and all other manner of monster, Rianne's split focus remained on the two kings. Like a serpent waiting for a mouse to emerge from its burrow, Vittoria watched through her eyes as King Jaekob of Wyndsel paced the marble floors.

Whillow whispered, *"One prick of the bloodwitch's finger and vengeance will be ours."*

Rianne could still feel the boiling skin of the unnamed queen, the bite of the ax on her own throat, the thousand deaths living inside her. The memory of the kings watching each death.

Samantah crooned, *"Their descendants deserve what's coming."*

"Two thousand eight hundred and seventeen are confirmed dead with several dozen missing," Captain Laurier informed Theo. "Not counting the Eyrand arena."

Theo stared at the floor with a darkening expression. "Four thousand one hundred and nine dead altogether."

"King Theo," the cold voice of Milah intonted. *"The other target of our vengeance. Once the Juri and Aradey lines are stamped out, none remained who originated the Ascensions or stood by while the wicked dragged queens to slaughter."*

"My beloved coven will one day rest peacefully with our final vows of vengeance fulfilled," a quiet voice, Kairya, whispered.

"We all will," the first queen, Vittoria, agreed.

Around Rianne, the conversation hadn't slowed.

"Double the search parties," Theo said. "If they're not found by morning, add their names to the dead."

Sentinel Kolten straightened his military jacket. "They could still be found. It's early yet to call off search parties."

Theo gripped the edge of the table. "The Mooncursed don't take prisoners, and if the bodies can't be found it's because there are no bodies to be found."

"They eat them," Captain Laurier replied, his eyes growing distant and watery.

Rianne swallowed. Distant memories of Mooncursed attacks danced at the edges of her vision. Torn limbs, spurting blood, feasting beasts.

"We're leaving at once," King Donovan announced. "I won't endanger my family by remaining in a city where werewolves run rampant."

Rianne's head snapped up.

"It could be months before we are provided another chance to exact our revenge if he leaves," Rebekkah said.

"We must keep them here! Scare him." Samantah, the other returned queen slithered around Rianne's collarbone.

"I don't know how," Rianne replied.

"Let me," Vittoria said.

Rianne hesitated, but finally gave up control and allowed herself to fade to the background of the other voices.

"The Mooncursed aren't werewolves, exactly," she heard herself croon. "They're close. Werewolves are cursed by the moon goddess and have been around centuries before the Shadow War. The Mooncursed specifically were men or beasts twisted by the magic of the Shadows. They often resemble werewolves, but they also take the form of many other beasts too. And who's to say the roads aren't swarming with all manner of Mooncursed beast waiting for your caravan?"

King Jaekob frowned but did not push the matter. He plopped into a chair.

Callysta's fragmented voice pushed through. *"There is still time to take what's ours. Oh, how the kings shall die."*

Blinking, Rianne grasped for control, pushing the others aside. Then Rianne met gazes with Aurienne.

The High Seer. She was watching Rianne with those impossible-to-read cloudy eyes gifted to her by the so-called Goddess. As if some of the queens in her bones had not been there, did not remember the events of the Shadow War that started all of this. Yet, something in Aurienne's steely gaze promised that the seer might have an inkling of what Rianne was up to.

"The seer may become an obstacle to remove," Samantah observed.

Rianne gripped her arm until her silver-tipped nails dug in—feeling the influence of the others in her mind.

"Speaking of obstacles—where has that wretched elf gotten to?" Rebekkah asked.

"Have you decided whether to join the alliance?" the seer interrupted Rianne's thoughts in a clipped tone that spoke volumes.

Rianne forced her face to remain expressionless, as she fought against Whillow—whose words poured from her mouth. "It's something I shall be discussing with your new *king* later. Since you're no longer regent, you should worry about the religious health of the nation and leave politics and wars to us. We'll have much to talk about, won't we *Theo*? Perhaps it will go late into the evening."

"*Stop it.*" Rianne slammed Whillow down, pushing her will against the bloodwitch.

Vittoria's voice was loud. "*If we can get Theo away from the guardians and monsters in this room, and most importantly away from that hellsdamned Sword of Souls and the pesky seer—we have a chance at completing our revenge.*"

"*He seems like a good man,*" Rianne protested. "*You'll be killing him for the sins of his bloodline.*"

"*You made us a promise,*" Vittoria reminded her. "*You've seen what good men have done when they believed it right. You see what Theo himself has done. With his sword, he's too powerful. He could force another ascension.*"

Rianne squeezed her fists harder. She hated that their arguments made sense. But she wondered how many of her thoughts were her own.

Aurienne's jaw clenched, and her fingernails dug into the arms of her chair. If looks could kill, Rianne would be twice dead from the darkness in the seer's eyes. She heard leather groaning behind her— likely the hilt of the seer's guard crushing the leather under his fist. Theo eyed her warily, his hand drifting toward his Sword of Souls.

Whillow's flirtatious comments were not well received. Perhaps a tactic she would have to try in private then.

"*No!*" Rianne shouted internally.

Rianne folded her hands, forcing them to be steady as the battle raged internally. "I expect to receive a reply from the emperor any day now. I'll give you all my answer then. I hear you're trying to figure out what he's looking for. I'm interested as well."

"After all you've seen, you're still considering his offer?" Aurienne snapped.

Rianne didn't want to. She believed in her heart it was the wrong call, but the queens whispered to her of the past. They called her naïve, and she knew they could be right. Her naivety had cost her life. She didn't want it to cost anyone else anything.

Rianne replied, "A true queen doesn't make a hasty decision."

Aurienne's clouded eyes narrowed. "A true queen isn't afraid to act."

Whillow glared at Aurienne through Rianne.

"Until you're an ally, perhaps you ought to leave," Aurienne said.

"There could still be Mooncursed roaming the forests." Whillow replied, this time with Rianne's consent, "I will stay until they've been dealt with, and then shall take my leave. It's only hospitable of you."

Aurienne's expression remained icy. "Maybe you should ask your potential ally, Rexil, to keep you safe."

Theo stood. "We'll make sure your path to the Way is secure and then you'll leave." Looking to a captain, he asked, "Captain Laurier, what have the sentinels discovered about the attack?"

"The Demorrans raided libraries at the temple, university, palace, and several public libraries," the captain said.

"This was a targeted attack," the seer replied. "What were they looking for in the libraries?"

"Maps. The location of whatever it is they've been scouting for," a master sorcerer said. "All the maps are gone."

"Adonis," the seer said, "tell us about the research into the Pillars."

The young sorcerer wrung his bandaged hands. "The closest Pillar to Karme and Heartspring is the Flame Pillar, but from our studies it's farther south than they've been scouting."

"We have to assume they have the location now or will soon," Theo said.

King Jaekob leaned forward. "If they're heading to the Flame Pillar, the roads to Wyndsel will be safe. We can all leave."

Callysta's mad mutterings filled the silence in Rianne's mind. *"Only your bones will leave. You'll be dead."*

Rianne felt her gaze narrow on his daughter, sitting meekly beside her new husband. Crown Princess Arissabett had not said a single word since arriving in Avyllon. Rianne had known the princess while alive. Recently they traveled together to Avyllon before the continental summit.

"She can help us," Rosalindt said.

As the group dispersed, King Jaekob remained in the room.

Perfect.

Rianne sauntered over to Arissabett, watching King Jaekob conversing with advisors in low tones. She sat primly beside the princess, feeling her face fall into the wide-eyed innocence she once possessed.

"Congratulations on your wedding," Rianne said.

Arissabett blinked as if just noticing Rianne's presence. "Rianne, it is good to see you." Her eyes darted to Rianne's throat. "I heard..."

"Yes," Rianne said, forcing a small smile. "No need for apologies. It's done. I guess I did return after all. Look at the pair of us, you married, me queen. So much has changed in a few short weeks."

"I'll be queen one day too," Arissabett murmured.

Rianne felt Whillow cock her head, studying the princess. Her eyes opened to the magics swirling around the girl. She wasn't of the king's bloodline.

Interesting. A puzzle for another time. But it meant they wouldn't have to kill her.

Rianne said, "Of course you will. I didn't mean to offend you."

The princess blinked again and took Rianne's hands in her own warmly. "You said nothing wrong. But ever since the wedding, I've felt so invisible. Everyone only cares what Donovan thinks, but he's not even a trueborn Juri. I am."

"I know all too well what it means to be invisible for the crime of being born a woman," Rianne whispered. "Change your fate, if you want to."

Aurienne, sitting on the other side of Arissabett, watched Rianne with a feral intensity that only Nesryn could rival.

"Where has that elf gotten to?" Samantah muttered in the background.

Rianne glanced around, checking the shadows and corners of the room to be sure that the hellsdamned elf had not appeared out of the air to haunt her.

"Your fate is your own," Rianne murmured.

Arissabett simply nodded.

King Jaekob strolled out of the room, surrounded by a cadre of guards.

"Now. This is our chance," Vittoria said.

Theo might not deserve to die, but King Jaekob certainly did.

"Excuse me, it's been a long day. I shall retire," Rianne announced.

Rhydian started to follow her out of the room.

Kingshit.

She had forgotten about the silent Warbringer. This would complicate matters. She had to head off the king before he reached his rooms without her constant shadow catching on.

"Rianne," Aurienne called, the musical quality to her voice ringing with falseness, "I See all."

Rianne held her gaze for a moment, before slipping out of the war room. She took a servant's hall toward the guest wing.

Rhydian looked around. "Why are we—"

"It's faster, and fewer people around," she replied.

She hurried down the winding hall that let out at the entrance to the guest wing. Her slippers danced on the marble tiles as she hurried to the end of the wing where her rooms waited.

"Would you check the suit for intruders?" she asked sweetly.

He smiled and unlatched the door. Once he was inside, she grabbed a blanket from an ajar linen closet and wrapped it around her head like a shawl—hiding her gown and crown.

Voices. The king was coming.

Rhydian's boots circled her rooms, and he would soon return to her. Seconds remained to accomplish her task. She hurried back down the hallway and slipped along the wall, willing herself to remain unseen. She could see King Jaekob's entourage, and she slipped into their ranks.

Passing several suites, they reached his door. The king was just about to walk inside. He was too far away! She reached out with the bone needle, stretching toward him. His guards were in her way. She leaned so far someone would soon notice, and she had to get back to her door before Rhydian completed the room check.

No!

She stared at him, a thousand eyes peering out of her skull, whispering over the top of one another until it became an incantation.

Stop.

Look at us.

Know your shame.

Turn.

He froze at the doorway as his guards entered the room. He glanced out to the hall where the rest of his entourage waited, but she remained hiding behind a large man in front of her. The king shook his head.

Guilt, doubt, shame, and fear pricked through the numbness. It was quickly washed away by the rage of the queens. She reached out again. She reached and reached...

She pricked King Jaekob's finger with the bone.

A devious smile, one prompted by hundreds of the souls inside of her, spread across her face.

It was done.

She slipped away from the entourage as they filled into the Wyndsel accommodations. The towering wooden door, carved with trees and stars, closed with a boom. Racing down the hall, she abandoned her blanket and reached her door panting.

Rhydian stepped out. "All clear." His brow furrowed. "Are you okay?"

She held her breath, willing herself to appear calm. "Just nerves from the evening."

He nodded and held the door open for her. As she entered under his arm, she allowed a trace of her smile to return.

Callysta said, *"Oh, how the kings shall die. One bloodline remaining."*

VENDETTAS
CHAPTER TWENTY-EIGHT

Souls are malleable things, fragile and resilient at once, capable of withstanding great anguish but can crack when struck at a weak point. Once cracked, magic from beyond the veil imbues the blood with unspeakable power.

— GRIMOIRE OF KAIRYA, BLOODWITCH, 5 B.N.T.C.

1152 N.T.C. The namesake capital city of Avyllon.

Funeral bells rang as dawn rose, and Rianne knew the cause before she woke. King Jaekob was dead. The finger bone needle had done its work. A part of Rianne's heart felt heavy and twisted—vines over a tombstone—underneath the numb blanket that death left in its wake. The larger part began to mirror the sentiments of the queens, and they were pleased. King Jaekob's ancestors committed terrible atrocities against the queens over the years, and by the way he treated Arissabett and his wife, it was apparent he was no saint.

Half-dressed and wearing various stages of sleeping attire, the allies gathered in the council room.

"The king is dead." Arissabett was ashen but was yet to shed a tear.

"Did the emperor create another Way?" Seven Forest Elder, Dharek, asked.

Nesryn sat in an open window with a knee propped up, surveying the room. "The wards held. This wasn't Rexil."

Rianne blinked. The elf hadn't been there just moments before. Rhydian's leathers squeaked as he shifted behind Rianne and caught Nesryn's eye.

"We must return home immediately." Prince Donovan's face was redder than the bloodroses at home. "I can see that *King* Theo fails to protect his allies."

Theo slammed his fists against the table. "It wasn't the emperor, and it wasn't any of us. Only one person stands to gain from his death, and it's his replacement."

Donovan pushed back from the table, and Theo straightened his stance, broadening his shoulders.

"Mind your words," Donovan hissed.

"Or what?" There was an edge to Theo's voice Rianne didn't recognize.

The two new kings stared each other down. Just the thing a fragile alliance in its infancy couldn't withstand. Depending on the emperor's offer to Rianne, she may have to use this crack in Teridar's armor later.

"Who is responsible? We must catch the murderer," Dharek said.

The Wildegrove witch, Kassia, wrapped her green shawl around her shoulders. "His death does not appear natural, but it matches no known poison, curse, or malady."

Whillow chuckled, *"Good luck identifying this curse."*

"There were all sort of dark magics running wild last night. Any one of them could've been the cause," Rianne offered quietly.

Did I do the right thing?

Vittoria murmured, *"More must come before the day is through. Use the chaos to complete our vow. Only one king to go. Don't wait until he's grown in power."*

Rianne glanced toward Theo, to find Aurienne's hard gaze upon her instead. Rianne looked away, toying with the embroidered sleeve of her nightgown where the bone needle was concealed.

Rianne thought, *"I don't want to do this."*

Milah's icy voice echoed in her ears. *"The kings must die, or we'll never be safe."*

Rianne gripped the needle. *"There is no question King Cavendar and King Jaekob deserved their dues. Vile-hearted cruel cowards. Theo doesn't deserve it though, not that I can tell. He raced with Rhydian to try and save me. He risked his life getting his friend out and still came back to save Jordyn. His only sin is his ancestry."*

Bloodwitch Whillow argued, *"We made a vow. We must follow through. The fates demand it. Our magics demand it."*

Nataylia—ever the voice of reason—said, *"He just slaughtered an arena full of people who did nothing other than get infected with magics for no fault of their own. He's freed vampires. Don't be fooled. When this is done, he will be no better than the other kings. It's in his blood."*

"I can't kill someone with a good heart," Rianne thought. *"I won't become what we seek to destroy."*

Samantah scoffed. *"A good heart? Maybe once, but no more. He's already changing. He's just like* them.*"*

Vittoria cut in, *"We are leaving today. This is our last chance to fulfill a centuries-old debt. If you will not do your duty, we will."*

Rianne gripped the edge of the table. *"I won't let you control me."*

Rosalindt said gently, *"We will never go to rest as long as our debts remain. The Fates foretell that as long as the kings live, the queens will die. Ascensions always return. Would you damn more queens to the ravine?"*

Rianne remembered the small faces watching the ascending

queens. Blood spurting. Heads rolling. Corpses falling. The suffocating, endless dark.

Rianne swallowed, feeling her heart soften. *"Theo wouldn't do that."*

Whillow said, *"What wouldn't he do for his people? Look at what he's already done."*

Returned queen Morgana said, *"The only question is whether you intend to keep your promise to end the ascensions for good."*

"Of course I do," Rianne said.

Vittoria slithered across her ribs. *"Then you know what you must do."*

Rianne shook her head, realizing that the arguments of the room raged on while she was distracted.

"We're leaving now." Donovan stormed out of the room with Arissabett tripping after him.

Seven Forest Elder, Dharek, said, "We shall return as well and prepare our borders."

Stone'ward and Ore'spike followed soon after.

"I will gather the witches and see how we might help," Kassia said. "We can prepare healing remedies and protection charms."

"Thank you," Aurienne replied gently.

If everyone was disbanding, Rianne was running out of time.

"We should go too. Our answer for the alliance will arrive shortly." Rianne glanced to Rhydian. "Would you prepare our caravan while I finish breaking fast?"

Rhydian kissed the back of her hand, calling forth weak butterflies in her heart, before he left. Rianne nearly smiled, but the warmth faded all too soon at the chill of death in her bones.

The remaining Avyllon council members spoke quietly with one another. Rianne waited, stalking Theo. Waiting. Watching.

She didn't have long, and the window to act was closing. Theo rounded the table, speaking with Captain Laurier and Adonis. He was only a few paces away. Rianne carefully glanced around. All eyes were elsewhere. No one was watching.

She pushed her half-touched plate away and stood slowly, casually. She turned as if heading toward the door. She slid the finger bone from her sleeve down into her palm.

It ends the ascensions.

It saves the queens.

Rianne tried to make herself believe it as the rage of the others filled her bones. She felt her gaze narrow upon her prey as their hatred overtook her. She may not want to do this, but she'd be damned if she allowed any other queen to die. Nothing would keep her from saving them.

Theo's hand hung by his leg. Exposed flesh, perfect for pricking. He'd never even know what happened, and then he'd be dead. So close. He was within her range. She reached toward Theo.

A weight closed around her hand, squeezing her fingers until they nearly cracked.

Rianne's gaze snapped up to find a lethal expression darkening Aurienne's cloudy eyes. Rianne's lips parted in surprise as Aurienne snapped the finger bone and crushed it to dust. Shocked, Rianne took a large step back.

Concern laced Whillow's voice, *"She shouldn't have been able to touch the bone. It should have killed her. Yet she crushed it without a thought."*

Fear bubbled inside Rianne, and Whillow pushed to the front and took control.

Aurienne's hand disappeared into the skirts of her gown, no doubt closing around the golden dagger resting within. Whillow moved Rianne's hand to rest on her bonesword corset.

Samantah said, *"We must kill him."*

Morgana spoke up, *"We could cut the seer down and slash at him with the bonesword, but he'd have drawn the Sword of Souls by then."*

Nicollete's suspicion tasted of copper on Rianne's tongue, *"If we leave here without killing him, we'll lose our chance forever."*

Rianne's resolve solidified. The old Rianne would never have considered murder, but that version of her was dead.

Not one more queen would die.

Aurienne's voice was low but cut through the whispers in Rianne's head. "I see you thinking about it. Turning over your options in your mind. Searching for the path to revenge. Let me offer a word of advice: don't."

Rianne folded her hands on her corset as Safyrah and Noxanya prepared to summon the bonesword. "I have no idea what you mean."

"Stay away from him." Aurienne's skirts brushed Rianne's for how close they now stood. "Or I'll send your souls straight to hell."

Nataylia said to the others, *"Would the seer do it? Here in front of all these people? Would she really commit murder?"*

"She could be bluffing," Milah mused.

Rosalindt tapped her spirit claws on Rianne's ribs, watching intently.

Samantah hissed, *"I don't think so. She's got the heart of a killer."*

Vittoria said icily, *"I would believe her."*

Rianne studied the seer. A strange stillness fell over Aurienne—stealing away all unnecessary movement. The seer hardly breathed, and not at all in the right cadence—as if something else inhabited her. The air crackled with magic, causing the hairs on Rianne's arm to stand up as her fingers traced the bone corset. Nesryn's head snapped in their direction, but Rianne ignored the elf.

"It never ends well for you, Rianne," the seer said. "Not in ten thousand futures."

Rianne tilted up her chin, feeling an unknown presence stirring in the bottomless sea of souls and magic in her blood.

"I've never been one to rely on the fate I was dealt." The bonesword slithered from Rianne's corset to her hand, so silently the rest of the room didn't notice.

Aurienne's lips curled into a vicious, cold grin. The seer's eyes glinted like frigid steel in the winter sunlight as if they were glowing, and she held Rianne's gaze without even blinking.

Rianne's souls could feel the magic gathering around the seer, ancient and intense enough to split through the veil and rip apart its human host. It tasted like rage and death.

"I warned you," Aurienne whispered.

Every soul in Rianne's body felt an unfamiliar tinge of human fear, right before Aurienne's magic closed on them and ripped them into the spirit realm between worlds.

DARKER MAGICS
CHAPTER TWENTY-NINE

Death is not the worst thing that can happen to you.

— JOURNAL OF QUEEN ROSALINDT DANIELLA
LENORE, 579 N.T.C.

1152 N.T.C. A world beyond the veil.

In a nightmare realm between worlds beyond the veil of life and death, Rianne gasped for air. Steadying herself, she turned a slow circle. Shapeless forms prowled in the mist, and tree bark groaned and cracked. Sinister vines coiled around tree trunks inset with teeth and glimmering gold nuggets. Copper lanterns hung from twisted branches, emanating a gloomy light. Between the trees, a small section of crumbling granite wall with faded tapestries and lonely marble pillars marked this as an ancient palatial ruin.

Whillow's voice was louder here. *"The power it took to drag us here, waking, against our will was inhuman."*

Something bumped against Rianne's foot, she moved her skirts to reveal a skull with too-wide eyes, curling horns, and rows of teeth.

The High Seer appeared from the haze, wearing full goddess regalia. Tattoos swirled along her limbs as if alive.

"I know of your vendetta against the kings," Aurienne said, her voice laced with warning, and a slippery echoing quality—like oil on water. "King Cavendar is dead, and let's not pretend you aren't responsible for King Jaekob. The raiders of Thrymr settled the Seven Forests centuries ago, and the armada of the Titan Cliffs is gone, leaving only simple miners. It leaves one king in your revenge ploy, Theo."

Aurienne folded her hands, eyes glowing like purifying godfire. The layers of her gown whipped around her in an unseen breeze.

Rianne coolly considered her options. Aurienne was powerful—but not so powerful to take on nearly a thousand angry spirits trapped in this body. The time for subtleties ended when Aurienne showed her hand.

Rianne shrugged. "He has Aradey blood. I swore to end the line. And he's been crowned. He's a true king and my revenge is incomplete."

"I'm warning you, stay away from Theo."

"Or what?" Rianne made herself chuckle despite her apprehension.

Aurienne took several steps forward from the mist, and Rianne could now see a woman's spectral form faded in and out of Aurienne. Rianne inhaled. The seer and her Goddess occupied the same space, her Goddess like a shadow haunting her body.

Did Aurienne even know?

Rianne had known Aurienne was powerful, but now knew the extent of the connection. Faint cords of golden fate, spun into chains, wrapped around Aurienne's arms and legs, her chest and neck. It was a wonder the seer could even breathe with fate suffocating her like this.

Perhaps, it was a mistake to taunt her.

Aurienne scowled, her face twisting into a nightmarish shape in this place between worlds as she advanced on Rianne. "I won't warn you again."

Rianne slid her foot half a step backward. Now dead, she no longer felt fear the way the living did, but she did recognize when she was in mortal danger. Rianne caught sight of the dark smudge, the stain on Aurienne's soul. Hidden by the Goddess and the blinding chains, now Rianne saw it—the mark of spirit necromancy.

Kingshit.

Spirit necromancy was ancient, forgotten, forbidden, yet Aurienne wore its mark. Aurienne's threat held far more weight now; she could possibly devour or shred their souls and leave nothing behind. She had done it before, and with her Goddess so near...

"Distract her with painful truths," Vittoria said. *"Tell her what she doesn't want to hear to take her focus from the blacksmith king."*

Rianne inhaled. *"That's horrible."*

"But necessary to escape this place," Rosalindt's icy fingers scratched across her heart.

Rianne spoke, "You don't even realize the hold she has on you, your Goddess. How close she is. Or what she's taken. The life you could have had. The dark forces lurking between worlds, waiting for you to weaken."

Aurienne stopped her advance, the mist pooling around her ankles. "I don't want to be your enemy, Rianne, all of you in there. But if you come for him again, I'll be an enemy you do not want. I swear it on my soul." Her expression was too flat, too cold.

"Aurienne is serious," Rianne thought.

"I'll find us a way out, just keep her occupied," Whillow hissed, slipping through Rianne's veins, testing their surroundings.

"If you had to choose between saving your precious continent, and that man, I wonder what you'd choose," Vittoria mused aloud. "Do you protect him because you think he's destined to win the war or for other reasons?"

The shadows circled Aurienne's fists.

She's angry.

Rianne backed away, feeling Samantah's taunts escape her tongue. "The size of his sword or the deftness of his hands? Maybe I should take him for a ride myself if he's worth all that."

Aurienne clenched her jaw but said nothing.

Jealous, but not enough to make a mistake over it.

Rianne nearly gasped. "Or maybe you're in love with—"

Aurienne's face contorted into a shape impossible outside of the realm of dreams and nightmares. With a sharp motion, Aurienne reached into Rianne's brain and wrenched out silver chains of memories. The queens screamed as all the pain they'd had ever known in all their lives exploded in every inch of their borrowed body. Memories twisted and knotted in Aurienne's shadowed hands. Rianne fell to the background as the spirits erupted in a wild frenzy.

Spirit necromancy.

"You're risking your soul!" Whillow screamed. "You're dooming yourself to hell."

Aurienne's words were measured. "I would burn my soul to ash to protect him."

Light poured from Aurienne's eyes, mouth, nose, and ears now. Her hands curled into fists wrapped in unnatural shadows. The chains of fate slithering across her body glinted like the sun on steel. The seer was deadly serious and prepared to strike.

Aurienne's expression remained flat as her eyes and mouth glowed brighter. "I remember your histories." Her voice was hardly a whisper.

Rianne felt as though she were unraveling, as though all her souls were back in that ravine falling to madness and forgetting who they were. She reached for Aurienne, but the seer's skin burned her flesh.

"I've seen Vittoria, bleeding out from childbirth gone wrong, handing her beautiful daughter off to her sister. Giving her life to the land so her daughter might be safe," she said.

The part of Rianne that was Vittoria howled as the silver memory lit up. Aurienne captured it and wrapped around the spirit's neck. It burned her body and soul, ripping screams from her throat. Vittoria writhed and clawed at the memory chains, unable to get free.

Aurienne whispered, "During the Shadow War, they rounded up the rest of your family for imprisonment and sacrifice, and then only a few years later, they killed Vittoria's dear sister."

Isybel shrieked as her death threatened to rip Rianne in half. Emotions, so long buried rose to the surface. Pain, grief, longing, regret.

"And after that, they killed Vittoria's daughter, Lexyra." Aurienne's words felt like physical strikes. "And her daughter. And all the daughters of all the Queensblood."

The dark pool of power within Rianne stirred, bubbling, waking.

Aurienne tugged on the silver chains of memories again. They struck the spirits, catching them and holding them down. Rianne struggled, but it was no use. She was being ripped apart.

"I've seen Rosalindt uncovering the lies, and yet they still held her down and cut off her head," Aurienne whispered.

"No!" Rianne screamed, feeling Rosalindt writhe within her.

"Penelope, Nataylia, Samantah, Rebekkah, Morgana, Charlotte," Aurienne listed.

As Aurienne recounted the memories, the spirits remembered and were snared into the seer's waiting grasp. One by one, the seer was binding them all.

Rianne found that quiet, dark place inside of herself where all the emotions went to drown. The dark ocean of power at the core of the spirits rippled. The one she dared not think of 'til now.

"You harm him, and I'll end you," Aurienne promised. "I'll devour your souls, leaving only the empty husk behind. I'll bind you in a hell that makes that cursed ravine look like a Goddess-forsaken paradise. You will scream for death that never comes. For how long your torment will endure, that thousand years will be the blink of an eye. And when I'm done, I won't kill you. I'll erase you."

Rianne forced herself to be still, and the pain fell away. As she loosened her tight grip on the queens, she prepared to release the spirits from her bones. Her body might wither without them, and she'd lose herself, but she had no choice.

"I'll bow before no one ever again. Devour us then. Try it. If this is the way you want to do this, then let's test your mettle." Rianne and the others spoked as one as she tapped her elongated nails on the magical silver chains binding her. "Be warned, we are many. We are old, powerful, vengeful. Even a Goddess might not be able to devour us all. We'll find out."

Aurienne jerked the chains. "I only want one thing."

Rianne tilted her head, the bloodwitches in her bones testing the resistance of the memory-forged chains.

"You shall not harm Theo." Aurienne's breath was hot on her face. "You shall not trap, imprison, endanger, harm, hurt, maim, or kill him. You will direct no one else to do the same, nor take any action, inaction, or omission that places him in danger. If you discover he is in danger you shall take every effort in your ability and those under your command to warm him and me of the danger. You must protect him. If you break this vow, you agree that I shall sunder your body and souls, and you shall not resist."

Rianne leaned forward, the chains digging into her skin and souls. "And you shall never threaten me with this fate again."

"Done," Aurienne replied.

Rianne reached out her hand to seal their accord, but Aurienne shook her head. Aurienne took her ceremonial blade and sliced her tongue. She reached forward.

The Old Ways. Not quite as dark as necromancy, but every bit as powerful.

Rianne grimaced but opened her mouth, and her tongue was sliced open. Aurienne leaned forward and kissed Rianne, her tongue sliding against the queen's.

Aurienne pulled away. "You will drown in your own blood and your souls shall be sundered if you break this oath."

"It is done," Vittoria said darkly through Rianne.

The chains evaporated, and Rianne rubbed her wrists, arms, and neck. She backed away from the seer, eyeing her warily. A thousand questions on her mind, many of them her own. Many parts of her wanted to immediately attack Aurienne—for the oath did not prevent such, but Rianne held them at bay.

"You can control anyone this way? So why don't you," Rianne asked.

Aurienne grimaced.

Rianne's anger stilled.

He's the only thing you care enough about to risk your soul.

"It'll cost your soul and afterlife, but you're willing for this," Rianne said. "For him. Why don't you just murder the emperor?"

"He's guarded, veiled. I can't find him." Aurienne gave her a sharp look. "Why don't you try to kill him?"

Rianne gritted her teeth. "First, I'll see whether agreement can be reached. If not, I will pursue assassination. Whatever protects Rodarri best."

"Killing Theo doesn't protect Rodarri." Aurienne snapped.

Vittoria pushed forward. "No, Theo was a personal interest of ours—mine. You could have asked me to protect Teridar or Avyllon. Even yourself or your brother. You could have asked me to agree to kill the emperor. But you asked me to protect *him*." Vittoria leaned Rianne in and whispered. "I know your weakness now. I know what you're willing to risk your soul for."

Aurienne smiled, a wicked smile that might have haunted Rianne if not for the fact that all her souls were already dead. "You now know the lengths I'll go to protect him. You won't want to learn what I'd do to avenge him."

Rianne lifted a brow, allowing Vittoria to control her for the moment. "I could still kill *you* under our accord."

Aurienne shrugged. "If you feel you must. Best of luck. I'm not an easy target."

The seer grinned and vanished.

Rianne blinked and was back in the world of the living in the war room staring Aurienne down with the taste of copper and the queens' blackened, dead hearts full of only rage.

Lavendiir Palm Tea
Chapter Thirty

What if I no longer know what is real?

— Journal of the High Seer Aurienne Azarrah.

1152 N.T.C. The namesake capital city of Avyllon.

Dabbing at the golden soulblood dripping from her nose, Aurienne watched the Rodarri royal caravan stretch away from Avyllon, heading toward the nearest Way. Aurienne wondered whether threatening Rianne had pushed Rodarri closer to an alliance with the Demorran Emperor. They couldn't afford to lose any allies, not after they'd paid such high costs. Scowling at Rianne and feeling as though the queen sensed her ire from the carriage, Aurienne pivoted away from the window.

After avoiding her magic for weeks, she'd just expended the entire shallow pool she'd managed to refill. Hours later, she was still light-headed and coughing up dark crimson blood. She curled up on the couch, leaning against the armrest with her throbbing head in her palm.

All their allies were preparing to depart. The People of Living Stone and Seven Forest dwellers, along with forest giant, Alleson, and Wildegrove witch, Kassia. She prayed they would be able to hold up their end of the alliance or it would all be for nothing.

Saryll knocked and slipped into her room. "Are you alright?"

Aurienne covered her mouth with a dark purple handkerchief to conceal another cough. "Could you bring me more lavendiir palm tea? I've run out."

"How much have you had today?" Saryll asked carefully, glancing at the empty tea mug beside Aurienne.

"Not enough."

"You shouldn't take too much. It can dampen your gift permanently."

"If only that were possible," Aurienne replied dryly.

"I'll ask Kassia for more before she leaves." Saryll sighed, clearly wanting to say more but refraining.

"Thank you," Aurienne called as the door closed.

If her head would stop pounding, she could help Theo. She couldn't afford to be weak. There was simply too much to do. She needed to help the efforts to fortify the city, deal with the Moon-cursed corpses, and tend to the injured. They were counting on her guidance. Then there was the matter of protecting the Flame Pillar. They also needed to formulate a plan about their next move against Demorra.

A little rest, and then she'd start planning. She closed her eyes for just a moment.

A coarse scratching noise caused Aurienne's eyes to pop open. She sat straight up and reached for her golden dagger. The scratching continued, and she stood, searching the corners of the room for the source. The air felt oily and hot, and she fought the urge to vomit.

"Hello?" she called.

"All alone again."

That voice. She froze, feeling fingers of fear brush her spine, as her throat tightened.

The blond mason Guild Master stepped out of a shadow, face swollen, eyes bulging, and throat distorted with purple bruises from where she'd strangled the life out of him.

"No," she whispered. "You're dead."

He grinned, displaying gaps from where she'd knocked loose several teeth in their struggle. "And yet, here I am."

Two other men stepped out from other shadows in the room. One with his leg and neck still spurting arterial blood, the other with half his skull missing—the men who'd attacked her.

Aurienne backed away, holding her dagger as tightly as she could in her oily palm. "I killed you."

Obermeister Gotrik stepped out of a shadow nearest her, his flesh shredded to bits. One arm was nearly detached, his entrails were dragging behind him, and he limped forward on a stump of a leg.

Aurienne yelped and dodged his outreached claws by leaping over the back of the couch.

"What?" She blinked.

"Your new king fed me to the Mooncursed when I wasn't even infected. He murdered me in cold blood," Gotrik replied.

"You're lying. Theo wouldn't do that," she spat.

Gotrik raised his claws. "If you say so. Either way, I'm here to return the favor."

The four men advanced.

Aurienne screamed.

"Your visions won't help you now."

She swung her blade wildly, slashing at the assassins, but it was no use. Their hands were on her, choking her. She could feel her bones break, the slice of a blade into her flesh, the punishing club strikes. They choked her to death. Stabbed her to death. Beat her. Everything they tried in that dark room, this time they managed. Neither her

Goddess nor Theo were there to save her, but she never stopped fighting. She clawed and kicked until she nearly blacked out.

Falling to the floor, Aurienne found herself alone again. Tears welling, she fought to regain her breath. Her head whipped around, searching for the men, but they were gone, leaving only behind bloody trails and broken furniture.

A dark entity appeared. The same who came to Aurienne when she was last attacked by assassins in that dark room. Taking the shape of a woman covered in shells, bead, and feathers, the entity grew, taking up the entire corner. She was veiled in shadows, with glowing purple eyes and runes. Flexing her silver claws, she grinned mercilessly.

"You again," Aurienne snarled. "You did this."

The entity grinned. "It won't be long now before your power is mine," she crooned. "It's fate. Every choice, every deal, every cross-road leading you to *me*. You were never meant to win the Darkling War."

Aurienne gasped. It made sense now. The emperor's goddess was behind the visions sent to Aurienne, behind the interference with Aurienne's magic. The emperor was just the front. Their real enemy was this malicious, lunar goddess.

"I know your name, and you are not welcome in this holy place of the Triple Goddess," Aurienne rasped.

The other goddess smiled. "Oh?"

"Niamh," Aurienne choked. "You have no power here."

The goddess hissed at her name and vanished into amethyst smoke.

"Soon." Niamh's voice faded.

The walls oozed torrents of sticky, black blood. It splashed every-thing in Aurienne's quarters, filling quickly to reach her knees in just moments.

Skeletal corpses punched through the floor, reaching for her ankles. They pulled at her skirts and legs, tearing her skin and drag-ging her down.

"No!"

She scrambled away, fighting to wade through the rising blood. She tripped and fell face-first into the blood, coming up to find her feet no longer touched the floor. Her quarters faded away and she was lost in a dark, oily ocean of blood. Mooncursed beasts, Shadows, and ancient beasts circled the waters.

The sky caught fire, and the flames licked at her face. Her skin blistered under the heat as her body stilled in the freezing waters. Scales brushed against her ankles as thorny, golden threads of fate wrapped around her neck like a noose, dragging her up.

"Soon." Far away, Niamh cackled.

Aurienne covered her head with her arms as she started to scream.

"Aurienne! What's wrong?" Theo's voice cut through the nightmare.

She opened her eyes, finding herself on the floor in her empty room surrounded by broken furniture, with Theo gently shaking her.

Wildly, she glanced around, searching for the haunting images. The blood was gone. The bodies. The ocean. The assassins. Niamh. She looked down, expecting the injuries that left lingering physical traces on her body, but found none.

Her breath came fast as she blurted out, "You didn't see..."

"See what?"

She swallowed.

"I don't see anything." His voice was gentle, and he rubbed his hands down her shaking arms.

It was so real. She'd been right there again.

Theo wrapped his arms around her, and she leaned against him, taking in his warmth. The Obermeister's words echoed in her ear. *He murdered me.* She wondered if it was another lie or whether Theo had done what the specter had claimed. She pushed the thought away, nuzzling closer against Theo's neck.

The oily sensation. She should have recognized it. It always accompanied the dark spirit who'd been visiting her. In the Way. In the visions. In the aqueduct room. Her stomach churned.

"I was sent a vision. I was back in the aqueduct access rooms, with the assassins. I saw impossible things. Nightmares." She looked up at him. "I know who sent me this vision and the vision in the Way."

Saryll pushed open the door, holding a steaming tea pot. Aurienne desperately reached for it, and Saryll, seeing her expression, hurried forward. Aurienne grasped the tea pot in both hands and poured the hot, but thankfully not boiling, contents down her throat and finished the pot.

"What happened?" Saryll demanded.

"The emperor's goddess Niamh sent me a warning. She's growing powerful. She's trying to corrupt my visions before we can defeat Demorra. We can't wait for Rianne's decision. We have to protect the Pillar, all the Pillars. There's not much time."

Aurienne shuddered. The oily quality to the vision remained on her skin, but she wouldn't fall victim to it again.

Theo held her tighter. "We should hear back any day from the spies at the other Pillars and will assemble a small force to leave for the Flame Pillar in the morning. Nesryn's ward designs should be done."

"You need to go," Aurienne said. "It's your destiny, it always was."

He grimaced but nodded. "I will go, then."

"Saryll, could you fetch several more pots of lavendiir palm tea. I'm going to need it," Aurienne wheezed.

"But without your visions, we won't know..." Saryll's response trailed off.

Aurienne noticed the dripping sensation from her ears and nose and reached up to find both crimson blood and golden soulblood. Saryll's gaze darted from the blood to Aurienne's eyes.

Theo glanced down and inhaled sharply. "Aurienne, what's wrong?"

She quickly wiped the blood away. "I'm fine. The tea will make it all better."

If she couldn't have visions, she couldn't be haunted by what she saw.

WARDS
CHAPTER THIRTY-ONE

The magic of the elves was never meant to be shared.

— SUNDRYL OAKHAND.

1152 N.T.C. The namesake capital city of Avyllon.

Nesryn's summons were a welcome surprise, and the leaf and whorl decorated letter slipped from Aurienne's hand on her way to the war room. Four words changed everything.

The wards are ready.

Aurienne's beaded ceremonial gown ticked against the floor, and her many bracelets and rope necklaces clinked with every step. Nervously, she twirled her hip-length hair in her fingers before shaking it away. She couldn't let the elf see how unnerved, how disoriented she'd become.

Theo's sure footsteps were just behind hers, boots softly thudding against the immaculate palace tiles.

Nesryn was waiting with her feet up on the war table when Aurienne and Theo arrived. She was leaned back in one of the tree-carved oak high-back chairs with her arms behind her head. Her feet hit the floor as she leaned forward with amused lightning in her stormy eyes.

The elf's mottled-gray hands pushed five scrolls toward Aurienne. "A ward for each Pillar, and another set of wards for the other cities to match Avyllon's."

The knot in Aurienne's chest loosened. "Thank you."

"The fourth pillar was hidden when the mountains moved. It will not be easy to find," Nesryn said.

Aurienne nodded. "Adonis is searching for it as we speak. He believes he will be able to narrow down potential locations."

"Not without traveling there," the elf observed. "In any case, we should start with the Pillar closest to Demorra. From the location of the Mooncursed scouts, we need to ward the Flame Pillar first. I planned to travel with you to ensure the wards were done correctly, but I notice the Warbringer has returned with *her*."

Theo stepped forward. "We have a small force scouting the area around the Pillar, and now that the wards are done, we can leave immediately to complete this."

Nesryn tilted her head. "Are you informing the Warbringer?"

Theo looked to Aurienne, who grit her teeth. She removed her cards from a spelled bag at her hip and shuffled.

Breathing on them, she asked her question. "Can we trust Rianne and Rhydian with the knowledge of the Flame Pillar?"

She drew cards.

The Vines.

The Falcon.

The Stars.

Nesryn scoffed. "It seems your cards believe we can. I wouldn't have been so optimistic. The queen is not to be trusted, and the Warbringer is blinded to the truth. However, if your cards tell us we need them, then I will allow it."

Aurienne squinted at her cards.

"Are you sure?" she whispered.

They did not change.

"You do not trust the Returned Queen either?" Nesryn's too-wide eyes narrowed.

"I do not." Aurienne's tongue burned with memory of the blood-oath.

"Do you trust your cards, then?"

Aurienne sighed. "Yes. They're never wrong."

"Be careful with them. They're becoming a powerful artifact," Nesryn warned.

Theo stepped forward. "I'll send a coded message to Rodarri immediately."

Nesryn tapped a location on the map with her short gray claws. "We'll meet him here."

"That's where the Flame Pillar is?" Aurienne asked.

"Near-abouts." The elf shrugged. "The land has changed in the thousand years since its creation. We'll find it, but we mustn't draw too much attention to ourselves."

"I'll send these scrolls to Wyndsel and give them to the Titan Cliff dwellers before they leave for the Water and Earth Pillars." Theo paused. "Are you sure we can trust Wyndsel to hold up their end of the bargain? Donovan isn't immune from the lure of Demorran gold."

Aurienne shuffled again.

The Siren.

The Hammer.

The Knot.

"For now," she replied. "They'll do their duty for the wards because it benefits them. Beyond that, I would not count on their support."

Nesryn adjusted the laces of her leather hunting vest and the line of daggers across her chest. The movement allowed white starlight to seep out from the scabbard on her back.

"I don't know the extent of Emperor Rexil's understanding of elven magic," she said. "He shouldn't be able to break these new wards, but it is possible in time. Once we've protected the Pillars, you should think about your next steps. You can't remain on the defensive forever with what's coming."

The words weighed on Aurienne. "I have seen no futures beyond this. I will continue to beseech the Triple Goddess and Fates for guidance."

Nesryn left the scrolls on the table and strolled out of the war room, calling, "You may have to find answers yourselves."

Aurienne met gazes with Theo, eyes lingering upon his face.

"I'll prepare to leave at once," he said.

DEADLY PROPOSAL
CHAPTER THIRTY-TWO

Gold-flecked rings and diamond stones,
Onyx shackles and rattling bones.

— HIGH SEER AURIENNE AZARRAH, PROPHETIC
VISION.

1152 N.T.C. Castle Rodarr, Rodarri.

Glossy banners and bright ribbons fell from the castle ramparts and walls. Balanced precariously on high ladders, castle workers cut them all free. Metal-tipped spires were now unadorned as discarded flags fluttered to the mud below. All that remained were the stark gray walls and stained-glass windows. Black bloodrose vines with spindly thorns and brilliant crimson roses strangled the castle from every direction.

The strangely chilly wind that settled upon Rodarri whipped Rianne's silver hair and the scarlet skirts of her gown. The cold may not affect her now, but it was all too similar to that hell world Aurienne dragged her to. She shuddered. How close had she and the queens come to being ripped apart? Her fingers traced the bone corset hidden under a layer of lace as she watched the workers return the castle to its proper state. No longer gilded in splashes of color that attempted to conceal the sins of the past, the castle was as it should be.

She followed the ramparts, Rhydian trailing her.

Rianne said, *"I'm not sure inviting the emperor here is a good idea."*

Milah was dispassionate as ever. *"We would be fools not to consider every option. If the alliance with the emperor is a farce, we must learn it from him not a seer's visions that can't be trusted."*

Rianne argued back. *"The entire continent is allied together. If we go to war with them, we'll be caught right in the middle."*

First Queensblood Vittoria's voice swirled around her throat, *"The High Seer's power in Avyllon is tenuous, as is King Theo's hold on the crown. The alliances with the Seven Forests and Titan Cliffs are shaky at best, and Wyndsel is looking for an excuse to realign with the emperor."*

Rianne said, *"I trust the High Seer's visions. She's never been wrong, and you saw how powerful she is."*

Rosalindt felt cold swimming in Rianne's blood, the queen never staying in one place for long. *"All the more reason to explore all our options."*

Rianne appealed to the fears of the three returned queens who'd crossed the elf and met the consequences. *"I don't think it's a good idea to be on the wrong side of Grimfall."*

Samantah hissed. *"She can be trusted least of all. It's why we must send her and the Warbringer away. They both threaten our potential alliance."*

Rianne sighed. *"I don't like keeping secrets from Rhydian."*

Whillow said. *"Secrets are necessary."*

"I don't want to leave you," Rhydian said, unaware of the conversation rattling around Rianne's head. "Are you sure I must go?"

"I don't want you to leave," she replied.

I really don't.

Milah tried to comfort her, sliding up against her shoulder. *"It's for the best."*

Rianne swallowed a sigh. "But I need you to protect the Pillar. It's rumored to be outside our borders, and if something goes wrong, we'll be right in the middle of the war."

Rhydian gripped his sword. "Why haven't you formally joined the alliance? What aren't you telling me?"

She looked away. "I'm exploring our options."

"What options?" He looked taken aback.

"If there's another way to protect our people, I'm going to find it before I commit us to a war that could decimate us. The prophecy says we can't win, but perhaps winning looks different than we expect. Maybe it's just about surviving." Rianne tasted Whillow's words along with her own. "Until then, you need to ensure we are safe."

"There's only so much fighting I can do," he said.

Rhydian studied her closely, a habit he'd picked up since her return. Questions lingered in his eyes. Suspicion. Like he was trying to solve a puzzle where he was missing half the pieces—and he was.

She took his hands. "Don't trigger your curse. There is plenty you can offer to the men from the sidelines. You're my general. Your strategy may prove more necessary than your blade."

He nodded.

"I assume the elf will be going with you." The bite of her tone came from Rebekkah—who'd never forgiven the grudge she held for Nesryn murdering her returning.

He worked his jaw as his shoulders tensed. "I assume so."

Samantah's disdain tasted sour. *"Good."*

"Starlight devours, blade's edge hungers," Callysta cackled.

"Be careful of the elf," Rianne said aloud. "She's a powerful asset but is unpredictable."

"I'm the one she's been stalking for weeks." He shuddered. "I feel her eyes on me even now."

Rianne glanced around, Whillow using her eyes to search for their foe. Balling her fists, she managed to push the spirit back down.

Queen Samantah crawled down her spine. *"The elf could be anywhere."*

Callysta hissed. *"Demon. Wraith. Monster."*

"Shush."

"What?" Rhydian asked.

Rianne blinked. She'd said it out loud. "Nothing. Sorry. The voices. The queens don't like Grimfall. She riles them up."

He shifted his weight. "I can't blame them."

A whisper of a smile tugged at Rianne's lips, one of the few since her return. "Inform me of news. And Rhydian—please be safe."

He lightly touched her chin, eyes darting to her lips briefly, before he straightened and backed away. "I will."

In another life, he would've kissed her. But they both must have sensed how much had changed.

He bowed and descended the ramparts. She noticed the flash of a gray cloak on a high tower following him.

Samantah's discerning eye caught it. *"There she is."*

"She will go with him," Milah observed.

Vittoria's focus never strayed from strategy. *"Good, the emperor arrives tomorrow. We need her far, far away."*

Rianne thought, *"I hope you all know what you're doing."*

They all replied, *"We do."*

Frigid spectral tendrils slipped between her bones and marrow from that dark pool she did her best to avoid, and she shuddered.

Rianne waited in the throne room with her hands clasped. Her hair was braided upon her head, with only a few delicate locks escaping. The gown was dark red and black, with a matching choker to hide her never-healed wound. She'd been waiting for hours, but her body never tired. Or... if it did, she no longer took notice. When the emperor arrived, she'd be here to receive him as if she knew the exact moment of his arrival. If he arrived. Uncertainty crept into her mind. The queens attacked it, washing it away in a torrent of anger.

Vittoria said, *"He will come. He won't be able to refuse the chance at sundering Avyllon's alliance."*

Rianne worried at her sleeve. *"He may suspect a trap."*

"He'd be a fool not to suspect a trap," Vittoria replied. *"He will bring adequate forces. And his priestesses or sorcerers will have attempted to scry the future."*

Rianne paced. *"How will I convince him to believe us?"*

"Leave that to us, darling," her mother's voice was a balm on her nerves. *"These are games we long perfected."*

Rianne swallowed, fighting the urge to fidget. She froze, feeling the frigid fingers of an unnamed queen trace the back of her neck. She pushed the queens down again, shaking her head.

"You're fighting us," Whillow said. *"Let us help you with this. This is not your burden to bear alone."*

Rianne exhaled and let go. The queens grew louder until Rianne was hardly more than an onlooker. While she watched, she kept her own thoughts locked tightly away as she began to formulate a plan. Queens were meant to have their secrets after all.

A Way opened in the throne room, splitting the air with cracks and snaps of light. Several priestesses, and an entire host of soldiers wearing purple velvet cloaks and gold armor stepped through. His entourage posted themselves around the room, filling the space. The emperor stepped out, slightly pale and closely flanked by two imperial soldiers. The Way closed behind them with a loud pop. He stepped through, and she noticed a bead of sweat roll down his hairline.

Milah said, *"Creating a Way fatigues him. Remember that."*

The emperor didn't move for long moments. His gaze remained locked upon her, not even scanning the room for assassins.

Rianne could feel Samantah rolling her eyes. *"He isn't even looking for evil elves."*

"Does he not suspect us of treachery?" Morgana asked. *"Or does he believe we're too naïve for such attempts."*

"Perhaps he has spies here. He had spies in Avyllon," Rosalindt said.

"Or it's simply worth the risk," Vittoria mused. *"Maybe there's something to those prophecies and visions the seer saw."*

The tendrils of Callysta's soul floated through Rianne's blood. *"The future is the past is the future and back again. None of it is real."*

The emperor's hands were clasped in front of him, mirroring her pose. He approached with intentional clacks of his boots that echoed against the barren stone walls. Three paces from her, he stopped. A bandage peeked out from beneath his robes.

"You kept your word," he said. "No sign of the Grimfall."

Elisabel placed a demure smile upon Rianne's face before answering. "I am serious about a possible alliance."

"As am I." He stepped closer.

This close not a single queen could ignore the thick muscles on his chest, the curve of his smirk, or the devious glint in his eye.

"This is going to be fun," Rosalindt clapped her spectral hands.

"If you'd told me of your plans to attack, I could have been absent." Vittoria spoke through Rianne.

"You might've warned Avyllon," he said.

She tilted her chin. "I didn't. And I didn't partake in the conflict."

"Why were you there?"

"Old debts to settle," she said. "Vengeance."

His gaze was sharp as a blade. "And were you successful?"

Rianne blew out a sharp annoyed breath. "Not fully. The High Seer got in my way." It was Rianne, but also Samantah that shared the same sentiment.

He chuckled but stopped with a wince, holding his ribs. Whillow's gaze snapped to him, looking for the source of the weakness.

"She does that." Anger laced his tight tone.

Rianne feigned concern. "Were you injured in the battle?"

"Nothing major."

Rosalindt's voice was sharp. *"A lie."*

"That elf was there," he said. "Trust me, my wards will be remade to account for errors made. We'll have surprises in store for her."

Rianne's mind raced, trying to pick apart the layers of his response.

Samantah pushed through the sea of spirits and spoke through Rianne with a hiss. "Our hatred for the elf runs deeper than you know."

He tilted his head. "Our?"

Milah offered her cool analysis. *"He's perceptive. Searching for every weakness. He can't know our secrets."*

Other voices spoke over the top of one another so loudly, she struggled to discern their origin.

"We should ignore his comment. Distract him," Isybel said.

Rianne's mother argued, *"No, we should make a polite excuse."*

"Purple blood sprays on knots of bone." Callysta's mad voice drowned the others out.

Rianne pushed through the voices to put on her best and sweetest smile. "My family. You'll meet the other Queensblood at the banquet tomorrow. My aunts, cousins, and sister. Unless you need rest from your journey and injuries."

"I need no rest." His meanings layered. "You'll find it takes much more than that to exhaust my stamina."

Whillow said aloud, "I don't tire either."

His smirk grew to a grin, making several queens' hearts flutter.

Rianne snarled to the others, *"Absolutely not."*

Outwardly, she said to the emperor, "Can we expect more favorable terms than previously offered? Our alliance is more valuable now."

He leaned forward to whisper in her ear. "I'll see what we can do."

Rianne swallowed. "Thank you. Please accept our hospitality and we will summon you for the banquet later to discuss terms."

"Looking forward to it."

The emperor followed the attendant out of the hall, half his entourage surrounding him and the other half disappearing into the wings of the castle.

Rianne rose through the spirits, taking back control and pushing them down. *"I don't like any of this. We've invited a wolf into our home, and he won't hesitate to devour us."*

Bloodwitch Noxanya replied, *"He doesn't know our teeth are bigger and our appetite deeper."*

Rianne thought, *"I wouldn't underestimate him. He conquered all twenty-seven tribes and nations of Demorra for a reason."*

Vittoria's voice quieted the dispute, *"We've been planning for centuries. Don't fret, darling. We have this under control. He will bend to our will."*

Rianne had seen too much and lived through too much to believe them. Better than most she saw the lengths those in power would go to keep their power. She saw the dangerous and violent glint in his eye.

Rianne said, *"Don't be so sure."*

Harps and violins filled the gray-washed banquet hall with soft melodies as the eleventh course was set before Rianne and the emperor. The soft glow from the Vittoria's Gift lighting fixtures pulsed behind the fogged glass with a steady beat. The tension in the room couldn't have been cut with a dinner knife—it would've taken a sword.

Rianne toyed with the sponge of the seven-layer trifle as she and the queens watched everything. Sensing the emperor's eyes on her, she speared a thin slice of peach dipped in whipped sweat cream and slipped it between her lips. She forced herself to chew and swallow. Food rarely had any taste since her return, and when it did it tasted of ash.

"I've heard rumors since arriving," the emperor said. "Of the ascensions. Of *your* ascension."

She squeezed her fork to keep her hands from going to her throat. "Ah, yes."

Whillow said, *"The best lies are founded in truth. If he hears what he wants to hear, he will believe it."*

He leaned forward. "They say your head was cut off and yet here you are."

Rebekkah forced Rianne to laugh softly. "The rumors have already taken lives of their own. The executioner did cut me but missed the killing blow. I was thrown into the ravine but landed on a ledge not far down. I was able to crawl out."

The emperor's eyes narrowed as he studied her. "No magical intervention then?"

"I won't say I don't encourage such talks to keep the coups at bay," Whillow tugged Rianne's lips into a devious smile. "I hear the whispers of discontent by the displaced, but who wants to attempt such when their queen is unkillable."

The emperor released an amused breath. "Reputation and fear are powerful deterrents." His gaze unfocused. "They keep you from taking more drastic actions."

Vittoria said, *"You've almost convinced him."*

Rianne tugged down the lace choker revealing just a hint of her jagged, unhealed wound on the side of her neck, keeping hidden the worst of it. "I should've died but for the commotion that caused the ax to slip." She returned the choker into place. "I should be dead if not for that."

"I'm glad you're not," he said keenly. "You're the only one on this godsdamned continent who seems to see reason."

Whillow pressed, *"Probe him on this. Find his motivations so we can use them."*

"I do see reason," she said. "I am not governed by fear or uncertain prophecies, instead making each decision on cold fact. Tell me, what is your vision for all of this? You've conquered all the warring tribes and nations of Demorra—you must have a vision."

"I do." His eyes darkened. "An end to the pointless fighting. Various tribes have been at war for centuries. Lives are lost and borders shift barely a few paces. The soil is ripe with blood. As a child, I quickly learned the harshness of such an existence and the loss of kin."

Rianne tilted her head, utterly confused. This sounded nothing like the evil emperor of destruction Aurienne foretold.

Samantah said, *"This is why the seer's prophecies and visions cannot be trusted."*

Milah's dispassionate tone pushed through. *"Listen carefully to what he does not say."*

He continued, "I traveled across the continent to the mountains of Nyx'ela, the realm of the gods, and was favored by Niamh. She gave me the power to cease the in-fighting. With her blessing, I can achieve true peace. Order. There are enough resources in the empire that no one should starve, if managed correctly."

"Some personal freedom is a small cost for greater prosperity, is it not?" Vittoria filled Rianne's mouth with the words.

The emperor nodded. "With the magic of Teridar, I could expand Niamh's presence and end all the suffering across all lands. The power I could unlock... And all I asked was coin to build infrastructure, troops to enforce the laws, and magic users to expand our knowledge. Yet I was met with rigid defiance and pointless resistance. I conquered a much larger continent with fewer soldiers. Teridar cannot stand before the might of my empire."

Rianne tapped her finger on the edge of her champagne flute. "What's the cost of Niamh's blessing?"

The emperor shifted in his chair. "She requires offerings of supplication. And sometimes, offerings of blood—but only from the faithful. The High Seer lied about that. I do not send the unwilling to their deaths."

Rianne studied her stained-glass goblet, finding herself believing him. Or at least, believing that he believed his words. Growing up as a Queensblood, she'd been an avid pupil in deception and found none here. If anything, he was lying to himself.

"Maybe he doesn't lie. But someone does," Rosalindt said.

"Or the seer is lying," Samantah said.

Rosalindt was in Rianne's hand now. *"Unlikely. She has no cause to."*

Whillow replied, *"The seer used necromancy; threatened to use it on us. Who knows what she's capable of, even lying to achieve her own ends or rise."*

Rianne found herself saying to the emperor, "I believe you."

And she did, but something was off about him. Something about his small mannerisms didn't fit right. The glances off into the distance. The darkness in the corners of his eyes. His staunch devotion. It told a story she hadn't yet put together. And the vague way that he spoke of his goddess was disconcerting. It reminded her entirely too much of how she lied to him about her ascension. There was far more to Niamh than he let on, which might explain the strange hue bloodwitch Noxanya saw in his soul-energies.

He met and held her gaze. "Then do we have an alliance?"

The queens all spoke at once, whispering or shouting over one another but Rianne silenced them with a wave of will.

She spoke for herself, "I can send offerings of resources and gold, but I am not keen to send all my forces to a foreign land, leaving myself unprotected. While I believe your intentions, I will not be unwise with my trust."

He tiled his chin thoughtfully.

Whillow slipped past Rianne and said, "Trust must be earned."

Rianne's stomach flipped as she immediately knew what the queens were suggesting. Her throat tightened, but she didn't resist. She'd said to Rhydian she had to do terrible things for her people, and this might be one of them. It fit into her secret plans, even if she loathed it.

A suggestive grin parted his lips. "I see. And how could we ever truly trust each other?"

Rianne allowed Whillow to smile, sweet and seductively. "I have some ideas."

He took her hands in his and set his gaze upon hers. "Then I believe I have a proposal."

Shivers of discontented anticipation rolled down her spine, and Rianne's cheeks heated. She faded behind the queens, allowing them to take control in this less enjoyable part of their schemes.

"Marry me and we'll achieve prosperity for everyone," he offered. "We'll rule the two continents together."

Beneath all the spirits, the part of Rianne that remained her closed her eyes. Outwardly, she smiled demurely.

"I accept your proposal," she said.

He leaned forward and brushed his lips against her earlobe. "I look forward to this partnership."

"As do I," Vittoria said, cunning dripping from her words.

"I have *matters* with our friends from Avyllon to attend to in the next days, but when I return, we shall wed," he said.

While Vittoria and Whillow might believe they had him under control and Elisabel believed his declarations, Rianne still had her doubts. While some of the others didn't believe Aurienne's visions, Rianne did. She'd seen too much not to, and something about it all unsettled her.

The queens all schemed, but Rianne made her own plans.

THE FLAME PILLAR
CHAPTER THIRTY-THREE

Four pillars hold the crown of the world.
The fifth holds back the Shadows of old.

— *JOURNAL OF THE SEER NARAINA CARYDALIS,*
25 N.T.C.

1152 N.T.C. The Flame Pillar, outside the Hunger's Teeth Mountains.

Splashing through another of the thousands of small streams in the Heartspring Valley, Rhydian pushed through another dense wall of trees to yet another clearing. The landscape was the same for a hundred miles in any direction, a cool, coastal forest with a lush mixture of broad leaf and evergreen trees that thinned to large meadows. The valley was so densely packed they'd foregone horses. The cool air and frigid runoff from the Hunger's Teeth Mountains caused Rhydian to bury his hands into the fur lining of his pockets.

Somewhere in the midst of all this, the Flame Pillar was said to be waiting—and Nesryn seemed confident that they'd be able to ward it as they had the city walls upon her arrival.

A dour expression darkened his brow at the thought of the elf—one he could feel as it sharply etched into his features, and he stomped toward the dense woods before pushing into the clearing. Three dozen sorcerers and a full unit of sentinels followed through the gaping clearings he left in his wake. Thankfully, Theo tried to scout ahead for him, tracing Nesryn's steps as best he could to make the group's trek easier. He paused to survey their surroundings with Theo coming to stand beside him.

The elf leapt past him, easily clearing a stream before darting between two saplings into the clearing.

"I thought you said you knew where the Pillar was?" Rhydian found himself snapping toward her.

"The forest has changed somewhat, but it is close," she replied.

"If it's a monument, shouldn't we be able to see it?" Theo asked. "It should be obvious right? A massive Pillar in the middle of nowhere?"

Nesryn grinned and forged ahead, disappearing from view.

"I wasn't expecting an answer anyways," Theo mumbled.

Rhydian closed his eyes, forcing air slowly in and out of his lungs. They'd been searching the forest for a week, and all they had to show for it were blisters and ill tempers. It was far too much time to silently stew over his concerns about Rianne, and it'd put him into a dark mood. Nesryn's antics might very well be the final straw that pushed his patience over the edge. Finally opening his eyes, he adjusted the ax and sword on his back and continued.

Crunching through the dead grass in the meadow, he paused to look for the elf, who'd disappeared again. He couldn't even hear the rustling of branches or the crunch of dried leaves under her boots. How did she do it? Shaking his head, he followed the faint outlines of her boots, picking his way over fallen logs and dense grass clumps. The boot outlines suddenly stopped, and he glanced around for any sign of where she'd gone but found none.

Driving forward, he cut across the meadow toward the next partition of trees. The sorcerers and sentinels followed his every step, creating a long, snaking path through the growing shadows.

Rhydian glanced up. The auburn afternoon sun peeking through the canopy warned that they'd have to stop and make camp in about an hour. The next potential camping site would have to do.

His boot sank into a frigid, snaking stream he hadn't noticed, and he bit back a curse. Shaking off the water, he pointed it out to Theo and continued ahead.

The red and black fox popped out of a cluster of saplings, prancing through the meadow with golden, glowing eyes. Ahead, Theo reached into his pack to produce several dried strips of fish they'd caught a few nights ago. He tossed them to the fox, eliciting a contented rumble from its throat. The bushy red tail flicked back and forth as it hopped from stump to rock. It turned its intense and expectant stare upon Rhydian.

After seeing it brandish immensely powerful magic at the summit battle a month ago, everyone had been too wary to pet or scratch it—as they were all unsure whether it was disrespectful to an entity with that level of magic—but they'd supplied the creature with an unending supply of treats whenever it showed up. It really was the least they could do.

Rhydian reached into his own pack and tossed the creature the largest fish from within, along with a handful of juicy berries. "Here, friend."

"Do you know where the Pillar is?" Theo asked it.

The fox bared its fangs, in what might've been a grin, much like Nesryn did at times.

Theo leaned forward. "Are you going to tell me?" The fox darted away, and Theo sighed. "Of course not."

Rhydian nearly laughed. That fox kept its secrets well hidden. It was one of the first moments since Rianne's ascension that had warranted any mirth.

The thought of Rianne stripped away any happiness. She was

keeping something from him; he could feel it. And—judging from the subtle changes in personality—the queens were far more present than she let on. He shoved the doubts away. The last thing Rianne needed was one more person questioning her. She'd be fine.

Rhydian stopped at the unending wall of branches before him, reminding him somewhat of the living walls of the Seven Forests city. Theo trudged up behind him as Rhydian unhooked his ax from his pack.

"We'll have to cut through." Rhydian said as set his pack on a dry, flat rock and shed his cloak.

The rest of the party took their seats. The sorcerers panted underneath their heavily laden bags beside grim-faced sentinels casting alert gazes on every shadow. By now, no one was a stranger to the dangers that lurked these lands. Theo pulled off his jacket and rolled up his sleeves before freeing his own work ax.

Rhydian's boots dribbled water as he took a stance to begin chopping their way through the woody foliage. Bark and branches flew quickly as the pumping blood in his veins felt amazing. Swinging metal was one of the best sensations in the world. The only thing that would be better was blood dripping of the blade. Gritting his teeth, he pushed the violent urges away.

It took most of the remaining hour of sunlight to hack a path to the next field, but he didn't mind as the effort kept his thoughts occupied. Sentinels took turns clearing wood and setting their backs to the ax until the sun dipped below the horizon and the skies darkened. By the time they broke free, they were covered in sweat and sap.

Rhydian stepped into the dusky meadow, sensing a presence nearby as his Warbringer senses gave warning. He felt sluggish and slow with every stride, his brain pounding. His feet wanted to take him a different path, an easier path. He nearly relented, but his determination to find the Pillar urged him on.

The air popped, and Rhydian stumbled forward, all at once free of the unseen resistance. His chin lifted upward, now seeing the once-invisible monument.

The Flame Pillar towered over the treetops, an unmistakable presence. The square stone building was about five paces by five paces with an immense bowl at the top holding a brightly burning flame that shed light upon the entire valley. The warmth from the flame licked Rhydian's face even from this distance.

How did I miss it before?

Nesryn appeared next to him. "The builders warded it from view to protect it. It's why the emperor couldn't find it. You have to nearly be upon it."

The fox prowled by Rhydian's feet, settling itself into the tall grasses. Rhydian glanced back toward the party, still struggling against the protective barriers and wandering in circles.

"This way," Rhydian called.

Protests and grunts followed. Theo pushed through next, followed by half the sentinels, the sorcerers, and the rest of the sentinels bringing up the rear. Awe colored every face as the Pillar's flames came into view.

With a crack of thunderous wings, Stellan and a host of vampires appeared between Rhydian, Theo and Nesryn.

The vampire tilted his head toward the Pillar, a predator assessing a threat. "You found it."

"Let's set up camp," a sentinel announced, shepherding the sorcerers away from the vampires' hungry gazes.

Stellan's eyes tracked the humans, though his face never moved. Turning his gaze back to Theo, he said, "We'll ensure the Moon-cursed scouts do not venture close enough to discover it."

Rhydian stepped forward, a warning in his tense movements to the vampires about what would happen if they harmed Theo.

"Thank you," Theo replied to Stellan. "We'll work on solidifying the wards."

Stellan slid forward, within a pace of Theo, and inhaled deeply. The vampire's black eyes glittered with an unreadable expression. "I see."

Rhydian took another step forward, hand sliding down to his ax. If the vampire took one step closer...

"You meant it when you said you'd bear the burden and give up your soul to save the continent," Stellan hissed. "You're already well on your way."

Rhydian blinked, unsure of what the vampire meant. The air cracked and Theo stumbled back as Stellan took to the skies with several beats of his leathery wings. Rhydian took his place by Theo, offering his presence as support.

The dark shapes disappeared into the clouds, and Rhydian clenched his fists. The vampire's words echoed in his mind, wondering if Theo was alright or if there was more than he let on. Rhydian studied Theo's distant expression, searching for answers. The fox barked at Theo, drawing his attention back.

"What was that about?" Rhydian asked.

Theo shrugged, before laying out his bedroll and climbing inside. The blacksmith's dark stare at the crackling fire told Rhydian that he knew exactly what the vampire meant.

Rhydian stretched out on his own bedroll and tucked his hands behind his head. Searching the night sky for answers, his thoughts drifted back to Rianne. She should be keeping him close. There was still so much to do in reorganizing the army, training, preparation, and yet she sent him here.

It made sense that she would want to keep the Pillar protected, and possibly that she wanted information on the movements of Avyllon. He clicked his teeth. That wasn't it. No, it was something else. The answer was staring at him, but he couldn't see it.

The night's watch changed before Rhydian fell into a restless sleep.

Theo settled into his bedroll, knowing all too well the sins staining his soul. Stellan had been right. The weight of his actions wore Theo down. Ghastly faces, mournful howls, and piercing screams haunted every one of his dark dreams. And more than that—fear of what he might have to do next.

He shifted in his bedroll, looking up at the winking stars. A flash of spurting blood flooded his mind. He rolled over, staring at the campfire instead. A Mooncursed dragged away its victim into the trees. Squeezing his eyes shut, he focused his thoughts on his Ma's garden—the breezy wildflowers and fresh vegetables. The Eyrand arena doors slammed shut before the screams started. He exhaled, trying to push the images away.

He searched for more powerful memories. Aurienne laying eyes on him in the Foretelling crowd, summoning him to her chambers. Licking the blood from his palm. Smiling and laughing as they exchanged monster stories and filthy ditties. Kissing under a witch moon. Every thought of her chased away the pain. Finally, he drifted into an uneasy slumber.

As dawn broke, the camp was a flurry of activity.

Nesryn handed Dean Chellaes a crisp parchment with ancient symbols scrawled in red ink. "Copy these wards exactly. A single mistake could be disastrous."

Wide-eyed, Dean Chellaes cradled the scroll, bowing low, and smoothing it over a flat stump.

"You think this will really protect it?" the dean asked.

"With these wards, the emperor won't be able to create a Way atop the Pillar," Nesryn replied. "Even if he creates one nearby, if the wards are up, he won't be able to find and destroy it."

Rhydian breathed a sigh of relief. They were so close.

"Why weren't they warded before?" Theo asked.

Her expression grew distant. "They were hidden and protected by armies until the Shadows were fully defeated and banished. They... should have been protected better, but at the time they didn't know. Now we know that the threat has returned and must be fully warded."

Rhydian asked, "How do you know so much about the Ways? The magic?"

"Who do you think created it?" Nesryn smiled at him, baring her fangs.

She'd said her people created them, but her grin told him she knew more than she let on.

Her severe smile faded. "The emperor should not have the knowledge of how to create them at will as he does. That knowledge should have been lost."

Rhydian's ears rang at this knowledge. "Can you create Ways at will like him?"

"How do you think I get around so easily?" She tossed her hip-length silver hair.

He sucked in a breath. It made sense why her tracks were hard to follow. How she appeared and disappeared at will. He thought he'd been going crazy, that his curse had been taking deeper hold of him than he realized. It had been her magic all along.

"Of course, I can," she said. "And not those messy, noisy, adolescent Ways the emperor creates. There are limits of course, but yes."

Beside Rhydian, Theo's jaw dropped as he sputtered.

She narrowed her eyes on Rhydian, her easy expression turning dark. "Remember there's no escaping me."

His blood spiked and the edges of his vision blurred red as his anger rose to meet her challenge. It took all his control to bite down on his urges to attack.

The elf sauntered away, whistling and inspecting the careful red paint strokes and chisel marks of the sorcerers.

Beside him, Theo shuddered even though he was not the target of her icy glare. "It all comes back to the Shadow War, doesn't it? There are so many ancient secrets."

Rhydian's lip curled toward Nesryn. "It seems like she knows most of them."

Maybe she had relatives that were there when it all began? Perhaps the stories carried through only a few generations.

Rhydian's blood ran cold.

Or was she there?

He pushed the thought away.

Impossible.

It would make her well over a thousand years old.

Danger prickled his senses, and he looked around. Something was still nagging him, about Rianne and the Pillar. The emperor. It wasn't adding up. His curse gifted him with mastery of strategy, and he knew something was wrong. He paced as the sorcerers continued their work.

Finally, he said to Theo, "I need to get back to Rianne. She won't tell me, but I sense something is wrong. I need to be there."

Theo clapped him on the back. "Go now if you need. We can handle this."

"She ordered me to secure the Pillar," Rhydian replied. "I'll return to her as soon as it's done. It's probably nothing. She's just adjusting to being back."

"Once we get this one warded, you return home," Theo said. "I'll go ward the others."

Rhydian watched the meticulous work of the sorcerers, warding the walls of the Pillar as the noon sun rose. Another few hours and they'd be done. He closed his eyes and took in the warm sun. Did the Fates smile upon them?

"To arms!" Nesryn appeared from nowhere, starlight exploding from her enchanted blade.

Rhydian shrugged off his cloak as Theo drew his Sword of Souls.

Extinguished

Chapter Thirty-Four

The eternal flame once extinguished might never burn again.

— Unknown.

1152 N.T.C. The Flame Pillar, outside the Hunger's Teeth Mountains.

A Way split the air near the pillar with a crackling hiss of lightning. Instead of sharp lines, the unstable edges resembled torn fabric with purple starbursts. Fifteen priestesses stepped through to form a circle around the portal. Light flared from the glowing ring branded upon their foreheads and formed an interlocking protective sphere.

Coldforges and bonedust.

Theo gripped his blade, dread draining the blood from his face. How had the emperor found them so fast?

Nesryn raced forward, meeting the first of the Mooncursed in the center of the grassy field. Her starlight sword cut through the air, downing the beasts with quick arcs.

Theo glanced toward the panicked sorcerers, looking to him with chisels and brushes hovering in mid-air. Hours had remained before they'd be done. He had to buy them as much time as he could.

"Finish the wards!" Theo ordered.

A flurry of robes and paint followed as they returned to the work. Several sorcerers opened their packs, swirling explosive liquids and mixtures. Fireballs sprung to life in their palms in a defensive circle around their companions. The Avyllonian soldiers formed protective rings around them.

Mooncursed poured out into the field. Wardens and sorcerers followed, taking up position defending the Pillar. The emperor stepped out last behind the priestess's protective sphere. His expression tightened at the sight of the Avyllonians, and he urged his forces on.

"Destroy the Pillar!" Sweat beaded on the emperor's brow as his arms shook.

Theo's head whipped as he studied the battle. Nesryn's sword made quick work of those unfortunate enough to get in her way, but there were so many. She couldn't possibly catch them all, especially while dodging fireballs.

The grass and leaves churned beneath the Mooncursed paws as they thundered toward the Pillar. Theo's hands shook as fear threatened to overtake him, but he gripped his sword and readied himself, feeling the spikes of adrenaline.

You can do this.

Flashbacks of the coronation attack threatened to empty the contents of his stomach. Blood, carnage, screaming civilians, falling buildings, smoky fires.

Focus.

He blinked as the beasts and soldiers raced toward them.

"He can't hold the Way for very long, not long enough to destroy the entire Pillar," Theo hissed to Rhydian. "If it closes with his forces outside, they'll be trapped here without reinforcements. What is he doing?"

"He understands the importance of this battle," Rhydian said. "He'll risk an army for the Pillar."

Or he is planning something else.

There was no time to think about that.

Theo stood his ground between the advancing beasts and frantic sorcerers. "We can't let him tear down the Pillar's protection. It's the only thing keeping out the Shadows."

Or... they could try to end it all right now.

"Can we kill him?" Theo glanced toward his friend.

Rhydian hefted an ax in one hand and a sword in the other. "We can try."

They charged toward the oncoming Mooncursed.

Clang.

Scrape.

Clang.

Steel met titan ore claws, and sparks flew. Theo slashed at a Mooncursed hybrid, with a human torso, elongated arms, and double sets of claws. It dodged and slammed its shoulder into his chest. He slammed into the hard ground and scrambled back to his feet, trying to keep the blade between himself and the quick creature. Theo slashed again, and it dodged again.

Rhydian lopped the foot off a Mooncursed with a man's body and a wolf's head. The Mooncursed roared, and Rhydian slashed it deeply in the chest with his sword.

"Theo?" Rhydian called.

The Warbringer had nearly downed his foe and needed Theo to dispatch it for him. Theo darted forward, but the cat-Mooncursed slid into his path. It raked at Theo's leg, scraping against the armor and slashing through the leather beneath. The cuts burned, causing Theo to stumble. He brought the sword up again, snaking toward the Mooncursed's neck. It cut through some of the thick fur on the hybrid's neck, but the cat spun and flipped away. Only a few droplets of blood wet his blade.

A charcoal-gray, prowling Mooncursed circled Theo from the other side. And the rest of the army was moments away.

"Theo!" Rhydian hacked another limb from his opponent, and dark blood rushed out as it fell to the dirt with a tremor.

The cat hissed and lunged for Theo, he dodged the same way it had been dodging him and dove for the downed beast. His sword clanged off titan ore embedded beneath the chest, and the beast hit Theo with the back of its massive paw, and he tumbled toward the mountain lion's waiting jaws.

Rhydian's eyes were turning bright red. He jumped between Theo and the lion, hammering it in the skull with the butt of his ax.

"Hurry!" Rhydian shouted.

Theo scrambled to his feet and drove his sword through the ribs of the twitching wolf-man. The Mooncursed shuddered and breathed its last.

Theo spun toward the charcoal wolf and sprang forward with a series of alternating horizontal and circular defensive maneuvers. Back-to-back with the Warbringer, he hoped he'd killed it in time.

"Switch!" Rhydian shouted.

Spinning, Theo slashed at the limping mountain lion Mooncursed, catching it under the chin.

A scream cut the air.

A sorcerer was dangling from the powerful, deformed paw of an eight-foot tall Mooncursed, thrashing and kicking. His eyes bulged Theo's direction begging for help. With a crack, the beast snapped his neck and hurled the body into the trees.

Theo ran toward the sorcerers and the Mooncursed that had slipped around them. Another beast darted into his path, snapping at his neck with its teeth. Theo slammed his spiked bracer into its maw and its sharp fangs closed on his arm. The fangs dug into his flesh. With a shout, Theo ripped his arm forward. The bracer spikes tore through the beast's mouth. It released him with a snarl, and blood dribbled down his fingers. He slammed his other bracer into its nose as he brought up his sword. The sword bit into a large artery under its arm and blood sprayed them both. It collapsed, and Theo continued to run.

Panting, his chest ached from the blows of the creatures and his fingers were growing numb. His leg burned from the lion's claws as warm blood oozed down his boot, but he couldn't help that now. He had to protect the sorcerers so they could finish warding the Pillar.

Rhydian was ahead of him, slashing through the Demorran soldiers attacking their sorcerers. Theo cut and chopped at the injured humans, delivering only targeted death blows to protect his friend's soul. Beheading was the most efficient way to ensure not a single death remained tied to the Warbringer. He lost count of how many died beneath his blade.

Heads bumped against the sorcerer's ankles, and the pale scholars braced against the Pillar walls to keep their poor hands from shaking. They were doing better than Theo, who struggled to keep up with the Warbringer. Orange fireballs and bubbling vials flew from the Avyllonian sorcerer's hands toward the incoming beasts. The small force of Avyllonian sentinels and soldiers they'd brought fought in groups of three against the Mooncursed.

A purple-skinned Mooncursed snatched a sorcerer from the Pillar, and Theo raced after it. He lifted his sword to cut across its lumpy, twisted back. It spun and smashed the back of its tree-trunk size arm across Theo's face.

He crumpled.

The darkness finally cleared, and he choked on each breath. Ears ringing, he shook his head and pushed himself to his hands and knees. His vision blurred. Screams drifted faraway, and he blinked hard.

Furred figures darted from the trees, dragging flowing robes away. The Demorrans stormed into the spiral stairwell of the Pillar. Flashes of silver and starlight were buried under a horde of dark fur. Rhydian was so far away.

Hellsdamn it.

Hazy red shapes on the ground formed a trail around the Pillar.

Theo stabbed at the nearest groaning lump, and a blurry fountain of blood sprayed. Tripping over clumps of yellow grass, he chased his friend.

"Rhydian, slow down!" Theo called as he swung his sword again and again.

The Warbringer wasn't slowing.

The sounds of hammers striking stone echoed from the top of the Pillar. Chisels scraped across the bottom of the Pillar as ink splashed the ground. Sentinels held their ground against the Demorrans. Head still pounding, Theo blinked, his vision returning slowly.

A green fireball from the Demorrans crashed into the Pillar, and Theo ducked under the falling debris.

Dean Chellaes picked up a fallen ink pot and ward after ward took shape with sharp strokes of her brush. She stepped over a choking companion, glancing at Theo with worried eyes. They weren't going to make it.

Theo looked between Rhydian's diminishing form with its trail of bodies, and the frantic sorcerers. The forces poured out of the distant Way, and he'd lost sight of Nesryn. Somewhere above their heads, Demorrans attacked the elemental bowl. He glanced upward, seeing the eternal flame flickering.

He had to stop them—but couldn't help with the wards and also save his friend.

Gritting his teeth, Theo circled the Pillar. His muscles fell into familiar defensive and offensive patterns he'd drilled with Rhydian as Demorrans swarmed him.

"Rhydian! Come back!" he shouted.

He couldn't hear or wasn't listening. Theo's heart sank. There was nothing he could do.

Six Demorrans circled him, blades raised, with a dozen more approaching. Somewhere in the depths of his skull, Theo knew there was no escape.

One night several years ago, he'd been guarding free-roaming sheep and cattle in the mountains. The flock had been attacked by a pack of starving wolves. Armed with a blacksmith hammer, a shepherd's staff, and a short knife, he'd kept them mostly at bay through the night by keeping the fires going. The wolves managed to steal one of the older sheep, but the rest Theo had saved. He remembered the terror he'd felt at the circling, prowling beasts. The yellow eyes in the dark. He remembered the feeling that he might not make it out.

Now it was something more like begrudging acceptance. The wolves only wanted a meal, but the Demorrans wanted his death.

"Bring me his head!" the emperor shouted.

The steely eyes of the men warned Theo they would die before they disobeyed or failed.

It was as good a place as any to die.

Theo gripped his darkly glowing blade. He charged the closest, blade slamming against the ax. He didn't stop. His blade carried forward to the soldier beside the first at a diagonal angle. A soldier he hadn't seen stuck a knife into his ribs. Theo faltered, grateful his leather armor kept the wound shallow, but still it seeped his energy. His body was bruised, his head pounded, blood trickled out of a litany of injuries. He raised his sword again, feeling the strength dwindling away.

An orange fireball exploded in the face of a soldier behind Theo; the sorcerers were protecting their king. The Avyllonian sentinels fought through the onslaught to reach him.

It wouldn't be enough.

Rhydian's mind thundered with bloodlust. The world was bathed in red as he repeated a mantra he hardly understood anymore.

Don't kill.
Wound.
Don't kill.
Wound.

Sword and ax threaded together in an unending pattern of blood-shed. The screaming soldiers fell behind him.

Don't kill them.

Nothing fatal.

Don't kill.

It was important. He knew that, but he'd forgotten why. They were his kills. Why shouldn't he have them?

Just one kill.

Then you'll be free.

Just a little deeper, and they'll die.

Then you'll be free.

He ignored the demanding impulses. It was important not to kill. It was the last thing he remembered before everything turned red.

A woman's face was watching him. Brown hair that was some-times white, rosy cheeks, kind blue eyes. They looked sad now. She was saying something to him, but he couldn't hear. It didn't matter. She wasn't here.

"You are not your curse," someone whispered.

But they weren't really here.

Don't kill.

Wound.

Don't kill.

Wound.

Sword and ax continued to fell foes. His impeccable control ensured that none died yet, none would die for a while. They'd lay there in agony for hours, but they wouldn't die.

Why not?

His instincts screamed at him to turn around. He spun just before a silver demon slammed into him, knocking him to the ground. The silver shape kicked him in the ribs, and he flew across the field. He launched to his feet, but knuckles struck his cheek repeatedly, and immediately his skull throbbed.

"Warbringer, snap out of it," the elf was snarling.

He opened his mouth, but the silver wraith knocked him down again.

"Do you want me following you around making sure you don't accidentally kill someone, or do you want me protecting the Pillar? What helps us the most?" she was demanding.

The red was fading from his vision. The groaning trail of bodies was silent—all deceased now by her hand. The bloodlust was waning.

"Your friend needs you. Theo is going to die." The demon-elf was shaking him so violently he could hardly think. "Rianne is going to be disappointed."

Slap.

Her hand cracked against his cheek. "Snap out of it!"

Rianne? He promised not to let her down again, right? *Theo.* His friend? Somewhere in the aching depths of his mind, he didn't want his friend to die. The memories were fleeting and slippery.

"I need to get back to the Pillar," she snarled. "I can't just wait for you to decide. Do I kill you now or can you handle your shit?"

He blinked.

"You told me you'd be strong enough," she hissed. "You promised to fight. Are you a liar, Warbringer?"

A palace room. The Grimfall elf hunting him. Angry words. Blades clashing. Promises made. It all came rushing back. His friends. Rianne. The curse. The Pillar. He remembered.

Eyes clearing—Rhydian stared her straight in the face. "I am *not* my curse."

Forced to his knee, Theo looked up at the ever-growing circle of enemies. Many died, but more arrived from the cursed Way. Theo pushed up to standing. If he was going to die, he'd do so on his feet.

The sorcerers at his back scribbled the wards, but he knew they were hours away from being done. He didn't have hours left in him.

Nor would the vampires leave their shadowy tombs to help until nightfall.

Theo raised his sword.

I tried, Aurienne.

A flash of silver, too fast for his eyes to follow whirled around him. Screams and spurting blood blinded Theo. Wiping his face clear of the carnage, he saw Nesryn darting toward the Pillar.

"He doesn't need to destroy the Pillar; he just needs to extinguish the flame at the top," she yelled as she darted up the stairs.

Theo's head snapped up. The flame was still flickering.

No. No. No.

A small Way exploded just over the Pillar. Dark shapes shot out of the Way, smothering the flame before the screeching Shadow burned up in a loud crack.

"No!" Nesryn shouted.

The Shadow wraiths sizzled as they struck the flame again and again. The flame sputtered under each attack.

"Get to the flame!" Theo shouted at a nearby sentinel.

Theo ran for the Pillar. Shadows barraged the flame and Mooncursed ripped through their forces. Flashes of silver in the windows of the towering stairwell told him that Nesryn was nearly at the top.

"Hurry!" Theo dragged himself forward, desperate to save them.

A deafening crack stopped him in his tracks.

The flame went out.

A translucent white line retreated across the skies from the coast to the heart of the continent. The protective barrier passed over them with a heady whoosh of air. Then it was gone. This region of the continent lay unprotected, and now Shadow magic was no longer banished.

Theo froze.

The emperor stood taller, striding forward and abandoning his attendants. He lifted his arms with a thin sneer. The edge of his Way solidified into a seamless line. The Mooncursed roared.

Theo stared at the lifeless Pillar and the empty bowl that once housed the eternal flame.

"Theo!" someone shook him.

Theo blinked.

Mooncursed formed an unbroken line and charged at the remaining sentinels and sorcerers.

Nesryn slashed her starlight sword into a long arc, cutting a Way to the amber fields outside Avyllon. "Theo! Now!"

"Retreat!" Theo bellowed.

SILVER MASKS
CHAPTER THIRTY-FIVE

We have a long memory too, and you're not the only one who collects secrets.

— QUEENSBLOOD VITTORIA NIGHTFLAME
LENORE.

1152 N.T.C. Castle Rodarr, Rodarri.

Emperor Rexil came up behind Rianne and pulled her into a tight embrace. His breath was hot on her neck, and his muscle-corded arms held her in place. Several queens relished it, but Rianne fought the scowl creeping onto her face. The mask she painted on required the strength of every spirit within her.

"The Pillar fell," he crooned. "I finally found it and destroyed it. After searching for so long, its mine."

Rianne had to struggle to spin around to face him and painted on a wide-eyed expression. "What does that mean?"

He released her, smiling a bit too wide. "It means, dear one, that I am no longer weakened on this half of the continent. I can create Ways. I can bring my forces here. All of them."

"Forces?" She tried not to sound like she was prying.

He kissed the top of her head. "Don't you worry about that now. We'll be married in just a few days, and you will not have to worry about any of this unpleasantness."

"Wonderful. Congratulations." The smile hurt to maintain.

Taking a deep breath, he exhaled. "Before, it was constantly fighting for every breath, but now, all that weight has just lifted. Nothing is hindering my magic."

Then he winced. It was small, quickly erased, but the queens missed nothing.

"He still will not admit weakness to us," Safyrah said. *"He does not trust us."*

"Don't let him think we're prying," her fellow coven-mate, Noxanya, added.

"I'm glad to hear you are well," Rianne replied out loud.

His expression heated. "I wouldn't let anything delay our nuptials."

Rianne felt a myriad of emotions all at once and hoped he could not read them on her face. Arousal. Displeasure. Excitement. Apprehension. Annoyance.

"Nothing will," she said.

At least that was the truth.

The triumph on his face outshone all else. "Matters require my attention, but I am looking forward to it."

She swallowed. The Pillar fell. Nothing would stop him now.

With a smirk, he marched away, a dozen guards and priestesses following his every step. He never went anywhere without them. Never gave away any vulnerability. Layers of deception and lies colored his words. Rianne realized why she didn't trust him. It's because he reminded her too much of herself right now.

Reeling, Rianne wondered when she'd become so duplicitous.

Was it death? Or was it the influence of the other queens? Or was she changing in small ways that added up.

She glanced toward the emperor's disappearing entourage. She didn't trust him. He'd agreed to marriage too fast. She was one nation of many and not even the most powerful. Why bind himself permanently to her? He'd conquered dozens of others. Why hadn't he married any of them?

He must be willing to do anything to tear the continent's alliance apart. It begged the question of why? Was there more to Aurienne's prophecies and readings than the other queens gave credit for? And after he achieved what he wanted, would he remain the steadfast spouse or would he toss her aside. Would she be added to a royal harem no different from the Queensblood she'd once been?

"He's a strong ally. We will use him for now," Milah said.

"He won't outsmart us," Willow agreed.

Rianne argued, *"Troops, gold, and resources will soon depart through a Way after the wedding ceremony, and the consummation is to occur before that so we can leave directly after the official binding. Once that happens, we'll be powerless. This is a bad idea."*

"Rianne, what are you doing?" Jordyn demanded.

Rianne turned, hand sliding toward her bone corset instinctually.

Her sister stormed toward her wearing beat up leathers, voice rising with each word. Jordyn's gaze was harder now, older. And she walked with a deep-seated confidence that even ballgowns never allowed. Her hair was woven into braids pinned against her scalp, and ink stained her fingertips.

"Why are you marrying him?" she pressed. "What about the alliance? What about Rhydian?"

Rianne said, *"I hate keeping secrets from her."*

"It's necessary to protect her," Willow said.

"Focus on your training, your region." Rianne said. "The sons of the commanders will not give up their territories easily, so you need to be vigilant."

"You need to be vigilant," Jordyn retorted. "Your betrothed has been meeting with the sons of the commanders *you* executed. Bram Tavish has been seen with him multiple times. There are whispers that they're demanding to be recognized as the true *heirs* of Rodarri. If the emperor had your best interests at heart, why would he be taking these clandestine meetings in quiet corners of the castle?"

Anger simmered deep in Rianne's bones. She knew what he might be meeting with them about. There was one request she'd never granted. One condition she never agreed to. Emperor Rexil was too interested in the Queensblood. If he was meeting with her enemies, who currently held less power here, it would be to satiate his magical curiosities. He'd want to hear about the old tales and rituals. The ascensions.

No. Not again.

She'd be damned if she allowed the ascensions to continue. The emperor had kept his word so far, but once the shackles of matrimony were fastened, would he change his mind? Would her sisters fall to the ravine?

"This alliance is still smart," Vittoria said.

Rianne retorted, *"You're blind. You're going to allow history to repeat."*

"We will not allow it," Rebekkah said.

Rianne threw up her hands. *"And when he's taken our army? When our sorcerers are gone? When the commander's sons call for our blood? We should join our allies before it's too late."*

Samantah said, *"Then we will kill him."*

Rianne felt a flare of anger through the numbness. *"And if it's too late?"*

Vittoria said, *"If we can control him, he is powerful protection for our people from outsiders."*

Rianne rolled her eyes. *"He* is *the outsider!"*

"Rianne?" Jordyn demanded.

Rianne realized her sister couldn't hear the arguments in her head, and what it must look like.

Jordyn's brows furrowed as her gaze darted up and down. "What is wrong with you?"

"I hear you. I'm thinking."

Her sister grabbed her hands from their resting place on the corset. "I can't imagine what you went through. Even watching it." Jordyn swallowed. "I will never get that image out of my head. I know being back must be difficult. I don't even understand how it's possible, how the queens brought you back. But I'm here, okay. You can trust me."

Rianne's resolve softened.

Whillow murmured, *"We've trusted our secret to others before and we regretted it."*

Shoving them all down, Rianne ignored that and squeezed her sister's hands back. "I don't fully understand the magic either. The wisdom of the queens is rattling around my head, and I'm just trying to make sense of it all. I see their memories, feel their pain. They're with me."

"With you?" Jordyn squinted.

"It's the best way I know how to describe it," Rianne said. "I'm sorry I've been harsh with you. I just don't want to see you go through what happened to me. I don't want that for any of you ever again. Trust that. I'm maybe a little different, but that will never change."

Jordyn's scowl relaxed. "I know. I don't understand why you're entertaining our enemy. I don't trust him."

Glancing around, Rianne pulled Jordyn into one of the many secret rooms in the palace. After closing the door, and ensuring no one was around, she leaned in.

"I am not telling him everything," she whispered.

The war machines, the trips, the spells, the poisons. They'd be well under way by this point. She glanced at the fresh stone dust near the wall, a trace of the anti-Way wards being carved in all secret passages. And the dire plan she had stashed away in the corners of her mind where even the queens couldn't reach.

Jordyn raised her brows. "Why?"

Rianne straightened her gown. "I make sure he sees what I want him to see. I let him see me as weak, so he believes he has the upper hand. I keep him distracted from my true plans. As for why, I don't fully trust him either. Just know that I have a plan. I would only enter into an alliance with him if it was the best thing for Rodarri. And I'll break an alliance with him for the same reason."

"Do you promise?"

Rianne nodded.

Jordyn lunged forward and enveloped her sister in a hug. Rianne patted Jordyn's back. The warmth of her sister's skin almost made her feel alive.

"Your skin is cold," Jordyn observed.

Rianne pursed her lips. "Death will do that."

"I suppose I should return to my studies. The Dazewood region won't run itself." Jordyn slipped out of the secret room.

Underneath the glowing Vittoria's Gift lichen behind the fogged glass, Rianne let out a frosty breath. If the emperor was already having meetings with the so-called heirs of the commanders, he was more dangerous and treacherous than they'd guessed.

"*Trust us,*" Vittoria whispered.

Rianne traced the lines of her bone corset, weighing her impossible options. Now, there was no choice in what must be done. The question was whether she had the strength to do it.

SHATTERED HOPES
CHAPTER THIRTY-SIX

Dreams were all we were ever going to have.

— UNKNOWN.

1152 N.T.C. The namesake capital city of Avyllon.

Every soul in Avyllon felt the sting of failure. From the high palace windows, Theo watched thousands fleeing the unprotected quadrants of the city toward the temporary housing where the remaining three Pillars still offered protection. Stone masons stacked stones underneath the veil of the protective shield—bisecting the city—and sorcerers painted wards before the mortar even dried. Nearly a quarter of Avyllon's inhabitants had been displaced, and there was little space to house them all.

The skin tugged where Aurienne stitched the fang marks on his forearm, and he winced. Her kind eyes found his as she carefully continued her work.

"This could have been much worse. Your armor kept you from losing the arm," she murmured.

He ran his hand through his Moonwater-slicked hair. She'd found an ancient ritual to bless several of the large pools in the city and demanded they all douse in it before entering the city. She'd mandated everyone bathe in it before every full moon to avoid another repeat of the massacre in the arena.

His heart sank.

How much blood was on his hands? He'd lost count of the deaths staining his soul. He replayed the recent battle over, trying to tally them up.

Ninety-seven dead from the first Mooncursed attack.

One frozen Titan Cliff dweller.

Sixty-four killed at the coronation attack.

Twelve hundred ninety-two at the Eyrand arena, including the Obermeister.

Two hundred thirty-six dead at the Pillar.

Thousands of Avyllonians he couldn't protect.

Unknown dead from the vampires' dark hunger.

Aurienne's hand pulled his face away from the evacuees, so he was looking back at her. Her fingers were warm on his cheek as she stroked the stubble.

"I'm glad you made it back," she said.

"I wasn't sure I would," he said. "He came out of nowhere, and we weren't prepared. I thought we had more time, but we underestimated him."

"He must have spies in the city who alerted him despite our best efforts." Her voice was sad.

He squeezed her hand. "When we were surrounded and overrun, I was thinking of you."

With her other hand she patted the expertly wrapped bandaged on his arm. "I prayed for your safe return every day. The Goddess blessed me."

Theo glanced back out at the dusky city torches. How many families were displaced, wondering where they'd sleep tonight, what they'd eat tomorrow. How many homes were no longer safe because the barrier moved? He rubbed his temples. Tomorrow, he'd make sure each and every one were given lodgings, even if he had to build them with his own hands.

Aurienne stood and offered her hand to him. He looked up at her, feeling as though she could read his every thought.

"The others are waiting to regroup," she said.

A heavy weight loomed over him, threatening to crush him.

"We haven't lost yet," she said.

Theo nodded and took her hand.

They strolled toward the war room, past tapestries and portraits, gilded griffons, and crystal fountains, and he found himself missing home. None of this opulence was necessary, and he certainly didn't want it. Not when the people outside these walls were searching for a straw mat to lay their head. Feeling Aurienne's hand in his, he savored it, thankful she was with him in such unfamiliar surroundings. Her presence was a comforting balm on his ragged nerves. It made it all worth it.

The war room group dwindled since the allies left. The ally delegations had dispersed to the four corners of the continent. Rianne too was gone, still considering an alliance with the emperor, leaving their southeast borders undefended. It left Theo, Aurienne, Saryll, Kolten, Miella and the vampires, Marco, Adonis, Rhydian, Nesryn, and the fox. They were all waiting when Theo arrived.

Miella fingered her heartwood pendant, the center now pulsing with an amber light. Stellan and Julietta stood to one side of her, and Marco, with his glowing tattoos, waited at the other.

Theo took his place at the head of the map table, leaning forward. "We've sent word to our allies already to let them know, but those hit hardest will be those on the east side of the continent."

"Are the representatives of Avyllon coming?" Saryll asked.

Aurienne's mouth set into a thin line. "Not since they might've tipped off the emperor to the Flame Pillar."

Theo continued, "The Pillar no longer keeps the Shadows out, and it's just a matter of time before they arrive." He glanced toward Nesryn. "How long will that be?"

"Not long," the elf replied. "They will want to avoid what remains of the protective shield, but they will be on our shores soon."

Rhydian shifted uncomfortably.

"Part of the university is beyond the new barrier. We're in the process of moving the tomes to the palace," Adonis said.

"The eastern part of the city should be evacuated in a few days." Aurienne glanced toward Stellan. "Would you be able to protect the people until then?"

Stellan's onyx gaze flicked to Miella, who nodded. A reminder of just how important Miella was in this war.

The vampire said, "We can protect against Shadows. However, our deal remains. We may feed upon those with the blackest hearts, even if they are your civilians."

Theo opened his mouth.

"Agreed," Aurienne said.

Theo snapped his mouth shut.

"We need to decide what to do in the long term," Aurienne continued.

"Isn't that where you come in?" Nesryn asked.

Aurienne looked away. "My visions are weak, and the cards have provided no answers."

Nesryn clicked her fingernails. "I can tell you that tipping him off to the location of the other Pillars would be a mistake until we find the leak of information. Wynds has promised to ward theirs, and the Titan Cliffs dwellers are warding theirs as well. It only leaves the Sky Pillar, which has been well-hidden. And there is no point in warding it until we reclaim the Flame Pillar."

"How do we do that?"

Stellan cleared his throat. "Yes, *Grimfall*, how do we do that?"

The fox growled deep in its throat at the vampire, tail flicking back and forth angrily.

The elf glared. "We can't."

Theo gently said, "How were the Pillars created before?"

"It's not possible," she said, tone flat.

"We have to do something," he said.

"The Pillars cannot just be recreated," she said. "They were constructed with significant sacrifice and great magic, and now the Flame Pillar is within the emperor's control."

"We have magic," Theo started. "We can—"

Nesryn sighed. "None of you are powerful enough to create a Pillar. Even the heroes of old barely managed it. Now that it's gone, I don't know that it can be revived. I'm sorry."

Her words stung. Theo knew he'd been less than helpful at the Pillar; he knew these failures were piling up around him. He glanced at Aurienne, bearing the burdens of a continent. He couldn't just give up.

"You know how it was created then?" Theo pressed.

The elf didn't answer.

"Please?" Theo asked.

"A firewyrm breathed life into the bowl," she said. "If you think you can find one of those rare creatures, bring it to the Pillar, get past the emperor's troops, and coax it to share its flame then go ahead."

Hellsdamn it.

The elf glanced around the room. "Nothing else that I am aware of still existing in this world has the power to re-light the eternal flame. As I said, it can't be done."

Outside, angry voices drifted through the city, and the sound of glass breaking against the palace walls rang out in the night. Theo winced, knowing he was already fast losing the support of his people.

"I'll try to find us another path forward," Aurienne said, hands shaking beneath the table. "With my magic weak, it'll take time. I will consult the cards."

"In the meantime, what do we do?" Miella asked.

Theo sat back in the carved wooden chair. "Fight for our lives until we find a way to defeat them."

Rhydian stormed through the palace, searching for Dean Chellaes or anyone who could open a Way back to Rodarri. Adonis had slipped out of the room muttering about the Sky Pillar before Rhydian managed to catch up to him, and he got a sense that the young sorcerer was still avoiding him.

He stopped a red-haired sorcerer in apprentice robes in the hall, "Can you open a Way?"

The woman shook her head, and he released her. Nearly at a run now, he stopped another robed figure. "Can you open a Way?"

"A what?"

He grumbled, continuing his war path.

"You look ridiculous," the elf chuckled.

He found her leaning against the wall.

"We need to return to Rodarri Castle," he said. "We have to warn Rianne."

"If you haven't forgotten, I can open a Way anywhere. I could set you down right in the middle of Rodarri castle if I wanted, yet you didn't seek me out." She twirled her silver hair between her fingers mercilessly.

He snapped, "I would rather ask anyone else."

"Are you still upset I punched you?" She scoffed. "It was the only way to knock sense back into you after nearly losing it. Do you know how close some of those Demorrans were to dying when I found them? You need to work on injuring them a little less or you're going to slip."

Rhydian clenched his fists.

She sauntered away, not waiting for him to ask for help, not offering it either.

"Just say it, you blame me for our failure," he called.

Her steps slowed. "Do you *want* me to blame you?"

He stopped completely. Was he seeking blame? He knew that his rampage drew her away from the Pillar just before they lost it. If she'd been able to stay with the Pillar, the flame may never have been extinguished. It was his fault. If he'd held his sanity, they might've had a chance.

"I blame me. I know you must too," he said.

"If you *know* I blame you, why do I need to say it?" she asked. "Why do you want to hear it? I thought you didn't care what I think."

Did he care what she thought? He shuddered. No. Definitely not. His guilt was just eating at him, and he wanted everyone to stop being so nice about it. He stomped away.

"Warbringer, we were going to fail," she said. "Once the emperor found the location before our wards were up, you must know there was nothing we could do. It was lost."

A scowl etched itself into his brow. "Then why did we fight?"

Her too-wide feline eyes blinked at him as she replied, "There are things worth fighting for, even if you're going to lose."

Bloodroses and Thorns

Chapter Thirty-Seven

Bloodroses bloom with sweetened lies, but their thorns drip with poison.

— *The warning of the bloodrose.*

1152 N.T.C. Castle Rodarr, Rodarri.

An unfamiliar face scrutinized Rianne in the mirror. Pale skin. Pearly white hair tucked into a long braid. Faded blue eyes. Gaunt cheeks. A jagged, wine-colored gash on her neck that never fully healed. She hardly recognized herself. In some ways, she looked as dead as she'd once been. She dragged colored powder across her cheek bones and dabbed perfume on her wrists and behind her neck. The kohl stick darkened her lids and lashes in an attempt to mimic life in her features.

Leaning closer to the vanity, she saw more profound changes. Her eyes flashed with intention; the innocence long burned away. She rarely twirled her hair between her fingers. No tears wetted her cheeks. Questions no longer shaded her brow; now she was filled with resolve.

How much of it was Rianne finding herself and how much was it the queens taking over? She hoped it was the former, especially with what she had to do tonight.

Wedding preparations filled the castle for the morrow, which sealed the alliance. Troops, gold, and resources would depart with the emperor through a Way after the ceremony, and there would be no going back. Tonight, the union would be consummated ahead of the vows. The timing was unusual, but it gave her the opportunity she needed.

Burned rose and sage bundles left wisps of white smoke in the corners of her quarters. White lace veils hung from the ceiling. Bloodrose petals drifted across the floor on a frigid breeze. A roaring fire threatened to escape the colossal hearth, setting the atmosphere for the evening.

Most importantly, Rianne was garbed in a sheer crimson and black chemise with hip-high slits. Twin panels of diaphanous fabric draped over her shoulders, barely covering each breast, and hung to the floor. Strategic cut outs offered peaks of porcelain skin. The perfect package for the conquering emperor.

She adjusted the lace choker to hide the reminder of her death and prepared for what came next. She was no stranger to intimacies. There had been a number of nobles before Rhydian. The emperor himself was charming, attractive, and powerful. In another life, she might've found him intriguing. She was not particularly enthused at the promises made for the evening, but nor was it unpleasant. She felt slivers of guilt at doing this when the one she truly wanted was Rhydian—but neither had made any promises to the other, and she'd warned him that she had to do unwanted things. She hoped he'd understand. Giving herself a final look in the mirror, she took a steadying breath. For her people, she would do this.

"There are worse options for a husband," Marialynn thought.

Vittoria reassured her, *"Do not be afraid."*

Rianne's resolve hardened. *"I'm not."*

"Your Warbringer will understand," Samantah said.

She gripped the edge of the table, focusing on keeping her secret plans to herself. *"He knows my time here is limited. He knows there's no future. I'm not betraying him."*

"We can take over if you prefer," Rebekkah said.

Samantah agreed, *"Yes, we're more experienced in the arts of deception."*

Rianne straightened. *"I'll allow you some control, but I won't shirk my responsibilities. I don't need to be protected."*

Vittoria murmured, *"No, you don't."*

Circling to a low table, Rianne poured two glasses of wine in crystal goblets. The long fabric of her chemise floated behind her. The roaring fire staved off the cool temperatures frosting the windows.

The doors opened, and the emperor entered wearing a loose velvet robe revealing his chiseled and scarred chest. Beneath the robe, low rising flowing pants dusted the floor. Twenty guards flanked him and filed inside. He waved them away. His guards glanced in the room before closing the doors again. And they were alone.

Rianne stepped around a hanging panel of lace and sauntered toward him, holding both wine glasses. She offered both. Brow lifting, he glanced from hand to hand. He was careful, wary of poison, but it would be foolish, dangerous, to attempt such a thing. She sipped from one, then the other, and licked the mulberry liquid from her lips. He stepped forward and wrapped his fingers around hers as he took one of the glasses.

"Does being with me require the courage of wine?" he asked. "Do you not wish to remember every second?"

Whillow giggled through Rianne's lips. "Such an occasion deserves to be celebrated, savored."

"There's only one thing I want to savor tonight," he said.

He brought his glass to her mouth and poured the wine. Yielding, she opened for him and took in the once sweet tasting drink while maintaining eye contact. His gaze smoldered watching her. Before she could swallow, his mouth was upon hers, tongue pushing her lips open. The kiss was demanding, and he claimed the wine from her. Her body went limp as he wrapped his free hand around her waist and pulled her close. She melted against his hard body. His knee pressed against the thin fabric between her legs, forcing them apart and sending sparks through her veins.

The kiss broke, and Rianne was gasping for air. The queens murmured their approval, relishing in the power of this man. He held his fingers beneath her chin for a long moment before he released her.

Smirking, he sipped his wine. "We're the perfect match."

Rianne set down her glass and drifted toward the bed, hips swaying. If only she could trust him. The queens in her head whispered she should, but she remained dubious. After tonight, there would be no choice.

"I want to believe that," she replied, leaning back against the edge of the bed.

The emperor emptied his glass and set it down. "I'll show you."

He crossed the room in a flash and pushed her against the bedding. She nearly yelped as he pressed against her, leaving her nowhere to go. His mouth claimed hers again as his hands roved beneath the sheer panels. His touch was firm enough to bring sinful pleasure. He slipped the straps over her shoulders, nearly revealing her breasts to the cool air. She gasped as the touch set her body on fire. A conquering emperor who took what he wanted without asking.

Part of her wished her body did not respond to his touch as it did, but the queens drowned out any reservations with their eagerness. She let it all go.

Shirtless, he positioned himself against the plush pillows. He put his hands behind his head, waiting.

Whillow pushed her forward. *"Go to him."*

Rianne knew what he wanted and obeyed. She climbed up and

straddled his silk-garbed hips. He leaned up to kiss her neck, hands upon her thighs.

Rianne's hand drifted behind her back as she isolated Safyrah and Noxanya in her bones. She roused their magic while they were distracted. It twirled within her fingers, and she traced them down the scars on his chest. He smirked before reaching up to kiss her lips.

Now!

Rianne summoned her bonesword from the corset on the chair and drove it down toward his heart with all her strength. The point speared into his flesh before an unseen power deflected the sword with a pop of purple light.

The emperor shoved her off with inhuman strength and a gravelly, beastly snarl.

Rianne rolled across the floor and skidded to her feet. She lifted her bonesword and inspected the crimson beads on the blade. She wasn't strong, but at that angle, even just her body weight should have driven the sword into his chest, but there he stood. She'd merely wounded him. There must have been invisible wards protecting him from a lethal blow.

Kingshit.

Inside—the queens were screaming.

"What did you do!" Whillow snapped.

"You tricked us!" Samantah hissed.

"How dare you? Now the alliance is broken!" Rebekkah said.

Vittoria raked her icy claws against Rianne's bones. *"You impudent—"*

Emperor Rexil sputtered, "Wh-what are you—"

Several queens giggled inside Rianne, her secret conspirators. "Can't blame a girl for trying." Rianne smirked.

The emperor pressed his fingers against the shallow cut, eyes widening. His eyes snapped to her sword, to her, to his wound.

"How?" he hissed through his teeth.

She stood, forcing her limbs into the familiar regal pose while smoothing the lacy garment.

"What is protecting you? Or... who?" she asked.

The emperor pursed his lips. "Here, I thought we could be allies."

She grinned wickedly. "I had to try."

"You'll regret this."

Her mouth snapped shut as her eyes narrowed. "You can't forgive a little knife play in the bedroom?"

"You don't want me as an enemy," he warned.

"No, I didn't." Whillow's lips curled into a smirk. "I wanted you dead."

The emperor's hand clenched and purple light burst to life around it. With a few quick strokes of his hand, he drew a series of shapes. A purple Way ripped through the air.

"Consider us enemies now." He stepped into the portal. "I'll discover what you really are, and then nothing can protect you."

What in the worlds and hells did that mean?

Rianne banished her bonesword and crossed her arms.

"Rianne, I need to speak with you—" Rhydian pushed open the door just as the Way cracked shut.

Rianne's heart sank as Rhydian's eyes darted from the portal to her garb to her flushed cheeks and swollen lips. He took a small step back, cheeks paling. His eyes roved down her body as if he could see every touch, like recreating a battlefield. She'd seen him nearly losing himself to bloodlust, but she'd never seen the expression darkening his features. The sounds of battle filled the castle, and he stormed out of her chambers.

"Rhydian," she whispered.

The nearly dead pieces of her heart shattered.

TIES OF BLOOD
CHAPTER THIRTY-EIGHT

Ties of blood ne'er come untied,
From this truth, one cannot hide.

— *HIGH SEER AURIENNE AZARRAH, PROPHETIC*
VISION.

1152 N.T.C. The namesake capital city of Avyllon.

Straw spewed out of the training dummy in the hidden courtyard tucked at the end of a cramped alleyway. The high city walls cast shadows on the milling vampire hunters. It'd grown to nearly a thousand malcontented individuals set on obtaining their vengeance. The people wore mismatched, dented armor, and their swords were rusted and bent.

Miella nocked another training arrow and sighted the roughly painted rings on the hay bale. She released and it struck the outer ring, but at least it hit the target. It was an improvement. She was tired of being relegated to the outside of the war plans, to be coddled in the battlefield, and serve as nothing more than a liability. She'd taken to training with Marco's growing group, in the many training centers popping up in hidden courtyards throughout the city. Miella tore her attention away from the growing militia and back at her target.

Marco strolled up beside her. "Stellan is never going to let you fight. You're wasting your time."

She gritted her teeth, nocking another arrow and releasing. "I have to do something."

Marco gestured toward the alley. "Come with me."

Without waiting for her, he strode back toward a covered cart in the alleyway.

"Gather 'round!" Marco exclaimed loudly to the group. "I know their weakness." He adjusted his heavy leather coat, the sunlight tattoos sparkling within his bronze skin.

The new hunters gathered around him.

"We once believed only the sun or my tattoos would work, but I've found ancient tales of heartwood being used to destroy them."

A man called out, "When do we get tattoos like you!"

The gift of the sun. A permanent way to protect against vampires, to be able to defeat them. To be able to defeat Shadows. But at what cost? If offered, would she even take it?

"Heartwood will suffice until you are ready for the gift of the sun," Marco said.

The hunters exchanged hungry looks, and Miella's stomach rolled.

"Here, I've fashioned heartwood stakes for all of you." Marco threw back the tarp on the hand-wagon.

The reddish wood reflected the noon sun, each crudely carved. The hunters circled the cart, eager hands taking their new weapons. The crowd dispersed, taking the stakes to the training dummies.

She blinked. He'd just given lethal weapons to several hundred angry vigilantes who were severely outmatched by the vampires. It was a recipe for disaster.

Miella grabbed Marco's arm. "We're trying to save the continent and you're out for revenge."

"The continent needs saving from those beasts. One day you will see exactly what they are."

She squeezed his bicep in annoyance, feeling the heat of the tattoos through the coat. "How can we hold off our enemies when you've attacked our allies powerful enough to face them?"

He patted her hand in a brotherly fashion, with just a hint of condescension. "We'll wait until the vampires attack an innocent, but they will."

"And who will save us from the Mooncursed and—worse—the Shadows if all the vampires are gone? They're the only ones keeping us alive right now."

Marco flexed his jaw.

"You're being foolish, not even waiting until the fighting is done," she prodded.

Marco grinned, the displeasure falling from his face. "You're right. We should allow the monsters to destroy one another before taking out those that remain."

Miella snapped her mouth shut. That's not what she had meant.

Marco continued, "But if they lose control in battle, we must protect our troops."

Miella toed the dirt with her boot. She'd seen the aftermath of the vampires' hunger. That quiet bloodbath in the forest still haunted her nightmares. She'd seen them tear into humans and Mooncursed alike at the coronation. If they lost control in battle and turned on Avyllon, it would be terrible. Her throat constricted at the thought.

Finally, she nodded.

"Good." He patted her shoulder again.

"Why does heartwood destroy them?" She fingered her heirloom pendant carved of the same.

"As long as it works, does it matter?" he said.

She narrowed her eyes. He'd evaded her question.

"How do you know it does?" she asked.

"It's what our kin used on them all those years ago," he said.

Reaching into his coat, he presented a polished stake to her, but she looked away. He pressed the stake into her hand, and the wood was smooth and warm. She refused to look at it, knowing that even touching it was a betrayal of Stellan and the vampires sworn to her.

"One day, you're going to use this," he said.

Miella glanced down at the stake, tasting the acerbic betrayal heavy on her tongue.

Darkness rolled across the skies, and Miella peered out of the library window, lost deep in thought. A sudden gust of wind from behind her blew her dark hair past her cheek. Turning, her gaze settled upon Stellan.

He wore a silken tunic and leather pants, and a hungry expression. His chiseled jaw, strong nose, and strong physique made him impossibly striking—and she knew he hardly needed his hypnosis to lure prey. His good looks nearly made her overlook the elongated fangs, the black talons, and leathery wings. The ultimate predator. She'd inherited his almond-shaped eyes, wavy hair, and olive skin. She wondered whether she also received the darker impulses his vampiric curse unlocked. The thought sent squirming sensations through her rolling stomach.

The vampire's black eyes bored into her, as though he could sense the heartwood stake that was hot against her hip under her tunic.

"How have you been?" His voice, once gravely and rough, was now smoother than spun silk.

"Bored. There's not much for me to do," she replied.

"Boredom is a gift few enjoy, especially in war." His wings shifted. "Those who fell protecting your homeland would wish for uninteresting days rather than the cold embrace of death."

Shame flooded her cheeks. "I don't mean to sound ungrateful. I just want to do more."

"The best thing you can do is live." She hadn't even blinked, but he was standing beside her now. He stared out the window at Avyllon's thousand fountains reflecting the starlight.

"I don't want to just stand by while everyone else fights for their home." She crossed her arms.

A chuckle rolled out of his lips, throaty and rumbling—startling her. "You have a fighter's spirit. I remember feeling the same when I went into the forest, desperate for the power to save everyone."

"Then you understand why just hiding away like this is killing me." She reached for his arm, his skin painfully cool beneath her palm.

He was quiet, the starlight glittering against his pitch-black gaze. Unbreathing. Unmoving. His claws clicked against the stone windowsill.

"I do," he replied.

"You cannot ask me to do what you yourself would not," she said. "Please."

The vampire turned toward her, and she was snared in his heavy gaze. "I have not forbidden you from anything. If you wish to join the fighting, no one will stop you. I would ask you to let me know so we can be there with you to fulfill our oath."

Her heart soared.

"Will you teach me?" she pushed. "I'm good with a bow; I used to hunt for the shepherd's pie at the tavern."

He licked his fangs, brows pulling together and forming deep lines on his otherwise granite-smooth face. "I will have Julietta train you. Know that a few months of training will not turn you into a soldier, but it might keep you alive."

Unable to contain her glee, she leapt for him, wrapping her arms around in him a tight hug. His talons patted her back in a fatherly embrace, gentle against her spine.

"I swore to do anything for you, my dear," he murmured. "Nothing is more important than family."

Her heart sank, as her guilt threatened to consume her.

LOVE & HATE
CHAPTER THIRTY-NINE

I hope this hurts.

— HIGH SEER AURIENNE AZARRAH, PROPHETIC VISION.

1152 N.T.C. The namesake capital city of Avyllon.

Bruises, blisters, and cuts colored Theo's knuckles as he pushed open the door to Aurienne's chambers. Midnight's moon long drifted across the sky, and vampires patrolled the city, but he'd refused to retire until every displaced Avyllonian was provided shelter. There was more work to do, but tonight, every head had a place to rest. He could breathe easier having done something. So much of his last weeks were spent making plans with unseen results, but today he set out before dawn with tools on his hip. He'd asked for volunteers to build houses in an undeveloped district, not expecting much, but people had shown up. Hundreds. If good people could be counted on like that, maybe Avyllon had a chance. It was just enough hope to cling to. And he could retreat to his safe place: Aurienne.

Theo tugged his shirt over his head and dropped it on the lustrous, white stone floors. He leaned against the doorway, pressing his forearm against the wood frame, watching Aurienne remove the jewelry from her neck and wrists at the vanity. She caught sight of his reflection in the mirror and her face lit up as she turned in the chair to face him.

Moonless night, she was stunning.

She glided over to him, hips swaying underneath a sheer maroon dressing gown. The gown was cut low to display the tops of her breasts and a hip-high slit showed more than a little leg. His breath hitched as his heart pounded. She was everything. He pressed away from the door frame and took her hand.

"Come to bed," he said.

Her gaze was lidded behind thick lashes. Slowly, he tugged her to the bed by the fingertips before he grabbed her by the hips, lifted her up and set her backside on the edge of the bed. She pressed against him, and a trace of vanilla filled his senses. She ran her hands through his hair, her nails scraping his scalp, and he found himself kissing her deeply and slowly.

Inside the room, stars twinkled, and rivers of color pulsed. The walls fell away, bathing them in light. Trees rustled from far away and elder rose petals of every hue rained down on them. The velvet brush of the petals felt so real in the vision, he nearly forgot it wasn't real. Though Aurienne avoided her magic, this did not fatigue her. She wouldn't admit it, but he knew it was because they were meant to be together, despite what the Fates claimed.

The golden cords of magic wrapping around them sparked against his skin with pinpricks of pain and pleasure. The bed faded away, and they were left laying on a mountain of clouds.

Her lips tasted of sweet, honeyed roses, and he needed more. With firm pressure, he pushed her back on her elbows—savoring the view and tracing the moon and star patterns inked into her skin.

When her head dipped back into the ethereal lilac clouds and her breasts heaved up, he nearly lost control. It took all his self-control to instead rub his thumbs against the bottom of her foot, summoning a moan.

Starting at her ankle, he drew a line of kisses toward her knee. His fingers followed, reaching up toward the apex of her thighs. Slowly, he made his way up her other leg, kissing and nipping until he reached her thigh. In a single motion, he dragged his tongue up her thigh to her entrance, pulling her other leg atop his shoulder. He licked with slow, rhythmic motions, gripping her thighs and backside.

Her breathing grew faster, and he reached up to caress her nipple —drawing forth another throaty moan. An urge rose in him to claim every part of her just as thoroughly as she'd branded herself onto his soul. He'd given his heart, body, mind to her, hells he'd offered her his whole future. He didn't care about her title, her magic, her destiny— he just wanted *her*.

He crawled atop her, the phantom flower petals brushing his back and clouds sinking underneath his palms.

"Theo," she breathed into his neck.

The urge to possess her just as fully as she owned him ignited within him.

He brushed his lips against her ear lobe. "Tell me you're mine."

He slipped another finger inside of her and continued drawing lazy circles across her nipple.

"I'm yours."

His shaft pressed against the inside of his pants. *Gods*—he loved to be her undoing.

Fingers buried, he bent down to drag his tongue against her, writing his name with his tongue—claiming her as she writhed beneath him.

"Make me believe it."

"I'm yours!" she screamed.

The sight of her was more than he could handle. "I want you."

"Take me." She reached down and stroked him.

Theo stood and let his pants fall to the floor. She glanced toward his length and swallowed before meeting his gaze. She moved one leg to the side, and then the other.

"Take off your gown," he commanded.

She shifted out of the gown and dropped it next to his pants.

He lifted her and flipped her over onto her stomach, then with a sharp tug pulled her legs off the edge of the bed so she was standing in front of him. Pressing her against his chest, he nipped the soft skin of her neck with his teeth. Dragging his hand up her stomach and breasts, he threaded his fingers into her silken hair and pressed her forward by her nape.

She inhaled sharply but complied. Seeing her respond to his touch would be his undoing. He would never be owned as completely by anyone as he was by her.

"Please," she whispered.

Theo pressed his shaft against her heat and slowly thrust inside of her. He pulled out halfway and thrust in again, and again. He took up a rhythm, thrusting as she rocked in tandem.

Sunless days, she felt amazing.

"Aurienne." Her name was a prayer and a promise.

He thrust again and again, feeling himself tighten and fill. She pressed her backside back against him, grinding. Faster and faster, the rhythm climaxed.

"I'm coming!" she said, and it drove him over the edge.

Her hips bucked as he thrust a final time and came just as his vision blacked out and stars danced in front of his eyes. She collapsed against the bed, and he pressed a kiss to her spine, smelling roses and vanilla on her feverish skin.

Theo gently took her wrist and dragged her to the bathtub. Sinking into the warm water, with her straddling his hips and her breasts pressed against his chest—they kissed until both of their lips were swollen, and they coupled again. This time, she set the pace, rolling her hips and grinding against him—taking her time with their pleasure.

Falling into bed, Theo drew Aurienne's naked body against his chest. He kissed the top of her head, and she snuggled up against him. He slipped into a dreamless sleep, wishing he could stop time forever, but time never stopped, and fate conspired against them.

In a dream, Aurienne overlooked a battlefield outside the city of Avyllon. Her feet sank in pools of hot blood.

Vampires battled Mooncursed beasts. The giants and Seven Forest naturalists battled shadowed monsters. The People of Living Stone fought towering mountain stone giants. War machines boomed in the valley, sundering one another to splinters. Adonis hurled fireballs and spells at misshapen monsters. Kassia twisted bloodmagic, trapping enemies into the earth itself with cords of imbued blood. Beside Miella, Marco burned Shadow creatures with sunlight. Rhydian roared in bloodlust. Rianne wielded her bonesword at Demorran soldiers.

Everywhere Aurienne looked, men and monsters battled gods and beasts, and howling souls departed beyond the veil. The city walls crumbled, crushing thousands. Fires broke out, and people ran screaming. Floods crashed through the aqueducts.

Death reigned as the emperor's forces and the continent's allies ripped one another apart. Turning a wide circle, she searched for Theo. Was he safe?

A fist yanked her shoulder and as she turned, Theo drove the Sword of Souls through her chest with hate in his eyes.

Blood bubbled out of her mouth, and time stilled. Winds gusted in her face, whipping her hair back. Glaring at her, he twisted the blade, cracking ribs and shredding her heart. The spirit-rending magics attacked her soul, leaving only ragged tatters dripping golden soulblood.

"Burn in hell, you monster." The words hissed from between his teeth, knocking her back.

She blinked, and the Sword of Souls was gone. Her fingers were hot and wet. Looking down, she found her dagger was buried in his ribs. She stared up at him and his scowl was replaced by a shocked expression as he fell.

"Why?" he asked. "I loved you."

She gasped. "Theo! No, I'm so sorry."

He was gone, but his whispers slashed her skin, leaving bleeding welts in their wake. She covered her face with her arms as the hateful words cut her to the bone.

> I hate you.
> You're a fucking coward.
> I'm well acquainted with monsters.
> I will enjoy watching you die.

"Theo," she screamed.

Stumbling through the ropey blood, she searched for him amid the uncontrolled battle. Boulders crashed nearby, and smoke joined the clouds. Rampant, wild magic exploded in every direction.

Theo!

She had to find him. Bile gurgled in her throat as she dodged the silver, lashing words that ripped into her skin. She would never hurt him. Wouldn't dream of taking his life, no matter what.

Please come back, please come back.

Theo appeared before her, wearing scarred, golden armor and the same hateful glower from before. The Sword of Souls glimmered in his hand. The whispers surrounded them both in a silver whirlwind that kicked up dust and ash. Prophetic words assailed her.

> Death is all you deserve.
> I hope this hurts.

May all the darkness staining your spirit drag you to
    the eternal hell you deserve.
Do you know what I've done? For you.

Blood pouring from his mouth and a gaping hole in his chest, and he fell to his knees, looking up at her with betrayal and hurt.

"Please, no," Aurienne begged.

A hand whirled her around, and Theo was driving his blade into her chest. She screamed as the sword's rending magics ripped through her. Over and over, they killed the other until her mind nearly broke.

He whispered, "It's always one of us that dies. One of us always dies."

    It's one of us.
    One of us.
    One of us will die.
    It's always one of us.
    Me or you.

Aurienne felt more than heard the words tumbling from her mouth in response, acerbic words that tasted of poison. "One of us will die, and it's not going to be me."

Theo leaned forward, his lips brushing her ear. "Burn in hell, you monster."

Aurienne woke choking on golden soulblood, chest aching as much from the phantom sword as from the hateful words.

TRUST ONCE BROKEN
CHAPTER FORTY

You have caused me more pain than our enemies ever will.

— *KING ATHEODOREN WILLEM THATCHER*
ARADEY.

1152 N.T.C. Rodarr Castle, Rodarri.

Swords clashed and Ways sizzled the air as Rianne shouted commands. "Complete the wards!"

Her sorcerers etched the final details in the wards she'd secretly commissioned that would prevent the emperor from opening Ways. They had to wait until the final moment else he discovered the magic.

From the crackling sounds echoing from the throne room, Rexil was gathering his regiment stationed in Rodarri and preparing for a full-scale attack. If the wards were completed in time, the his forces might be trapped here.

The Grimfall elf darted past, running down the Demorran sorcerers launching fireballs at the Rodarri soldiers. They didn't even have a chance to scream as she raced by. Somewhere in all the chaos, Rhydian roared, and the castle walls shook. Rodarri troops hurried toward the throne room.

She leaned over her sorcerer, watching the hammer strike chisel. The wards began to glow.

"Almost done!"

Calls to evacuate filled the air.

Kingshit.

"Done!" the sorcerer called.

The wards flared to life. Rianne held her breath, but silence filled the castle. He'd escaped.

Damn it to all the hells.

Vittoria's tone was flat. "*What did you expect?*"

"It was a backup plan," Rianne retorted. "He should've been dead."

Vittoria snapped, *"But he is not, and now he will come for us."*

"I know!" Rianne screamed aloud.

Thunderous steps approached from behind, and Rianne spun as the elf stormed up to her.

"What did you do?" Nesryn demanded.

The queens hissed as one, *"Grimfall."*

"Why was he here?" the elf continued.

Nesryn's approach didn't slow, and Rianne was forced backward. She felt her face tensing into a glare from the ire of the queens.

"I was considering an alliance, and decided not to accept," Rianne said.

"He was here?" Nesryn roared.

Rianne refused to back up any more, leaving her face-to-face with the elf. "That's usually how negotiations work."

The elf growled, her breath hot on Rianne's face.

"Nesryn." Rhydian came up beside them, a threat lingering in his voice.

Rianne's expression softened as she looked to the Warbringer. "I tried to kill him with the bonesword. It's magic should have worked.

I got him distracted and tried to kill him. I had to lure him into a sense of security," she tried to explain. "But it was my plan to assassinate him."

Rhydian's scowl didn't break.

"I've been trying to get through his wards for weeks, and yet, he was here," Neseryn said. "Unprotected? If you'd let me in on your plan, I would have killed him. *I* wouldn't have failed."

Bloodwitch rage bubbled in Rianne's throat.

Returned queen Rebekkah clawed her way to the front of Rianne's mind and hissed, "We will never trust you, Grimfall. Not after what you've done."

"Every death in the war from this moment forward is on your hands," the elf replied. "I could've ended this all tonight, and yet your foolish, misplaced hate has doomed us."

"How does it compare to the blood on your hands?" Samantah shot back through Rianne.

Rhydian pushed between them; his empty palms raised. The bloody, starlight sword trembled in Nesryn's hand as she looked over Rhydian's shoulder toward Rianne.

"At least I'm no liar," Nesryn growled. "Lying to those closest to you is the first step on the path of corruption. I thought you'd last longer than the other returned queens, but it seems my faith in you was misplaced, Rianne. I'll be keeping my eye on you from now on."

The elf stormed away, leaving Rianne alone with Rhydian.

Rhydian slowly turned to face her, and his cold glare was an icicle piercing her heart.

"I'm sorry," she whispered. "I thought I was doing the right thing."

"You've been pushing me away since your return and yet you—" He shook his head.

"I know," she said. "I tried to tell you I'm not the same."

"Clearly." Pain was painted across his face. "I'm not angry at you for doing it. Hurt, sure. You warned me you'd have to do things for our people, but I thought you'd tell me the truth. I never thought you meant *this*. Instead, this entire time you've been keeping secrets from me. Sending me away so you could enact your schemes."

Guilt wracked her. "I know."

"I don't even know who you are. And if you'd let me in, we could have ended this, but you didn't trust me enough."

"It's not that I didn't trust you!"

"Then what?"

She pursed her lips. How could she explain the war in her head? The choices were hers but not fully. She could not claim innocence for any act, yet the queens were so loud. Their pains were hers. Their memories shared. The fury joined.

She looked away.

"Rianne, I don't understand." His eyes searched hers. "I've been honest with you about everything. Why couldn't you trust me?"

Tears burned in her eyes. "I do trust you."

"Just not with this?"

Rianne's lips quivered. "I told you that I hear the other queens. I am in control for now, but they grow stronger. I won't be around for long and being around you hurts because it reminds me of everything I can't have. It's easier when you're away, even if I grieve what we've lost."

"You're really gone then?"

Yes. No. Sometimes. I don't know anymore.

Rhydian clenched his jaw. "How can I believe anything you say?"

With a hoarse scream, Rianne tore down the lace veils in her chambers and tossed them into the fire. She hurled the glass goblets into her vanity. Shattered glass rained down from the cracked mirror and cut into her soles as she stomped across the room. Bloody footprints trailed in her wake. She ripped the bedding off her mattress and dragged it to the fire. It caught flame, pouring smoke through the hazy room.

Kneeling on the cold floors, she scraped the rose petals from the floor until her fingernails bled. The brush of the gossamer fabric against her legs brought another scream. She tore the chemise off and threw it into the fire. Sinking to her knees, the magnitude of her failure was crushing.

All that planning for nothing.

Vittoria said, *"I thought we agreed. You would listen to us, and we wouldn't fight you. You've ruined our chances at avoiding an unwinnable war."*

Rianne said, *"I don't regret it. It was the right thing to do. The alliance with the emperor would have doomed us."*

Rianne lifted her head, speaking out loud. "You were never on my side. You never listened."

Whillow whispered, *"You never trusted us either."*

Glass cut into Rianne's palms as she leaned forward. "Maybe none of us know how to trust anyone. We were all too busy fighting one another to see clearly."

Rosalindt caressed Rianne's cheek. *"We are only here to help."*

"I went along with your plans because I trusted your wisdom, but I should have been questioning your clarity," Rianne whispered.

"We have lived far longer than you, girl," Milah's dispassionate presence was soothing amidst all the rage.

"Some of you are so angry, so hateful, that you will do anything for revenge," Rianne said. "And I understand. I'm furious. You don't trust anyone because you've been let down by everyone, but you lost sight of our duty to our people. *I* believe Aurienne."

Rebekkah snarled, *"You can't trust the seer. Seers whisper twisted truths and pretty lies. You saw what she nearly did to us. She stole our revenge."*

Samantah agreed, *"We still have plans for the seer. One day she will suffer."*

Rianne lifted her head. "No. There has been enough vengeance. It's a cycle that circles overhead until we're caught in its noose. That vow is complete. Now, we must focus on protecting our people."

The queens all murmured, a thousand replies bouncing around Rianne's skull.

Rianne watched the roaring fireplace, consuming the remnants of her failure. "I never trusted the emperor, and it's my fault for not speaking up. I let this go too far, but I won't again."

Vittoria's claws scraped Rianne's ribs. *"So what do you plan to do?"*

"Trust in our allies so we have a chance at survival," Rianne said. "Fate said we must all come together. And I don't believe we've seen the worst of what Emperor Rexil has to offer."

Vittoria asked, *"And if they betray us?"*

Rianne beat her fist against the ground. "We're going to do this my way."

Whispers of begrudging agreement filled Rianne's skull.

A flash of silver hair around a corner revealed the elf's location. Rhydian stormed around the corner, but the hallway was now empty. His hands shook, vision bled red, and he sucked air between his teeth.

"I know you're here," he shouted, voice echoing off the austere gray walls.

"I wasn't aware you were looking for me." Her tone was as bored and icy as ever.

He whirled, finding her standing behind him cleaning blood from her starlight sword. Those mercurial eyes stormed and the points of her short claws flexed. Even standing before him, her camouflaged gray skin blended into the shadows.

She tilted her head. "Are you looking for a fight?"

"No."

She continued cleaning her sword with the tattered, bloody rag.

"Maybe," he growled.

Grinning, the points of her fangs dug into her lips. "I'm up for a few rounds if you are, Warbringer."

The thought of them battling until they tore the castle down had him seeing red, and he wanted nothing more. Blood would spray the walls as the stones rained down. Then the memory of Rianne cut the festering rage and left him empty.

"You were right. Go ahead and gloat," he said.

"I'm usually right," she said. "It rarely brings me any satisfaction."

He backed away and took several long, steadying breaths. His fingers itched for the ax at his hip, but he crossed his arms instead and leaned against a stone pillar. The spiked rose carvings dug into his back as he thumped his head into the wall.

"Rianne... she's not the same," he said.

Nesryn's brow lifted. He could almost hear the "*I told you so*," in her frosty tone. She didn't say it though. Sheathing her blade on her back, she waited for him to continue. It could be his waning grip on sanity, but she seemed less irate than usual.

"She was my purpose. I fought the curse for her. Everything was for her. Now that she's..." He blew a breath out of his teeth.

"Love is a powerful motivator," she said. "Wars have been won for much less."

Rhydian had loved Rianne more than he thought possible, especially when he'd always believed his life was hopeless. He would have done anything for her. Anything. That love blinded him to what he should have seen. She was there, but a little less Rianne every day. Where did that leave him?

"I'm not sure what the point is anymore," he said.

Nesryn sighed and leaned back against the wall across the wide, empty hallway. "Isn't that the question? I've asked myself that many times."

"I don't have any reason to fight." His shoulders sagged.

In a blink, she was propped against the column beside him, sharpening a dagger. "You fight for you."

NECROPOLIS
CHAPTER FORTY-ONE

There are monsters at our gates.

— HIGH SEER AURIENNE AZARRAH, PROPHETIC VISION.

1152 N.T.C. A world beyond the veil.

Dregs of sleep clouded Aurienne's mind as she woke in a nightmare graveyard world far from the strong arms she'd fallen asleep in. The skies were burnt red, and the air smelled of decay. Rows of crumbling headstones atop rolling hills stretched as far as her eyes could see in any direction. Thunder rumbled in the distance, and the skies flashed with scarlet lightning.

Bones littered the ground.

Fabric scraped against stone, and Aurienne glanced up.

Rianne perched on a rose quartz and marble vault, half sunken into the crushed black grass, the name of the deceased lost to time. The diaphanous layers of her black gown danced in the putrid breeze. The gilded bones around her corset gleamed in the hazy twilight. Her glassy eyes revealed she might've been crying.

Rianne straightened her skirts and painted a ghastly smile on her face that looked like she had forgotten what the expression was supposed to look like. "We've decided not to kill you."

Aurienne stared warily. Her lips opened but no words came out, for none were polite, and Rianne looked like she was actually *trying* to be civil. Yet she had the *audacity* to drag her from Theo's arms and into a deserted apocalyptic necropolis to tell her that she was not planning on killing her. How had she even managed it?

"Thank you?" Aurienne gestured to the hellscape surrounding them. "And all this?"

"You're not the only one who walks between the veils," Rianne replied. "I died. Now I can see all the hells of all the worlds."

Aurienne folded her hands across her chest. "You picked the creepiest hellscape that you could and dragged me here as payback."

The twinkling in the queen's sad eyes reminded her far more of Rianne than the souls that, every so often, wore the queen's skin.

Rianne slipped off the vault and lingered before Aurienne with a thin smile. "I thought you'd like it, seeing where you brought *me* the last time that we spoke like this. And it's not the worst one."

"It's sufficiently creepy, well done. Your point is made."

Rianne laughed, and her voice sounded genuinely and unmistakably her.

"You are still in there," Aurienne said.

"I'm more Rianne than you give me credit for," Rianne murmured.

In this world between worlds where magic and reality collided, Rianne's crimson beating heart glowed inside her chest like sunlight behind fogged glass. Obsidian bramble vines wrapped around her pulsing heart and bones. The spirits moved underneath her skin.

"You're less her than you know," Aurienne said gently.

"Perhaps." Rianne's expression tightened. "Your own soul is in danger as well. Your Goddess' presence is dangerously close, and knotted ropes of fate surround you. Together, it's more power than you can contain. Even now, it's seeping from your bones. And another goddess wants you, is waiting for you to weaken. With the necromantic corruption, you too are at risk of losing yourself."

Aurienne felt her shoulders sag. "I know."

A mausoleum crumbled on a nearby ridge, sending boulders tumbling into the valley. Lightning struck a headstone, which exploded upon impact underneath skies rumbling with thunder.

"Maybe none of us are meant to survive this war," Rianne said.

"By the end of it, maybe none of us deserve to," Aurienne said.

Rianne smiled sadly. "We don't, but some do."

Most of us will die in these coming months.

Aurienne replied instead, "I hope that's true."

"I'm here to accept your alliance." Rianne straightened. "I considered Rexil's terms and found them wanting. With the Pillar down, and the Shadows and Mooncursed here, I see that though he believes his cause righteous, our people will all suffer. My armies will join yours."

Aurienne's chest tightened as she gasped before sweet relief spilled into her lungs. "What changed your mind?"

"Something is off about him," Rianne shrugged. "I did not trust him. So, I seduced him and tried to assassinate him. Unfortunately, it did not work."

Aurienne blinked.

"He's personally warded by something," the queen replied. "I did not see the wards even with my eyes opened in death until my blade nearly pierced his flesh. The wards are powerful magic and hidden. They only became active upon a threat of danger. My bonesword only grazed him before the wards deflected the blade."

"He's invincible, and warded against all harm? Who even has the power to ward like that?"

The crimson lightning splitting the distant skies reflected in Rianne's gaze. "Only gods."

Rising Guilt
Chapter Forty-Two

The worst is yet to come.

— A promise of the Fates.

1152 N.T.C. The namesake capital city of Avyllon.

Nightmares haunted Aurienne's waking and dreaming hours. She wandered the palace halls, searching for Theo—her only reprieve from the pain. Around a corner, a dark-eyed version of him sank his sword into her chest. Choking on heart's blood, she looked down and blood coated her hands as her own dagger slipped between Theo's ribs. He fell before her, glaring up with hateful eyes. She nearly stumbled, coughing as each attack leeched her strength. Blinking, the nightmares vanished once more.

Vile whispers echoed in her mind.

I hate you.
I will enjoy watching you die.
Death is all you deserve.

Do you know what I've done? For you.
One of us always dies.

She stumbled beneath the relentless onslaught and slipped to the floor. Catching her breath, she pulled herself to standing and leaned against an oak door frame.

"Are you alright?" Kolten asked.

Aurienne straightened; she'd forgotten about the loyal guard who never left her side. And how terrible was that? His entire life revolved around her, and she forgot he was even there. His kind eyes searched hers, revealing the depth of his feelings. Feelings she didn't reciprocate. He'd be just another casualty in a long line. They all deserved better than her.

"Yes, fine," she said. "Just tired. Thinking."

"Do you need anything?" Kolten asked.

"High Seer, there's an update." Saryll's arrival saved her from having to answer.

Aurienne looked to Kolten, "Could you give us a few minutes please."

"I should really stay," he said. "Threats are everywhere."

"I'll be fine," she reassured him.

He hesitated.

"You're dismissed, Kolten," she said as gently as she could.

With a tight nod, he marched away, hand on his sword.

Aurienne returned her attention to Saryll. "Are our armies ready to march?"

"Yes," Saryll said. "The builders finished the new wall and wards, the vampires are defending the city, and the standing army has mobilized. New recruits are joining the training every day. They're ready to leave whenever you give the order."

"It's Theo's order to give now," Aurienne replied.

Saryll inclined her head, knowingly. "Either way, they're ready. The nameless one has sighted the emperor's army on the isthmus. We suspect that opening the Ways here and in Rodarri weakened him, but we must remain vigilant."

"How many did the nameless one see?"

"We're going to have to send nearly all our troops," Saryll replied. "And most of the vampires will have to go with them. The nameless one also confirmed that the Rodarri army has been posted at the border as well and is prepared to provide backup."

"Rianne is keeping her promise then." She swallowed. It meant Theo would have to leave soon. "I'll let him know. They'll likely be leaving for the isthmus tomorrow."

"Do you want me to let our allies know?" Saryll asked.

"I'll do it." Aurienne paused. "But you can let Kassia know."

Saryll stiffened, cloudy eyes turning glassy. "There's no need."

Her heart ached for her sister seer. They really were cursed to lives of loneliness. Every glimpse of happiness ripped away.

"What happened?" she asked softly.

"Kassia left," Saryll said. "She asked me to go with her, but I told her I had to stay. My place is here, serving the Goddess. There is no life for me long-term away from Avyllon, and there is no life for her here."

"I am so sorry."

"Don't be. We've been given so much." A tear slipped down Saryll's cheek despite her claims of being fine.

I know that pain all too well.

"It is the curse of the seers," Aurienne said quietly. "Seers must watch the lives we were meant to live but can never have ourselves."

"I think I saw Theo in the forge," Saryll clasped her hands before slipping around the corner with a swoosh of her ceremonial gown.

The whispers returned.

> *I hope this hurts.*
> *You've taken everything from me.*
> *Burn in hell, you monster.*

Aurienne wrapped her arms around herself. The sharp words only quieted in Theo's presence, and she needed the peace.

Cutting through the palace, she passed the main library. At this late hour, it should have been empty, but several lanterns flickered within. She glanced inside, seeing Adonis buried in a stack of books, alone. Not so long ago, he would be out with his friends causing trouble. Since he watched Mathis die, he'd never been the same.

Maybe I shouldn't have sent him on the journey?

Was this all her fault? If he'd never left Avyllon, he wouldn't have been caught in the Mooncursed attack. He wouldn't be grieving his mentor and his own perceived failures. She'd tried again and again to reach him, but he was locked in his own world, searching for some scrap of redemption.

Leaving the library behind, she slipped out of the palace toward the adjacent forge. She crossed the square when a familiar voice caught her attention.

"Coppers for the poor?"

Aurienne froze.

A small, young woman leaned against the temple walls, shaking a dented bowl. "Coppers?"

Her eyes were burned into empty sockets. Evani, the seer Aurienne had condemned.

"A blessing High Seer?" a woman with a child asked.

Evani's head snapped toward Aurienne.

Aurienne tried to smile at the mother. "Blessings of the Goddess," she whispered, placing her hand upon the babe's forehead.

"High Seer?" Evani struggled to stand, using the temple wall for support. "Aurienne?"

Evani's ribs showed through her threadbare sheath, and her knees and bare feet were dirty. Her lips were cracked, and her hair was pulled back into a grimy knot.

Aurienne backed away, hardly daring to breathe.

"I know you're there," Evani called. "Please have pity. I made a mistake, but I can serve Her. The seers won't let me in; they won't even speak to me. Please."

Aurienne wanted to reach for the girl but stopped. What could she do? The Goddess's will was clear, and she could not defy her. If Aurienne hadn't failed, if she'd been strong enough to survive the visions, maybe she'd been able to stop Evani before it was too late. Another failure in Aurienne's growing list.

"I'm sorry," Aurienne whispered, backing away, and leaving the girl alone.

Syaoran stepped out of the shadows of the temple, the silver in her hair catching the torchlight. The former High Seer's brown eyes were somber. From her place behind the a pillar, Aurienne realized she'd been watching Evani.

"Your gift is killing you," the older woman said, absently touching the scars on her arm. "I warned you."

"I know."

"I never told you about the day I gave you your birth reading." Syaoran drew nearer, voice nearly a whisper. "Something tried to take you. It was dark and... slippery. As though this world rejected her presence. She will take advantage of your weakness, and it will bring destruction to us all."

Aurienne blinked. Niamh had been after her for that long? Since she was an infant?

"I know who it is," Aurienne said. "The emperor's goddess Niamh. She's tried to corrupt my gift."

Syaoran folded her hands before her, still wearing her ceremonial robes though her prophetic gift had long been taken from her. "I had a vision the day you were brought to me. In one hand you held life, and in the other death. You were always meant to be our salvation or destruction. I didn't tell you because it was too great a burden to place on someone so young, but you need to know."

Aurienne balled her fists, hissing at the tender bones in her healing hand. "Why me?"

Syaoran glanced toward Evani. "Why do any of us have the fates we're dealt? Perhaps you're the only one who could bear this burden." The older seer turned back toward Aurienne. "I sense you're fighting something else. It's taking away your focus and strength. Whatever it is, end it. You can't afford to let her get to you."

Syaoran tentatively reached out to squeeze Aurienne's hand before disappearing back into the temple.

Heart heavy, Aurienne continued around the temple toward the forge. Niamh had tried to take her as a baby. The evil goddess had been after her power her entire life, but why? What was she planning? If Niamh really was after her, it put everyone around her in even more danger.

Holding back tears, Aurienne entered the forge. The fires were dead, anvils silent. Theo sat alone in the cold room with no trace of the glow he'd once had. Even without her Second Sight, she saw all that weighed him down. The bloodshed, his own choices, the necessary sins, the unpromised future.

She swallowed. He'd killed for her. Not only in the heat of battle, but he'd cursed the Titan Cliff dweller, and if the stories were accurate—he murdered the Obermeister in cold blood. What else had he done that should be laid at her feet? What else would he do?

A bleeding image of Theo appeared beside her, and whispered, "Death is all you deserve." Then it vanished.

She couldn't let anything hurt him, least of all her.

"Theo," she called.

He looked to her, and his face lit up as he placed the steel sword on the bench. "Is there news?"

"The last divisions are readying to leave for the isthmus to reinforce our troops," she said. "They're ready to leave at your command."

"Ah. I see."

Her words doused the light from his face. Everywhere she went, she brought pain. She hurt everyone around her, even the person she would protect with her own soul.

Face contorting, Theo stood and lunged toward her. She choked on a gasp as he drove his sword under her ribs. Her back slammed against the wall and rattled the hanging tools. The blade twisted, tearing through her flesh.

"I hate you," he hissed against her ear. "I hate what you've made me."

"Aurienne?" The nightmare vision of Theo vanished as Theo stood from the bench he'd been on the whole time.

"Are you alright?" he asked.

It's getting worse.

She tried her best to portray a bland expression. "Sorry, I just remembered, I have a few things to finish up, but I'll see you later?"

He called after her, but she darted out of the forge. It hurt too bad. She retreated toward her chambers, breaking into a run. She slammed the door and stumbled out to the balcony. She saw it all again.

Theo's face filled with rage as he drove his sword through her and whispered hateful truths in her ear. She deserved it. Her presence in the world was one of destruction and chaos, and everyone was worse for it. She just had to hold on a little longer, and then she could be done.

With shaking hands, she retrieved her cards. She closed her eyes and shuffled. There was only one question on her mind. One she'd been too afraid to ask.

Are Theo and I destined to die if we fall in love?

She opened her eyes and drew the first card. Death. The fourth time in her life. Gasping, she pulled another card, and then another.

Death.

Death.

Death.

Death. Death. Death. Death. Death.

Every card showed Death, and the cards never lied.

WICKED REFLECTIONS
CHAPTER FORTY-THREE

I hear all the dead queens screaming, screaming, screaming. They do not live, but they do not die, and they are here with me always.

— JOURNAL OF QUEEN REBEKKAH FAYE LENORE,
72 N.T.C.

1152 N.T.C. Castle Rodarr, Rodarri.

Bloodrose thorns bit into Rianne's palm as she squeezed the black and crimson bloom. Her blood pattered against the uneven cobblestones in the secret passage overlooking the deserted Courtyard of Queens. She ignored the call of the ravine within as she watched the traitors. Several of the commander's sons huddled in the corner. After hanging their fathers, she hadn't reappointed their positions officially. Quietly, she'd been turning over many of their duties to the other Queensblood. Yet, the self-purported *heirs* continued to claim their *birthrights*.

Her gaze narrowed. As if they had any right to anything other than the end of her bonesword.

Rianne blinked, sensing Whillow and Samantah's incensed influence over her thoughts. She took a steadying breath as she sought firmer control over the spirits. Anger wouldn't help, and she didn't know what the commanders' sons were up to yet. But the fact that they sought a meeting *here* of all places was worrying. Rianne's instincts for danger were impeccably honed after generations of oppression, and right now, they were screaming.

Rejecting the emperor's proposal on what should have been the night of their consummation had sent shock waves through Rodarri. Discord and unrest infected her city, and these foolish young men didn't hesitate to capitalize upon it.

Bram Tavish glanced over the shoulders of the others, as if he could sense her prying gaze from the cobwebs of the hidden spyhole. But she'd ensured that the secret passage doorways had been repaired and rehidden after the skirmish after her ascension, so there was no way for him to notice her.

He and the others wore leather vests in the fashion of armor but adorned with velvet and gaudy buttons. A pathetic attempt to look noble while maintaining the air of a warrior. She shook her head.

Whillow's hateful voice filled her bones. *"We should kill them."*

"At the very least, we ought to arrest and question them," Morgana agreed.

Callysta hissed in a mad, sing-song voice, *"Voice full of lies, betrayal in their eyes, don't trust the ones, with the hate in their bones."*

"Quickly, hurl their bodies into the ravine," Whillow murmured. *"No one will know."*

Rebekkah's wicked grin had settled on Rianne's mouth, and she wiped it away. She'd promised to work together with the spirits, but she was still uneasy with every bit of herself she was losing.

Rianne said, *"They're talking about why the alliance fell through. Everyone is talking about it. For now, we'll leave them be."*

First queen Vittoria said, *"When war comes, send them to the front lines. They'll never return."*

Rianne replied, *"For now, temperance. I don't want to kill anyone else if we don't have to."*

Milah's ruthless indifference was cool in Rianne's throat. *"Temperance and mercy have only ended with our bones littering the ravine. Now is the time for blood."*

Rianne ignored her. *"With the emperor gone, it's time to reveal our plans to Jordyn. I don't want to keep any more secrets from her, and we will want her help eventually."*

The queens grumbled but did not protest.

Rianne released the bloodrose and crept along the secret passage. These secret meetings were trouble. She chewed her lip as she exited the hidden door. They would have to be dealt with soon, but she didn't want every choice she made to end in death.

Smoothing her skirts and straightening her rosebone crown, she strode through the halls. Towel-laden aids, sunlight-starved administrators, and burly guards quickly stepped aside with a bow. Leaving the castle behind, she approached the witchshield-hidden training rings.

Jordyn scowled in one of the rings, twirling a dagger that kept falling to the ground. After picking up her fourth dagger, she noticed Rianne.

Rianne paused outside the wooden fencing. "There's something I want to show you."

Jordyn slipped the knives into her training gear and stepped underneath the wood beams. "Where are we going?"

"You'll see."

Inside the castle, Rianne followed her ancient memories below the Queensblood quarters to a rough-hewn stone wall on the highest floor in the basements. Her fingertips hovered over the faded stones.

"You wanted to show me a wall?" Jordyn crossed her arms, leathers squeaking at the elbows.

"Do you see anything different about this section of the wall?" Rianne asked.

Jordyn squinted, holding the lichen lantern closer. "It's a little greener than the rest of the wall. They aren't the same stones."

"A door was walled up a long, long time ago."

So many years ago, there was a nameless, rebel queen, standing in that very room, mixing the darkest of poisons before being found out. Before fighting for their lives and nearly freeing them all. She met a fiery end at the stake for her efforts. The dark pool of magic in the depths of Rianne's shared souls stirred.

Calling for the spirits of Noxanya and Safyrah, bloodmagic filled her palm. She summoned her great sword. One by one, the bones around her ribs flew from the corset and formed the bonesword.

Jordyn stumbled back as Whillow easily twirled the sword in Rianne's hand. Rianne might not have been a warrior, but their strengths were hers. Gripping the hilt with both hands, she drove the end into the mortar between the stones. Magic erupted and the wall crumbled. Pebbles tumbled in every direction.

The dust cleared and revealed the outline of a wooden door with a circular metal handle.

"Some secrets were never meant to remain hidden." Rianne ordered the sword to rest again, and it floated back into the corset of her gown.

Jordyn's wide-eyed stare only grew wider. "How can you do that?"

Rianne gestured Jordyn forward. "The power of the blood-witches runs through our veins. We come from a line of warriors; we need to live up to that legacy."

Swallowing, Jordyn opened the door. Dank air flooded the basement corridor and cobwebs hung from the ceiling. Rianne entered the windowless room behind her sister. Broken glass crunched beneath their feet. There were no shelves, no furniture other than the large laboratory table.

"It's a poisoner's laboratory. I believe it was our ancestor's," Rianne said.

Rianne followed the wall until she found the crack in the mortar.

She opened the door to reveal stacks of grimoires, ancient ingredients, and tools.

Gaping, Jordyn put the lantern on the table and stood before the secret compartment. "What is all this?"

"It was the makings of a rebellion." Rianne sighed. "War is won by a multitude of means. It's time to ready all the tools of war. The secret knowledge may save your life if you manage not to kill yourself."

Jordyn reached for a vial of swirling liquid, but Rianne gripped her wrist.

"There are forgotten potions in here that could bring down the hellish beasts in the emperor's army. Read first." Rianne guided Jordyn's hand to a grimoire. "I will share it with the others in due time, when they're ready."

Jordyn started to free the grimoire from the layers of dust inside the hidden compartment.

Rianne interrupted. "There's more. Come with me."

With a longing look at the grimoires, Jordyn closed the compartment and followed Rianne out of the room.

In minutes, they were outside and disappearing into the forest.

"Avoid those brambles, they'll catch the gown." Whillow's warnings echoed in Rianne's mind.

"Rock. Grass patch. Rock. Dirt," Milah chimed in.

"Don't step on the twig," Whillow continued. *"Mind the puddle."*

Sticks cracked under Jordyn's boots, as she hastily ducked under branches and tripped on unseen obstacles. "How are you walking so quietly?"

Rianne chuckled, a rare and genuine response. "Perhaps you need more practice."

Vittoria murmured, *"We're being followed."*

Whillow growled, *"An heir."*

Rianne paused. She could not lead him where they were going, and no explanation would suffice venturing out into the forest alone.

Snap.

Jordyn was swinging her legs over a fallen tree when she froze. "What was that?"

"If you recall there are certain protections we could use," Safyrah murmured. *"So many traps in these woods."*

Noxanya agreed, *"It would be so easy. Just lead him that way a little."*

Rianne swallowed. "I can't."

"Can't what?" Jordyn asked.

"It's that or risking discovery," Milah agreed. *"Once they know there's something in the forest, they will tear it apart until they find our secrets."*

Rianne worried at her sleeve. *"Can't we just lead him back to the castle? Pretend we were picking berries?"*

"They'll never believe it," Whillow replied.

Another twig cracked, and the rustling was getting closer.

"Rianne?" Jordyn whispered.

Milah heated Rianne's blood. *"Mercy can only go so far. We've agreed not to kill them all, but this one must die."*

"You promised to trust us, to listen." Vittoria's tone was gentle, but firm.

Rianne wrung her hands. There had been so much death already. Cavendar. Jaekob. The Commanders. The Demorrans in her castle. She was no stranger to violence, but she feared it would consume everyone.

Vittoria sighed. *"It is the cost of war."*

Rianne grimaced as she turned due east, not bothering to conceal her steps. "Step only where I have."

"What are we doing?" Jordyn whispered. "Who is following us?"

"It is important you do as I say. Do not stray from my path," Rianne answered.

Rianne searched the trees. There. A bloodrose vine was wrapped around the branch of a tree, nearly invisible unless you knew exactly what to look for. She scoured the ground until she spied the trap.

Sidestepping it, she glanced back to ensure Jordyn followed. Rianne ducked behind a wide oak tree and waited.

Crack. Snap.

The footsteps neared.

Crash.

The heir howled and shouted profanities. His wails shook the forest, before they quickly quieted into shuddering pleas.

Rianne emerged from behind the tree and approached the pale, sweating victim. He was somewhere between his teens and early twenties—just a boy. He frothed at the mouth as he frantically tried to free his leg from the buried trap. Sadly, the stakes were well-placed, and the poison was already working. There would be no escape.

Jordyn darted out from behind Rianne and knelt beside him. "We have to do something!"

"Nothing can save him now." She forced the guilt from her throat. "That is one of the poisons you will learn to make, and you will find the antidote will never reach him in time."

With a violent shudder, his pleas quieted.

Jordyn sat back into the piles of decaying leaves, looking up at Rianne slowly. "Did you know? Did you do this?"

"Yes."

"How could you?" Jordyn's voice was barely a whisper.

Rianne wanted to say that she didn't want to; that watching the poison destroy his body broke her. She wanted to admit that the memories of the commanders' bodies swinging in the wind clashed against the memories of the sacrificed queens, and both haunted her. Death dampened most of her emotions, but at times, they came screaming through. She wanted to admit that sometimes she no longer knew who she was, and she was drowning.

She didn't say any of that.

The skirts of Rianne's gown spread into an emerald halo as she knelt beside her sister and offered her a hand. "This is war. Mercy isn't a luxury we can afford."

Jordyn searched Rianne's face and eventually took the offered hand. "Are we at war with our own people?"

"We always have been."

Standing, Rianne continued through the forest silently. The rose-bone crown weighed heavily upon her brow, but she'd brought Jordyn out here for a reason. Milah's discerning gaze located a ring of vetiver root, red salt, and white dust.

"We're here," Rianne said.

Jordyn glanced around at the empty, quiet forest. "I don't see anything?"

"Exactly."

Rianne reached for Jordyn's hand and pulled her through the thick air of the witchshield. Loud hammer booms, clanking metal, and voices accompanied the construction laid out among the low-cut tree stumps. Lines of temporary housing filled one corner of the work site beside blacksmith shops and crates of supplies. Serious guards patrolled in tight overlapping rings.

"What is all of this?" Jordyn asked. "And how?" She looked back at the witchshield.

"Witch magic," Rianne said. "They can do impossible things with the right combination of herbs. It's not so different from the magics of our ancestors, even if they claim moral superiority. I was able to convince some witches in nearby villages to create this for me in exchange for certain promises."

"I didn't know—"

"Witches keep their magics well hidden. Several of our ancestors had knowledge of this, or I wouldn't have known either."

Architects with rolled up parchment plans argued with sorcerers as builders hammered large nails into place.

Jordyn turned a slow circle. "What are you building?"

Rianne stepped beneath the shadow of a towering wooden struc-ture inside temporary scaffolding. "War machines."

"This is what you were hiding from the emperor?"

"Among other things," she said. "They've been sequestered here since my return, preparing for war. No one else knows of this place except Rhydian. Upon my command, they will mobilize."

A flash of a furry red tail darted by, before the crimson and black fox leapt upon the crossbeam of a completed trebuchet. It blinked at Rianne with golden eyes.

The fox from the summit?

It was gone moments later.

"This is amazing." Jordyn's awe highlighted the tender age she'd been forced to mature out of. "I can't believe such things exist."

"They're made for killing monsters." Rianne wondered whether the elf was right about her, and that it was only a matter of time before she was one herself.

Jordyn leaned her head on Rianne's shoulder. "Are you okay? Really?"

No.

"Don't worry about me. What more can anyone do to me?"

Back from the forest, Rianne dabbed at the thin line of blood at her throat. The unhealing wound was a reminder that her heart now beat slowly, barely pushing the sluggish blood through her drying veins. Aurienne's words haunted her. *"Who you think you must become, and who you can choose to be are not the same."* Was she choosing right?

Rebekkah scoffed. *"The seer knows nothing."*

"We could test her Sight. We could see just how binding her blood oath is," Morgana suggested viciously.

Whillow chuckled. *"Just a little drop of poison, and Theo would—"*

Rianne choked as dark crimson blood spilled from her lips. Pains wracked her heart and ribs, and she nearly slid from her chair. She gripped her throat as her vision darkened.

"Now look what you've done!" Rianne thought.

"Fine! Fine! We will leave the blacksmith alone. I was just wondering," Safyrah's voice echoed through her teeth.

The pains eased, and Rianne wiped the blood on the back of her hand. Sweat dripped down her brow. The blood oath was not to be trifled with.

"My Queen, a message for you?" a messenger knocked on her bedroom door.

Rianne ripped open the door and took the message with a curt nod to the messenger. She tore open the letter to find three words scrawled on the moon-stamped parchment.

"I'm not amused."

Rianne laughed, and once she started, she couldn't stop. Aurienne must've been absolutely livid to find that Rianne would even consider breaking their blood oath. Rianne could see it, days ago, Aurienne seeing a vision or reading her cards and scribbling the furious message.

Rianne's emotions bubbled through the silver shield of the spirits and overtook her. She held her sides as her hoarse laughs filled her chambers.

"I'm sorry," Rianne called, wondering if Aurienne could See it. "I didn't mean it. Theo is safe."

She returned to her chair and leaned forward on her elbows. It seemed impossible to avoid missteps. As if right and wrong didn't matter because in the end, it was all so tied together and impossible to detangle. Every choice set her on a desolate path, with all roads winding down to the darkest of hells. At the heart of it all was justice and mercy, and what to do about her growing enemies.

Milah pushed to the forefront of the sea of spirits. *"You should kill the commander's sons. The heirs."*

Rianne rubbed her temples. *"We can't kill everyone who ever disagrees with us. There will be no one left."*

Samantah argued, *"We've seen the glint in their eye before. It ended with our blood on the blade of an ax."*

"Let's try to earn their trust," Rianne said. *"I hear you, and at the first sign of betrayal, we'll do it your way."*

Rosalindt whispered, *"Your soft heart will be our undoing."*

Rianne replied, *"I know."*

The queens might be right. She wanted to be merciful, but when had it ever worked? Maybe she should become what they wanted.

Her heart ached for Rhydian, but she'd kept him away to protect him and now he might stay away for good. How could he forgive the things she'd done? The lies? She didn't deserve him.

Her bloody fingertips brushed a line in the cracked mirror. "I don't have much time left, and Rhydian can never know my secrets. I can't hurt him anymore."

Vittoria said, *"Love is more than most of us had. You were fortunate to have any time with him."*

Rebekah said, *"You have a new duty now."*

"I know," Rianne whispered. "The people don't need my blood. They need my blade." She traced the shape of a skull into the broken shards of the mirror.

In life, she was weak. In death, no one could defeat her.

NEVER
CHAPTER FORTY-FOUR

The wishes kept closest to your heart,
Are truths best left unspoken.
One day they all will soon depart,
Never to be remembered again.

— WOES OF THE HEART, A BOOK OF POEMS BY
TALIESIA, 508 N.T.C.

1152 N.T.C. The namesake capital city of Avyllon.

Dark circles lined Aurienne's eyes above her gaunt, pallid cheeks. Her heart was numb. If she had allowed herself to cry, she never would've stop. Pulling a thick shawl around her shoulders, she stared at her reflection.

After this, she may never be able to face herself again. Even now, she hardly knew who she was looking at anymore. Deciding who lived and died. Forcing people to make terrible choices in the name of fate. Calling upon forces she could never hope to control. Turning to necromancy and dark magic. And now... now she had to do the thing that might break her.

Her cards showed her the terrible truth.

If she and Theo fell in love, it would only end in death.

Goddess—please don't let it be too late.

Even at the Foretelling Rite, she'd seen Theo's fate, held him dying in her arms before she even knew his name. Now, her dreams were plagued with horrible images. She choked on blood as he drove his sword through her heart before he fell to the ground—dead.

It'll be me or you, and it won't be me.

She could accept that he killed her one day; it was only what she deserved, but she couldn't stand him hating her or, worse, him dying because of her. She'd been warned before by the Fates but paid it no heed. Foolishly, she let her heart guide her judgment and now Theo might pay the price.

"I will die before I allow that," she whispered. "I will let my soul burn in the hells before I take anything else from him. I've already asked too much."

Taking her golden athame, she pricked her finger before placing her hand on the mirror and smearing the offering of blood.

"If I do this, you must protect him." She stared at her reflection, waiting for an answer.

Her door opened, and Theo strode in. "I gave the orders. We leave for the isthmus tomorrow. This is my last night in Avyllon for a long while."

She watched his reflection sit on a chaise and rake his hands through his hair.

Aurienne clenched her fists until her long nails dug bleeding gouges into her palms. Pivoting on her chair, she turned to face him.

He looked up, and his eyes rested upon her.

It has to be done.

His gaze narrowed as he clenched his jaw. Sitting up straight, he squared his shoulders. He always could read her face too well.

"No," he said firmly.

Her lips parted to speak, but he interrupted her.

"No," he repeated.

"Theo—"

"No. I already know what you're going to say. You've done this before. No."

"But you don't—"

He threw up his hands. "You're going to say fate doesn't want us together. We've been through this. I'm tiring of you finding excuses to run away when it's plain that you want to be with me as much as I desperately want to be with you."

"The Fates are warning me against this," she said. "I would be a fool to disregard them. You've seen my other visions come to pass. You know these omens are not to be ignored."

"Your visions don't always come true, and there are many paths to the same future," he argued.

"Fate demands that one of us will die." She searched his gaze, trying to impart understanding to help him accept this. "And it won't be me. They won't let me die so easily."

"Then I die." He took her hands. "None of us may survive this war anyways. Perhaps I die either way, and the Goddess is merely warning you of it. Or the Fates are wrong. Or we both die together so the war can be won. I would take a few precious moments with you over a lifetime alone. Be it a day or a week or a month, we matter."

She studied him sadly. "Not more than the fate of the world, Theo."

"Don't you feel this. When we're near, when we touch." He squeezed her hands. "It's magic that transcends time or war or fate. This is bigger than all of that. Our souls know one another, recognize one another. We're meant to be. Believe in us."

She did. Goddess, she did. More than he would ever know. In only weeks, he made her remember what it meant to live, that life mattered. He'd given her hope and woken her heart from its eternal slumber. Unfortunately, Aurienne knew her life had a singular purpose, and Theo was too good to be washed away in the wake of her endless destruction.

"Fate has other plans for us," she said.

"You just won't take a chance on me."

Her voice quieted to a whisper. "In my visions, I watch your face contort with hate as you drive your sword into my chest, over and over again. One day, you'll see me for the monster I am and realize how cold this heart is, and you'll only view me with disdain. I can't..." She swallowed.

She found his gaze with her own, pleading with him to hear the words she would not say within those she spoke. "I don't want to watch you grow to hate me."

"That can't be the reason."

"Every time I close my eyes, I have to experience your death." Her voice broke. "The visions are as real as you are now. I feel your hot blood between my fingers, and your last breath on my cheek. I watch the life drain from your eyes as I hold your cooling corpse. Do you know what that's like? Living and reliving your death over and over. And each time it comes with a warning: that your death will be *my* fault. Could you live with that? Watching me die every night?"

He said nothing.

She looked away, hating herself for being what she was. "I won't let you die."

"It's not your decision to make for me."

"Could you do it?" she demanded. "If it were the other way around, could you live with my blood on your hands?"

He worked his jaw.

"I won't apologize for doing this to save your life," she said.

Your life matters even if mine doesn't.

She knew he wasn't going to let this go, it wasn't his nature. He would fight and fight until it killed him. She was going to have to break him to save him.

"Fine. I've been trying to let you down easy, but here's the truth," she said. "I never really cared about you. Fate just needed you, and it still needs you."

One day you'll forget my name and have the life you're destined to have. If you must hate me, at least you'll be alive to do so.

He stepped back as if her words knocked him back.

"I don't believe you," he said. "You don't mean it."

She willed him to believe her. "Fate wants you to fight this war, and it was my job to push you into doing it. So I did, by any means necessary. You believed what you wanted to believe, and I just let you. The truth is, you're not worth dying over."

Already the contempt crept into his eyes, and her heart ached.

"Are you serious?" His voice raised. "You set me on an impossible quest to gather our allies for a summit with no guidance of how to accomplish it. You let me fall for you with every conversation, every kiss, every quiet moment. Then you break my heart and abandon me halfway through to figure it out on my own. I freed nightmares for you. Every life the vampires take, every drop of blood they consume is on my hands. Not yours. Mine. And the Mooncursed... I had to watch our friends get torn apart. And then at the Titan Cliffs... I might've murdered someone in cold blood. Then you steal my future by naming me king during a war. Where I locked thousands in an arena to die. You've asked so much of me."

"I have, and I don't regret a thing," she said. "I'd do it again."

They stared at each other for long moments, breathing hard and glaring.

"You are as cold as everyone believes," he said.

She willed him to believe her, pouring all her anger and intention into her voice. "I'm never going to love you."

"I wish I'd never met you," he muttered under his breath as he stormed toward the door.

Each word stung. She pressed her hand against her chest, hoping to dull the sharp pain of grief lodged beneath her ribs from his words. Her eyes prickled with unspent tears.

"Theo," she called.

His knuckles were white on the door frame as he stopped, looking back as if he willed her to say something, anything to keep him there. A glimmer of hope lingered in his gaze, yearning for her to beg him to stay. Goddess knew she wanted to. She simply couldn't. She wouldn't survive if her weakness doomed him to a painful death.

Aurienne looked away as she spoke another raw and painful truth. "I wish you'd never met me too."

PART THREE

INTERLUDE

Praise be to Niamh for her many blessings. Our devotion is unwavering for we are the heart of the goddess, and we bind ourselves to her in this world and the next.

— PRAYER OF THE FAITHFUL.

1153 N.T.C. The heart of the Demorran Empire, in the capital city of Rexila.

Soul-bound priestess Maddelena pressed the Nyx'elan crystal ring in her forehead to the cool temple floors. The glowing brand was a sign of her enduring loyalty and devotion to Niamh—the one true goddess.

"May the faithful of Niamh receive everlasting blessings," Maddelena intoned. "Bless the favorite son, the wolf emperor is the head, for he speaks with the voice and wisdom of the Goddess. The united Demorran army is her mighty hand of justice. Our ancient protectors are her teeth in the world. The sorcerers are her lifeblood, granted the gift of her magic. The priests and priestesses, we are doubly blessed for we are her heart."

She lifted her head, the ring casting light on the floors around her. "Together, we shall bring forth the body of Niamh."

Another priestess kneeled beside her, pressing her own purple brand into the floor to complete the unbroken daily cycle of prayer. "Niamh, grant us your wisdom."

Maddelena stood and backed away from the sculpture of Niamh's likeness, her head bowed. She took slow steps, feeling woozy. She always felt unsteady after her prayers, but it was to be expected. Prayer was the closest a mortal could get to the divine without entering the innermost sanctum that housed their goddess spirit. Returning to the mortal coil taxed the body.

The light of Maddelena's crystal flickered, and she quickly glanced at her fellow priestess to ensure the other didn't see it. Their light should never waver else their faith faltered.

My light was once so strong, what happened?

Was it her dreams? She shuddered at the horrible images that plagued her. Purple chains connecting every altar and offering bowl in the city, coating in dripping blood. Shadows opening like doorways. Mountains of bones. Twisted and corrupted beasts lurking the streets. Worlds crashing into one another in fiery infernos.

Her light flickered again.

No! They're lies!

All lies.

Maddelena immediately dropped to her knees, pressing her forehead to the ground in prayer.

Flicker.

Blessed Niamh would never allow those horrible images. She protected her people. In the span of months, she'd allowed the emperor to unify the warring tribes to avoid such violence, such want, such pain. None went hungry. Her glimmering city was a beacon of peace and bounty. It was justice and mercy. All things in balance.

Flicker.

My life was meaningless before Niamh. She gave purpose and clarity. I do not doubt her. I am not worthy of her blessings.

The light of her brand steadied, casting shadows on the rune-etched walls. She raised her head, relief coursing through her.

Finally standing, she straightened her iridescent gown, fingers brushing the painstakingly stitched runic patterns. The thread of marbled onyx, diamond, and gold was reminiscent of the titan ore worn by the noble Male'una'di. The ancient creatures had been called forth by Niamh so she may bring the world under her protection and blessings.

Suppressing a shiver, Maddelena continued. Today was a glorious day. Niamh had deigned it time for the acolytes to ascend to priestesshood. She could not allow the doubts darken this day. The time for the binding ceremony was upon them. Her skin prickled with anticipation. Today, she would see the face of her goddess. The glorious light would fall upon her unworthy countenance as the acolytes received her gift.

She hoped her light didn't falter before all of them. No matter how much time she spent praying, her brand's light did not shine as brightly as before the summit. She rubbed the back of her hand where the elf they called Grimfall brushed her skin. Had the elf laid a curse on her?

If a curse had been laid, it would explain the dreams.

Her pulse quickened. She should immediately tell one of the other bound priestesses and be brought to Niamh for cleansing. The bell sounded again. There was no time. She would have to be cleansed after the acolyte binding.

Maddelena approached the inner sanctum of the goddess. Few entered it, aside from the binding ceremony. A line of eager acolytes waited with flushed cheeks. Their lives were about to change forever. She smiled, watching them.

The doors opened on their own, and the bound priestesses

entered first. They filled the grand room, facing the waving curtains on the platform. White incense swirled near the floors.

Male'una'di and their wardens were posted near Niamh's dais. The towering, pristine wolves watched them with keen eyes.

"The time for binding is upon us." The goddess' voice was sweeping and musical. "Those with the most devotion will be chosen to be bound to the goddess for all time."

Caught up with emotion, Maddelena held her breath as a vision of Niamh emerged from the curtains.

Ten feet tall, Niamh herself was a rare beauty. Ethereal. Rainbow glimmering skin that changed colors. Fluffy feathers wound into her hair. Her large eyes blinked slowly, watching them all. Her limbs moved with a divine grace. Not fully in their realm, she faded in and out of sight.

A wave of power raced through them in shockwaves, and Maddelena's mortal eyes were opened to the beautiful violet vines connecting the city to Niamh, extending her blessings. The crystal ring connected them to her, drawing them closer. Tears slipped down Maddelena's chin.

The power in this room was tangible. She was not worthy to breathe the same air as a goddess.

Her hand began to ache—the hand the elf had touched. Her vision swam, head pounding. She gasped as her pulse spiked. She should have warned the others before she came into this room of her curse.

God's blood—I've brought the curse into the sanctum of our goddess.

Niamh placed the crystal circle upon the brow of the next inductee, the ring working its way into the woman's flesh.

The goddess glanced toward Maddelena For a terrible second, a purple shimmer twinkled across Maddelena's vision.

The illusion dropped all at once, and Maddelena's heart froze.

The color drained from Niamh's divine countenance, leaving her gray and dull. She had long teeth and ears, with spindly claws for fingers. The feathers in her hair were ratty. Her eyes sloshed liquid silver.

She was no goddess.

Maddelena bit her tongue until it bled to keep from screaming.

Twisted, knobby purple ropes floated in the air, magically connecting each bound priestess to Niamh. The light pulsed from the priestesses to the demon—as the devil devoured it. Each priestess dulled as the light left their body. Maddelena nearly choked, looking down at her own bulbous tie, watching her light pulse within it.

She's using the Nyx'elan brands to steal our life force.

Inside, Maddelena *knew* she was finally seeing the truth. This was no curse. No twisted nightmare. The elf's touch had somehow broken an enchantment, and Maddelena was no longer blinded by pretty lies.

Tears poured down her face, but she couldn't force herself to move.

Niamh pressed another crystal ring into a woman's forehead, and she didn't move as it settled into his flesh. Blood dripped to the floor, but the enchantment must have numbed her, as it had Maddelena and the others. Why they never noticed how painful and invasive the binding was. Immediately a purple cord connected the woman to the so-called goddess. The light of her soul began slowly following the cord back to Niamh.

The next acolyte, a well-muscled woman, was not found to have enough devotion and was led toward the same corridor where the two sisters from earlier had gone. She could now hear the faint screams from that direction. Perhaps the rumors of people being turned into monsters was real. Tears continued to fall as reality slammed back into her.

The next acolyte was not found to have enough faith and was led behind the curtains. Blood sprayed the linen, and Niamh opened her gaping maw to swallow the woman's light whole.

This was evil, corrupted magic. Slowly, Maddelena backed away. She had to leave.

The crystal ring in Maddelena's forehead grew hot. She screamed as it seared her skin, crackling and pouring out angry light. Niamh's gaze snapped to her, as did every other bound priestess in the room.

Then her crystal snapped in half, and the enchantment fully evaporated.

Reality crashed into her like a wall of stone, sending her staggering backward at the horrors she now faced.

The male'una'di on the outside of the room became clear. Gone were the noble, silent beasts, and in their place were horrible, contorted creatures.

Mooncursed.

The stories were true. A long, low whistling noise mixed with a howl slipped from one of their uneven mouths. Its fur was matted, and bloody drool dripped from its broken fangs. The bony spurs and titan ore plates screwed to its body seeped dark blood that pattered to the floor. She nearly wretched. It met her gaze, and she could hear it screaming in her mind.

So much pain.

The other priestesses had hazy, unfocused gazes. Blind to their reality. They looked upon her with confusion. The acolytes poured blood from their foreheads as their energy was sapped by Niamh.

Blood flowing down her own forehead, Maddelena backed away from the horrors in the room. The truth of what she'd been doing gripped her with icy claws.

Niamh's hoary gaze snapped toward her, resting upon the broken brand in her forehead—signaling her escape.

"Seize her!" Niamh growled.

Maddelena ran.

THE TRENCHES
CHAPTER FORTY-FIVE

We all bore scars of those years, both body and mind.

— THE KING'S JOURNAL, DATE UNKNOWN.

1153 N.T.C. The Contested Territory of the Terre Isthmus.

FIVE MONTHS LATER.

Swords clanged as blood-stained mud squelched underneath Theo's boots. The battle raged. The snarling, six-legged Mooncursed bear-lion hybrid circled him with a maw that could easily crush a skull, gnashing its rows of incisors. The titan ore collar and plates gleamed in the afternoon sun underneath patches of matted brown fur. One of the legs had been hacked at the elbow, now connected only by a sinewy rope of flesh.

Theo's sword arm burned. He rolled his shoulder, trying to keep the screaming muscles loose. Finding a firm patch of soil, he paused and waited for the beast to lunge as they always did. It roared and leapt. He drove the Sword of Souls upward into the beast's protruding rib cage. Fangs and claws raked for him, and he narrowly dove out of the way, rolling through the mud.

Cursed things.

He spun and barely got his arm up before the beast was on him again, snapping inches from his face and tearing at his metal armor with three of its legs. Meaty, foul breath heated his face as the Mooncursed drove him backward through the mud. Twisting, he brought the sword up and sliced at an approximation of where its neck would be before slipping away.

The beast shrieked and shook its head. Theo glanced toward the nearby tree line, glimpsing the warden urging the Mooncursed on. Theo's gaze narrowed as he picked up a fallen ax and hurled it toward the warden. It struck her deeply in the chest. She was dead before she fell.

Theo turned back toward the Mooncursed, now glancing around the raging battle with an unfocused look. Without a warden, it was just as likely to attack its own as it was to attack Theo's soldiers, but it was dangerous, nonetheless. Theo gripped the enchanted, glowing sword with both hands and brought it down on the Mooncursed. The enormous head rolled away.

On the next hill, Rhydian slashed at three Mooncursed. Each bled from a dozen shallow wounds that could have been lethal. Pulse racing, Theo charged through the fighting, the bodies, and heavy mud. As he was nearly to the beasts barely holding onto life, Nesryn leapt over his head and cut all three down in a single slash of her starlight sword. They fell before they could scream.

"Where were you?" Rhydian snapped at her.

Theo took a deep, steadying breath and slowed to a jog.

Nesryn nodded toward the corpse of a colossal stone giant surrounded by thirty downed Demorran soldiers and several wardens. "Busy."

She narrowed her gaze upon Theo. "Still haven't worked out how to tap into your sword's power?"

Not for lack of effort.

Tensing, he shook his head.

"Without the magic, it's nothing more than a sharp hunk of metal." She huffed and stalked away.

Rhydian came to stand beside him. "You're bleeding."

Theo squinted at a jagged wound on his shoulder and a matching one on his hip. "It's nearly night. I'll get it looked at then."

"The vampires should be out soon," Rhydian said. "We should call the order to regroup back at camp and count our losses."

Theo surveyed the crude barricades stretching across the isthmus, watching the movement of the various units. The building-sized stone giants were already lumbering back behind the Demorran wards as the Mooncursed slipped into the trees and the human soldiers slowly retreated.

"They're already heading for the wards for the evening, ahead of the vampires' arrival," he said. "We might as well head back to camp. Hopefully, there's hot stew waiting for us—"

An air-splitting, crackling hiss preceded an immediate drop in temperature that froze Theo's blood. Theo and Rhydian exchanged a glance, knowing it could mean only one thing.

A Shadow.

Mooncursed were bad enough, but even they paled in comparison. As fast as vampires and bloodthirsty as Mooncursed, Shadows nearly destroyed the continent a thousand years ago. Instead of beasts, they were nearly human—which was somehow worse. Theo had seen the aftermath of entire units cut down, the rare survivor describing a sound they'd never forget. He swallowed before looking for Nesryn who'd already vanished again.

"Hellsdamn it," Theo muttered.

An otherworldly, throaty wail echoed across the plains. It pulsed, bouncing from the lowest tones to a sharp crack. Theo winced, and reached up to his ears, finding blood.

He hefted his Sword of Souls while Rhydian readied his sword and ax. They searched the nearby hills for the source. Theo's blood pounded in his head and sword arm, as chilly spikes of fear raced down his spine. He had to remind himself to breathe.

A strangled scream, and then two more, turned Theo's focus toward a rolling hill just beyond theirs.

Rhydian hissed, "Where's that damned elf when you need her?"

Nearby troops shouted to one another. "Protect the king! Protect the king!"

Eight soldiers formed a line before Theo and Rhydian, calling for reinforcements in shaky voices.

The Shadow crested the hill, its gaze trained directly at them. Theo realized it was a man, painfully thinner and taller than any found on the continent. His features distorted into twisted, slithering shapes beneath the shifting charcoal skin. Gleaming, black oversized eyes regarded them coolly. He reminded Theo somewhat of the nameless spy, except the wraithlike spy was entirely noncorporeal, and the Shadow flickered in and out of existence.

Twin rings of pure darkness orbited the Shadow's torso, crossing over his chest at the front and spine at the back. He bared his shortened fangs in a cruel, anticipatory grin.

Theo wasn't sure what he'd been expecting, but after the monstrous, animalistic Mooncursed, it wasn't this. In fact, the Shadow looked eerily similar to—

The Shadow moved, as if too quickly for reality with part of his body remaining behind his soul for a fraction of a second.

Theo reacted instinctively, sidestepping and bringing up his glowing sword. The Shadow's daggers pinged off Theo's sword, sliding instead into the heart of the soldier at Theo's flank. She fell to the churned mud without a sound. Blindly, Theo brought his sword up again, covering his open ribs.

Clang, clang.

The daggers bounced off the sword.

He willed the sword's magic to awaken, but it remained inert in his hands.

The Shadow slid to a stop, body and spirit finally catching up to one another. "*Rei'i*," he hissed. "*Te'fata eaci'jam te'cric raltas.*"

The Shadow appraised him before lunging. Theo stumbled back, trying to bring his blade to bear. He knew he'd be too slow. The Shadow moved nearly as fast as vampires, faster than Theo could even see.

Rhydian's ax stopped the darkened daggers mid-strike before he ducked a pitch-black flaming orb of magic aimed at his head. Rhydian didn't hesitate to slash upwards with his sword, keeping it hidden behind the ax until the last moment. The Shadow nearly didn't see it. The sword caught the Shadow's forearm before it half-teleported several yards away. Blackish gray blood dripped to the churned mud and grass.

"*A'dart etrem atua'me ufri,*" the Shadow promised.

Rhydian tore across the distance, blades raised.

"Attack!" Theo ordered to the troops flanking them.

Theo darted in, slashing and slicing in the most complicated pattern Rhydian had taught him—praying the glowing sword would respond to his will. Rhydian danced around the shadow, ax and sword blurring in a brutal flurry of steel. Seven soldiers tried to attack, but the cursed daggers cut through their weapons. One soldier fell and then another, and his sword remained dormant.

"Back!" Theo cried.

The soldiers continued to fall as Theo barely managed to keep his sword between himself and the Shadow's relentless onslaught. A dagger caught Theo from underneath, piercing the armor on his shoulder. Theo twisted his sword underneath a strike meant for his throat as Rhydian slashed low and caught the Shadow in the leg.

Rhydian charged again, and the Shadow deflected his blades with one dagger, but caught him in the chest with an elbow strike that hurled the Warbringer across the plain.

Rhydian rolled several times before crumpling into a heap. He struggled to stand and stumbled toward Theo while gasping and holding his chest.

Panting, Theo stood amongst the corpses of his fallen soldiers, facing the Shadow down. His sword arm burned with effort. There was no defeating the Shadow. Just like the stories, they appeared from nothing and once their dark work was done, they returned to nothing. He wasn't sure he could take much more.

The Shadow teleported away, spinning the daggers between his fingers. "*Mec'ul tn'aroved aerbenet.*"

Theo gritted his teeth and forced himself to stand tall. He faced death daily these last months, but he never feared it as much as in this moment. Outmatched. Helpless. Magicless. He knew it was inevitable.

Rhydian staggered forward. Theo prepared his next, and possibly last defense. The Shadow darted forward, soul and body splitting in the attack. Theo brought up his sword.

Nesryn appeared between the Shadow and Theo. "Enough." Her voice rang out across the bloodied field.

The Shadow froze mid-teleport, its face contorting into an ungodly expression. It surveyed Nesryn for long moments.

Nesryn's expression was tight. "*Jur'mt'ne gl'dio tdot'su mar'ret.*"

The Shadow dragged its fingernail through the air, slicing the sharp, cleanest and smallest Way Theo had ever seen. It snarled at Nesryn before stepping through and disappearing.

Nesryn released a heavy, troubled breath.

Rhydian stormed toward the elf. "Where were you?"

Seeing the crimson glint in his friend's eyes, Theo stepped in front of the Warbringer.

"You are not my only concern, Warbringer." She snarled. "With all your promises of controlling your violence, I should be able to leave you alone for a few minutes."

Shaking, Rhydian roared his frustration before storming away.

With a flick of her sword, Nesryn created an even sharper Way. "I'll track it down," she said to Theo.

"Nesryn, the Shadow, is it—" Theo stammered, searching her gaze for answers.

The steely sheen to her expression silenced him, but he knew what he'd seen.

"Leave it alone, Theo." She vanished.

Surrounded by corpses and blood, Theo's sword hung limply in his hand. These were not foes they could best. Mortals couldn't defeat monsters. This was not a war they could win.

Beside a crackling fire, Theo took another long, angry swig of the potent ale that burned all the way down. The medic stitched the day's injuries closed, and the needle went in and out over and over again. Theo's scars layered over one another now, all various shades of healing. He relished each prick of the needle, knowing he deserved much worse.

The screams outside of human Demorran troops falling to vampires was all the reminder he needed of his sins, and yet they continued to stack up. The Living Stone warrior at the Titan Cliffs hadn't woken yet, still frozen solid stone, and he may never wake. That quiet grouping of houses where he'd found the two young survivors of vampire attacks remained abandoned with the corpses still inside. All those terrified screams in the arena as Avyllonians changed into Mooncursed. The Obermeister he'd allowed to enter, knowing he wasn't infected. Every life that had fallen at his hand these past months weighed on him.

Theo hissed as the skin pulled taut, and he tipped back the leather waterskin until his vision swam.

"Don't tell me our king is squeamish at the sight of a little blood?" One of the Rodarri soldiers around the fire called out.

Theo forced a false smile. "You only get injuries in the thick of battle, besides a little ale won't stop me from downing more Demorrans than the lot of you."

Hearty chuckles echoed from the fire, spreading to the surrounding camps of allied forces.

An Avyllonian soldier leaned forward with a devious grin. "You willing to wager a night in your fancy tent on that?"

Theo snorted. "Go for it. My eyes weren't made for maps and math. I'd prefer a night under the stars any day. Remember, whoever sleeps in there is responsible for the work within."

The soldier chuckled and leaned back. "All yours, Your Majesty."

Theo took another long swig, searching for solace in the tenuous camaraderie with his troops. "That's what I thought."

Rhydian claimed the stump beside Theo and began sharpening his swords and axes.

The needle continued going in and out of Theo's flesh between dabs of seer-blessed moonwater. Not all his injuries were from the afflicted, but the healers were overly cautious. The soldiers were practically bathing in the stuff, especially nearing the rise of the full moon. Theo refused to have another repeat of the coronation day attack. The seers and witches now blessed water all hours of the day to keep a steady supply.

He wondered whether Aurienne blessed any he'd used these months, whether she'd secretly used her visions to aid them. Did he cross her mind as often as she did his? Had she shed any tears for him, or was she truly as heartless as everyone believed? He should've listened to her warning that she would never love, but she shouldn't have led him on. His daily battles were a constant reminder that she just needed him to fight this war. If only he could stop thinking about her.

Just stop breaking my fucking heart.

"You owe me another coin," Rhydian said. "You're thinking about her again."

"I wasn't," Theo lied.

"Your brows do this thing, and then your mouth does this other thing whenever you're thinking of her." Rhydian made twirling gestures with his hand toward Theo's face.

Theo grunted.

"All done," the medic said. "Here's another flagon of moonwater.

Be sure to douse your wounds in the morning. We can't have our king turning into a wolf."

Theo nodded his thanks, tipping back the flask one more time. He slipped slowly for an hour, chasing the delicate balance of keeping his thoughts muddled while still waking up without the headaches.

Eventually, he crawled onto his cot and fell into a restless sleep full of nightmares and regrets.

In his dreams, he was at the Foretelling Rite watching Aurienne sink into that ceremonial pool, drowning. He turned away and let her die. In another dream, a great chain barred the vampires into their mountain tomb. With his Sword of Souls, he cut through it and released a wave of darkness that blocked out the sun. Avyllon's walls fell beneath a mountain of cursed bones. The titan ore collar on the Living Stone man turned into a serpent and struck. Dream after dream, twisted versions of reality collided with sinister memories.

Ghastly ghosts watched him from mirrors and pools.

Golden tethers of fate wrapped around his throat until he suffocated.

His bones cracked; claw and fang emerged as he became a wolf.

The first light of dawn peeked over the mountains, chasing away the dark thoughts that haunted Theo's forlorn nights. He rose, feeling the stretch of fresh stitches and healing scars, and the throbbing of overused muscles. From daybreak to nightfall, he'd fought hard every day since Aurienne broken his fucking heart to pieces. He'd been used to hard labor at the farm and forge, but this pace was relentless.

Rolling out his neck, Theo buckled his pauldrons, breastplate, and bracers. He exhaled long and low, before ripping off a piece of jerky with his teeth. Another endless day of fighting.

Rhydian and Nesryn entered the tent, wearing dark expressions that told of another quarrel. Rhydian was nursing a purple bruise on his jaw, and Nesryn flexed her hand absently.

They're going to tear each other apart.

"The vampires have gone for the day, and the Demorrans are beginning to push across the isthmus again," Rhydian said tightly.

Theo sat on a stump, pulling on his boots and shin guards. "How far did the vampires push them back last night?"

"Not far enough," Rhydian said. "The men are already taking positions beyond the barricades to hold them back."

Theo shook his head. "We can't keep doing this. Hundreds die as we exchange just a few miles back and forth. Our armies barely hold their ground during the day and the bulk of their army hides from vampires behind their wards at night. And his armies seem endless. The emperor can keep throwing bodies at us until we fall. It's ended up in a brutal stalemate we won't win. And for what?"

Aurienne was wrong. There was no winning. There was no surviving. He hated that he'd ever trusted her.

"One of the provisions caravans from Avyllon was attacked," Rhydian said. "The seers must have seen enough to send them in batches, but we need to request a replacement."

Supplies and troops were running low. Theo hung his head in his hands. "We've got to do something, or we won't be able to hold out much longer."

Shaking off the misery, he stood and strapped the Sword of Souls to his side.

Nesryn's crystalline voice caught him by surprise. "The winds are changing."

The elf's gaze flicked toward the entrance seconds before a soldier stepped into the command tent and hastily removed his dented helmet.

The soldier extended a hand with a gold-adorned missive. "Your Majesty, the High Seer has requested your immediate return to Avyllon." He glanced at Rhydian and Nesryn. "The three of you."

Forget-Me-Nots
Chapter Forty-Six

Divination cards are a powerful tool to open the mind and focus the gift of Second Sight. Powerful seers can infuse their own soul's essence into their deck, but this should never be done lightly. These cards could end up with a mind of magic all their own and would no longer be controlled.

— Cards of the Triple Goddess: A Study of Divination Cards by Seer Delthenea Ivyvein, 997 N.T.C.

1153 N.T.C. The namesake capital city of Avyllon.

Earlier that day.

Months passed since Theo left, and in that time not a single vision came to Aurienne. The depleted well of magic filled and filled, yet the Fates remained silent. Her entire life, even before she could remember, the visions came daily, hourly. Now nothing. Occasionally, visions tickled the back of her mind, but she kept them at bay with meditation and doses of dampening lavendiir palm tea. Her soul needed to heal as much as her body. The eerie silence left her alone with her dark thoughts and darker regrets.

The gardens outside the palace had become her refuge as she resorted to the nature magic of the witches. When she wasn't blessing moonwater or organizing war efforts, she strolled through the midnight blue ghost orchids, indigo poppies, and orange fire lilies, tracing her fingers across their petals. Bubbling fountains and quiet ponds were tucked between the weeping willows and red-leaf ash trees.

Settling in the swaying olive-hued Northwind grasses, she smoothed a divination blanket and began to shuffle her cards. With a practiced flick of her wrist, she spread the cards across the blanket.

"We're going to lose this war," she said. "We're losing now. The Flame Pillar is down, and half of Avyllon is left unprotected. Every day the Mooncursed creations are pushing our armies back, and their human armies are hounding our borders. People are dying, towns are burning. We need an answer. A weapon. Anything to help us gain advantage. Please, show me the answer."

She poured cleansing moonwater from a small flask into a rune-carved bowl and dabbed a drop of the blessed water onto each card. Ripping petals from her gathered blue forget-me-nots, she placed a one on the back of each card before smearing them with white ash. The cards quietly hummed.

"I can't rely on the visions or Fates for now," she murmured. "It nearly killed me. But you, I can always rely on you."

Leaning forward, she breathed on the deck and watched as the enchanted paper absorbed the offerings. She collected the deck and shuffled again, listening to the lazy sway of the branches. The cards remained cool and dormant, but she continued to shuffle.

"I've given you offerings of the four elements. You've taken my blood, sweat, and tears. What more can I give?"

Her hands dropped to her lap as she stared wistfully at the peaceful gardens.

"You're all I have now. I've never had a family. The seers fear and avoid me after what happened to Evani, even Saryll and Syaoran keep their distance. Adonis has pulled away. I cannot look to the Fates. The Goddess has been silent. And Theo..."

Theo.

She sighed. "I've given my life to undoing my birth prophecy. Don't let it be in vain."

Silence.

"My only friends. The only constant in my life that I can always count on. Even my magic has failed me. I've given all I have." She touched the cards to her forehead. "Please, can I count on you?"

The cards began to buzz loudly and tremble in her grasp. They tore free of her hands and rose into a hovering swarm of black and gold. A gasp escaped her lips as sixty-three grinning cards floated above her.

Blood of the Goddess.

The cards shot like arrows toward the palace. Aurienne scrambled to chase them, tripping over shrubs and grasses.

The cards soared inside, flying through the royal halls.

Aurienne's eyes remained trained on the deck, and she bumped into a maid carrying a stack of linens.

"Sorry," she called.

She passed several groups of people, who stopped to point at the enchanted deck soaring overhead.

They flew up the grand griffon staircase. Lifting her heavy skirts, she skipped stairs as she ran. She heard gasps of shock and footsteps behind her but focused on keeping them in sight. They paused for the briefest moment, suspended in the air, before sliding under the door to the war room.

Aurienne flung open the door to see her entire deck hovering over the carved table map in a rotating, perfect circle. One card plummeted and stuck into the wood. The rest of the cards floated to the floor.

Panting, she held her still-bruised ribs and crept forward. The card had sliced into the wood and was stuck in a location on the map, nestled between the border of Avyllon and Rodarri.

"Thank you," she whispered to her deck.

Behind her, a crowd of seers, guards, palace attendants stared at the quivering card.

Aurienne glanced toward an open-mouthed messenger. "Send for Theo."

Now.

Hours later, Aurienne paced the war room alone, waiting for Theo. He should be here any moment. Her hands shook at the thought of seeing him again, and she rubbed them together to steady herself. She glanced at the card still sticking straight out of the map table. One last chance to save them.

Theo entered, causing Aurienne's breath to hitch. He wore dented and marred leathers splattered with mud and blood, and faded patches revealed where his metal armor ordinarily set. His hand never left his sword hilt, and his eyes darted around the room. Freshly stitched scars on his brow, chin, and hand conveyed tales of what he'd endured these last months.

His gaze settled upon her and roved up and down, and though worry pinched his brow, his tone was flat. "High Seer, you summoned me."

She pursed her lips. "I didn't *summon* you. I informed you that I had information that was best shared with everyone in person rather than by missive."

He crossed his arms and leaned against the ceiling-height solid walnut bookshelves that lined the walls between the clear-glass windows looking out over the fountains and pools of Avyllon. "And you always know best."

The sharpness in his gaze stuck Aurienne in the chest.

Self-righteous bastard. Do you think I want any of this?

Just because she Saw the future didn't mean she always controlled it. She was a slave to it just as they all were, and she was sick of carrying blame.

She darted forward, causing her silk skirts to eddy around her ankles. "*Fate* knows."

"And fate is never wrong?" A challenge danced behind his eyes.

"Not even when we want it to be," she snapped.

She realized she'd stormed close enough his breath tickled her chin, and she could feel his body heat through her gown. Her gaze darted down to his mouth, and his lips parted. They each froze, neither daring to cross the line. Her heart hammered.

Echoing boot steps filled the hall, freeing them from their paralysis, and Aurienne backed away as Rhydian entered the room.

"I'm fine, elf." Rhydian said.

"I saw your eyes, Warbringer, and you are most certainly not fine." Nesryn entered the room on Rhydian's heels. "You need to avoid battle."

"If you haven't noticed, we're in the middle of a war," he shot back.

Aurienne glared at the floor, unsure whether she was relieved or disappointed at the interruption. She glanced toward Theo who avoided her gaze.

Nesryn flicked her long, silvery hair. "A war you're determined to fight until the bitter end, and I hate to tell you, but we are nowhere near the end. If you want to stick around for that hell-queen of yours, you need to listen."

"Don't talk about Rianne that way," Rhydian said.

"If you insist on keeping this up, I will abduct you and leave you to rot in a forgotten cell until you can keep better control of yourself," she said. "The next time your eyes go red, I won't have a choice. You. Are. Too. Close."

Rhydian puffed out his chest, but she stared him down in response. Finally, he shook his head and plopped down in one of the chairs around the table.

Adonis strode in, the golden insignia branding him a full sorcerer on his robes gleaming in the light. Miella, Marco, and General Laurier took their places around the table. Sentinel Kolten followed the last of them in, posting himself behind Aurienne once more.

"Well?" Theo crossed his arms.

"What have you learned?" Adonis asked more gently.

She cast her brother a soft smile. Haunted as he was these days, he was the only one who didn't seem to blame her for their predicament.

Aurienne pointed to the center of the sprawling table map, where a divination card remained embedded in the striped walnut. "The cards have told me that the answer to our next step is there. More than that, I do not know."

The group peered over the table's location—a marshy wildland just outside the small town of Sunfyre.

"What do you think is there?" Sentinel Kolten asked what they were all likely thinking.

"I have no idea," Aurienne admitted. "But we need it."

"We can't keep this up much longer without the Pillars." Theo refused to look at Aurienne as he spoke. "Adonis, would you prepare to take us to the Way nearest the Sunfyre Wilds?"

Adonis nodded but remained silent. He said very little these days.

"We will join you," Nesryn cut in. "It would be good for the Warbringer to be removed from the front for a time."

Rhydian scowled.

General Laurier bowed to Aurienne, "If the king is needed on this quest, I'll return to our army and hold off the Demorrans as long as I can."

"Good luck," Aurienne said—praying her goddess would keep them safe.

Theo glanced toward Rhydian and scoffed. "Great. Another impossible task."

She flinched, his ire catching her off guard. She stilled her features, willing an unreadable mask to appear.

"The answer is there. It's up to you to find it," Aurienne said.

"Enlightening as ever," he replied.

She cut him a glare. "Let me know when you've found the solution."

Theo bowed deeply with a scowl, keeping his gaze fixed upon her. "As you command." He straightened and stormed out of the room, and she could only watch him go.

Why does everything I touch turn to ash?

FRAGILE AMENDS
CHAPTER FORTY-SEVEN

Even death cannot silence the yearning of the soul.

> — *THE CURSED BOOK OF POEMS, AISLINN FURY,*
> *3 N.T.C.*

1153 N.T.C. Castle Rodarr, Rodarri.

Silencing the ceaseless whispers rattling her bones, Rianne watched through the stained-glass window overlooking the cobblestone courtyard where Rhydian, Theo, and Adonis approached. Rhydian dismounted in a single, easy motion and strode toward the guards at her front gate. Longing sliced through the numbness that had consumed her in his long absence.

Hellsdamn it, how she'd missed him.

She couldn't ignore the unexpected butterflies filling her stomach or the way her sluggish blood raced. Five long months passed since Rhydian departed for the front lines with hasty, harsh words leaving a lingering, bitter taste in her mouth. For those five months, she'd been preparing for the invasion they knew loomed just over the horizon. The Mooncursed scouts grew bolder, roaming the wilds and forests in packs. Her auxiliary soldiers drilled and patrolled relentlessly as the threat grew ever nearer. Deep in the forest, her war machines and poisons readied for her summons. Her Queensblood kin trained every day and studied each afternoon.

She never allowed her thoughts to stray to the Warbringer. She told herself she'd put her attachment to him away, that it had faded with the rest of her emotions.

A lie.

Even in death, nothing could fully untangle the hold he had on her. She would love him until she faded away.

Milah murmured, *"Do not forget that he's not yours to keep. You have a greater purpose now. Your heart is not only your own."*

"I'm well aware of my duty," Rianne replied.

Rhydian glanced up at the window, as if sensing her presence. Retreating from sight, she straightened her gown. He wouldn't have returned without important news, and she'd best face it. Taking a measured breath, she withdrew from the hall and approached the courtyard.

With the main gates in her sight, Bram Tavish stepped into her path. Rianne stopped abruptly, her crimson lace skirts brushing the tips of his boots. Barely taller than her, Bram slicked-back his hair while wearing a weaselly expression on his pursed lips. He leaned in, his mulberry wine breath hot on her face.

"The general returns," Bram sneered.

Rianne clasped her hands, fingertips brushing the bonesword corset.

"When are you going to return what is ours?" The venom in his tone bubbled under the surface. "The heirs and I have been waiting patiently these months to have our lands, titles, and regiments. Our patience has been met with silence."

"He makes no effort to hide his disdain. He does not fear us. We should rectify this problem before it's too late," Whillow whispered.

"If seeing his father's boots swing from a noose doesn't instill fear, nothing will," Nicollete hissed. *"Let's end them all before they rise up."*

Straining, Rianne pushed them down. *"Now is not the time to lose more men. When the time comes, we will send them to war with everyone else and let the gods and Fates decide."*

Rianne narrowed her eyes at Bram. "No decisions have been made. Your father and the other commanders committed treason. Before I make any appointments, I must first confirm your loyalty."

"Then why have I heard whispers of the Queensbl–"

"Careful what you say next," she warned.

"Whispers of your *kin* visiting the regions owed to the commanding families," he finished. "Untrained. Unseasoned. Unworthy."

"They are merely carrying out *my* orders. And I do not answer to you." Her words were slow, daring. "I'll make my edicts on my own time and to whom I please."

His voice was low. "You don't want me as an enemy."

"Who are you to question me?" she snapped, feeling the queens bristling within her blood. "You're no one and nothing unless I say. What you seek must be earned, and so far, you're owed nothing."

Barely contained rage twisted his features.

"His muscles tense for a strike," Whillow warned.

Bram took a step forward, hand drifting toward the gilded ornamental dagger at his hip, but Rianne refused to retreat. The bone corset heated under her touch as she readied for an attack.

"You–"

"Take a step back," Rhydian's large frame stepped between Bram and Rianne, pushing the noble backward. "I hope you're not threatening our queen."

Rianne's heart lurched into her throat. That Rhydian would protect her even after everything...

Bram snapped his mouth shut as he was forced to look up toward Rhydian's scowling expression.

"Even *considering* insult or threat against our queen is a poor idea." Rhydian glanced toward Bram's hand resting on his dagger as Rhydian's own hand drifted for his ax. "Because you answer to me."

Bram's lip pulled back.

The Warbringer's tone grew dangerously low. "Do you understand?"

Bram released the hilt. "We were just having a friendly chat." He dark gaze lingered on Rianne. "This conversation isn't over."

"It is for now." Rhydian stepped into his eyeline.

Bram backed away before turning on his heel and stalking down one of the wide, austere halls.

Rhydian turned to Rianne. "He cannot speak to you like that."

"What would you have me do? You disapproved of how I handled his father's treason," she replied.

The muscles in his forearms tensed as he squared his shoulders. "There are many options between kissing your enemy and hanging them without a trial."

She flinched as the comment hit its mark. "What brings you back?"

"I have news."

"I'm surprised to see you," Rianne murmured. "After how we left things."

"I swore to serve you. I keep my promises."

Her heart fell just a little. "I see."

The silence stretched between them. She played with the woven edges of her sleeve.

"I don't want things to be like this between us," he finally said. "Our lives will be too short to dwell on past hurt."

Her breath caught as unfamiliar bolts of hope prickled her pulse.

"We both have our afflictions, and we're trying to do our best in this war," he said. "I won't begrudge you a decision I might've made in your shoes. I've seen what the emperor's army can do and if there was any chance to defeat him, it was worth it. I just want us to be honest with each other from now on. I could've helped you if you'd trusted me."

"My secrets aren't only mine anymore." She lifted her gaze. "But I will be honest with you, I swear it."

He reached for her hand, and for the first time in a long while, she did not pull away.

"I know what you're fighting," he said. "It's not so different from my own curse. Let's fight it together. Just trust me. Stay with me."

She nodded. The words would not come out; she could not agree to something so far out of her control.

Finally, she whispered, "I'll do my best."

Rhydian leaned in and brushed a soft kiss against her brow. She closed her eyes, savoring the feel of his lips. She'd missed the warmth of his skin, the stubble upon his jaw, the smell of him.

Her heart raced. The sensation didn't last as long, and she quietly gasped for air as the crushing numbness stole it back from her. These moments with him were the only ones anymore where she felt alive. And they were gone too soon.

He released her. "Aurienne's reading indicates there's something in the Sunfyre Wilds that can turn the tide of this war. With your consent, I will go with Theo and the others to search for it. Nesryn —" He hesitated. "Thinks it would be good for me to be away from the front lines for a while, but I will return to our troops if you command it."

"If the seer's visions are to be trusted," Samantah muttered.

"Seer's cards take flight with beating wings bleeding, falling," Callysta said.

Rosalindt pushed to the forefront. *"The seer hasn't been wrong yet."*

"Do not trust the words of the Grimfall," Morgana snarled.

Rianne took a steadying breath, clenching her fist within her long sleeves. *"Silence."*

Sweat beaded along her brow at the effort of holding them back. Her head throbbed as her heart thudded weakly. Controlling them grew harder by the day.

Just a while longer.

"Thank you for informing me," she said to Rhydian. "Of course, go with them. Anything that will help us end this."

"When we find it and bring it to Avyllon, I'll return to you," he said.

"I'll be looking forward to that."

He grinned. "Let's go mad together."

Rhydian bowed, taking her hand and kissing the back of it, before returning to Adonis and Theo in the courtyard. They were back on the road in moments, and she watched as their dust cloud faded into the distance.

Milah's presence filled Rianne's skull. *"I've warned you about him."* Her emotionless tone was flat as ever. *"It will only end in disaster and hurt him."*

"I'm done listening to you about Rhydian," Rianne replied. *"You're wrong. When he returns, I am going to give us a chance. I won't let anything keep us apart."*

Milah settled back into Rianne's marrow. *"You'll regret that."*

"Nothing could make me regret loving him," Rianne said.

SUNFYRE WILDS
CHAPTER FORTY-EIGHT

A demon stalks those parts. Feral. Dangerous. Unpredictable. Do not venture to the wilds around Sunfyre village alone.

— TORN SCRAP OF REWARD POSTING.

1153 N.T.C. The wilds outside Sunfyre village, Rodarri.

Acrid fumes poured from rocky volcanic vents surrounded by steaming pools. Standing atop a rocky mountainous outcropping, Theo surveyed the Sunfyre wilds nestled between southern Avyllon and eastern Rodarri. Below, green swamps and impenetrable mangroves filled the valleys where freshwater met stagnant ocean inlets. Theo dabbed his neck as the hot, humid air left salty trails. Only about a hundred miles south of the Heartspring Valley, the thermal vents and hot springs heated the land for miles. Winter storms avoided this valley, leaving it hot year 'round. Yellow crystals nestled in the craggy peaks and fiery orange-yellow leaves on the trees gave the place its name as much as the heat.

The reward posting Theo had taken from the nearby town flapped in the brackish wind. Of course, Aurienne had to send him to a swampy, reeking hellhole with no idea of what they were searching for, but the reward posting might provide some clue—a demon.

"What do you think the demon is?" Theo mused aloud to his three companions.

Beside him, Nesryn narrowed her stormy, silver gaze. "If it's the so-called demon, it could be a firewyrm or a skilled sorcerer." She didn't sound convinced, and that unsettled him.

Theo swallowed, having come just a little too close to a cavern-wyrm when he and Rhydian were trapped underneath the Titan Cliffs. "How big are the firewyrms?"

She gave him a withering look. "Keep your eyes peeled for whatever person or creature that calls this place home. We might be looking for an artifact or monument."

The elf muttered to herself as she crept down the craggy hillside toward the volcanic vents. Theo suppressed a shudder. Nesryn's fluid motions and tendency to appear and disappear at will always left him guessing, and he could never read the expression in her otherworldly, ancient eyes. He'd watch her dispatch monstrous enemies with ease, and he never felt quite safe under her discerning gaze.

Rhydian came up beside Theo. "Well, where do we start?"

Theo studied the map. "The cards said there." He pointed to the heart of the wilds.

"Is that where the demon is?" Adonis asked.

Theo glanced toward the hissing, orange steam vents. "It hasn't been seen for a while. If it exists, it'll be deep in the wilds. Let's be careful."

Adonis shouldered his bag, weighed down by tomes and vials, before following them into the valley.

The rocky path down was easy compared to the steep heights of the Heartspring mountains they'd recently traversed. Before they released the vampires and everything changed. He blinked away the visions of blood and broken bodies, the unrelenting reports of lost loved ones and protests that they couldn't have been criminal, the rising death count.

Adonis and Rhydian were as silent as Theo, each lost in their own thoughts. Up ahead, silver flashes signaled Nesryn's progress. The gravel path led them straight into the heart of the swamp.

Theo's next step splashed down in a hidden murky pool, splattering the steamy water up his pant legs. He pressed his fist against his temple, annoyance burning his tenuous patience to a crisp.

Coldforges and bonedust.

He hated this place. He hated being on another stupid, impossible mission. Most of all, he hated the seer who sent him here. Except, he couldn't really hate her, and that pissed him off even more. He pulled his dripping boot out and shook his foot, stepping onto a twisted mangrove root.

Adonis avoided the puddle, stepping onto the root and across a sandbar separating two pools. His foot slipped on stringy moss, and he stumbled. Theo reached to steady the young sorcerer.

Hissing erupted beside Theo, and he dove at Adonis at the last moment. A geyser erupted where Adonis had stepped, sending boiling water upward. They stared at the lethal green cloud.

"Thanks," Adonis said.

"We'll need to watch for those, and who knows what else," Theo said.

Gods, this really was the worst place on the continent. Is she punishing me?

"You owe me another coin," Rhydian called.

Theo grumbled. He was going to owe the Warbringer a treasury if he kept it up. He needed to forget about her.

"Look at this." Rhydian pointed to a burnt mangrove branch.

"Is that..." Adonis trailed off.

Five smeared lines of ash blackened the bark of the branch at eye-level. Like a small hand. Or a claw. Theo stared at it, feeling his skin prickle. He glanced around, not seeing any other signs of life.

Theo shouldered his sword uncomfortably. "Be ready for anything."

As the hours passed, Theo began to find a pattern to the wilds. Swampy inlet fingers of ocean water were separated by small peaks of lava rock or sand bars. The lava rock was sharp, cutting through the leather of the boots, but it made for the safer terrain.

"Nesryn," Theo called as night set.

She appeared behind him. "What."

Theo nearly jumped. "We're going to make camp."

"Hmphf. Follow me." She stalked due south, splashing through the water and gliding over overturned trees.

Theo glanced at Rhydian before trailing the elf. The ground grew firmer as the stars rose in the sky, and soon they were on nearly solid, flat ground. She stopped in a thick grove of oaks.

"At least it's warm enough we don't need a fire," Adonis quipped.

Theo forced himself to smile in response. It was rare that Adonis ever acted like his old self. Rhydian's sheepish expression was quickly replaced with a grin to match Theo's. Rhydian and Adonis hadn't yet cleared the air, and Theo knew Rhydian was keen to make amends.

"No chance of us getting cold," the Warbringer replied.

Nesryn's expression remained flat, but was it his imagination or did it soften just a touch as she studied the teen?

"I'll keep watch for predators," she said.

Theo glanced at Rhydian. "Does she ever sleep?" he mouthed.

"I hardly need to," she replied.

Theo's eyes grew wide as he quickly put his head down and prepared to camp for the evening.

The muggy heat of the valley barely dipped that night. Theo sat atop his bedroll, chewing strips of dried meat and aged cheese. He finished the meal, sipping only on lukewarm water. Finishing his food, he propped himself against a tree and crossed his arms.

Sleep eluded him.

Aurienne's reading of him curled in the corners of his mind. *"You want to make the most beautiful blades, to fall in love, and live a good life. All of that will happen. And it won't. You shall make the most powerful blade in the world, but it will break. Or it shall break, and then you make it. You will fall deeply in love and lose it, three great loves. You will save lives and take them. You shall live on for centuries, though your death looms near. All of it and none of it. Your fate is sealed."*

He hadn't known it at the time, but her words damned him. He understood none of his destiny, yet, he knew the Fates were far from done with him.

"And if they hate you for what you've done?" Stellan had asked him. *"There is anger and death lingering about your soul. I had the same darkness when I made my deal. Beware of it."*

Theo glared at the stars in the sky. In the quiet of night, his thoughts were too loud. Only battle freed him of them.

"Stop. Can't think. So slow," the stone warrior's words slurred as it ceased to move at all.

The image of the Obermeister pushing past him and strolling toward the arena flickered between the other images. The Obermeister falling to the changing Mooncursed. Theo had known he was not infected and let him go to the arena anyways. Another murder.

The arena.

Theo squeezed his eyes shut.

Godsteeth, it's all too much.

A branch cracked. He stilled, listening for the telltale signs of a creature advancing—more cracking twigs, shuffling dirt, or rustling. None came. He looked to Adonis, who'd already fallen fast asleep inside his bedroll, and then to Rhydian. The Warbringer dozed fitfully, breath catching and limbs twitching. It hadn't woken them.

A sharp hiss cut the night, a geyser somewhere releasing the pressure. He glanced that direction, waiting for more sounds. A breeze rustled the leaves.

Minutes passed before Theo's heart stopped beating so fast. He tried to breathe slowly, forcing the tension from his muscles.

He stared at the twisting roots pushing up trails of yellow crystalline sand from below the dirt.

"You can't rest." Nesryn was suddenly sitting beside him.

He glanced at her. "I keep hearing branches break. Leaves rustle. In my mind, every sound is an attack waiting to happen. A Mooncursed beast about to explode from the dark. A Shadow lurking nearby."

"But that's not what keeps you awake." Nesryn's too-perceptive gaze bore into him.

"No," Theo finally replied. "It's not."

"Be glad the guilt eats at you," she said. "When your acts no longer bother you, then you have cause to worry."

"Do you still regret anything?" Theo asked

She tapped her fingers on her leg. "Not as much as I should."

Standing, she brushed off her leather pants and disappeared into the trees.

Morning came, and Theo readied his pack. He stuffed the bedroll and water flask inside as he gnawed on dried fruit and bread. Shouldering the bag, he stood and prepared for another long day.

Nesryn climbed the tallest mangrove, disappearing up into the twisting viny branches. A flash of red fur blinked through the orange and yellow foliage. Theo approached the base of the tree, glancing up to see the little fox following Nesryn. How had it even gotten here? It didn't come through the Way with them. One day, he was going to figure out who and what the fox was.

Theo turned to Adonis to comment on the fox. Under Adonis' feet, Theo spied a strange spot on the ground he hadn't noticed in the dark. Smeared lines of ash trailed between the trees, as if someone dragged a burning torch. The scattering of the ash told him the trails were old, but what could make that?

He followed the trails toward a grove of orange-leafed trees. Everything smelled of ash.

"Theo?" Rhydian called.

Theo was about to turn back when his boot struck something hard. He bent down, the sand had turned to glass.

Theo stood quickly.

"Over here," he called.

Adonis and Rhydian pushed through the vines and leaves to join him.

"What could have done this?" Rhydian asked.

A rumbling growl nearby shook the ground. Theo drew his Sword of Souls as Rhydian readied his axes. Adonis already had four vials of swirling liquid in his palms. They followed the sound, pushing toward another of the swampy ponds.

Nesryn appeared in front of them, holding up her hand in warning. They stopped. The elf grew unnaturally still, pointing toward a jagged opening in the earth. A volcanic vent spilled steam and molten rock into a briny pool. They must be near the ocean now.

Scrape.

Rumble.

Scrape.

Hiss.

A beast the size of ten horses slithered out of the volcanic vent, sunning its golden scales in the rising sun. The firewyrm shook itself, lifting its nose to the air. The ground rumbled as it shifted its weight.

Adonis paled, Rhydian's eyes were turning crimson, and Theo's muscles shook with adrenaline. This beast wasn't as big as the cavernwyrm he'd seen under the Titan Cliffs, but it was plenty big enough to snap a man in half with its armored jaw. Nesryn waved her hand at them, motioning them back. They backed away slowly.

The firewyrm sniffed, and its head snapped their direction.

"Run," Nesryn whispered.

Theo grabbed Adonis by the collar and ran as the young sorcerer hurled his concoctions at the beast. The vials exploded on its nose and cheek in plumes of smoke, and the beast snarled and hissed.

Running, Theo dragged Adonis with him. Rhydian followed,

keeping himself between then and the firewyrm. Nesryn shouted something, either at them or the firewyrm—Theo wasn't sure. But he'd fought enough Mooncursed to know when they needed to flee. Nesryn might be able to hold her own, but they stood no chance.

Crashing sounds chased them through the groves. Trees fell. Geysers erupted. Blasts of fire from its throat singed whole lines of trees. Its claws raked against the piles of volcanic rock as it narrowed the gap.

"Faster!" Nesryn shouted.

Adonis' collar was up by his ears as Theo pulled him along, the bag with his tomes bouncing across the ground. The firewyrm burst through the trees, sending flames right at them. Theo ducked, shoving Adonis down. The flames rolled over their heads, and Theo was hardly able to breath under the plume of unimaginable heat.

"Stun it!" Nesryn shouted.

Rhydian charged and slammed his ax into the beast's hide. The ax bounced off the scales, and the firewyrm roared again. It spun and slammed into Rhydian, sending him flying. He rolled to his hands and knees, gasping and struggling to rise.

"How do we reason with it?" Theo shouted.

"You don't, you trap it," Nesryn replied.

The firewyrm snarled and opened its maw. Flames shot every direction Theo lifted the Sword of Souls, and it redirected the flames from his face. His stubble was singed, but his skin remained unharmed. Adonis was covering his face with his hands on the ground.

Nesryn leapt out of the trees, slamming her boots into the firewyrm's snout. It roared, backing away and shaking its head. She hauled Rhydian toward them by his arm, running full speed.

Just as she was about to reach them, a flash of flame sped by. It was... a person? Theo blinked, staring at the human flame that darted between them and the firewyrm. The figure spun toward him.

Theo's skin prickled at the new danger. Time slowed as he swung his Sword of Souls at the figure. Nesryn's starlight blade intercepted, preventing his steel from descending on the living flame. The figure ran away, drawing the firewyrm away with it.

Faster than he could blink, Nesryn sheathed her sword and reached for him and Adonis, holding Rhydian's with her other hand.

The world turned dark as Nesryn touched him, and they fell through the Way.

BLOODRIGHTS
CHAPTER FORTY-NINE

This was a city built on bones and death.

— *UNKNOWN.*

1153 N.T.C. The forest outside Castle Rodarr, Rodarri.

Winter sunlight snuck glimmering rays between the canopies over the long laboratory tables set out under the tents. Vials of herbs, glass tubes, grimoires, dried flowers, and other tools were neatly spread down each. Rianne paced down the length of the table, hands clasped against her bone corset.

The hundred or so Queensblood were gathered, wearing simple apron dresses and daggers on their hips. Gone was the ornamentation, the jewels and ballgowns and rouge. Nearly six months of daily training and studying, of doing the accounting and administration for their assigned regions had changed them to the core. They were now ready.

The whispers filled her mind.

Vittoria's voice was loudest. *"We told you they could rise to it."*

"I didn't have to be so harsh with them," Rianne said.

"You did," Milah replied.

"They needed to understand the gravity of what comes," Whillow said. *"You won't be able to save them forever. One day, they will have to save themselves. When that day comes, you'll be glad how hard they trained."*

"Shackles clanking, bars shattering, blood dripping, poison flying, death fills castle walls," Callysta cackled.

Rianne stood at a large cauldron, with the long tables all facing her. The pot bubbled with a charcoal liquid that smelled of bloodroses.

"Why are we out here?" Jordyn asked. "Why not inside the castle?"

Rianne grimaced, thoughts settling upon Bram Tavish and the other noble sons. "Our enemies are everywhere. I do not trust their prying eyes."

"This is the grimoire of our bloodline." Rianne lifted the worn leather book. "It began with Kairya's coven, with our kin Noxanya and Safyrah. Our first queen, Vittoria, gave it to her sister, who gave it to Vittoria's daughter. Bloodwitches through the centuries added their knowledge to it. I have added mine, and you shall add yours."

Glancing toward her sister, Rianne found Jordyn in rapt curiosity. The others watched her carefully, a mix of interest and distrust. Her heart ached, but the queens' spirits quickly numbed her pain.

"Do not regret their fear. Change is never easy," Noxanya said.

Rianne pursed her lips. "It is time I taught you the bloodmagic of your ancestors. You've earned it with your dedication, and we will need your aid to win this war."

Jordyn spoke up. "What do we learn first?"

"First, we test your power to see how much you each possess," Rianne said. "That will tell us the extent of your abilities and guide your training."

She sprinkled dust from a crushed mirror into the cauldron.

"A mirror for truth." She dropped in a few more ingredients.

"Hellebore lily for protection. Witches' tears for grief. A letter between lovers for love. A length of steel hardened by forge and battle for vengeance. A knot of rope for justice."

Jordyn craned her neck, absorbing every detail, quill scribbling furiously.

Rianne collected a pinch of royal cemetery soil from the small vial on the table beside her. Dirt still stained her fingernails from last night's collection. With her other hand, she lifted the obsidian petals of a nightflame flower.

"Cemetery soil to represent death. Nightflame for life," Rianne said.

The two ingredients dropped into the cauldron, the smoke rising to form a skull. Rianne smiled. The testing potion was ready. It only required one more ingredient—their blood.

"Add a drop of your blood to reveal your gift in bloodmagic," Rianne continued. "You all will be able to use it, but some will have more natural affinity. Aunt Yllicea, as the most senior of us, would you go first?"

Yllicea straightened her back and walked toward the cauldron. She sliced her finger, the skin paper-thin from age, and dripped a droplet of blood into the cauldron. Black smoke plumed out of the brew.

"You have a high affinity," Rianne explained.

Her aunt grinned. "I'll put it to good use killing our enemies."

"Her spirit is strong," Whillow whispered.

Rianne motioned to Marta. "Next."

One by one, the Queensblood tested their blood. Nearly half had a weak affinity, and white smoke hardly sputtered out of the cauldron. Twenty-seven had a moderate gift with a misty gray. The remaining twenty-one possessed great power. They were trueborn bloodwitches. Soon, only Jordyn remained.

"Jordyn," Rianne said.

Her sister's eyes were fiery as her mouth set into a hard line. She drew the dagger at her hip and pricked her finger. Squeezing it, she dribbled blood into the cauldron. Flames and dark smoke exploded from the mix, sending the bubbling liquid flying.

Queens ducked behind their tables as the brew hissed and crackled.

Mouths open, they all looked to Rianne. She could not conceal her smile, feeling the warmth of her pride through the numbing blanket of the spirits within.

"Your power rivals that of Kairya and Whillow," Rianne said. "One day you will be one of the most powerful bloodwitches to live."

"When you are gone, she will rule," Whillow whispered. *"She is a worthy successor. Loved by her people, and her power will be respected."*

"Yes," Rianne whispered. *"She will be the queen the people deserve."*

Vittoria's presence wrapped around Rianne. *"A queen like her cannot exist in our cursed land until a queen like you clears the way."*

"I will," Rianne said, pushing away the brittle feelings in her chest.

The others clapped for Jordyn, touching her on the shoulder as she passed by to regain her position at the laboratory table. She was beaming the whole way.

"Those of you with the highest gift hardly need vials or potions at all," Rianne said. "Your will and your blood will be enough to create any curse, any destructive magic you desire. The rest must study the grimoires. The brews within will elevate your magic. Adding your blood will weaken, maim, kill."

Her eyes settled on Jordyn. "Before you are copies of the grimoire. I've had one copied for each of you and prepared it with magic. Place your blood upon the spine. Once you do, it will be locked to you. None can open it but one of our blood. It binds us together as a coven."

The queens pressed their blood against the grimoires, and the air filled with heady magic. The bloodwitches inside Rianne showed her the crimson knots connecting them all now.

"Ours will be the largest coven in history," Kairya said proudly through Rianne.

"Their magic will strengthen one another," Safyrah whispered.

"Open the books and begin preparing deathlung, bloodboil, and other curses," Rianne said. "Create as many as you can. You will come here every day after weapon's training."

The Queensblood bowed their heads and began their work. Curses grew under the golden canopy as the bloodwitches learned their craft.

"I hope it's enough," Rianne murmured.

"If only we'd been able to combine our magic like this before. We might have saved generations," Whillow said.

Vittoria said, *"Alone we are weak, but together we are strong."*

And how much must I fade to achieve this strength? Will any of me remain?

FLAME ELEMENTAL
CHAPTER FIFTY

Elementals once roamed the land, humans transformed by powerful magic into beings of water, fire, earth, and air.

— JOURNAL OF THE SEER RHEIA, DATE UNKNOWN.

1153 N.T.C. The wilds outside Sunfyre village, Rodarri.

Opening his eyes, Theo found they were in a quiet, cool field in the mountains overlooking the Sunfyre Wilds. Nesryn's Way had been so fast and smooth compared to even the Way portals, he'd hardly noticed the journey. The chill of the winter air settled upon him. In the distance plumes of smoke peppered the landscape—the firewyrm's breath igniting the combustible clouds below.

Adonis brushed himself off before rifling through his bag. Rhydian paced, muttering. Casting sharp glances back at the Warbringer, Nesryn perched on the cliffside overlooking the valley below. Theo came to stand beside her.

"Which one was the demon?" Theo asked.

"Either," she replied. "Both. But if I were to guess, the wanted poster was talking about the elemental. Firewyrms are hardly seen above ground these days and only attack if provoked or if their territory is challenged. Besides, people would know what a firewyrm looks like. A flaming human? That sounds more like a demon. It's possible people got too close to the firewyrm, but my gold would bet on them having seen the elemental."

"What's an elemental?"

She stood, crossing her arms. "You've seen them, you just didn't realize—the Living Stone People."

Theo blinked. He should have realized.

"When magic becomes concentrated around one of the four elements, it can turn a mortal into something else. It's rare. There have been none in this world in a very long time, not since the magic grew dormant. Perhaps the Pillars are influencing the magical energies around them. The People of Living Stone near the Earth Pillar, a seafaring nation near the Water Pillar, and now a flame elemental near the Flame Pillar. We may very well find magic coming to life near each as the land readies to defend itself from the corruption of foreign magic."

More riddles, ancient magic, and impossible quests. Why couldn't anything be simple?

Theo glanced back at the valley. "Can the elemental relight the Flame Pillar?"

Nesryn licked her fangs before finally answering, "Yes."

Relief washed over Theo. They were so close to fixing the failure that haunted his every moment. With the Pillar repaired, they would be safe from Mooncursed and Shadows. Aurienne had been right. The answer was here all along. Resentment bubbled inside him.

"If we can find him or her and convince them to help," she said. "I've found that those transformed by the elements tend to be... unpredictable."

"I have practice convincing others to join the cause," Theo said. "Can you take us back down?"

Nesryn cocked her head. "Do you think it easy opening Ways for others on command? Your bodies were not made to go through, they fight the magic. Even I have my limits."

Theo pursed his lips. "Then we'll walk. I think she was headed that way." He pointed toward the coast.

Rhydian approached, finally breathing slower with his eyes back to brown instead of the cursed red. "Let's find the elemental and convince them to join us."

"If you can't, you'll be taming a firewyrm." Nesryn chuckled.

Adonis swallowed as he slung his vial-laden bag over his shoulder again. "How much humanity remains in an elemental?"

Nesryn's small grin faded. "Depends on what transformed them. It's rarely a happy miracle. More often than not, it's a nightmare."

Turning, she scaled down the cliffside in a flash without another word. Her desaturated skin shifted to mirror the pattern of the shadows.

Theo trailed behind, trying to follow the path she'd taken down the mountain. He stepped over a pile of rocks, following the winding game trail between the sparse trees. His boots crunched on the flaky snow, a reminder of the long trek back down to the steamy valley.

As the hours passed, Theo studied the changing landscape. Rocky cliffs gave way to rolling grass knolls as they approached the jungle marshes.

"Where would a flame elemental live?" Theo asked.

He couldn't see Nesryn, but he knew she never strayed too far.

A chuckle rattled the leaves to his left. "Why would I know that?"

"You know just about everything." He glanced toward the direction of her voice. "Including about the Shadows."

Nesryn was right in front of him, blocking the path. His boots slid on the gravel as he pulled up to a stop.

Her voice threaded with a hiss. "I don't know what you think you know, but I suggest you pick your words carefully."

"Why do you speak their language?" Theo pressed.

"I know it because I've been alive a long time." She spun and stalked away. "I won't warn you again. I'm not in the mood for your inquiries."

The prickling on Theo's skin warned him to drop the issue for now, but her continued reluctance to discuss it meant his suspicions might be too accurate. He tried to ignore the far-reaching implications if he was right.

Theo changed topics. "The flame elemental, where does it live?"

Nesryn didn't answer.

Rhydian chuckled.

Theo lifted a questioning brow at the Warbringer.

"You'd never believe it, but I think Nesryn actually likes you," Rhydian snorted.

Theo removed his jacket. In the hours they'd been walking, the temperature had risen back to an uncomfortable level. Steam wafted off the rocks.

"Everything the elemental touches burns," Theo said. "The grass under its feet. The branches that touched its arm. If it was hiding or trying to sleep somewhere without setting a fire, it'd have to sleep in a cave."

"You're thinking a cave near the ocean?" Rhydian asked.

"Not on the beach. There's too much naval travel. The elemental seems to avoid people. Probably one of the secluded inlets," Theo said.

"Let me check the map for places like that," Adonis said.

Stopping near a stump, Theo dropped his bag, stretched his shoulders, and downed his first waterskin. Beside him, Rhydian leaned on a tree, taking his whetstone to his ax blade as Adonis searched the map for landscape that might have caves.

Adonis pointed. "There's a stream that way not too far."

"Thanks."

Theo gathered up their empty waterskin and headed the direction Adonis pointed. Stepping around the hanging mangrove branches, he continued in the direction until he heard the trickling of water up ahead.

He could nearly see the stream when his boot stepped into a stagnant puddle. The scent of salt water assailed his senses. He nearly ignored it until the briny smell mixed with a charred-smoky aroma.

Pausing, he glanced around. The stream fed into a small inlet lapped against the mountain. Perfect for a flame elemental to hide. Adrenaline filled his veins, and his hand went for the dagger at his hip.

He crept toward the scent of flames. It led him to a secluded break in the hillside, covered in shale and rocks. Outside the rocky cave, there was a small fire with a rat on a spit over it. Ash and embers coated every inch of the space. Small animal skeletons lay in a pile.

The scent of hot flames, hotter than even his forges, caught his attention. He released his dagger and lifted his hands.

"I mean you no harm," he said. "You surprised me earlier, but I'm not here to hurt you."

A hunched-over living flame slunk out of the cave. "As if you could harm me."

He took a step closer, keeping his hands raised high. "I'm glad I didn't. My sword is enchanted. It unravels magic."

The figure crouched behind a large boulder, peering at him carefully. "Why are you here?"

Nesryn stepped out from behind a mangrove tree, Rhydian and Adonis at her heels. "You found her."

Her?

The flame elemental stood, and Theo realized it was a young girl —perhaps only thirteen years old. Her entire body was made of fire that never seemed to go out.

"What's your name?"

"Hana."

He nearly smiled. It was progress.

"Hana, we've come to ask for your help," Theo said. "There is a Flame Pillar, a giant monument, at the border of Avyllon. It has been doused. There's an invading army who wants to conquer the continent with ancient magic. If we relight the flame atop the Pillar, it will keep them out. Can you help us relight it?"

She scratched her chin, sending sparks flying toward the grass. "All you want me to do is light a fire on top of some tall building?"

"Yes," he replied. "It seems like a small task for one with your gift."

She crossed her arms. "Give me one reason I should help you?"

"You'll be saving hundreds of thousands of lives. Maybe more."

Hana shrugged and continued to turn the spit over the small fire. "Not sure why that's my problem."

Theo stifled the irritation growing within him. He'd forgotten how infuriating it was to ask people to help save a continent that they themselves had to live on. He forced himself to remain calm.

Nesryn knelt, "You can come with us where you'll never have to be ashamed of your power, with freedom to burn to your heart's desire. You can kill without sanction."

Hana pursed her lips. "I can kill? Without getting in trouble?"

Theo was taken aback. How could one so young possess bloodlust to rival that of a Warbringer, and without a curse to match? What must have happened to her to make her this way?

"Thousands," Nesryn said. "You can burn armies. Mooncursed beasts. Villages. Siege engines. Anything that stands in your way. No longer hiding what you are or what you can do. And you won't be alone. You'll be surrounded by people with magic, with afflictions, with power. Or... you can stay here alone in this swamp eating rats. The choice is yours."

Hana dragged her finger through the mud. "What if they were right to banish me?"

Nesryn grinned, baring her fangs. "If you can't convince them otherwise, then prove how dangerous you are."

"And you just want me to relight this pillar?" Hana let go of the little spit.

"Yes," the elf said. "We want you to burn so brightly that the entire continent sees your light and knows your power. They will know it was you who saved your people and damned your enemies. Your village will know what you've done."

Theo caught on to Nesryn's tactic. "I don't much like people telling me what my destiny is, do you?" he said.

"No," Hana answered with a smile.

"Will you help us relight the Flame Pillar?" he asked.

Hana looked up. "I'll go. And I'll burn them all."

Sunlight and Darkness

Chapter Fifty-One

Vows made on heartwood three,
All impossible to keep.

— High Seer Aurienne Azarrah, prophetic vision.

1153 N.T.C. The forests outside Heartspring.

Beneath the dense cloud cover, the night should have been pitch black. It would have been if not for the young flame elemental setting the clearing alight with orange coils of fire. Stellan hovered in the clouds, watching his prey stray so far from the safety of the group.

Hissing, he stalked her. Theo hadn't even warned the vampire of their plan to find this elemental. They'd left the city without a word, expecting the vampires to protect them like loyal dogs. Stellan knew better than to trust.

And now, he saw what they were after. Anger rippled through him. A flame elemental with the power to burn him. Stellan knew they'd been searching for a way to relight the Pillar for months, and while she'd likely be the key it was a risk he couldn't take. Soon, she'd be just as formidable as Marco, and those he was sworn to protect would be in danger. He could put an end to it right now.

A grin curled his lips.

Little flame all alone.

The hunter with his sunlight tattoos was threat enough, but a flame elemental? It was a risk to his vampires he couldn't take. No one would notice if he snuffed out one little light; they'd find another way to push back the emperor, and no one would ever know what he'd done. The deaths already staining the girl's soul technically met his oath to Miella, even if the stain was yet to be set deeply enough to determine her future.

The only question was how, and it was one he'd been working out for an hour. So young—she had no control over her powers. She was not yet able to turn them off. If he dropped her into the sea, the waves might douse her light, and she'd never escape.

He licked his long fangs. She'd probably burn through him before he could get her there. But... he could command her to walk straight into the sea and she may very well drown, especially if she was susceptible to the hypnosis.

Can flame elementals drown?

It was a slow death, compared to some. Stellan supposed it would be unpleasant business either way, but unfortunately it was necessary. Just one more casualty of war. Finding a downdraft, he silently drifted into the trees and landed. She wandered farther and farther into the dark woods away from the camp. No one noticed. Not Theo or even the elf whose gaze never strayed far from the Warbringer. Not the sorcerer.

Perfect.

He crept through the shadows, no more than a wraith. She stopped in a wooded clearing, staring off into the mountains. He could smell the charring wood of the log she now sat upon. Felt the woosh of the night breeze. His icy skin prickled with anticipation of the hunt. Perhaps he'd try to hypnotize her to extinguish the flames, and he could drain her powerful blood, consume her death. *Delicious death.* Maybe the compulsion would be strong enough to overcome her lack of control.

Close enough now, he dragged his claws through the flames near the nape of her neck. He prepared to lunge.

Soft sniffles broke through the bloodlust brought on by the hunt. He stilled, smelling the salt of her tears.

"I just wish... someone loved me," she whispered. "But I have no one."

He flexed his claws, hesitating.

"But they turned on me, so they all deserve to burn." Bitterness filled her voice. "By the end, everyone will burn."

The words pierced all the way to the sliver of humanity remaining in his heart. The thrill of the hunt fell away. The rushing of blood in his ears faded. His fangs no longer ached. He was left feeling empty.

Drawing back his claws, he took several steps back into the darkness—conflicted. His upper lip curled into a snarl. What weakness was this? All weakness, all hesitation had been stamped out centuries ago. He shook his head and crept closer once more, readying himself to hypnotize her.

With a flap of his leathery wings, he shot over her head and landed in front of her. The girl gasped and nearly fell backward off the fallen heartwood tree. Stellan lifted his hands as non-threateningly as he could with six-inch claws.

"I heard you crying." Stellan sidled closer, keeping his hands raised "May I sit?"

Gaze narrowed, her eyes crackled a burnt red. She nodded finally, wiping flaming tears from her cheeks. He sat at the edge of the log, trying to catch her gaze so she could lose herself in his eyes, and he'd *command* her. Then he'd kill her and eliminate the threat. But she stared at the ground.

"Did you come to kill me?" she whispered, wrapping her arms around herself. "I won't be an easy prey."

How had she known his motives? He tilted his head, trying to look up into her face. It would only take a few moments for her to be lost in his dark gaze. "Why would you ask that?"

"There's a darkness in your eyes that I've seen before. The hate. The fear." She looked up into his face.

Perfect.

Now he could compel her. He began to deepen his gaze, allowing her to fall into his will.

Douse your flames.

"I saw it before my family cast me out," she whispered. "So I would understand if you did."

"What?" he asked before he could stop himself, compulsion falling away.

Her flames flared, the sadness and anger warring for dominance in her tone. "I see the way they looked at me. Like a feral beast about to turn on them. Maybe I am." Her lip curled. "I hate them."

She looked up at him, and he felt her falling into his web again. Though her suspicions and dark desires formed a wall, he slipped past her defenses, drawing her into his control.

"I just... I can't help what I am," she whispered.

Strength drained from his arm, causing it to drop limply to his side. His bloodlust cleared, and he saw a young girl with no family who couldn't help what she was. It was all too like the dark deal he'd made to become a vampire and the rejection he faced upon his return. He sold his very soul to protect them, and they so quickly cast him aside. Nothing angered him more than the betrayal of family. How could he harm her when she had none to protect her?

Hellsdamn it.

All visions of eliminating this fiery threat washed away. And that vexed him. He turned to leave, but her quiet sobs locked his limbs in place. He sighed.

The space in his chest where his heart once was grew heavy. "I mean you no harm."

And hellsdamn him if his words weren't true.

She looked up with fiery tears. "Really?"

Apparently.

"Tell me what happened, child?"

She sniffled and ash floated out of her nose. "One night, late, I was sleeping. I heard a noise, my younger sister leaving our cabin. I ran after her, but she was sleepwalking right toward the town bonfire. I grabbed her arm, but she fought me. I fell into the bonfire and burned. The next morning, I woke covered in ash but unharmed. The town said it was a miracle."

Stellan clasped his claws, listening intently.

"It wasn't a miracle though," she said. "It changed me. Several nights later I woke screaming from the memory of burning. Screaming from pain. My entire house was on fire. I was on fire. I ran into my parent's room, screaming, but they saw me and fainted. I dragged them out. Fire was everywhere, I couldn't hardly see anything. I dragged my three siblings out too."

Sacrifice that only earned betrayal.

She sniffled again. "But then they chased me out of town with pitchforks. I didn't know why until I passed a stream. I was burning all over. And from that night on, I never stopped burning. I hid in the wilds, foraging for what I could. Several times I tried to return but they attacked me each time saying I was a demon." Her eyes were glassy with liquid flame. "I'm not a demon, am I?"

"No," he said. "You're not."

She looked down. "They think I am. That's why I'm all alone."

He knew he'd come to regret the next words he uttered. "If no one else, I will protect you. I will come for you."

"Thank you," she whispered.

"We monsters must stand together," he said, watching the skies begin to lighten.

Her flaming tears dripped into the long grass, and he quietly stamped them out.

Hana's pain spoke to whatever humanity remained in him. Her words found purchase in the dark depths of his rotted soul. Nothing was so terrible as betrayal by one's own blood. His vampiric instincts recognized the darkness in her, and demanded she be claimed into his colony.

He sighed, gritted his teeth, and placed his hand on hers. His palm sizzled upon contact, smoking and filling the meadow with the stench of flesh. He didn't move. She looked up, and the gratitude in her eyes kept him from pulling away. He gave her a gentle squeeze and held on as long as he could, trying to send some comfort to the girl before he released. When he finally let go, his hand did not heal. It would take many kills before he recovered, but he found he did not regret it.

A Hero's Welcome
Chapter Fifty-Two

Seers must watch the lives they were meant to live but can never have themselves.

— Curse of the seers.

1153 N.T.C. The namesake capital city of Avyllon.

Avyllon's fortified gates cast long shadows across the golden wheat valleys surrounding the city. From the ramparts, archers nocked their bows, preparing to draw. Armored sentinels rode out to meet Theo's small party, swords drawn.

The sentinel at the front recognized Theo, and immediately pulled up. "Sheath your weapons," he ordered. "It's the king."

Theo urged his horse forward. "Well met, Eryk. Anything to report?"

Sentinel Eryk glanced toward Hana, whose flames burned violet-red as she wrung her hands in agitation. "A few Mooncursed attacks on the eastern villages, but they were quickly hunted down by the vampires."

As the sentinels fell in line to escort them back to the city, one of the sentinels mumbled, "They've brought back another one."

Theo gritted his teeth. He couldn't expect them to acclimate to the waking magic all at once. He glanced toward Hana, who was staring at the ground.

Internally groaning, Theo said, "This is Hana. She is a royal guest and the only thing we've found that can relight the Flame Pillar and push back the Demorrans. Be sure she is treated with the utmost respect."

Hana's head lifted, and the sentinels nodded in acquiesce. Theo knew it wasn't the last he'd be hearing about it.

The smooth, white sandstone walls dotted with sparkling crushed glass stretched high into the sky. He heard Hana gasp as they walked through the gates. Her head whipped back and forth, sending embers tumbling onto the white stone roads.

"There are so many fountains and pools. And waterfalls!" she exclaimed. "The buildings are tall as mountains. And there's glass in the roads showing underground rivers! Do people really live here? They get to see this all the time!"

Theo followed her gaze to the thundering aqueducts and crystalline water splashing down the layered pools between the buildings. He wished for the awe he'd once had at this glittering city, but all he could see now were the patrol patterns of the sentinels, the boarded-up homes, and the abandoned streets that were once so lively.

Sentinels bordered Rhydian and Adonis, and Hana walked between them. Even under the blinding noon sun, her flames caught the suspicious gazes of all they passed. Families gathered in doorways, murmuring to one another. Guildmembers stopped their work. Vendors emerged from shop fronts.

".... Eyrand arena..." someone whispered.

Theo's gut clenched. That word would haunt him the rest of his days. The screams of the shifting Mooncursed and their victims. The blood soaking into the stones and dirt. The piles of bodies they burned.

He swallowed.

"King... Theodoren... Seer..." The whispering continued. "Beasts... Cursed."

Fear radiated through the city. He could sense it. His battle instincts alerted him to the growing danger. All hope had been drained of the people after half a year of attacks and monsters inhabiting their city. It didn't help that he'd been fighting a war since his coronation. He hadn't had the chance to earn their trust in person as much as he'd like.

They passed a home with boards on the windows, claw marks on the door, and the ash of a sorcerer's fireball on the wall. Several men and women were scrubbing blood from the sandstone entry. They stopped to look at him as he rode by.

Theo gripped the reins tighter.

"Look at this!" Hana exclaimed.

Theo whirled to see the young elemental sprinting toward a vendor stall with stained glass candle holders and blown glass bowls.

"Hana, wait!"

She brushed by the sentinels' horses, singeing their tails and hair, causing them to rear and whinny. Their hooves wheeled in the air as the soldiers struggled to remain seated. Onlookers shouted. A horse spun, knocking into a fruit cart and sending the apples and pears rolling down the street.

The vendor yelled, bringing his hands up in front of his face and stumbling backward. One of the tables overturned, sending the fragile goods crashing into the stone. Glass shards went flying.

Theo jumped off his horse to chase her. Rhydian and Adonis were blocked by the rearing horses, leaving Theo to deal with her on his own.

Hana continued to run, arms outstretched for the booth. "They're so pretty!"

The vendor scrambled for a nearby wastewater bucket and a metal glassblowing rod leaning against the door.

"No!" Theo called out.

The vendor tossed the grimy bucket in the elemental's face and the water exploded into a cloud of steam. She screamed in pain, scratching at her steaming face. The vendor swung the metal bar, and it struck her across the arm. It thunked as it struck before it bent from the intense heat.

She cried out, cradling her arm and backing away. Theo glimpsed the twisting, furious expression darkening her face.

Hellsdamn it.

Hana clenched her fists, the reddish flames growing hotter until they turned a bright blue tinged with white. She shrieked and the flames coating her flesh erupted into a firestorm. The glass all around her melted into a prismatic puddle. The wooden stall burst into flames. She screamed louder and clawed at everything around her. Beams liquefied. The stones warped. Black smoke poured out of the inferno.

Nearby vendors grabbed hammers, axes, and clubs before approaching. Sentinels rushed toward the gathering crowd.

"Keep them back," Theo called to Eryk and Rhydian.

The sentinel captain and the Warbringer reached out their arms, blocking the crowd.

Theo circled around, standing between Hana and the vendor. "Hana, you need to calm down."

"He hurt me!" she screamed.

Slowly, Theo drew his glowing blade. He held it out horizontally, the flat of the blade angled toward her. She snarled, but he lifted his non-sword arm.

"You frightened him. He hasn't seen an elemental before, and you came running at him. If you saw something powerful come running for you and you didn't know what it was, you'd be afraid too wouldn't you?"

Hana's flames turned indigo as the heat reduced around them.

"She's a demon!" the vendor cried.

"Get inside, now," Theo snapped.

With a frightened yelp, the vendor crawled inside his shop.

"Hana. You promised to help," he reminded her.

Her eyes glinted turquoise. "I promised to burn people."

"Our enemies. These people are not our enemies. Not unless you make them so." Theo gestured behind him toward the crowd, signaling them to put down their weapons. "You wanted to see the palace, right? We have a room for you there made fully of stone."

"My own room?" She angled her head.

He nodded.

She looked down, shame marring her brow. "I can't control my flames. I never could. Any more than I can control my temper."

Theo swallowed. A flame elemental with no control over her magic was dangerous, and it was going to make relighting the Pillar more difficult.

Coldforges.

It hadn't occurred to him that she might not have control over the magic consuming her.

"It's alright. You're trying," he said.

Her flames lightened to a yellowish orange. "I'm sorry for causing a fire," she said brightly to the crowd, before skipping back to the waiting sentinels.

Theo's chest was tight and his limbs jittery with unspent energy. He glanced back at the vendor hiding within his shop.

"We'll pay for the damages. Send a bill," Theo muttered.

He trailed the elemental back to the sentinels, who watched her cautiously. The crowd hesitated, lingering in doorways.

"Back to your homes and work. There's nothing to fear," Theo announced.

To Rhydian and Eryk he whispered, "Let's go quickly."

The group moved toward the palace, Hana once again between Adonis and Rhydian, and nestled within a growing group of sentinels.

Nesryn leapt off a nearby rooftop and landed beside Theo, her boots silent on the sandstone. "You did well. I wondered if we were going to have to return to the Sunfyre Wilds to capture a firewyrm."

Theo mounted his horse, squeezing the reins. "I'm hoping this wasn't a mistake."

Nesryn grinned mirthlessly, canines on display. "We'll find out. If you succeed, you're a hero. If you don't, you're a monster."

Hana was safely tucked into a stone room on the first floor with Rhydian and Nesryn. The elf had been difficult to convince into babysitting Hana, but Theo finally persuaded her that Hana was as great a threat to the city as Rhydian, and Rhydian agreed to remain with them so she could keep an eye on them both. Theo was fairly certain she'd called him unseemly names in an ancient language.

He found Aurienne in the gardens between the temple and palace, staring at the swaying wildflowers while shuffling her cards.

"We found a flame elemental," he said. "Nesryn says she can relight the Flame Pillar. We just have to get her to it, but the emperor put wards around the Pillar for a few miles, so we can't get very close."

"That is good news," she said.

Theo rolled his tongue over his teeth, irritation flashing in his skull. "I supposed you already saw it in a vision."

"I haven't had a vision since you left for the front." She turned, and he could now see the bags under her eyes.

Concern filled his throat. She wrapped her arm around her ribs, her wrists looking frailer than they had. Had she not been eating? Her long hair was tucked into a messy plait. The gown she wore, simple. Hardly any jewelry adorned her skin. He swallowed the concern, hating it was always his first response for her.

"My cards said you were returning soon," she said. "I hoped you were successful."

"Why aren't you having visions?" he asked, unable to help himself.

"My mind needs to heal."

He gestured toward her deck. "But you can use those?"

A faint smile crossed her lips, one he hadn't seen in a while. "They've taken on a magic of their own. It seems they hardly need me at all these days. Their magic doesn't drain me."

The golden King figure on the front flipped him off with long claws before disappearing into the black ink. Theo scowled.

Same to you.

"Nesryn says Rexil has the better part of an army posted at the Pillar," he said. "I don't know how to get Hana there covertly. We can try to sneak her to the Pillar from the Way. Do we wrap her in heavy blankets and... hope she doesn't burn them before we get there."

Aurienne's expression was flat. "You're going to sneak a flame elemental miles through enemy camps? Hiding her under blankets? She'll burn them, and you'll be caught, you know this."

"I want to just open a Way a few miles out and have the vampires fly her to the Pillar." Theo raked his hands through his hair.

Aurienne shook her head. "She'd burn right through their hands before she arrived. Even taking turns, it's likely they'd drop and kill her before they got there. And the Shadows would ensure it. There's also an army between the nearest point we could open a Way and the Pillar."

"I know. Do you have a better idea?" he snapped. "One that doesn't involve us sending our entire army?"

Aurienne knelt into the wildflowers. She shuffled the desk, pressed a kiss to it, and then pulled three cards.

The Living Flame.

The Dusk.

The Bones.

Theo didn't need to be a seer to know it was an ominous portent. She met his gaze, pursing her lips.

"Then what do we do?" he said.

Aurienne shuffled again, breathed on the back of the deck, and turned over three more cards.

The Moon.

The Stars.

The Sword.

Theo glanced at her. Frowning, she turned over three more.

The Coin.

The Knot.

The Scales.

She leaned down and whispered, "I do not understand," before drawing three more.

The Emperor.

The Scales.

The Sun.

Aurienne sat back into the grass. "We'll have to fight our way to the Pillar. The Fate of the continent rests upon whether we succeed."

Theo gripped his sword hilt. "Did they say when?"

"The full moon, when else," she said bitterly.

"That's in a week."

She looked up at him. "We'd better prepare then. We have a battle to win."

Theo strode out of the garden without glancing back.

WOLF GOLD
CHAPTER FIFTY-THREE

Give me Queen Rianne and, in exchange, enough gold to fill a castle shall be yours.

— A LETTER FROM EMPEROR REXIL TO LORD BRAM TAVISH, 1153 N.T.C.

1153 N.T.C. Castle Rodarr, Rodarri.

Howling winds echoed off the stone walls, bringing a bone-deep chill to the castle. Rianne slid the crisp parchment into the orange flames that filled the wide fireplace of her chambers, absorbing the news. Rhydian and Theo found a flame elemental. They could relight the Flame Pillar and drive back the Shadows. Without the might of the Shadows, the allies could withstand the emperor's armies. In just one week's time, Theo called the allies to meet at the Pillar. Rhydian would gather Rodarri's forces from the isthmus and meet her with the rest of their army at the Pillar.

At first light, she would go to her secret war camp and mobilize the war machines.

"The emperor won't know what hit him," Rosalindt whispered.

"The element of surprise will be needed to reclaim the Pillar," Rianne thought. *"It will take everything to get past the forces he's stationed there."*

And then when I see Rhydian again, I'll tell him everything.

Memories of his hands against her skin, his lips on hers, the rare smile that brightened her whole world warmed her chilly heart. She latched onto those memories, focusing on every detail to keep them from fading to gray again.

She glanced up at the pastel dawn, it was time.

The door to her room burst open, rocking on its hinges and slamming against the wall. Rianne spun, preparing to summon her bonesword as sixteen of the commander's sons charged toward her, weapons drawn. She raised her hands, the bones of her corset readying to reform her weapon, when shackles closed on her wrists.

Burning. Searing. Rianne screamed as bone-deep pain she'd never known ripped through her. Her hands and knees hit the stone floor. The voices of the queens faded to nothing, just whispers so very far away. Her life force was draining; what kept her alive dwindled. Her flesh sizzled and bled where the metal touched her skin.

Bram Tavish yanked her up by the shackles, forcing her to stand on wobbly legs. "The emperor left us with these titan ore shackles in case you needed to be contained. It seems he was right. This will keep you tame."

Titan ore? Her brain struggled to process what he was saying. Titan ore negated or enhanced magic. If she could no longer hear the queens, it was cutting her off from the very power keeping her alive. Silver tears welled in her eyes, the pain nearly too much to bear.

"I warned you that you didn't want me as an enemy." His sneer slithered across his face.

The other young men sniggered, glaring daggers into her skull.

She couldn't think, couldn't move. The pain was so great, her strength nearly gone.

"You shouldn't have made the queens your commanders," he said. "They weren't experienced enough to see this coming."

Tears burned her eyes. She'd known it was a bad idea, but the former Queensblood were the only ones she trusted. She'd wanted so badly for them to rise to the occasion. It asked too much. Perhaps she should have hidden them away to never be found rather than asking them to seize their full potential. The thoughts blended as the pain hammered her skull.

"I'm going to make you beg for mercy, just as my father begged." His breath was hot on her face. "But you didn't show him mercy did you?"

Stars exploded across her vision as the back of his knuckles smashed her temple. Her knees buckled, the shackles searing her flesh the only thing keeping her upright.

"You're going to regret this," she hissed between her teeth.

"I learned from my father's mistake," he said. "I didn't tip my hand. And I learned from you to be ruthless."

He grasped her leather and lace choker and ripped it away, exposing her never-healing death wound.

"No!" She brought her hands up to her throat.

He only laughed harder. His hands groped at the corset around her ribs, trying to pry the enchanted weapon from her gown, but it would not budge. He wrenched on the fused bones, jerking her around violently.

"Why won't this thing come off!"

She lifted her head, trying to keep her lips from quivering. For the first time in months, she was all alone.

"You can't take what's not yours," she said.

His fist cracked against her mouth, sending blood flying across the room. "I didn't give you permission to speak."

Her head lolled as her vision swam. She blinked, trying to clear her eyes.

Bram stroked her cheek, grinning as she tried and failed to pull away. "The emperor wants you alive, else I'd be taking my time savoring your death."

She gritted her teeth.

He leaned forward. "But don't worry. I'll take my pound of flesh from the *Queensblood*, starting with your sister."

Her feet dragged against the gray stone floors as strong hands found her arms. Memories of dead queens being dragged to their deaths filled her mind. It was happening again. With all she'd done, all she'd accomplished, Rianne had failed at the one thing she vowed to do: end the ascensions.

Maybe she could warn them.

"Jordyn!" Rianne screamed. "Jordyn run!"

"It's too late," Bram sneered. "They're being rounded up as we speak."

"Jordyn! Hide!"

Bram grabbed her arm and shook her roughly, knocking her head around. "Quiet or I'll hit you again."

"Jordyn!" Rianne screamed down the hall.

He growled as he shoved her to the ground and continued dragging her through the deserted halls. She strained her neck to try to glimpse anyone, the pain creating a thick fog in her head. Maybe they could hear her and slip into the secret tunnels. The *heirs* may be more reckless, but they lacked the foresight of their fathers. Maybe her kin could escape the castle this time. Tears slipped down her cheeks.

The uneven ground scraped against her legs and back as the titan ore shackles burned into her skin. She scrambled to her feet just as they made it to the dungeon steps.

Stumbling down the uneven stone, she barely managed to keep her balance. He dragged her toward the cell at the back where the barred door was open and waiting.

Rianne slipped on a stagnant puddle and slid to the floor. Bram shoved her inside. She crawled toward the door just as it slammed in her face.

"You don't need to do anything to the Queensblood," she pleaded. "They did nothing wrong."

"Our fathers did nothing wrong either." He kicked the door, inches from her nose. "And we weren't even returned their bodies to bury."

She gritted her teeth, from the pain as much as from keeping her mouth shut.

He reached through the bars, gripping her wounded throat. "You tried to steal my birthright, my inheritance."

Her silver-tipped fingers dug into his hand as she gasped for air.

"I was born to rule, and you were only ever meant to die." He released her and stepped away.

She tried again, "We've already had an ascension. More are not required."

Bram crossed his arms, displeasure washing over his sharp features. "Rexil wants the Queensblood. Once we figure out how to disable the wards, he'll return and collect them. He will decide if ascensions are required."

She breathed the smallest sigh of relief. There was time before her kin would be put to death. If they could keep Demorra at bay and relight the Pillar, she could keep them safe for longer.

Rianne's hands found the bars, and she pulled herself up halfway. Even if she was imprisoned, they needed to join Avyllon at the Pillar. All would be lost if Avyllon fell.

Her blood ran cold, and she fell to the ground, the last of her energy gone. The emperor's gold and false promises bought them off.

Bram pushed off the bars and strode away.

"Rexil betrayed me," she shouted after him as loudly as she could. "He will do the same to you!"

The dungeons were silent but for her voice and Bram's fading footsteps. Faintly flickering torches cast ethereal shadows across the mossy stones.

Rhydian was in Avyllon. Jordyn and the queens had likely been rounded up. Her army would easily accept the commander's sons given their history with the commanders she'd hung. Her secret army remained hidden, waiting for her summons. The spirits were silent and her bonesword dormant. Nothing and no one could save her. If only she'd better listened to the queens and they'd better listened to her, none of this would have happened.

There was no way out, and without her, there would be no stopping Demorra.

DRYING INK
CHAPTER FIFTY-FOUR

My life was a lie.

— UNKNOWN.

1153 N.T.C. The namesake capital city of Avyllon.

Ink dried on the letters to Wynds, the Seven Forests, and the Titan Cliffs. Aurienne put the quill back into the inkpot before rolling up the paper. She hoped the requests would reach their allies in time. A letter to Rodarri had already been sent by Rhydian on the road.

She glanced around the war table where the assembled prepared for the coming battle.

The nameless one used his staff to position carved horses and men where the Demorrans were stationed around the Pillar while Theo studied the formations carefully, scrawling notes on a large parchment. Saryll shuffled her cards, laying out sets of three for question after question. Beside her, Adonis studied a thick tome, quiet as ever.

Days from now, they'd be marching to the valley south of Heart-spring and facing off against the emperor's army stationed there. Nesryn had agreed to open a way for Avyllon's army, and they hoped Rodarri and perhaps their other allies would meet them there on the coming full moon.

Aurienne's cards began to chatter within the spelled box, and she looked up.

"You're supposed to stay in your room," Rhydian's voice cut through the tension.

"I'm bored," Hana whined before she stomped inside the war room.

Her flames licked at the walls, leaving trails of ash on the sandstone.

"There are books in here. Paper. Wood. It all burns. You need to stay where there's stone," Rhydian said.

"If I'm going to light this giant fire, I need to listen to the plan." She crossed her arms. "So what's the plan? What do I do?"

Aurienne answered before Theo could. "We'll have to fight to get you through their line to the Pillar. How far can you throw your flames? We'll need to get you close enough to do that."

"Throw them?" Hana tilted her head. "What do you mean?"

Adonis lifted his head. "A fireball?"

"I can't do that."

"Imagine some of your flames separating and send them," Adonis said.

"Can you just imagine your hand falling off and hucking it?" Hana wiggled her burning fingers. "No? Same thing. I *can't*."

Theo exhaled, casting a glare in Aurienne's direction. "We'll have to get her to the top of the Pillar then."

The elemental's flames flickered back to a bright orange. "You promised I could burn people."

Aurienne glanced toward Theo, brows pulling together. Hana was young, perhaps thirteen or so only. Why would Theo fuel her thirst for violence? He shouldn't have made that promise. Aurienne's cards rattled in her dress pocket.

Theo ignored Aurienne, answering Hana. "Just touch anyone who gets too close to you."

Miella and Marco entered, the former's face drawn and heavy while the latter's jaw was set.

Hana clapped excitedly upon seeing Marco. "You're like me!"

"Yes, close enough," he replied.

"Will you be joining us, hunter?" Nesryn asked.

Aurienne glanced toward the now-open window where the elf swung her leg outside. She hadn't been there moments ago. Beside her, the small crimson and black fox flicked its bushy tail.

Grinning, Aurienne held out her hand to the fox. It bounded toward her, stopping to arch its back under her hand like a cat. She scratched behind its ear,

Marco stroked his chin, studying Hana thoughtfully. "They found you."

Aurienne stopped scratching the fox, gaze panning toward the vampire hunter. Something about his tone sounded warning bells in her head.

What is he up to?

She shook away the unease. There was no time for that.

"I propose—," Theo said.

"We'll need to prepare all forces to march," Aurienne started saying at the same time. "The majority of our troops will have to be called back from the isthmus as well. If we mean to go through the Way in formation, we'll gather outside Avyllon's gates. I would propose seven hundred vampires travel to the pillar, leaving three hundred with the city to defend against Mooncursed attacks. We'll send a seer with each company and put together agile groups of sorcerers that can maneuver between the foot soldiers. The sentinels can accompany the sorcerers and seers, they're used to guarding them and know how to fight beside their magic. I think—"

"Anything else?" Theo retorted. "Or might I get a word in?"

The room grew silent.

"Let's reconvene in the morning," Nesryn interrupted.

The room dispersed quickly, leaving only the two of them alone.

"Have you fought in a battle?" he pressed.

"No."

"Have your visions returned?" Theo asked pointedly.

She gritted her teeth. Anger rumbled in her chest as she glared daggers at him.

"So why are you giving orders?"

"What is your problem," she snapped.

"You tell me I'm supposed to lead our armies, yet you don't trust me to do it," he said." Is it my destiny to fight this war, or is it just another one of your lies?"

The words were a blow straight to her heart. And he wasn't wrong. She had forced this role on him and now didn't let him do it. The pain snapped her control on her rising temper.

The words were out of her mouth before she could stop them. "I may not be the ruling regent anymore, but I remain the Goddess-chosen High Seer, and you'd do well to heed my warnings. I've led this nation for thirteen years. You've been king for less than six months, and most of that was at the isthmus. You haven't ever ruled. Not really."

Aurienne was breathing heavy, and found she'd taken two large steps toward Theo.

Theo's jaw tightened. "I haven't had the chance to rule because I've been risking my life every day to keep you all alive, but I guess that counts for nothing."

"Of course it matters!" Her face grew hot.

"Not to you," he said. "No one matters to you. You're just going to point us all in the direction of battle and watch us die, like you always do. You never have to risk anything or get your hands dirty because the rest of us do it for you."

"I expect to die in this war!" The words fell from her lips before she could stop them.

He stared at her.

"Just go," Aurienne said.

"Fine," Theo snapped.

The doors to the war room slammed open as Theo stormed out, footfalls echoing off the palace walls.

Wynds of Betrayal

Chapter Fifty-Five

Beware the siren's call. Once ensnared, there is no escape.

— *Wyndsel sailor's wisdom.*

1153 N.T.C. The city of Wynds, Wyndsel.

Salty squalls gusted through the open-air windows in the royal dining room. Queen Arissabett pushed the fish and vegetables across her plate in small circles. She set down the silver fork and sipped on the blackberry wine. Rolling the goblet in her fingers, she studied the empty room. The king's food cooled on his plate an hour ago, though he'd never deemed to join her.

Her gaze went to the letter resting on the golden tray, waiting for his eyes. She reached for it. The wax crest of Avyllon sealed it shut. Her fingers itched to open it.

Donovan pushed open the doors to the banquet hall, stumbling and laughing, one of Arissabett's ladies under each arm. Her stomach twisted into knots. She laid down the unopened letter.

"My queen!" he called out, clearly drunk. "I'm glad you're still here. We've worked up quite an appetite. The ladies taught me a riveting card game."

The ladies giggled, exchanging flirty glances.

Arissabett gripped the edge of the table. "The cook didn't send up enough for guests."

"Tell him to send more!" Donovan waved his arm about.

He walked up behind her and pressed a kiss against her neck, smelling of wine and perfume.

She pursed her lips. "The messenger left this for you. It's from Avyllon."

Donovan's hazy expression darkened, and Arissabett's chest constricted. She'd seen that look too many times.

He waved the ladies away. "I've work to do."

Exchanging puzzled glances, the ladies detangled from under his arms and slipped out of the grand room.

Donovan broke the seal and ripped open the letter. He skimmed it quickly before tossing it on the table.

"Avyllon," he said. "Fools all of them. They're going to attack the Demorran forces guarding the Flame Pillar. They want us to join them."

Her breath eased up, sensing no sign of his temper. "Are you going to?"

He scoffed, reaching down to pick up a candied pear. "No."

"Why? Doesn't it keep the emperor farther from us?"

Donovan threw up his hands. "We've warded our Pillar and are guarding it. The entire fleet patrols the seas. We'll protect ourselves."

Arissabett stared. "But they're our allies? We must answer their call for aid."

"They were fools to lose their own Pillar." Donovan sat back in his chair, kicking his feet up on the table. "Your father allied with Avyllon out of fear, but we need to consider the fact that they might fall. If they do, it's better if we didn't send our armies against the emperor's."

"And if they don't?" Arissabett asked.

"If they don't, then we haven't marched against them either. It's not like we could march our army all the way to Heartspring anyways."

"I don't think—" she began.

His feet slammed against the floor as he stood and grabbed her arm. She cried out as he yanked her forward, his fingers leaving bruises upon her skin.

"You're not meant to think," he snarled in her face.

She brought her hands up fearfully. "I'm sorry," she squeaked.

He jerked her again, snapping her head back and forth like a rag doll. "I am your king! You do not question me."

"I'm sorry!" Tears ran down her face and dripped onto the pearl embroidery of her gown.

"You're no warrior," he hissed. "You're just a stupid girl who needs to learn to keep her mouth shut."

"I'm sorry. I will."

His grip softened at her compliance.

Donovan stroked her face with his knuckles. "I'm sorry. It's been a long day, and talks of war are stressful. I can't stand anyone else questioning me. You know how much I need you, don't you? I just need your support."

She nodded.

"I love you." He kissed her mouth.

Gods.

She wanted to believe it.

Arissabett returned to her rooms and meandered aimlessly out onto the open-air balcony overlooking the cliffs. She leaned against the chilled redstone balustrade, dropping her face in her hands. Wine splashed from the half-empty glass hanging from her fingers. Seaglass wind chimes chimed quietly from the windows.

Only months ago, she'd thought everything was perfect. Where had it gone so wrong? Now, her father was dead. Donovan was king. She'd been reduced to a silent, figurehead queen. Her voice mattered not. Her dear husband dallied with whores every night before climbing into her bed smelling of wine and sweat. And she was supposed to ignore it and keep a smile painted on her pretty face.

She'd loved him once, believing he loved her. Had it been an act? Could someone be so cruel as to play with her heart the whole time until he'd been seated into power? Tears slipped down her cheeks.

Donovan said abandoning their allies was the best way to keep Wyndsel safe. Why march to fight a battle halfway across the continent, leaving their home undefended. Arissabett knew nothing of battle and politics, but they'd signed the alliance. Didn't that mean something? Shouldn't they at least warn Avyllon they weren't coming? Or was she just a foolish girl who should keep her mouth shut?

Arissabett rubbed her bruised olive-hued arms against the chilled ocean air and retreated into the warmth of the lonely chambers. The blazing fire and plush blankets called to her. She could drink wine until it numbed the thoughts in her head, and she fell into a deep sleep.

Her hair blew past her cheeks in a frenzy as a strong gust whipped her skirts past her ankles. The sensation of being watched prickled the flesh on the back of her neck. Heart hammering, she turned slowly—squinting to search the shadows cast by the hearth.

A man, the most painfully striking she'd ever seen stood on the balustrade, eyeing her hungrily. Almost black eyes. Tall. Muscled. Long, dark hair. Wearing fine silks that caught the breeze, exposing his muscled chest. He grinned, fangs on display, tilting his head as his gaze roved over her. Tall leather wings moved in the shadows.

With a gasp, she blinked, and he was gone.

Shackles

Chapter Fifty-Six

Titan ore can be warded to enhance, dampen, or transform magic. With the right combination of wards and materials sealed with Etherian power, the possibilities are endless.

— Scrap of paper stuffed within a faded textbook.

1153 N.T.C. Dungeons of Castle Rodarr, Rodarri.

Gold-flecked onyx shackles bit into the raw skin on Rianne's wrists. The torn and bruised flesh chafed beneath the searing magic of the titan ore. It didn't hurt as it would have if she'd been alive, but if the pain caught her notice at all, her injuries were severe. Days had passed, though it was so dark she couldn't be sure how many.

The voices of the queens, once loud, were so far away. It took every ounce of strength she had left to hear them at all.

Milah's flat voice swirled through Rianne's ears. *"We should have killed them all."*

Samantah snarled, *"Mercy is a weakness we can't afford."*

"We warned you," Rosalindt whispered. *"Your soft heart was our undoing."*

Rianne leaned against the chilled wall, head bowed. The will to argue fled as the titan ore sapped her strength with every breath.

"My soft heart and your thirst for vengeance equally damned us," Rianne said aloud. "If we'd better worked together, we would have succeeded."

The door at the stairs slammed open and heavy footfalls followed. Rianne lifted her head and shielded her eyes as a bright torch stopped at her cell. Bram held a small wooden bowl and flask in one hand.

He hurled them into the cell, the first provisions she'd seen. She hated herself for the way she launched at them. Throwing her head back, she gobbled up the precious drops of fresh water. The stale bread was so hard it hurt her teeth, but it filled the gnawing void in her belly.

"How quickly the queenly pride is stripped away," Bram chuckled.

She refused to look at him.

"I sent word to the emperor that we've taken the castle. We haven't managed to disable the wards, but it's only a matter of time before Rexil returns." He grinned wolfishly. "We'll betray your precious Avyllonians and attack their army from the rear. Pinched between the two forces they'll collapse. They won't be able to retreat into the Pillar's protections, and, come daylight, Rexil will defeat all threats."

He reached through the bars to finger her titan ore shackles. "Rexil told us to take these off soon after we'd gotten them on you. He said they sapped the strength of a magic being too quickly."

Hope trickled down her throat into her heart.

He released the shackle chain. "But I've seen the truth. Whatever happened to you in the ravine made you too powerful to remove these. They'll stay on until you're in his control and he strips your power permanently."

The hope dried up as quickly as it came. Tears burned her eyes.

"I hope he'll let us keep your sister as breeding stock." He chuckled darkly. "I'm sure it's all the emperor has planned for you. Maybe this dead thing can still bear life."

With an animalistic snarl, Rianne slammed her fists against the bars and bared her teeth. He blinked as he took the smallest step back, but quickly recovered.

"He'll be here soon to take you and the Queensblood to Demorra."

She laughed. "And give up the protection of a thousand years of spilled blood? He will take all of your power. Why would he do anything he said once he has everything he wants?"

Bram shifted uncomfortably. "Shut your cursed witch mouth. You know nothing."

"I know that a person who's willing to betray someone is willing to betray anyone," she said. "He will stop at nothing to get what he wants. Between the two of us, he's the greater evil."

Bram glared at her. "I won't let your lies infect me. You can rot in here until he arrives."

The torchlight faded with his footsteps, and she was left in near pitch black. She dug her nails into the peeling, rusty layers of the cell bars.

She'd given no one a reason to, but if *one* ally in Avyllon noticed her absence, they could save them all. She just needed one person to believe in her. No one had saved her from her ascension, and she'd betrayed or alienated all her allies, but she still prayed to any gods listening that someone would see what she'd been trying to accomplish and believe that she wouldn't leave them to die. Please let Rhydian's faith in her remain steadfast. He just needed to believe in her one final time.

She lifted her head. There was one person she could still communicate with across time and leagues through her blood oath: Aurienne. She had no way to harm Theo, but perhaps even thinking of it would send the seer a message.

I will kill him once I am free. I will drive my bonesword through his chest.

Blood trickled from Rianne's mouth. She breathed heavily. The seer would receive her message now. If only she could get word to Rhydian.

"You can't trust the seer," Samantah hissed.

"If we'd been better allies, we wouldn't be locked in here," Rianne snapped.

She stared into the dark, whispering prayers over and over. Rhydian hadn't been able to save her last time, but he should know something was wrong now. He would come and save her.

The queens all whispered a haunting truth, one she knew but hoped to all the gods was a lie.

No one was coming.

BROKEN ALLIANCES
CHAPTER FIFTY-SEVEN

Oaths broken and souls returned,
Lies offered and truths spurned.

— HIGH SEER AURIENNE AZARRAH, PROPHETIC VISION.

1153 N.T.C. The namesake capital city of Avyllon.

Rhydian paced the war room, boots thumping against the polished, white sandstone floors. Rianne had never written back. Dusk was fast approaching, and it was time to open the Way. Their armies would pour into the valley surrounding the Pillar. Once they attacked, there would be no turning back. Wynds, the Seven Forests, and the Titan Cliffs never replied either. If Rodarri didn't show, Avyllon would be facing the emperor alone.

Theo, Aurienne, General Laurier, Sentinel Kolten, and Miella and Marco stood around the grand, carved table. Nesryn lurked around the exterior bookshelves of the room, always just in his periphery.

"We can't wait any longer," Theo said. "We need to get down to the barracks and lead our army outside the city wards to go through Nesryn's Way."

Aurienne clasped her hands, avoiding eye contact with Theo. "We must decide whether to attack as planned. We don't have the confirmed support of any allies, and they might be busy defending their own homes."

Rhydian shook his head and dragged his hands through his overgrown dark hair. "Rianne wouldn't not show up."

Theo sighed. "Rhydian."

No.

He was so tired of everyone believing the worst in her. She couldn't help what had happened to her and tried so hard to make it right. She'd made mistakes, but so had they all.

"Rianne wouldn't betray us," Rhydian said.

Aurienne shuffled her cards absently. "It's possible she didn't get our letter, or hers was intercepted. Even if her intentions were good, we don't know for sure that she's coming. And it's assuming a lot to believe her intentions are good."

Rhydian slammed his hand into the map table. Theo's head snapped his direction, but Aurienne didn't react—as if she were expecting it. Without looking, he could almost sense Nesryn edging closer.

"Send another raven. She will come," he said. "She allied with us and won't let us down. She wouldn't do that."

"She wouldn't?" Nesryn's voice was ice on steel.

"Why would she trick us? Before when she was considering breaking King Cavendar's alliance with us and joining the emperor, she told us. Why would she be so open about it then and lie now?"

"Because this is the emperor's chance to crush us," the elf said. "Maybe she did join him after all."

"No," he snapped. "We battled in the castle and pushed him out. She didn't join him."

Theo and Aurienne glanced between them as the others in the room backed away.

Nesryn took several steps closer. "Unless it was a clever ruse. Tell me again the state you found her in? Tell me how you could smell the emperor's touch all over her body."

Rhydian's anger turned his vision red. "I know her. She wouldn't leave us to die."

"No? Like she wasn't changed when she died? Like she wouldn't lie to you?" Her words lingered. "Like she would tell you the truth, let you in on her plans? Or you mean like she wouldn't court and become engaged to Rexil while sending you away? Or do you mean how the Rianne you knew wouldn't hang all the Commanders? Kill King Jaekob and Cavendar? Try to assassinate your best friend?"

Her last question speared the air from Rhydian's chest. Assassinate his best friend? He glanced at Theo who wore a puzzled expression. They both looked to Aurienne who refused to lift her head.

"She did what?" Theo said slowly.

Aurienne rolled her tongue over her teeth, remaining silent. Her silence was as loud an admission as any.

Rhydian's heart sank. "When?"

"After the coronation," Nesryn supplied.

Aurienne glared at the elf.

"There has to be some mistake? Some misunderstanding?" Rhydian pressed.

Nesryn scoffed. "You don't know her anymore. The Rianne you knew died in that ravine. What's left of her is crumbling, fading into the other spirits that *returned* with her. The spirits are ancient, angry, powerful. It was never a fight she could win."

Rhydian's face burned. Thankfully, General Laurier and Sentinel Kolten had slipped out the door while Miella and Marco had strolled over to the windows overlooking a sparkling pool of crushed glass.

"You knew more than you let on," he said. "You knew what she was fighting, and you didn't tell me?"

"I tried to tell you," Nesryn sighed. "You didn't want to listen. Not to any of us."

"If you knew what was going on you could have helped her," he shouted. "But you're a heartless, bitter—"

"Rhydian," Theo warned as Nesryn's hand drifted toward the hilt of her glowing, brilliant sword.

"You could have helped her," Rhydian hissed, forcing himself to breathe through his teeth.

"Nothing could help her but the release of death," Nesryn replied. "Then she would be free. If there was a way to bring her back, to bring any of them back I would share it. Such a power does not exist. It never did. Nothing cheats death. You can push it off for a time, but it always comes for you."

Rhydian slammed his fist into the table again, causing the wood to groan. As Aurienne wrapped her arms around herself, paling at Nesryn's words, Theo stepped toward him.

"Maybe she will show," Theo said. "Her letter could've been lost, an eagle could've killed the raven, we don't know. Arguing about it gets us nowhere. We have to decide if we going to attack the Pillar with or without her."

Rhydian shook his head. "It's too dangerous to go without her." He looked to Nesryn. "Take me to her and let me see for myself."

She crossed her arms, tilting her chin. "I won't be able to hold open the Way for an entire army if I take you to Rodarri and back. As it is, the task will reach the limits of my power. I'm not sure I'll be able to open a Way back already."

"I have to see her," he said. "I have to know."

"Accept that she's gone," the elf said bitingly.

"Please," he implored.

Nesryn worked her jaw.

"Witch!" Aurienne shouted as she coughed up dark blood dripping from her tongue onto the map table. "Rianne betrayed us."

Rhydian gripped the edge of the table. "How do you know?"

Aurienne wiped more blood away, her mouth an angry line. She gritted her teeth.

"Aurienne?" Theo said quietly, firmly.

Aurienne finally met his gaze for the first time since they'd all been in the same room. "We made a blood oath that she would not harm you, after she tried to kill you with the same weapon she used on King Jaekob. I caught her trying to curse you with an ancient dark object. This blood, the burning at the back of my throat, the whispered promise we made tells me she's thinking about harming you now. I'd guess she joined the emperor and plans to attack or leave us to die."

Rhydian's heart hammered inside his chest as his temples pounded. "No. It can't be."

Aurienne has to be wrong.

Rianne didn't have a violent bone in her body. She was kind and soft, forgiving, loving. She wouldn't try to assassinate an innocent, an ally.

Aurienne looked toward him sadly. "I saw her with my own eyes. After she tried to assassinate you, I had to threaten her with spirit necromancy beyond the veil before she agreed to the oath. She meant to kill him so her revenge would be complete. You... didn't see her there. She's not the same."

"You did what!" Theo shouted.

Looking at Rhydian, Aurienne continued, "Rianne is still in there, but so are many more of them. I'm sorry. There is no reason she would be considering breaking the oath unless she'd betrayed us. We can't wait for her. We must attack the Pillar with or without Rodarri. No help is coming."

Rhydian paced, clenching his fists. Aurienne had never been wrong about her visions. Everyone was telling him to give up on Rianne, that she was gone. He'd promised to serve her, but if she wasn't here anymore, his oath meant nothing.

Nesryn said, "You can go to her on your own if you want. But we must go to the Pillar now."

Rhydian squeezed his eyes shut for a moment, trying to escape the growing heartbreak. "We go to the Pillar."

A secret part of him still held out hope that Rianne would prove them all wrong.

FORBIDDEN
CHAPTER FIFTY-EIGHT

This world makes monsters of us all.

— JOURNAL OF THE HIGH SEER AURIENNE
AZARRAH.

1153 N.T.C. The namesake capital city of Avyllon.

Heart hammering, Theo followed Aurienne through the halls outside the war room. What had she done? Walking quickly, he cornered her beside a bubbling fountain.

"Wait, stop," he said. "Talk to me."

She paused in the last rays of afternoon sun reflecting off the white, polished stone inside the palace. Turning, she squared to face him and lifted her chin—ready for a fight.

"Aurienne, what did you do?" he breathed.

"It doesn't matter." She glanced away, balling and un-balling her hand. "I did what I had to, as I always do."

Flexing and rubbing her hand were nervous habits she'd picked up ever since the assassination attempt.

"After the coronation, she was going to kill me and you..." he trailed off.

"I dragged her soul beyond the veil and threatened her," she admitted. "I tried to get her to see reason, but you've seen how she is sometimes. She wanted you dead out of some sick sense of justice and vengeance for the sins of your ancestors. I had to *make* her stop, so I threatened her with spirit necromancy."

The blood rushed out of his face, and he found himself gently grabbing her arms. "Spirit necromancy is dangerous. You're risking your soul!"

"I know that," she snapped back. "But I couldn't let you die. I would do it again. I would risk my soul for yours."

Theo took a full step backward, hand clutching at his leather armor as pain flashed through his chest.

She'd entered a blood oath to protect him. She knew the consequences of a necromancy, yet she'd been willing to risk her eternal soul for him. That wasn't someone who didn't care. He'd been wrong.

Realization dawned on him. It was someone who cared far too much. He hadn't been listening to her when she'd told him she couldn't watch him die again, that she wouldn't be the reason he died. At the time, it sounded like a hollow excuse. For someone forbidden from ever falling in love, she was going to great lengths to protect him. Even lying about it.

As if she could read the look on his face, she said, "I truly am sorry. I never meant to hurt you. I would do anything to keep you from pain. I would spare you from this destiny if I had any power to."

She spoke the truth. He knew it in his bones.

Exhaling, he backed away. "I'm sorry. I didn't know. I thought— well, it doesn't matter what I thought."

Her smile was small and pained as she looked away again. "I understand. I would hate me, too."

He stepped forward, and he carefully took her hands in his. "I don't hate you. I could never hate you."

"Don't be so sure," she said. "You don't know what I'm capable of."

Leaning down, he caught her gaze. "I know you better than anyone. You want what's best for our people, and you're willing to make the difficult decisions to ensure it. I understand the weight of that burden, and even when I wanted to, I couldn't hate you."

Pain flashed across her face, and she pulled her hands from his to wrap her around herself. "We can't do this, Theo."

The absence of her touch was physically painful. If she was hurting the same as he was, then it was torture.

"Before, when you said you didn't expect to survive this war, did you mean it?" he whispered.

She nodded. "I've never seen a single vision of myself beyond the war. I see flashes for others, read futures for them that extend into the future. Never for myself. It just goes black."

I'll never let you die. To get to you, your enemies will climb over my corpse. There is nothing I won't do to protect you.

He bit down on those promises. It would only hurt her to hear. Instead, he said, "Then tonight, we truly go to war."

BATTLE FOR TERIDAR
CHAPTER FIFTY-NINE

We all must make sacrifices.

— HIGH SEER AURIENNE AZARRAH.

1153 N.T.C. The Flame Pillar, outside the Hunger's Teeth Mountains.

Dusk fell upon the fields outside Avyllon, and Nesryn's Way burst to life. It ripped through the sky and peeled open, creating a portal as wide as a village. The sharp, violet edges were paper-thin. Avyllon's army marched through thirty wide. Alarmed shouts mixed with war cries as the battle began.

Theo lifted his gleaming sword and charged through the Way. "To war!"

Avyllon's armies followed, rows upon rows of their soldiers marching through and pouring out onto the fields surrounding the Pillar. The Demorrans were ready.

For all their secrecy and care, someone had tipped off the emperor.

Horns blew, sounding the alarm. Demorrans lined up and met the charging Avyllonians. Mooncursed snarled inside their metal cages, clawing and gnashing at the bars as the wardens set them free. Shadows took to the skies, alighting atop the Pillar. Scattered Demorran sorcerers hurled purple fireballs toward Nesryn's Way.

Theo charged up and down the advancing line, shouting commands. Sentinels Kolten, Edran, and Eryk flanked the king's unit with Rhydian, Nesryn, Adonis, Miella, Marco, the nameless one, and Aurienne. Aurienne's cards flew from her hands, floating before her in changing patterns. Even the little fox darted underfoot, a flash of red fur and glowing eyes.

"Forward left, they're regrouping," Aurienne called, and signalers relayed the commands. "Right, archers double time, fire!"

The sentinels hefted their short swords. A Mooncursed galloped toward his personal unit from the scattered, felled trees. Miella fired an arrow, and then another. Marco's sunlight tattoos flared, and he dripped the bleeding flames on the edge of his sword. He drove the sword through the beast. It fell with a roar.

"The center weakens," Aurienne said. "Send them now."

"Cavalry press center, archers support," Theo ordered. "First through fifteenth companies advance hard."

The cavalry rode hard for the Demorran camps as archers loosed arrows into their ranks.

"Our line is about to break at the twenty-seventh company," Aurienne said.

"Hold your formations!" Theo ordered, wheeling his horse.

The mortal, Avyllonian soldiers marched in groups of one hundred strong. The front line poised their spears toward their foe. The cavalry darted in and out of the Demorrans, breaking their lines and retreating and breaking them again. Squads of line-breakers hammered the scrambling enemy, while siege units focused on lighting the tents, wagons, and defense structures on fire.

"We make our own fate," Theo called. "We take the Pillar today or we die!"

Thousands poured through.

Avyllon's entire army and all their sentinels marched. Fifty thousand trained warriors entered the field, hardened by battles at the isthmus and raids on the city.

A seer accompanied every company, tossing bone runes and reading cards before calling out warnings to the commanders. The temple of the Triple Goddess sat empty as all her daughters went to battle.

Sorcerers were protected by squads of sentinels, tucked between the companies of foot soldiers. They hurled firecore, dreamsmoke, sightstealer, razorlung, and other swirling vials.

Vampires soared through the Way, seven hundred strong. They targeted the Mooncursed, sinking their fangs into the throats of the feral, cursed beasts. The Demorrans hurried to place their defensive walls of lashed-together trees, while Avyllon brought forth siege engines.

The nameless one flitted between the darkening shadows, a wraith among the battle, using his glowing shadow staff to strike enemies back.

Death and chaos reigned.

A mere five miles stood between them and the Pillar, but it might as well have been a hundred. Theo steeled himself, preparing for a long night. They had to reach the Pillar before dawn or the vampires would be gone, and they'd never be able to face the Mooncursed alone. Fourteen hours. It would save them, or they'd all be dead.

The armies clashed, and Theo entered the thick of the fray. Rhydian kept ahead of him, wounding the soldiers who ventured too close, and Theo or Nesryn finished them. Rhydian shook his head, and as he turned his head, Theo could see his eyes turning red. The call of battle was proving too much for him.

Horns sounded again and the Demorrans turned and all focused on Theo's group. They must have found the king and would strike at the head of the army. The Demorran cavalry had finally mounted and now rode for them.

Stone giants ripped open the earth, clawing upwards and lumbering across the field toward the Avyllon companies. Theo kicked his mount on, leading the charge toward the Pillar.

"Theo," Nesryn shouted. "You must use the magic of your blade. We need it now."

"I don't know how." Theo clenched his jaw as he blocked the strike of a Demorran's spear. "Maybe I don't have magic."

Nesryn hurled a dagger from her belt, which sunk into the chest of a snarling Mooncursed. She leapt, slicing her starlight sword through its throat. She flipped, dislodging her dagger before the beast fell.

"The magic runs deep in your blood," she said. "It's the only reason the sword responds to your touch. You just have to will it to obey."

Theo tried to will the sword to do something, anything, but it didn't seem to change. He continued to fight the swarms of Demorrans and Mooncursed. They were surrounded, cut off from the rest of the army that was getting hammered.

Gods—it felt hopeless.

Nesryn appeared before him, her stormy charcoal eyes boring into him. "Why are you fighting? Let that guide you, focus on it."

What am I fighting for?

Theo allowed his body to take over the practiced familiar motions of battle as his mind searched for his purpose. His attention split between the memories and the warfare.

Cool crystalline water rushed over his head as he dove after Aurienne into the pool at the Foretelling Rite. He dragged her out, before forcing the water from her lungs and breathing life into her. His skull cracked against the dungeon cell before all turned black.

Barefoot, he entered her chambers, lit with a hundred candles. Her skin was warm as she took his hand and sliced his palm. His heart hammered as she licked the blood from his hand and read his fate.

Ma smelled of wildflowers as he hugged her goodbye, and the eyestone she'd given him now bouncing against his tunic.

The blade at his throat in Wyndsel. The trial at Rodarri where he fought Rhydian and was nearly beaten to death. Being hunted in the Seven Forests and trapped in the dark for days under the Titan Cliffs.

Clang.

Thunk.

Splat.

Crunch.

Blood sprayed as Theo slashed a Demorran, the man falling from his horse and tumbling to the ground. His mind followed the memories, searching for his purpose.

Bonfires and stars lit the skies as he danced under the witches' magic. Aurienne's lips were soft against his as he kissed her. And then she spun away, and he remembered she was never his to have.

A long, low whistle rose in the night sky before turning into an unearthly howl. The Mooncursed ripping through the caravan in a flurry of claws and fang. Mathis straightened, clutching a vial of deep purple liquid. The veil of age lifted from his wrinkled face as he slammed the deathforce into the ground. They'd buried their friends in a grove of tamarack trees and planted hellebore lily on their quiet graves.

Burning eyes peered out of the Heartspring cave. A hot, damp breeze slithered out of the cave's mouth, before a horrible voice answered his pleas. He'd been knocked to the dirt as the vampires took to the skies for the first time in a thousand years.

Staking the Mooncursed head into the ground at the Seven Forests. The Living Stone warrior at the Titan Cliffs that hadn't woken. That quiet grouping of houses with blood smeared on the walls where he'd found the two young survivors of vampire attacks.

Hiss.

Clang.

Screech.

Clang.

Theo's unit was pressed together with barely enough room to turn. The sea of Demorrans threatened to drown them. His sword arm burned as he struck again and again, following Rhydian's bloody trail. The memories came hard and fast.

The screams of the dying and transforming at Eyrand arena. Long months battling at the isthmus. Companions falling every day. The Shadows. The Mooncursed. The dying. It all faded together into an unending nightmare. Every life that had fallen at his hand these past months weighed on him.

And through all the violence, he saw Aurienne telling him she couldn't watch him die again. Telling him she could never love, telling him to leave. The feeling of walking away from her to fight her war.

Rage, bitterness, resentment, regret, heartbreak pierced him to the bone. Yet, the blade remained as before. He knew what he'd faced, what he'd done, and he faced down what he must yet do.

Why am I doing this?

Theo brought his blade up to block a lion-Mooncursed's claws, twisting the blade with a flick of his wrist to sink it into its shoulder before sliding up to hack into its throat.

To protect my home, my family, my people.

Because I swore I would.

For the future.

For her.

He was doing this for love. His thoughts went to Aurienne.

Stillness settled upon him as his doubts fled in the face of his unwavering will. Failure wasn't an option. This was his destiny, and he'd be hellsdamned if he didn't take it.

Theo's glowing blade came alive, slicing through steel and bone —rending souls and magic. Enemies fell by the dozen, the hundred, the thousand.

FALLING ASH
CHAPTER SIXTY

Unbreakable vows are made on heartwood because its bark no longer burns.

— SIXTH FOREST WISDOM.

1153 N.T.C. The Seven Forests.

Ash rained down from the inferno racing across the Fourth Forest straight toward the Seventh Forest treetop city. Thaen and the other warriors formed a long line between the blaze and their home. Behind them, people scrambled to pour buckets of water on the city walls and their homes. Fearful eyes reflected the orange blazes.

"Hold!" Thaen's father, Dharek, shouted.

The elders fanned out ahead, bark-skinned arms raised as thick smoke poured through the canopies.

Thaen and other naturalist warriors formed a loose line behind the elders. He raised his hands, feeling the energy pulse through his veins.

Dharek glanced back. "Not yet. Preserve your magic. We'll need it when ours runs out."

Grimacing, Thaen lowered his hands. His father continued to prevent him from using his magic these past months, and his arms had fully cleared of the transformative barkskin. Strangely, he was itching to embrace it again—even with the painful consequences.

Dharek's hands tensed as vines and sprouts burst through the ground, forming a secondary wall to hold back the flames. The other elders called their own barriers. Magic popped in the air.

The unnatural orange and purple flames raced on.

"How did the blazes jump the streams?" Elder Emmesa asked, arms shaking from effort.

"Magic," Dharek gritted.

Thaen watched his father closely, taking several steps forward to stand just behind him. Barkskin covered Dharek's hands and arms up to the elbow. Thaen clenched his fists and slammed the butt of his spear into the packed dirt.

Forest giant, Allesan, lumbered over, each footstep booming. "We can't let the fire line progress farther. It'll burn through all seven forests and reach the saplings."

Thaen's father stared ahead. "We'll all be dead before it gets that far."

Gripping his spear, Thaen watched the barkskin crawl up his father's arm. He waited for the elders' commands. Howls echoed through the trees, followed by deathly screeches. The Mooncursed. And Shadows. They were coming.

"Forward!" Thaen ordered his warriors.

They slipped between the elders, preparing to defend them from the beasts. The barkskin crept up all the elder's flesh, toward their shoulders as the walls grew higher, thicker, denser. Hopefully the flames wouldn't be able to penetrate, and would suffocate and starve.

Ever since the Pillar fell, they'd been fighting off Mooncursed beasts and small fires, but nothing compared to this. Mighty trees centuries old were burning. What was lost this day might never return. This was the fight of their lives.

Avyllon sent word they planned to attack the emperor's troops stationed at the Flame Pillar. Dharek and the elders planned to send reinforcements before their forests had started to burn. Now, Avyllon was on its own. The Seven Forest people had to protect their homes before they could lend aid.

The first Mooncursed tore through the trees, shooting for Emmesa's throat. A spear struck true, and the wolfish beast fell. Two more spears pierced its chest before it finally lay still. Groups of three. Three strikes to take down a beast. In the long months since the Pillar fell, they'd learned. One-on-one the beasts were fierce, but they could be overpowered by numbers.

Another charged them, and Thaen slammed his spear into it. Two arrows struck in the lion-creature's neck and chest. It crawled forward for Dharek, and Thaen speared it in the skull.

"Hold!" Dharek shouted to the elders.

The unnatural flames slammed up against the wall, searing and sizzling the vines and bark holding them back.

A Mooncursed darted out of the brush, and Thaen dove to avoid its claws. Spinning, he shoved his spear up into it as it pounced. A fellow warrior speared it, before helping to drag it off him. Thaen pushed to his feet, already striking at the next attacking beast.

The black smoke was so thick, he could hardly breathe. Sparks drifted down and seared small marks into his shoulders and arms. The flames rammed the protective wall, searching for any gap to slip through.

Barkskin crawled up Dharek's throat. His movements were becoming shaky. His arms grew lower by the minute. Flames and beasts attacked the wall, as Dharek pushed back.

Thaen spun his spear, slamming the butt into the side of a Mooncursed's head before twirling it around and driving the tip into the beast's skull. Two more spears struck its chest, lancing in and out. The beast fell twitching.

"The sorcerers! They have to be nearby!" Dharek shouted through his teeth. "Find them!"

Thaen scanned the trees, searching for the bastards.

There.

Taking a measured step, he twisted his body and hurled his spear into the trees. The spear struck a sorcerer hiding behind a tree trunk, and the man fell. Thaen dodged the flames, hurrying to retrieve his spear.

Flames shot toward him, and he rolled forward, coming up with his spear ready to throw. He hurled it at the next sorcerer. The woman fell.

Thaen grasped his spear, twisting it to free it of the sorcerer's ribs. He backed up slowly, watching the trees for Mooncursed as he rejoined his warriors.

Arms shaking, Dharek continued to pour magic into the protective wall. The barkskin crept up his face, now covering every other inch of his body. The wall crawled forward—pushing back against the flames and the Mooncursed trying to get to their precious city.

Dharek looked at his son. "Don't let it consume you."

Thaen's frenzied heart stilled. "Father!"

"I love you, son." Dharek grunted.

Barkskin grew over his mouth, closing it forever, before reaching his eyes. The naturalist stopped moving—now fully one with the forest he'd wanted to protect.

"No!" Thaen shouted, knowing in his heart his father was gone.

Rage filling him, he raised his arms and called for every last ounce of magic. It exploded in his palms and full-sized trees tore out of the soil. The wall pushed forward toward the dwindling flames.

"Go!" Thaen fell to one knee. "Take out their sorcerers. I'll hold it as long as I can."

Sweat dripped down his face as the barkskin crawled up his arm.

LEXYRA
CHAPTER SIXTY-ONE

With spilled blood and eternal magic, I damn you. I lay a curse on this wretched place that will last a thousand years and a thousand deaths. Every pain we suffer shall be cast upon our enemies one-hundred-fold, and you will drown in the blood of the slaughtered. Death will consume your soul, and vengeance will be ours.

— FINAL WORDS OF QUEENSBLOOD LEXYRA DAWNROSE LENORE, BLOODWITCH, DAUGHTER OF QUEEN VITTORIA NIGHTFLAME LENORE, THE FIRST QUEENSBLOOD, 31 N.T.C.

1153 N.T.C. The dungeons of Castle Rodarr, Rodarri.

Never again. I won't be caged again.

Jagged, rusty bars of the damp cell dug into Rianne's fingers. The titan ore shackles clinked against the metal, and her skirts were damp and heavy from the brackish water. They'd come too far to fall now. If she failed, the ascensions would return and thousands more Queensblood would die in the centuries to come. The Flame Pillar would remain doused, and Rodarri would be overrun. Had the day of the attack come? Were her allies dying while she rotted in here?

My death must mean more than this.

Her fingers brushed her corset, willing the bonesword to come to life in her palm. The bones were icy under her touch with the titan ore silencing her magic. She'd never even known such an object existed. Maybe if she'd been a better ally, someone would have told her.

She leaned against the gray wall beside the door. The sons of the commanders had no idea what they'd done. They believed their cause just, and maybe it was as just as hers had been. Their rage was the same as hers. An unending cycle of vengeance that only stopped when the violence stopped or when everyone was dead.

The knowledge swirling in her skull and bones was endless. If only they'd better used it, this never would have happened. She wouldn't have been captured so easily. If the queens had listened to her about their allies, her friends, and maybe if she'd listened about the commander's sons... This all would have been very different.

Where was Rhydian? Why hadn't he come? Had she finally pushed him away too far? Had he given up on her? Had Aurienne misinterpreted or ignored her message? Would she die in here? Her mind swam as her dark thoughts threatened to drown her.

With the queens so far away, her hold on the mortal realm was tenuous. The titan ore sapped her strength, turned the deluge of power into a slowing trickle her failing body couldn't survive on. Her joints cracked as she shifted against the rough floor.

She closed her eyes, picturing the gardens just outside these subterranean cells. Cerulean sirenbells and amethyst foxgloves swayed in a warm summer breeze, their petals scattered across the blanket. Peach-colored clouds floated in a sapphire afternoon sky. Rhydian's hands were on her waist, pulling her in. His lips against hers as he whispered, "I love you."

Silver tears soaked Rianne's cheeks, and she opened her eyes. She'd made promises to Rhydian and wouldn't break them now.

I won't give up.

She released her hold on her body, allowing the faint magic to tether her to the queens.

The spirits shifted in her marrow.

Whillow whispered, *"It's time for the end to return to the beginning. The path has been laid to break the cycle. We now must destroy the curse."*

"I don't understand," Rianne replied. "How do I destroy this curse?"

Rosalindt pushed forward. *"Titan ore is strong enough to contain one of us. Not all of us."*

Rianne swallowed. "What do you mean?"

"If you joined us, we could escape," Samantah's rage was hardly contained.

Vittoria's voice was louder than all others, louder than it had ever been. *"We were always meant to fight together as one. The curse was only ever to gather us."*

Fear slithered down Rianne's throat.

"You know how," Noxanya said. *"She's been waiting. The queen you refuse to name. The answer has always been right there, hiding in the dark ocean of power."*

Vittoria's voice began to fade as Rianne's strength faltered. *"You know what you must do. You've always known. It's time to unlock the power that lays dormant in us."*

Rianne backed away from the bars. All too aware of the power they spoke of. The power she'd been avoiding. She could feel it beneath her feet, between her fingers, slipping across her neck like dark water. All it took was dipping her head below those cursed waves, and she might never emerge.

Scraping boots, and loud thuds filled the corridor. Rianne craned her neck to see down the hall, hearing feminine voices mixed with angry shouts of the heirs and turncoat guards. Shivers ran down her spine as she heard her sister's voice in the corridor.

Milah's spirit wrapped comfortingly around Rianne's shoulders. *"She's been waiting for you. So many centuries. We've all been waiting. Embrace your destiny."*

Her mother's voice was a cool salve on her aching heart. *"It's time to join us, daughter."*

Silver tears slipped down Rianne's cheeks. She'd been living on borrowed time knowing the end came near. This was always the fate she was a slave to.

Four guards fell to the floor before the bars, foaming at the mouth, clawing at their throats silently.

Her sister Jordyn, Aunt Yllicea, and several others stepped in front of the bars, hands glowing crimson—bloodmagic. Behind them, others held daggers and swords still dripping with blood. Jordyn strode toward Rianne, determination painted across her expression.

Rianne whispered, "You came for me?"

"We make our own destinies," Jordyn said. "If we want to escape our fate, we're going to have to fight for it."

"How did you overcome the heirs?" Rianne asked.

Jordyn smiled. "We let them see what we wanted. We didn't look like threats until it was too late. We poisoned their celebratory wine and then we struck as hard and fast as we could. Poisons, passages, blades. And those pampered prats hadn't been training. We may be small individually, but together we're unstoppable."

Rianne smiled and hugged Jordyn back. It was the same thing she'd told her sister about the emperor.

"I'm sorry I couldn't save you," Rianne said.

Jordyn's hands flared with bloodmagic. "You showed us how to save ourselves. The others are still fighting, we need to go to them."

Peace flooded Rianne. Her only true goal had ever been to keep her family safe, and she'd done it. By forcing them to train, by teaching them magic—she'd helped them find their strength.

"You don't need me anymore," Rianne whispered, a smile drawing across her face as happy tears rained from her eyes.

"Nonsense," Jordyn replied. "Now hold on, we'll get you out of there."

"No need," Rianne held her hand up.

The fear and anger melted away. Deep down, she knew that her family was going to be fine after this. The spirits were right. It was time. Now—the only threat to them was the emperor, and she'd best defeat him if she joined the spirits for good. This was the fate she'd embrace. She'd dive into that dark well of power, endless as the sea, and do what she'd promised to do—then she'd have her revenge. She would protect her land from the emperor, and then end the sacrifices once and for all.

I'm not losing myself.

I will become what I was always meant to be.

Her ascension had been brutal and horrific, the return worse. But this time when Rianne faced her fate, she would face it on her terms. It would be her choice, and she would meet it with a smile.

"I love you Jordyn," she said. "I'm not afraid of death. I understand now."

Jordyn's brows twisted, hearing the farewell in her voice. "Rianne?"

Rianne took a deep breath and allowed her soul to fall through the spirits inhabiting her body. She slipped beneath the sea of power.

There was a darkness in that sea, lurking near the bottom, and she could only believe that it was the cursed daughter. Rianne knew all the ascended Queensblood by name, and only one had remained dormant. Lexyra. The daughter Vittoria sacrificed herself for, who'd never received her birthright of life and instead eventually followed her mother to execution. The bloodwitch who'd led a revolt against the kings and been burned at the stake for it. The queen who'd cursed all their spirits to be bound to the ravine, waiting for their revenge. Silent. Waiting. She'd been amassing power for centuries as the sacrifices piled up as high as the bleached bones in the bottom of the ravine.

"Lexyra, I know you're there. It's time. Wake up," Rianne whispered as the darkness surrounded her.

The dark endless pool of power took shape. It roiled, crashing through Rianne and absorbing all the spirits in her bones and blood. Rianne felt herself joining the pool, becoming one with the death she was fated for, one soul in a sea of souls. One voice in a thousand. Rianne faded into the deep as another took control.

"Hello."

Lexyra's spirit awoke. It was forest fires and tidal waves. Burning bones and icy blood. It was a thousand deaths all at once and a thousand promises to keep. It was power. And now that she woke... destruction would follow.

Her spirit wove through Rianne's bones and blood, settling deeply into her new home. The titan ore shackles glowed, the dampening magic struggling against the combined might of all the queens. No longer was there a mere connection from Rianne to the others, now they all melded as one. Lexyra yanked Rianne's hands apart and the shackles crumbled, the magic rendered inert. No magic could stand against a thousand angry queens.

Lexyra reached Rianne's hand out and closed it around the bars. The bars snapped and popped as a thick layer of frost coated the splintering metal. The door fell from its hinges with a loud bang. Slowly, carefully, Lexyra stepped over the ruined mass, before walking past Jordyn and the other queens in the corridor.

Flexing her hands, she traced their bloody path through the dungeon and back through the castle, waiting to find her prey.

Three guards rounded the corner wielding spears.

"You! Stop!"

"Hands up!"

Whillow grinned through their lips. "Oh me? You want my hands up? As you wish."

Lexyra's hands shot up and bone darts from the corset flew toward the guards, burying deeply into their necks. Blood spurted down the uniforms as they choked and fell to their knees. With another jerk of her hands, Whillow called back the darts.

Behind her, Jordyn gasped—in awe and surprise.

Safyrah and Noxanya emerged, calling the bonesword into being from the corset. Samantah turned it a lazy arc, waiting for the boots echoing down the hall. Slash. Slice. Slash. Bodies fell. Blood coated the walls.

"We surrender!" A soldier dropped his sword to the cobblestones, and several more followed suit.

"It's a bit late for that. I don't accept surrender from traitors," Nicollete whispered as Samantah cut them down.

Bodies lined the dungeon as they made their escape. Shouts and the clanging of metal filled the stairwell. Lexyra followed the commotion, hearing the sounds of raging combat echoing through their castle.

Lexyra stepped out of the stairwell and followed the sounds toward the queens' chambers. In the center of the wading ponds, a brutal fight seethed.

Elderly Tamiira drove her sword through the gut of a captain as Atley held a man's head underwater. Marta stood over the smaller girls, holding a bloodied sword. Elayhna raised her blade and drove it down on the neck of the man Atley drowned. His head floated away in the water.

A captain grabbed an older queen by the neck and slammed her against the wall. She screamed and clawed at his eyes. He squeezed her throat, and her eyes bulged. From nowhere, young Ella appeared and drove a dagger deeply into his ribs. Blood spilled from his lips, and he fell. Another kicked a wounded man into the pond and held his head below the surface. The man stilled beneath her cousin's hand. Before

Lexyra even lifted her hand, the fighting had ceased as the men died.

Just then, the Queensblood noticed Rianne's arrival. To a one, the Queensblood wore stolen armor and cold expressions.

Rianne pushed to the front of the spirits, silver tears of pride dripping down her chin. They'd taken up arms and fought for her, for themselves. They'd stood up and taken control of their lives. It was all she'd ever wanted for her sister and the others. These brave queens before her would never be sacrificed again. They'd never be taken again.

Lexyra took hold again. "After tonight, the circle will be broken."

Jordyn's expression pinched, as if she could see the spirits slipping in and out of control, could see her sister step back for the others to step forward—a seamless dance.

"I'll come with you," Jordyn said.

Rianne touched her sister's cheek. "You have all done more than enough. Leave Bram and the remaining *heirs* to me. I don't want merciless blood on your hands. I don't want you to be like me."

Jordyn gripped her sword. "I want to be exactly like you. You were right. We were weak and nearly died for it."

Lexyra slipped into control. "Healing demands first cutting out the rot. I hope that my cruelty makes way for your goodness. The people will never love me, but they will love you."

Safyrah and Noxanya's souls wove together, whispering magic from their butchered coven.

Lexyra strolled through the castle toward the king's chambers. Undoubtedly, Bram had taken up residence there. The grating laughter within confirmed Whillow's suspicions. Lexyra grinned as she slammed open the doors, bonesword in hand.

Bram's chair tipped over as he scrambled away from the door, and the other dozen young nobles tumbled frantically out of their chairs. Her skirts danced across the polished floors. Her bare feet were silent. A slash of her blade took the head of the nearest noble. She wrenched it out and drove it into another's neck. Soon the floor was soaked with blood and only Bram remained cowering with his dagger in hand.

Callysta's crazed smile twisted Rianne's pretty features. "Oh, how they all shall die."

"How did you escape?" Bram's voice cracked.

Callysta only smiled.

Bram fell to his knees, tossing the blade across the floor. "I give up. I call for mercy."

Milah squared Rianne's shoulders. "We know nothing of mercy."

Bram scooted backward as Lexyra advanced. The bonesword glinted hungrily in the firelight.

"You can't kill an unarmed man," he pleaded.

Lexyra-Whillow slammed the hilt of the sword into Bram's face, as he had struck Rianne. Blood poured from the cut on his head.

"What are you doing?"

"Cutting out the rot," Lexyra whispered.

Lexyra-Whillow pressed the tip of the bonesword against his chest and slowly slid it past his breastbone as he thrashed and screamed.

Callysta's smile turned feral. "Oh how they all shall die!"

Lexyra threw open the windows and gazed at the evening sky. Safyrah and Noxanya sent shards of the bonesword flying into the night. The rest of the traitorous noble sons would die in their beds tonight. Their families would die. Their lines would end, and the cycle of revenge would be complete. There would be none left to oppose her.

Lexyra spoke, "We have a battle to win tonight, and the fate of the continent depends on it. Let's hope we aren't too late."

HUNGER'S TEETH
CHAPTER SIXTY-TWO

There is war and eventually there is death, but nothing more.

— QUEENSBLOOD RIANNE CHARLOTTE LENORE.

1153 N.T.C. The Flame Pillar, outside the Hunger's Teeth Mountains.

Horrors of war came to life all around Aurienne, the same as her Lunahain vision of destruction. Minutes turned to hours and longer. Theo led the army on, taking first a mile, then a second, and almost a third. The darkened Pillar, a single stone column taller than Avyllon's walls, stretched for the sky. They were so close, with five hours left before dawn.

A second Way burst to life, crackling and jagged around the edges and glowing with purple light. Reinforcements teemed through the emperor's portal, an endless stream of warriors and Mooncursed.

Aurienne's breath caught.

If their allies didn't show soon, they would be overrun.

"Is Wynds coming?" she asked her cards.

The Siren flew in front of her face, the figure on the card shaking her head sadly before diving into the water with a splash of ink.

"The Titan Cliffs?"

The Living Stone card just looked at her, unmoving. They'd be too slow to arrive in time.

"The Seven Forests?"

The Silver Tongue card showed a face coated in bark, burning. They were dealing with their own threat, they wouldn't come.

Aurienne swallowed. "Rodarri?"

The Dead Queen card hovered before her, the queen screaming.

Hellsdamn it.

"What?" Theo demanded.

She shook her head. "We must keep going."

Her cards spun, frantically dripping ink. She stepped forward, trying to see the beast painted on every card.

From nowhere, a Mooncursed slammed into her and threw her to the ground. The breath was knocked from her lungs, as she tried to scream for help. It began to drag her away by her skirts. She clawed for the ground, nails digging into the thick mud.

Spinning, she kicked at it with her boot, striking its nose several times. It shook its head, jerking her back and forth. Air finally returning, she shouted at it while kicking harder. Fingers fumbling, she drew her golden dagger out of her gown. She kicked again and the beast leapt on her.

Screaming, she brought up the dagger, blindly stabbing again and again. The beast roared and backed away, blood pouring from its neck and face. Several lithe wolfish Mooncursed skulked out of the trees. Fear ripped through her. The first beast opened its maw and dove.

Aurienne screamed again.

A deafening roar caused the largest beast to turn as a luminous sword cleaved its skull in two. Theo brought down his Sword of Souls as he leapt from horseback. The beast fell. Theo whirled, slashing for the gray-furred beast who darted out of the trees. A single slice and the beast fell, twitching and writhing.

Two more attacked, lunging for Aurienne. Theo stepped between them, standing over her in full armor with his enchanted blade that vibrated with energy. She looked up in awe. The hardened warrior who owed her nothing, protecting her with his life. Strong, agile, ruthless.

A reddish Mooncursed circled Theo from the shadows and sprang for his unprotected back.

"Theo!"

At the last second, he turned, crashing the hilt of the sword into its skull. The creature cried out, but with a flick of the wrist, he'd taken its head.

Theo turned and reached out his hand for her, breathing hard, anger and concern warring in his gaze. She took it, and he helped her to stand. He didn't release her, letting the touch linger as he searched her face. She couldn't look away from him.

"You came?" she breathed.

"I will always come for you," he said.

Her heart threatened to burst. He kept hold of her hand long past necessity, escorting her back to his personal unit. When he finally released her, he remained at her side.

The bloody conflict raged through the night. Evenly matched, the armies met again and again under the blanket of darkness.

Dawn broke, and Stellan landed beside Theo. "We must leave. We stayed as long as we could. We'll return at dusk," he said before taking to the skies.

If we survive.

The vampires all left with a thunderous beating of their wings.

Aurienne's heart sank. She glanced at Theo, a dark storm brewing on his face. He lifted his head toward the lightening skies before catching her gaze.

Their time had run out.

Nesryn swung her bloody sword. "I can try to open another Way. I'm not sure I can hold it open for long enough."

Aurienne didn't need visions to know Theo wouldn't call the retreat. Without the Pillar, they had no hope of standing against the Demorrans. They were losing the isthmus by the day, and now their army was decimated. If they couldn't get to the Pillar, they'd all die.

Theo lifted his sword. "We fight on."

Blood pounded through Rhydian's veins and in his skull. The crimson veil descended upon his vision, threatening he would soon lose control. He could taste the coppery tang of the blood, the salty aroma of the sweat, the steel around him. He launched himself at the nearest Mooncursed, wading through the sea of corpses. The beast was some horrible combination of a buffalo and a tiger, the skin half falling off its frame. He smashed his ax into the beast, and it fell.

A weight crashed into him, knocking him sideways. He caught his footing and roared, feeling his blood sing and call for death. He spun.

Nesryn was inches from his face. "Limbs only or they'll die, Warbringer."

Rhydian shook his head, trying to clear the fog from his mind. Had he been striking to kill?

He gritted his teeth, managing only, "Sorry."

Nesryn said, "I'll do the killing."

The pace was unsustainable. Too many were dying. Retreat. Charge. Fight. Maneuver. Charge. Retreat. Repeat. And each time hundreds died. Rhydian's thoughts blurred as he could only focus on the fighting. With the vampires gone, they could not hold their ground. Hours passed, the day wore on, and still they fought for their future, for their lives.

"Only a mile remains," Theo panted, sword arm shaking.

"A mile filled with enemies," Aurienne said, her cards hovering around her. "There is no path through yet."

Rhydian gritted his teeth, attacking the line with renewed effort. Sooner or later Theo or Nesryn was going to be too late, and his curse would awaken. He'd been lucky so far.

The nameless one stepped into existence from nothing, twirling a purple-tinged staff in wide circles. "The Shadows remain with the Pillar, but many are absent. They're planning something. You've not seen what Niamh is capable of."

Nesryn froze in the midst of the fighting. "Niamh?"

The bloodlust raged through Rhydian, but his instincts screamed when she stilled like that, sensing the nearby threat.

"Where did you hear that name?" Her voice was cold as death.

The nameless one spun the staff into a charging Demorran, knocking him into the mud. "The goddess that Rexil serves, the one who put up the wards. Her name is Niamh."

Nesryn's fluid ash gray skin shimmered as her eyes darkened to black slits. Her hand shook with anger as her nostrils flared. The tip of her starlight blade lowered as she looked into the distance.

"It can't be," she whispered.

Rhydian gripped his ax. "Who is she?"

Nesryn's jaw clenched. "If it's who I think, she must be stopped." She glared at Rhydian. "Keep fighting."

"Now! All forces to the Pillar!" Theo ordered.

Rhydian grabbed the reins of a nearby horse and pulled himself up. The army rallied and charged behind them. He kicked the horse into a gallop, staying seated with only his legs and swinging twin axes. Limbs went flying as he and Theo led the assault.

Rianne. We need you.

Avyllon's army crashed against the Demorran's auxiliary line surrounding the Pillar. Waves upon waves of Avyllonians smashed against the shield wall.

The Demorrans squeezed Avyllon's charging spearhead formation into a wobbly line, entire companies felling beneath the fang and claw of Mooncursed. And then the Demorran line took a step forward, then another. Avyllon was pushed back. Rhydian was jostled by retreating soldiers.

"Cavalry, regroup. Charge! Fiftieth through sixtieth companies forward! Drive hard now!" Theo shouted commands.

Fireballs flew over their heads. Shadows began leaping from the Pillar, racing forward toward them with their otherworldly throaty cries. They tore into the soldiers. Archers loosed arrow after arrow into them, but the beasts hardly slowed. The nameless one flew to their aid.

Rhydian couldn't go to them. He had to drive forward to the Pillar. If they couldn't relight it, it was all for nothing. He glanced back, seeing his allies fight for their lives. Aurienne calling directions to Theo. The king cutting down hundreds with his starlight blade. Miella nocking arrow after arrow until her quiver ran empty. Marco slashing at Mooncursed with his flaming sword. Adonis launching fireballs. The young flame elemental touching any who got too close and holding on as they burned—a wild light in her eyes. Nesryn's unnerving gaze following his every move, saving him from madness.

Another wave of Demorrans pushed them back. Mooncursed tore into their flanks. They lost a hundred paces. And then another. Rhydian glanced at Theo, who was bleeding in a dozen places, but determination painted his face. Rhydian glanced down, seeing his own small injuries bleeding. So close to the edge, he hadn't even felt them.

Rianne, please.

Avyllon lost a mile, the companies compressed, the sorcerers and seers being picked off. They couldn't do it. All their planning, all their magic, and they still couldn't succeed against the might of the Demorran empire.

Trumpets sounded, and Rhydian lifted his head. An army garbed in red marched in neat lines over the grassy knolls. The bulk of the Rodarri army arrived. And for a horrible moment, Rhydian wondered whether Rianne had come just in time to crush the resistance.

Queensblood bloodwitches hurled cursed vials and dribbled blood to the ground as they hurled curses into the Demorrans. Sorcerers sent fireballs into the sky that fell upon the enemy siege walls. With a war cry that echoed through the onlooking mountains, Rodarri attacked Demorra with unmatched fury.

Ballista crossbows fired steel arrows the size of fence posts into the Demorran front line. Trebuchets rolled forward, hurling flaming boulders. Dragon's maw machines spraying flames over units of Demorran cavalry. Behind the army, soldiers carried fang walls with sharpened tree trunks pointing out.

Chills raced down Rhydian's back. Rianne came. She hadn't betrayed them, and she might just save the continent.

The tide of the battle turned.

WEARY HEARTS
CHAPTER SIXTY-THREE

Let's show them war.

— RHYDIAN REDBROOKE, WARBRINGER,
GENERAL OF THE RODARRI ARMIES AND
QUEENSGUARD.

1153 N.T.C. The Flame Pillar, outside the Hunger's Teeth Mountains.

Whistling tones of the dead left bleeding ears in their wake. The Shadows had arrived in full. Hundreds split the skies with their eerie wails and gleaming blades, hovering around the top of the Pillar.

Weary faces looked to Theo. Thirty thousand bloody, beaten soldiers had faced monsters and survived, but the cost had been great. The corpses of almost half their companions now littered the battlefield.

Darkening skies released a fine mist that settled upon their griffon-crested armor and gore-matted weapons. Theo wiped the grime from his face, watching the Rodarri forces beat back the Mooncursed and Demorran soldiers. Flames, boulders, and steel arrows flew across the freezing mud toward their foe.

Dusk was hours away, and the vampires would not be coming to their aid. Wynds' fleet never arrived, but it wasn't going to. And Rodarri wouldn't be able to hold them off forever. The time to press the Pillar was now, or they'd lose it for good.

Theo stepped onto the back of a wagon, looking over the assembled. The golden griffon on his armor was dented and marred, and blood trickled from his injuries.

"We won't get another chance to relight the Pillar, to protect our families from the Shadows." Theo panned his gaze over the crowd. "I am willing to die for this, and I will be leading the charge."

The soldiers' gazes were glued to him, eyes shining with apprehension and begging for reassurance.

"If we can relight the Pillar, we can push them back. Without the Shadows or Mooncursed, the human soldiers won't remain for long." Theo turned slowly. "This isn't some royal cause; I'm not asking you to fight for more land or power. This is for your village. Your home. Your families. If we can push them back, the people you love will be safe. And if we can't—the darkness will tear across the continent, and nothing will be left. There will be nowhere to hide."

Determination washed over the army. Chins lifted, shoulders pushed back, and fear dissipated.

Theo raised his gleaming Sword of Souls, sending starlight across the field. "We must make this stand today. And if we die, history will remember what we fought for."

Shouts rose from the soldiers.

"Fate said we couldn't win this war, but I don't accept that!" Theo shouted. "We make our own destiny."

More shouts of agreement followed.

"Fate be damned!" Theo yelled.

Thirty thousand strong roared, "Fate be damned."

Theo breathed in the stormy air, readying himself for this final effort. Either they'd relight the Pillar and stop the emperor, or he'd die. It all led up to this. The travels and training, the attacks, the battles. The deaths. The blood on his hands. His whole life.

Blinking, he realized his best memories were of Aurienne. He could see her again for the first time, standing over the ceremonial pool. Dragging her out and watching as the life returned to her cloudy eyes. Horseback rides and tavern conversations. Monster stories and dirty ditties. A thousand tiny moments.

She'd brought him the most pain, but also the most happiness. Her rare smile lit up a room. Her touch consumed him. Her dedication and strength awed him.

His bitterness and resentment were for what? Was he going to ride off to die without telling her everything he'd been too afraid to? Life was too short to remain angry. Seeing Aurienne thrown to the mud, seeing the Mooncursed loom over her, he realized he would only regret the things he didn't say.

The king of Avyllon stepped off the wagon and mounted his horse, facing down the horde surrounding the Pillar with his army at his back. He kicked his horse toward their final stand, but before he met Death, there was one thing he must do.

"Fate be damned," he whispered.

Warring Goddesses and Unspoken Truths

Chapter Sixty-Four

I would have followed you through hell.

— *Journal of the High Seer Aurienne Azarrah.*

1153 N.T.C. The Flame Pillar, outside the Hunger's Teeth Mountains.

Underneath a mantle of bruised storm clouds, Aurienne planted her boots on the splintered wood atop the siege tower. She dug her fingernails into the railing, preparing for the hours to come. The fate of the continent hinged on the few hours between now and nightfall. The flickering path to salvation would remain open or it would close forever. Her magic had remained dormant for months, but it was time to unleash its fury. She felt it bubbling inside her chest, a living pool of liquid gold.

"Aurienne," Theo called below from horseback.

She tore her eyes from the Pillar to him just as the skies opened with misty showers. The rain stuck his hair to his head and turned the coarse dirt to mud. Droplets coated her hot skin.

"It's time," he said. "The war machines have arrived. Rhydian and Nesryn are here. We can't wait any longer. We're storming the Pillar. We're going to have to get Hana as close as possible. She'll have to touch it."

Aurienne clenched her jaw and glared at the writhing swarm of death and magic at the heart of the battlefield. Theo would be charging where the fighting was thickest, where the sorcerers and Mooncursed creations gathered. Amidst the stone giants, Shadows, and other horrors.

Please don't die. I won't survive it.

Instead, she said, "I'll do my best to clear you a path."

I'll protect you. Even if it kills me.

It was a promise. Their gazes met, full of unspoken truths, cruel regrets, and raw heartache.

A sorcerer's fireball exploded against a nearby siege wall, and Theo's horse spun beneath him. His gaze never left hers.

Weary acceptance marked his features. "If today is my last day in this world, I'm going to tell you the truth."

She knew that look.

"Theo, don't." Her tone was firm.

"I won't go without saying it," he said. "Not again."

Don't say it. Please don't say it. This can't be taken back.

"I love you."

No.

Chills raced across her skin as fates and futures collided. Everything changed in an instant. She could hear her cards rustling from miles away and threads of fate snapping. Ancient magic pulsed as the Fates looked on.

Sooner or later, death would come for them now. The fate she'd been trying to prevent was sealed. Nothing would stop it.

One of them would die.

"If I die today, I won't die with regrets. You can push me away and you can break my heart again and again. It's too late." He allowed a hint of his once-carefree grin on his face. "You can pretend you don't feel it too, but I'm going to love you either way. It's only you, Aurienne. It's always going to be you. I love you."

He drew his sword and, with a final backward glance, charged into the fray. She watched him go, unknowingly carrying half her heart with him.

I love you, Theo.

The skies opened and rain pelted the battlefield. Raindrops clung to Aurienne's lashes and trickled down her neck.

Closing her eyes, Aurienne reached her spectral fingers into the overflowing, boiling pool of magic surrounding her heart. The shock of power hit her harder than a lightning strike, and she screamed. Her soul was ripped from her body and thrown into the world of futures and possibilities. Gritting her teeth, she grasped at vision after vision and placed it atop her sight. Her mind ached at the effort of keeping so many competing and changing outcomes straight.

He will not die. I'll get him to the Pillar even if this magic kills me.

Futures flowed from the choices of each warrior, connected by golden threads. She traced them, watching the futures collide and separate, going as far forward as she could to where the path to the Pillar cleared.

Theo just needed a single opening to get through, just a break in the line that held for long enough. The shifting futures evaded her.

There.

She found it. A future where Theo broke through the line and charged the Pillar with Rhydian, Hana, Adonis, and a handful of warriors. They made it to the base of the Pillar. The future shifted, breaking. The flanks collapsed on Theo and his troops were overrun.

No.

It had been there. The future where he broke through. She just needed to find the choices that changed things. A sorcerer looked left instead of right and signaled a warden. The Mooncursed surrounded them. She had to change that. Sorcerers hurled fireballs that decimated the troops just behind him. Theo avoided the fireballs, but giants burst free of the ground beneath him. A single Demorran cavalryman noticed Theo and signaled them to circle back and attack. The Shadows caught sight of the cavalry and descended.

She could change it.

Aurienne wrapped the chain of futures around her fist. She held it tightly, as she traced each small act backwards in time. The future writhed in her grip like a viper, each deviating choice threatening to collapse the entire chain. A thousand intertwining choices, but she held the future in her hands.

"The Fate of the continent rests in our hands! Protect your king!" Aurienne shouted. "Everyone, on me!"

Signal flags directed the attention of the Avyllon and Demorran armies to Aurienne.

Her voice echoed across the field, to the nearest trebuchet. "On my mark!"

Her left hand gave them a heading. Her right hand hovered in the air, waiting. Waiting. She tracked the many decisions of a flamethrowing sorcerer until she found an opening. The Demorran sorcerer's attention fell to Theo.

Her hand dropped. "Fire!"

A trebuchet launched toward where she'd pointed, and the sorcerer disappeared beneath a pile of rubble.

She lifted her hand again, signaling a group of ballistas. "Mark!"

Theo's horse charged across the battlefield straight toward the Pillar. Hana followed, and behind them was the bulk of the remaining army. Theo raised his illuminated Sword of Souls, directing them to the smoking hole in Demorra's defenses. A group of Mooncursed gathered around a warden and, with screeching snarls launched themselves toward Theo's flank.

Her hand dropped again. "Fire!"

A ballista fired steel arrows as tall as a man toward the line of Mooncursed charging Theo's flank.

Her hand aimed again at the unbroken line of troops encircling the Pillar, then it dropped. "Fire!"

Trebuchets and ballistas launched steel and stone toward the Demorrans, sending up a cloud of rubble.

She found the cavalryman from her vision and pointed her hand toward him. "Fire!"

A steel arrow speared the enemy from his horse and pinned him to the ground. But the Demorran cavalryman beside him looked their direction and signaled the others. The future writhed in her hand as the cavalry started to turn.

"Fang wall! Advance! Protect their backs!" Aurienne ordered.

Rodarri soldiers led the enormous workhorses forward, dragging sections of the wheeled fang walls made from whole tree trunks sharpened into deadly points. The walls forced the cavalry to change direction. The Demorrans foot soldiers and Mooncursed attacked, but the Avyllonian archers picked them off behind the safety of cover.

The Shadows swirling the top of the Pillar began shooting down, picking off warriors.

"Load up the dragon's maw machines with corpseroot vials," Aurienne said.

She lifted her hand. "Fire!"

Vials flew toward the top of the Pillar, catching the Shadows and lighting them on fire. Theo continued pressing on, cutting down Mooncursed and Demorrans on his path to the Pillar.

Aurienne fell to her knees, in both her spectral and corporeal forms, nearly losing the grip on the elusive future she chased. She slipped out of the veil, too weak to remain. Her magic dwindled to a meager stream, and she was unable to hold on much longer.

"Do you think you can defeat me?" Niamh's voice slithered into her ear. "You're fated to lose this war."

The sight of Theo charging across the battlefield, relying on her to cut them a path through steeled her resolve. Nothing would harm him while she breathed.

"Love is stronger than fate," Aurienne replied.

A shadowy illusion of Niamh stood before her. "Your visions weren't enough before. Your magic wasn't enough. What makes you think you can succeed now."

Summoning the last of her will, Aurienne gripped the tenuous future. "You have no idea the lengths I'll go."

SILVER TEARS
CHAPTER SIXTY-FIVE

Every bloodmagic curse has a cure, however dark or impossible. For the Warbringer, it lies in a moment of true peace. Though, for one born with battle in their veins, who could ever be at peace?

— *GRIMOIRE OF KAIRYA, BLOODWITCH, 1 B.N.T.C.*

1153 N.T.C. The Flame Pillar, outside the Hunger's Teeth Mountains.

Chaos reigned. The Rodarri army, their bloodwitches and sorcerers and war machines attacked the Demorrans with fervor. Rhydian's blood sang. The intoxicating sounds of death, the taste of copper and salt on his tongue, and the energy vibrating the air with the souls of the departed had him gripping his ax, ready to unleash his curse.

The butt of Rhydian's ax crushed a Mooncursed's throat, and Theo charged forward to drive his Sword of Souls through its chest. Rhydian hacked down, severing a warden's leg from his body, and

Theo followed with a slash across her throat. Nesryn launched toward a giant in their path, using her starlight blade to cleave it to rubble. As their enemies gathered, Miella slung her bow over her shoulder and used her long spear to stab at enemies from behind the Avyllonian sentinels' shields. The glowing tattooed vampire hunter Marco dripped glowing blood to his dagger and set the Mooncursed aflame. Their tight group pressed for the Pillar.

Rianne stepped onto a knoll, surveying her forces, and his heart leapt—the call of violence slipping away. She wore an unfamiliar expression, bloodmagic pooling around her fingertips. Something was wrong. He glanced at his friends, surrounded by enemies, and then back to Rianne.

Theo caught his expression, "Go to her, we'll hold them off as long as we can."

"I just need a minute," Rhydian called to his friend.

Theo wheeled his horse, slashing through the Demorrans who swarmed them. "Give him cover!"

Adonis launched a vial of dreamsmoke, obscuring them from their enemies. "Here!"

The cloud bloomed around them, and Rhydian charged for Rianne. His horse's hooves thundered through the field, sending mud and blood spraying.

Her gaze settled on him, and his heart sank. All those subtle differences he'd been forcing himself to ignore painted every inch of her. The faded color of her once cerulean eyes. The way her gaze was sharp, her lips pursed, her jaw set. The calm fold of her hands without any endearing fidgeting. The stiff posture of her spine.

Sliding off his horse, he approached.

"Where is she?" he said, trying to keep his voice from cracking.

"She's here, with all of us," the one who only looked like Rianne answered.

He gripped his ax. "Who are you?"

Rianne's lips moved, but it was not her voice. "I'm Lexyra, the daughter of the first Queesblood Vittoria. The bloodwitch who bound the spirits to the ravine, who allowed for some of us to return."

Rhydian stepped forward, raising his ax to the specter's throat. "Give her back."

His fury made him want to tear down anyone who stood between him and Rianne. But it was Rianne looking back at him, and he knew he could never hurt her. Lexyra must have known too.

She lifted a finger, pushing the ax away. "No one took her. She died, Rhydian, at the ascension. You've always known she returned changed."

His heart hammered as his stomach churned. He'd known. Somewhere deep down, he'd known. Unable to let her go, he'd clung to hope and ignored what his instincts screamed.

"Please. Bring her back," he said.

"If only we had the power," she replied. "We used our magic for as long as we could to give her time. In the end, it was her choice to join us. She's here, always here. One voice in a thousand."

"Can I speak with her?"

"She's weak," Lexyra said. "Her soul is recovering from the transition, but I will bring her forth for as long as I can."

His eyes burned. "Thank you."

"Rhydian?" Lexyra waited for him to look into her eyes. "I must warn you... you can't be together. There's not enough of her left, and she's not alone."

He nodded slowly.

"Say goodbye," Lexyra said.

Rianne's eyes glimmered a brighter blue, a soft smile tugged at her lips, and her entire body softened. The spirits wore her body, but they'd never be her. This was the woman he loved.

"Rianne," he took her into his arms and pulled her close.

Her delicate arms wrapped around him. "Rhydian."

"Are you okay? What happened?"

"Rexil gave Bram and the others titan ore shackles. It's why I was late," she said.

Fury and guilt wracked him. "I should've come for you."

She shook her head. "This is how it had to be."

"Don't say that," he said.

"Lexyra told the truth," she said. "So much is lost. I feel flashes of emotion, of love, but more and more it's just numb. And when I do feel, it's lost within the thoughts of the others. I'm only still here to protect my people."

Rhydian took a stumbling half-step backward, pressing his fist to his chest. He couldn't believe this. The red veil threatened to descend again, as he realized he lost her. He'd failed all those months ago at the ascension.

"I'm sorry," she said, a twisted look on her face. "I wish we had more time, but that is our curse, isn't it?"

Rhydian stood paralyzed, looking on the face of the woman he loved desperately, and failed. He saw Rianne in the garden, smiling as rays of sunlight kissed her face. Twirling her around in the wildflowers. Her hand on his chest, banishing his curse. Him reaching for her through the gate bars. The ax coming down on her neck. Her head rolling into the ravine.

"I'm so sorry I failed you," he said. "I won't stop fighting for you. I will find a way to bring you back fully. After this war is done, we will be together."

Rianne's voice was soft as rose petals, and too quiet. "If I know nothing else, I remember I love you, but my soul is locked in death. I will always love you, but there's less and less of me every day."

Anger flared in his head, trickling down his spine like boiling water and thawing the frost in his veins. This was the end. He knew it.

"You will always be in my heart, and I will always come when you need me." He let out a slow breath. "But I just can't watch the woman I love fade."

"I know," she said.

Neither said anything as the battle raged. Soldiers screamed, Mooncursed roared, fireballs flew, and steel clanged.

Rianne whispered, "I held on as long as I could."

Rhydian closed his eyes and drew her into a hug. "No one can hold off death forever."

"I'm so sorry, for everything." Sobs wracked her body.

"You have nothing to be sorry for. I'm the one who couldn't save you," he whispered.

"When I died, I watched my entire life fly past. My best memories were those of you. Time we weren't meant to have, but took anyway," she said.

Rhydian pressed his nose into her silver hair, kissing the top of her head. "What I wouldn't give to go back to those lazy afternoons in the garden dreaming about running away and raising chickens and cows."

She pulled away and stroked his cheek a final time. "In every one of my dreams, I'm there with you."

Rianne held on for control, using all her strength to remain in this moment with him. She knew this was very well their last moment as they'd once been. Her soul threatened to shatter from the effort, and the other queens offered their own magic to sustain her for a final few seconds.

Rhydian said, "Dreams were all we were ever going to have. With our curses, there was never a future for either of us."

Rianne faded into Lexyra. "There is war and eventually there is death, but nothing more."

Rhydian hefted his ax. "Then let's show them war."

Lexyra pushed to the front, "I promise they will feel our rage at what our enemies stole from us in every bite of the blade."

The grief drained from Rhydian's face and was replaced by a cold, dark rage. "See that they do."

The Warbringer strode off toward the raging battle. Rianne watched him go, savoring the emotions warring within her. Soon, they'd all be numb again. The pain nearly sent her to her knees, but she'd choose pain over nothingness.

Nesryn stepped out of the shadow of a nearby tree, her ever-changing gray skin camouflaging her. The elf gave Rianne a long, sad look. The malice that so-often marred the edges of her eyes was replaced by knowing compassion.

Rianne swallowed, allowing kindness to shine through her eyes. "Keep him safe for as long as you can." She whispered, "Please."

The elf nodded and was gone.

A single silver tear splashed the crimson mud as Rianne faded and the queens took control.

CURSE OF HUMANITY
CHAPTER SIXTY-SIX

My curse is not the hunger that overtakes me at dusk, it's the guilt that consumes me at dawn.

— UNSENT LETTER FROM STELLAN ROTHBAIN TO HIS WIFE KADIYA ROTHBAIN, 2 N.T.C.

1153 N.T.C. The Flame Pillar, outside the Hunger's Teeth Mountains.

War cries woke Stellan from his diurnal slumber. He crept to the edge of the mountaintop cave to watch the battlefield below, wrapping his leathery wings around himself. The clouds were dark, but the hour of night had not yet fallen. The hunger had not returned. The crushing guilt of his own sins was why he seldom remained awake during these haunting hours.

The tide of battle had turned. Avyllon had been scarcely holding its own when he and his vampires were forced to flee the rising sun, but with the appearance of Rodarri, they had stood their ground.

Now, though, the endless forces pouring through the Way were beginning to overtake the armies of the continent. And somewhere down there was Miella. Hours remained before the protective cover of nightfall.

Miella needed him. They would not survive the next hours. The Demorran armies would overrun them, and she would be killed. He never should have let her into the fray. He should have carried her away to safety, but it hadn't been within him to crush her fighting spirit. Even his beastly side respected her fiery heart. And now he had to decide whether he would keep his oath.

This affliction was the result of the oath he'd sworn on the heart-wood tree. He'd sworn to accept whatever cost in exchange for the power to protect his family, his blood. He never thought the price of their salvation was his relationship with his kin. Their estrangement didn't matter to the oath. He would protect them from the Shadows and their cursed creations for all time. The Shadows had returned, and Miella was his blood. The oath demanded he fight for her. And she needed him to fight for her now.

Could he allow himself to hunt and feed with his humanity fully intact? It was terrible enough to know his darkest urges took over at night, but if he hunted during the day, he could not absolve himself of the fault.

Could he sink his teeth into the necks of his foes? His stomach churned at the thought of warm blood gushing over his tongue. He flexed his claws. Could he slash and tear limbs from humans and beasts alike? He swallowed as the memory of cracking skulls and breaking bones filled his pounding head. Sickening crunches. Sloshing blood. Ear-splitting screams.

Stellan turned from the cave's entrance and paused. He could hardly bring himself to even consider such a horror. But for Miella, who looked so like his young daughter once did, he must.

He called for Julietta. "Gather the others. We swore to protect our last surviving kin, and she is down there. They will not survive without us."

"You want them to attack before nightfall?" Julietta replied. "They risk eternal death in the sun."

"I know."

"You're asking them to hunt and kill without the hunger?"

The last time they'd hunted during the day, Stellan had locked them all away in the heart of a mountain for a thousand years. All night they starved, and during the day they slept fitfully with skulls full of nightmares. Their bodies withered but they did not die.

He caught her gaze. She'd been his loyal second for a millennium, and yet her expression tightened. The tilt of her brows, pout of her lip, imploring widening of her eyes—she looked all too human in these moments. They both knew what this would cost. Fighting this battle in full humanity would irreparably rend their lingering consciences. It was asking far too much.

"Summon them all," he said. "Our oath demands we fight, even if we go to the eternal death. Even if our souls suffer for another millennium."

Stellan unfurled his wings and soared toward the battle. He flew in circles, searching for his last living descendent. Stone giants, Mooncursed, Shadows, Demorran troops and sorcerers attacked in organized waves. Their formations crushed Avyllon from all sides, and now sought to cut Rodarri off from their ally.

The war machines were in place however, and Aurienne was directing the troops onward. Every shot, every movement, she shouted commands for. She reminded him very much of the powerful seer he'd known during the Shadow War. All Aurienne's efforts were focused on the Pillar. That's where Miella would be. Gritting his teeth, he fought against his body's weakness in the daylight hours. Every movement taxed him.

Gliding through the clouds, he spotted Miella trailing Theo, Adonis, Rhydian through a sea of enemies. War machines sent lances and boulders into their path in an attempt to clear the way. With a cry, Stellan fell upon their enemies. Blood sprayed the mud as he hacked them to pieces.

The beating of vampiric wings filled the air. A cheer went up from Teridar's troops. Vampires soared underneath dark clouds, staying in groups of five to attack the Demorrans. Like eagles, they dove down with ferocity before returning to the skies.

The clouds parted and a ray of sun shone through. Erelia was not fast enough to avoid the sun and flew straight into it. She disintegrated into a cloud of ash, her scream echoing overhead.

Stellan froze, blinking at where his friend had just been. Without the hunger to overpower it, the shock nearly paralyzed him. He beat his wings, searching the skies for any other breaks in the cloud cover.

He trailed Miella from the air, lunging for the enemies who stood in her way. Their progress was slow, but she hacked with her short-sword as Theo and Rhydian together cut down enemies by the dozen. Marco remained at Miella's side, searing any who would seek to harm her. Stellan ground his fangs. His human emotions around Marco were even more complicated than the vampiric ones. For now, he knew Marco would protect Miella and it would have to be enough.

"Keep going!" Stellan shouted.

He took another turn around the battle. Stellan's preternatural senses caught the darkening of an aura. Sin coated someone's thoughts, even here in this battle with death all around, their deceit was coppery and vile. He spiraled overhead, searching for the source of the betrayal.

Nico shot forward, slashing mortal enemies with his claws. "Keep the line!" he commanded, leading Avyllon's army forward.

An Avyllonian man crept through the battle toward Nico. Panic raked through him. All Stellan could see was Tomas and Erelia.

His eyes turned black as his dormant inner beast took control. "Nico!"

Stellan swooped down, his claws outstretched for the traitorous bastard who would attack an ally in the heat of battle. He didn't attempt to slow his descent. Nico spun just as Stellan crushed the mortal to the ground. Blood poured from the traitor's mouth and ears, and his limbs twitched. Stellan's limbs sat at wrong angles from the height, but he sank his fangs into the man's neck.

The warm blood was coppery and sticky, and Stellan fought the urge to gag as it trickled down his throat. He heaved, forcing the healing liquid to remain in his throat. Tears burned his eyes at the effort. Bones snapped, and he regained his form. Something caught his attention. He stepped on the man's limp wrist and pried the object from it.

A heartwood stake.

Because of their oath, it was one of the few objects that would do immediate, mortal damage to one of his kind.

Cocking his head, Stellan studied the unremarkable man who'd nearly taken Nico from him with secret knowledge he should not have possessed. Glancing up to survey the battlefield, he found his brother Marco staring right at them. Marco's tattoos flared with the intensity of the sun, but it did not match the heat of the hunter's gaze. Miella was beside him, growing pale.

Stellan glanced from the traitor back to the pair. No hint of surprise lined their features. Marco was resolute, and Miella was... guilty. An expression Stellan knew all too well. They had some knowledge of this.

His human heart cracked. Was there a plot? Did Miella have knowledge of it? He endured horrors of battle to keep her safe, to help her allies. He'd ordered his people, those he was charged with protecting, the ones he'd failed once before to fight in the daylight, knowing what it cost. Had she betrayed him?

The battle raged on, and Stellan took to the skies again. Once the killing was done, he would find just how deeply the deceit ran.

Veil of Death
Chapter Sixty-Seven

"I held on as long as I could."
"No one can hold off death forever."

— *Journal of the High Seer Aurienne*
Azarrah, prophetic vision.

1153 N.T.C. The Flame Pillar, outside the Hunger's Teeth Mountains.

Golden threads of fate and time wrapped around Aurienne in knots as she passed through the veil of death to face down a goddess.

Niamh was an illusion, an oily, shifting smudge upon the air. The shadows surrounding Niamh fell away, and out stepped a tall, lithe goddess with rainbow-shimmering hair falling to her hips, an effervescent gown that pooled at her feet, and luminous starlight skin. Her features were sharp, and she bared her fangs past violet-stained lips.

"Your power will soon be mine," Niamh said. "You can't fight fate."

Aurienne clenched her fist around the future, swaying with the effort. The future wiggled, trying to change, but she traced back the point of deviation.

Her corporeal form lifted a hand toward the giant springing to life as Theo charged past. "Fire!"

The trebuchet projectile cracked against the giant's head, and the giant stumbled away as Theo and his warriors slipped past.

Niamh shot before her in a flash, reaching out and gripping her throat. Aurienne gasped, her hand reaching for Niamh's iron grip. The future fought her, and she caught sight of an archer nocking a bow and sighting it toward Theo.

"No!" Aurienne choked.

She lifted her hand, signaling the Avyllonian sorcerers and dropped it. The vials flew toward the archer an instant before the bow released. The vials struck, and the archer fell. The arrow flew past Theo, pinging off his pauldron. He glanced back at her, not seeing the war she fought beyond the veil.

The golden threads dimmed as the final reserves of Aurienne's magic dried up. The future snapped out of her hand and vanished, lost. Her eyes watered as her body began to shake.

Niamh squeezed and Aurienne's vision went dark. "You have nothing left to give."

Aurienne's corporeal form wheezed as her magic slowed to a trickle, "You're wrong."

"So defiant," Niamh chuckled. "Just like Rheia was. It didn't save her in the end either."

Rheia?

Niamh continued, "I've waited too long for this, planned too meticulously. Magic you cannot comprehend has set these events in motion. They can't be stopped. Not by you, and not by your young king."

"Goddess, please help me," Aurienne whispered.

Niamh pulled Aurienne closer and lifted her feet off the ground. "Your Goddess can't help you now. She's left you all alone, as always."

Aurienne's boots dangled, her toes scuffing the ground. Her fingers clawed into Niamh's wrist as she fought for air. The armies waited for her signals, the incorporeal struggle invisible to them.

A heavy presence settled upon Aurienne's shoulders. Her Triple Goddess was here with her.

"My daughter, I am always here," her Goddess whispered.

Blinding, boundless magic burned into Aurienne. Her bones were on fire, her blood screaming.

Filled with new power, Aurienne slammed her palm into Niamh's face and sent the other goddess sprawling through the spectral mist.

Aurienne's Goddess stood before her. Olive-hued skin, black wavy hair wrapped in braids, and eyes blue as sapphires.

Niamh burst from the mist, short fangs bared and eyes feral. Purple light exploded from Niamh's fingers and her body faded into an oily wraith. She dove for Aurienne, slamming into her spectral body.

Aurienne screamed as pain erupted in her. Her Goddess stepped into her, and her body became a battleground for the two goddesses. Niamh's claws raked through her magic as her own goddess fought to heal the wounds. The immense clashing of power threatened to cleave Aurienne's weakened soul in half. Golden and crimson blood seeped from her eyes and mouth.

"High Seer?" someone distantly was calling for her.

Aurienne was wracked with pain as the two powers collided. She blinked her corporeal eyes, straining to see the battlefield. Her spectral form used the new power within her to find new golden threads of fate. As Theo fought his way toward the Pillar through a dense horde, she desperately searched for the future that would see him through. A Mooncursed charged straight for Theo.

"Fire!" Aurienne directed.

She aimed one hand toward a wall of Demorran shields and signaled the trebuchet. "Fire!"

The large boulder cut a path through the shields, but more soldiers took their places.

Niamh hissed as the Triple Goddess forced her from Aurienne's soul. The oily feeling remained and Aurienne shuddered. The Triple Goddess stepped free of Aurienne. Niamh rose, sharpening her ethereal claws, but she was blocked by Aurienne's Goddess.

A golden thread flickered, a path through the army to the Pillar. Aurienne clutched it, following each choice, each step, each death. Tracking how to force it to become real.

A Demorran lifted their sword, striking Theo down. Not if the ballista took him out first.

"Fire!" Aurienne ordered.

The metal spear pierced the Demorran in the chest, but a Mooncursed leapt over him and knocked Theo from his horse, pinning him to the ground. Its jaws snapped over him.

"No! Fire!"

Another spear shot through the Mooncursed's head. Theo pushed up to stand, finding his horse again. The Demorrans attacked the dragon's fang wall, threatening to collapse Theo's escape.

"Fire!" Aurienne commanded.

The trebuchet missed, slamming into one of the dragon's fang sections and Demorrans poured in.

Aurienne froze, staring at her hands. Each of her actions took her farther away from the future she sought. She blinked, searching her soul and finding an oily sensation on the top of her Goddess' pool of magic.

Slowly, she looked to Niamh who was grinning. "Can't trust your visions, can you? You don't know what's real and what's not?"

Her Goddess flung Niamh back with a chain of golden fates and put her hands on Aurienne's shoulders. "I will tell you a secret that Niamh desperately wants to hide from you. One I hoped you would discover for yourself. You never needed me. You have all the power you need in here." She tapped Aurienne's chest.

Aurienne glanced at Niamh who was already storming toward them. "How? I have no magic left?"

"It's not the only source of magic," her Goddess said. "You still don't see it? The power other than what is yours or what you steal by spirit necromancy?"

"What other magic is there?"

Her Goddess stroked her cheek. "It's all around you if you look closely."

Aurienne closed her eyes and allowed her consciousness to drift between her body and her spirit. She hovered in the space between time and reality. Opening her eyes, she looked around her. Time stilled as she really looked.

Each warrior on that battlefield was a person with dreams, hopes, memories, love. Every death was an ending of all potential and futures that might have come to pass. Their choices and wills were unpredictable, shifting, human. The smallest acts created impossible shifts. Fate wove it all together in a pattern she now understood. And in it all, was power.

She blinked, gazing back upon her Goddess. "I see it now."

"I knew you would." Her Goddess smiled before she vanished.

Niamh chuckled. "She leaves you again."

"You may have the gift of foresight, but you know nothing of fate," Aurienne said.

"I have more power than you will ever know," Niamh snapped. "Your spirit necromancy cannot match my own."

"It's not necromancy."

Aurienne reached through the veil for the golden threads of fate. She grasped as many as she could, allowing them to flow through her. All at once, she lived every potential future. The love they might know, the children they might have, the things they might accomplish. Their secret fears and hopes. In the potential of what each life might be, there was power.

Niamh reached for her, but Aurienne drew up a golden shield of futures. Niamh's spectral claws scraped against the shield, unable to break through. Aurienne grinned triumphantly.

"How!" Niamh shouted.

"I am a seer," Aurienne said. "I am master of past and present and future. I can use the messy, beautiful present of others. The limitless futures. The depth of their memories. Instead of consuming them as you have done, I'm setting them free."

Aurienne called forth her own memories, reliving each moment as she wove them into anchors of the magic surrounding her.

Aurienne was three years old, clinging to her mother's hand as they navigated the busy streets. The unfamiliar noises hurt her ears, and she whispered, "Mommy, can we go home?" They stopped on steps to a temple that looked like it touched the clouds. Aurienne screamed as her mother pried her hand open and left her in the arms of a stranger. Tears poured down her face. It was the last time she allowed herself to cry.

Ten lonely years later, Aurienne was trained in every form of divination and foresight. The day Syaoran woke with clear eyes, every seer in the temple cast runes, shuffled cards, offered blood, and conducted rites to find their next High Seer. She could feel the weight of their stares as every single one spelled out her name. Syaoran took her to the inner sanctum, and Aurienne made her vows to the Goddess that night under a Hallohaim moon.

The Rites where she risked death for visions of the

*future flashed in her memories. The flames on her
feet. The crushing weight of the earth above her
head. Standing for a day and night on the tallest
tower in the city. Slipping under the blessed waters.*

*Just weeks ago, kissing Theo under the moonlight.
Witches magic as much as the cool air and the
warmth of the fire sent chills down her skin. Music
and laughter surrounded her. Dancing, drunk on
wine, she spun into his arms and allowed her heart
to lead. Her fingers wound into his wavy hair, and
his strong hands pulled on her waist. He smelled of
pine-scented mountain air and hot forges as she
breathed him in.*

Every memory gave her power, anchored her to her identity, and allowed the memories and futures of others to flow through her. Every death she caused was power. Every life she saved, power. She was connected to every living thing in the valley, the threads of fate bound to her in a weave that she now knew.

A future where Theo reached the Pillar shone brightly as the sun. She grasped it, easily following every choice.

"Fire!"

"Fire!"

"Fire!"

The power ripped at her memory anchors, and she dug further into the most powerful memories.

*Seeing the Goddess for the first time.
Placing the crown on Theo's head.
Threatening Rianne to protect Theo.
Him whispering "I love you."*

Every pivotal moment, she lived again as she directed the battle.

"Fire!"

"Fire!"

She held the golden threads tightly, watching the futures change in her palms, and adjusting. Holding all futures in her mind, she overlayed them, watching them unfold in real time. A million possible outcomes all playing out at once.

Niamh's claws rattled against Aurienne's shield. "Impossible!"

The nameless one appeared, wielding his staff. Niamh flinched, retreating from the pair.

"You dare stand against me?" Niamh growled.

"We're not in Rexila with your priestesses and offering bowls and wards," the nameless one said. "We're in the shadow lands, the world between worlds beyond the veils of life and death. And this is my domain."

The nameless one advanced and Niamh opened a purple Way.

"You can't change fate!" Niamh screamed at Aurienne as she stepped through.

The golden cords of fate wove and knotted around the raging futures and fates—she reached out, calling more cords to her. She gripped them and was thrown backwards against the railing from the influx of power.

Past. Present. Future.

All wove together into an unbreakable force flowing through her as she surveyed the battle.

Then she felt it. The weak, arrhythmic beating of her heart. The slowing of the blood in her veins. The pressure building in her head. Pouring of what could only be soulblood down her face. Her hands were drenched in golden blood mixing with crimson. She cast a final glance at the battlefield, raging with retreating monsters and soldiers. Theo and the others were at the pillar, fighting.

Please, let it be enough. Please.

She sent another boulder hurdling toward their enemies. She choked as she pointed to another target. Her hands shook as her chest rasped for air.

"You can't fight fate," Niamh whispered from worlds away.

Aurienne rallied the last of her strength. "I *am* fate."

Sinking against the railing, she tightly gripped the future where the path was clear for Theo. She pointed to a final target as she coughed up golden blood. Swaying, her vision blurred as she sent one final command to the armies.

Aurienne collapsed.

An eternity later, she opened her eyes to see Theo, splattered with blood, gleaming sword in hand, standing over her. He shouted a battle cry as he downed another foe. A vision? A dream? A nightmare? She wasn't sure.

Everything went dark, and faraway Niamh laughed.

SPARK OF TERIDAR
CHAPTER SIXTY-EIGHT

A single spark can ignite an inferno.

— *JOURNAL OF MASTER SORCERER MATHIS*
MIVVEM KASTER.

1153 N.T.C. The Flame Pillar, outside the Hunger's Teeth Mountains.

Time slowed as Theo's heart seized. Feeling as though the universe shuddered, he turned to the siege towers to see Aurienne fall to the mud. She didn't get up. His heart shredded in half, torn between knowing he couldn't leave his task and needing to run to her. He had to believe she was going to be okay. And if not, she couldn't have sacrificed in vain. If he did nothing else, he would relight the hellsdamned Pillar before he died.

Kicking his horse, he charged ahead. Rhydian, Adonis, Miella, and Marco urged their mounts after him. Theo raced straight for the line of tall Demorran shields. No time remained. He would get to the Pillar now. His horse whinnied and snorted as its hooves pounded the mud. The horse jumped, clearing the shields. He focused on the sword's power.

> *Ma and Pa walked into the room, wringing their hands and looking around. Their eyes lit up when they saw him. They hugged him, smelling of home.*

> *The woods were dark as the caravan sat 'round a blazing bonfire. Theo was telling a monster story as the sentinels crept up on the unsuspecting travelers. Aurienne sang a dirty ditty with a sparkle in her eye he'd never seen.*

> *Theo sat beside Aurienne in the small tavern, downing mugs of bubbly cider in the corner. Clinking mugs, they laughed until they were gasping for air. She reached forward to grab his hand, and he'd never wanted her to let go.*

> *Rhydian and Theo were trapped inside a mountain, fumbling in the dark, convinced they were going to die but not accepting their fate.*

> *Aurienne was pressed against him in the Rodarri gardens, raking her hands through his hair as she kissed him. Every nerve in his body lit up. They laughed, lips still locked.*

Energy poured through his veins. *It was all for love.* Magic shining, Theo swiped his glowing sword across the shields and sliced them in half. He'd finally broken through the Demorran auxiliary line.

His party followed through the gap. Hana ran after them on

foot, leaving small burning footfalls in the crushed grass clumps and hardening the mud.

Nesryn swung atop an abandoned mount, cutting down enemies behind Rhydian.

Theo focused on the memories, willing the magic of his sword to awaken.

Aurienne led Theo to the royal forge at Wyndsel,
letting him learn from the masters and do what he
loved.

Aurienne ran down the temple steps for him, crashing
into his arms, smelling of vanilla and elder rose.
In front of the whole city, she kissed him.

His starlight sword found the chest of a Mooncursed. It raked its claws through his golden armor as it died. Another closed its jaw on his forearm, puncturing the bracers and lighting his arm on fire with pain. He slashed for the beast, nicking its face. It howled in agony, clawing at its jaw.

An arrow flew by, slicing his cheek. He ducked and another arrow narrowly missed him. Miella loosed her own arrow toward the archer, but missed. Adonis hurled a swirling vial, and it hit home. Theo didn't need to look back; the screams told him the archer was no more.

The mile was hard fought, blurring together in an endless stream of battle and violence. Theo's arm burned, and he struggled to keep his sword up.

Finally, they reached the bottom of the Pillar only to find another last line of soldiers. Theo charged forward but was beaten back by the shields and spears. He couldn't try to jump again as they were right against the base of the giant column. Packed so tightly, a hundred warriors faced him, standing between him and the wide entrance.

Theo's sword flared as he fed it all the memories he held so dear.

Rhydian surged forward, abandoning his mount and spiraling toward the troops with twin axes. Nesryn followed, her starlight blade snaking out and destroying all Rhydian touched. Marco focused on the Mooncursed, holding his burning short sword high to keep the Shadows at bay.

Retreating, the group regrouped and rushed the line again. A small team of Avyllonian sentinels followed their every move. A dozen paces stood between them and the door. They were so close.

"Keep going!" Theo ordered.

"We can't get through!" Miella cried.

"They've regained the line. We're cut off from the army." Rhydian's words were curt as his limbs shook from the effort of fighting his curse.

Adonis reached into his bag. "This is the last vial of firecore. We didn't think it was strong enough, but it's worth a try."

"Nesryn!" Theo shouted.

The elf stabbed her sword straight through the breastbone of a Mooncursed monstrosity. She flipped over a Demorran spearman and kicked him in the face. He fell and didn't get up. She took the vial from Adonis and sighted the Pillar.

Nesryn hurled his vial. It flew higher and higher in a straight line directly toward the enormous bowl topping the Pillar. The vial exploded against the stone, flames licking at the bowl for a few precious moments.

The flames died out.

"Light my arrow," Miella offered.

Hana closed her hand on the arrowhead, turning it molten. Miella nocked her bow and released the arrow toward the Pillar. The arrow struck the side of the bowl, but the flames died out.

Hellsdamn it.

It isn't enough.

He glanced around for vampires. Maybe one could get her to the top of the Pillar. They were too far away. They'd have to fight their way up the tight staircase, and he could see through the spiraling windows that it was full of Demorrans and Mooncursed, and the top was lined with Shadows.

Backup wasn't coming. Aurienne couldn't save them this time. Rianne was fighting her own battle. Reinforcements were pouring out of the emperor's portal. They were exhausted and battered, yet, they had to find a way to the top.

This was the last stand.

Theo lifted his sword. "We'll kill as many as we can. Hana, run for the top of the stairs as fast as you can."

The flame elemental hesitated, glancing toward the column rising toward the sky. "What am I supposed to do?"

Theo leaned closer to her, the heat nearly blistering his face. "You wanted to burn people, right? Now's your chance. Burn your way to the Pillar, and then set it aflame."

Hana grinned.

STEEL AND BONE
CHAPTER SIXTY-NINE

Heroes only stay heroes for a short while. Those of us cursed with immense power always fall.

— JOURNAL OF NESRYN ASHWILDES, 288 B.T.C.

1153 N.T.C. The Flame Pillar, outside the Hunger's Teeth Mountains.

Fate looked on as Teridar fought for its survival. With a flick of her hand, Lexyra sent her forces to the Pillar, pressing it from all sides so Theo and the elemental might relight the protective monument. Brave Avyllonians and Rodarrians charged toward ancient beasts, armed only with steel and their nerve.

A bloody battlefield raged around her as magic filled the land and skies. War machines hammered the ranks of the Demorrans. Sorcerers on each side launched fireballs. The Queensblood witches released poisons and curses. Giants lumbered through the ranks. Mooncursed and vampires clashed. Shadows slipped in and out of reality, leaving destruction in their wake. Thousands lie dead or dying, with more falling every minute.

A crackling purple Way opened before Lexyra, and Emperor Rexil stepped out wielding a golden sword. He caught sight of her, and his gaze narrowed. He strode toward her, the imperial robes under his golden wolf armor dragging through the mud.

Lexyra tugged Rianne's lips into a grin. Noxanya and Safyrah raised her hand, summoning the bonesword. The bones of the queens flew from her corset to form the enchanted weapon. Warrior-queen Whillow gripped it tightly, staring down their enemy.

He paused paces from her, tilting his chiseled jaw. "I underestimated you."

"So it seems," the queens all replied.

"You escaped the titan ore shackles," Rexil mused. "Interesting. No one has done that. And your magic—what are you?"

Lexyra bared her teeth. "You won't be alive to find out."

Rexil matched her expression with his own feral one. "I'm going to enjoy ripping every one of your secrets from you." He glanced up at the rising moon, seeming to grow larger before her eyes.

"But first, I'm going to stop your friends from reaching the Pillar." He turned toward the direction where Theo and the others battled for the continent's future.

From within the sea of spirits, Rianne rose.

Rianne whispered, *"Together, we can defeat him."*

She reached out among them, her soul the thread keeping them together. Her love, her passion, her hope. Rianne's kind heart wasn't a weakness after all—it was their greatest strength. She threaded their consciousness together. A thousand souls fighting as one. Combining all their strengths and none of their shortcomings. She absorbed Vittoria's wisdom, tempered Samantah's bloodlust, absorbed Whillow's warrior heart, embraced her mother Charlotte's love, channeled Safyrah and Noxanya's magic, and harnessed Lexyra's fury. Each queen had their strengths, but only Rianne could do *this*.

She was always meant to do this.

"Not while I breathe," Rianne replied.

He stopped, turning back toward her.

She grinned, truly feeling the pride lacing her voice. "And you'll find I'm hard to kill."

Rexil stalked forward, golden sword glowing with purple runes. Crackling, unnatural energy clung to him. His dark eyes promised violence and retribution.

Mud clung to Lexyra's boots and the bottom of her skirt as she advanced. The wind whistled through the trees and mountains around them. The cries of the dying and war cries of the living filled her ears.

Lexyra gripped her bonesword and swung. Bone met steel, but she did not hesitate. Whillow's training poured into her bones, sliding off Rexil's blade and slashing for his throat. Whirling back, the tip of her sword narrowly missed his flesh. His eyes widened. Immediately, she twisted the blade again toward his unprotected ribs. He dropped his armored elbow on the flat of her blade. She pressed on, bonesword striking for him in tight arcs.

They circled one another.

"You've been trained in the sword," he observed. "We could have made quite the pair. No one could stand against us. There's time to change your mind and ally with me."

Nicollete laughed. "We're not so naïve, Rexil. Your offer tastes of lies. They always did."

He shrugged, bringing his blade up again. "The rest of my Shadows are coming. They bring with them the *infer'ni uumbraen curtores*, the damned behemoths. They will crush your armies."

Vittoria and Lexyra snarled together. "The cursed tongue."

Rexil tilted his head. "What do you know of it? What has the Grimfall told you?"

A thousand long years of memories flooded her.

He swung before she could answer, and sparks flew. He spun mid-strike, the hilt of his sword cracking her in the mouth. Her blade snaked forward, slicing past his cheek as they separated again.

Lexyra reached up to wipe the blood from her lip. "Is that all you've got?"

Vittoria took over, the tight arcs looping into concentric circles that struck at him with alternating sides of the blade before slashing the tip toward joints in Rexil's armor.

Rexil could not match the change in style, and the blade caught him across his collarbone, slashing a cut through the leather. He backed away, pausing to dab at the blood before slowly looking at her in awe.

Lexyra's smile was a snarl. "Your wards do not protect you against all of us."

She lunged, a succession of quick, furious jabs toward every major artery.

Clang.

Clang.

Clash.

Crack.

Frantically blocking, he opened his mouth to say something, but Callysta's fragmented soul took over, swinging wildly at him in unpredictable, disorganized patterns.

"The teeth of hell devour even the wolf," Callysta cried.

Rexil met the attack, sidestepping and bringing down his heavy weapon. Lexyra barely moved out of its path, the honed edge slashing material from her gown. He slashed again, his blade finding her thigh as hers found his back.

They circled each other.

From the corner of her eye, she saw her army retreating. Aurienne was nowhere to be seen, and the war machines struck for their foes aimlessly. The Pillar was crawling in Demorrans as Theo's forces pressed to break the line.

Her heart leapt as vampires filled the skies, falling upon the stone giants, Mooncursed, and enemy sorcerers. Night had not set, but they fought valiantly. A vampire was caught in a rogue ray of sunlight burst into flames.

The Queensblood witches summoned bloodcurses as sorcerers hurled fireballs. Avyllonian seers in white ceremonial gowns stepped forward, aiming the war machines. Teridar's monsters were all that was holding back the emperor's unending hordes pouring through the Way.

She glanced toward Rexil, "How does failure taste?"

He lifted a finger to the skies. "I wouldn't know."

An otherworldly wail split the skies. Hordes of eerie figures ripped through reality, dragging with them the behemoths of nightmare.

REKINDLED
CHAPTER SEVENTY

Only a monster can defeat a monster, says the devil.

— PARABLE OF THE GOLDEN FOX.

1153 N.T.C. The Flame Pillar, outside the Hunger's Teeth Mountains.

Earth-shattering roars rumbled the ground from the tree line where Shadows slashed Ways into existence. Lithe creatures as tall as trees stalked out of another world. A dozen beasts—with scales on their backs, fur on their chest, and feathered wings—rumbled the earth with each stride.

Theo's sword nearly fell from his hand as the ground beneath his feet rolled. Nothing could stand before these beasts. Even Nesryn or Rhydian would be hard pressed to succeed. He glanced at the Warbringer who hacked at everything in sight with his axes and nearly reached the stone archway leading to the spiraling staircase.

They began to climb against the enemy defenders.

Legs burning, they fought through the Demorrans up the ending stairs. Theo kicked a corpse out of their way through one of the windows. The body fell the long way down before crunching against the ground.

The height was dizzying, and Theo stepped back against the interior wall. Keeping his back to the wall, he fought upward behind Rhydian's trail of carnage. Adonis, Miella, and Marco followed, preventing Theo from being flanked by foes.

Endless stairs.

Hundreds of foes.

The climb was unending. A blur of blood and screams.

Theo burst out of the stairwell, stumbling onto the flat rooftop of the Pillar. They were as high as Avyllon's walls, and a single misstep meant immediate death. The bowl was only a few paces away, but a wall of Shadows encircled it making the clicking, echoing noises promising death. The painfully thin and tall shifting humanoid shapes possessed distorted features flickering in and out of existence, with slithering shapes beneath the dark gray skin. Twin rings of darkness orbited their chests.

Hana waited behind, her hands leaving ash prints on the door frame. A Shadow darted forward reaching for her with its long, spindly hands. It touched her and both screamed in pain as the opposites connected. She retreated farther into the stairwell as Theo brought his sword down on the Shadow's arm. Upon touching his enchanted blade, the Shadow fell to the floor, writhing as his rending magic undid it.

"I feel cold," Hana said, rubbing the dark spot on her arm. "They can't touch me, it hurts and my flames dim."

Theo swore. He'd have to get her closer yet. They'd have to fight through this horde of Shadows, with more alighting atop the Pillar from the emperor's Way every minute.

He glanced down to the siege tower where Aurienne had fallen. *She can't have sacrificed in vain.* He pushed all his doubts away. Nothing would keep him from getting this Pillar relit. Aurienne had believed in him, and he wouldn't let her down.

Settling into his familiar fighting stance, Theo attacked.

Hana lit Miella's arrows on fire, and she shot them into the Shadows—who screamed in agony as eternal fire poured into them. Marco shielded them, defending them from all attacks. Adonis hurled fireballs and vials, tracing shapes in the air with his glowing fingers.

The nameless one stepped out of a nearby shadow, whirling his glowing purple staff. The Shadows hissed, changing forms and shapes. The nameless one was a shadow in human form, but the Shadows were shifting blotches of darkness—as if made of a substance not of this world, as if the world fought against their very existence.

Nesryn landed on the rooftop between their party and the Shadows. She brought her starlight sword to bear, baring her fangs as her dark eyes flashed.

A Shadow stepped out of the formation, inky black shades dripping from the once-human figure. "Rotidor. Tse'atua culp'ae."

"Te'moniue. Nun'ce more're," she replied hatefully, the ancient language lyrical on her tongue.

"Te'inveni'emu," the Shadow hissed.

"Infener'um te'ad expel'ear." Nesryn replied before launching forward.

The nameless one joined her, a blur of purple and white side by side dancing with the ancient warriors.

Rhydian roared incoherently and raced after them. Rattling hisses erupted from the Shadows and swarmed him. Theo lunged for the black mass, holding onto the memories that anchored him.

The flower petals falling around Aurienne at the Foretelling Rite.
The moonlight reflecting off her cloudy eyes.
The soft elder rose scent of her skin.
The way her smile tugged at the corners of her lips.
The sound of her laugh.

The first bite of his blade cut into the Shadow, and inky blood poured out of the changing form. It shrieked so loudly his ears bled, but he kept going. His blade cut through more Shadows, each nick bringing forth their demise. Magic erupted out of them, filling the air with unspent power that had the hairs of his arms standing up.

A Shadow called out, "Iidal'gh ami'ea."

Every gleaming pitch-colored eye turned to him.

"To Theo!" Nesryn cried as they swarmed.

His sword rang out as seven Shadows struck at him. He parried and blocked, slicing and stabbing everything in range. They dodged his blade, hissing and releasing their horrible cries.

A Shadow's blade slashed his sword arm, and blood began to pour down to his wrist. Theo shouted in pain, his fingers already beginning to go numb. He gripped the Sword of Souls with both hands, bringing it before him. Retreating, he blocked and parried the impossibly fast attacks. A sword sliced his leg above the knee. A dagger nicked his elbow. Another dagger wedged beneath his armor, scratching his ribs.

Blood poured down his sword arm underneath his armor. Something blunt struck him on the side of his head, knocking him sideways. He struggled to keep his balance. More Shadows were flocking to the Pillar from the open Way.

Hellsdamn it.

Hana was crouching behind the door frame, watching the conflict. Miella shot arrows she'd taken from the dead, Marco staying at her side. They were so close. They just had to carve her a path.

"Hana! To me! Take the first opening you see," Theo ordered.

The flame elemental dove between two Shadows to stand behind the king of Avyllon. She peeked out from behind his back. His head was woozy, his strength nearly depleted. Just a few more minutes.

Giant claws slammed down against the edge of the Pillar, causing the entire structure to shake. Theo stumbled, falling to his knee as the behemoth pulled itself up. It opened its mouth and roared, spittle flying.

Rhydian grabbed Theo by the shoulder and helped him up, eyes red as the bleeding eclipse. Theo met his gaze, seeing his friend on the brink of losing control. Rhydian was clenching his fists and frothing at the mouth. He stared as if saying goodbye. Then he dove for the behemoth, landing on its face and slashing with his axes.

Nesryn's head whipped from the Shadows to Rhydian and the behemoth. She danced around the Shadows, her starlight blade disintegrating all it touched. She looked to Rhydian again, grabbing the behemoth by the fur as it shook its head to try and dislodge him. Its giant maw opened with rows of fangs, snapping toward the top of the Pillar.

Theo dove to the ground and rolled. The beast snapped where he'd just been standing. He pulled himself to his feet, panting and vision blurring. His blood soaked his shirt in a dozen places.

The bowl was right there. He stumbled forward, swinging his sword as high as he could. A Shadow appeared, driving a dagger into Theo's ribs. Theo fell to his knees, lifting his blade to block their other hand. Twisting the sword, he contoured it behind the Shadow's arm and up into its chest. It fell.

Another few steps.

He could do it.

For Aurienne.

The red and black fox darted by, twice as big as Theo had ever seen it, with gold earrings in its ears and five tails. Gold light poured out of its eyes, ears, and mouth. Its fur began to glow with green and gold spirals. A large shield pushed outward from it, and the Shadows retreated against the light. The fox darted forward, pushing the Shadows back.

"Hana, now!" Theo shouted.

A Shadow gripped Theo by the throat, screaming into his face. Inches away, he looked into the cursed eyes, seeing images of a dying world, of ancient curses, of impossible truths. His strength drained. He brought his sword up behind him and drove it into the Shadow. The Shadow crumpled, and Theo fell beside it.

"Run Hana!" he called, blood trickling from his mouth.

The flame elemental darted forward toward the bowl. The behemoth smashed its giant clawed fist down, knocking the glowing fox off the side of the Pillar. The fox's golden shield went out as the Shadows' heads all snapped toward Hana. She screamed and sprinted the final few steps.

Hana dove between the Shadows, reaching for the bowl atop the Pillar in slow motion before a wall of crushing darkness consumed her.

QUEENSBLOOD ASCENDED

CHAPTER SEVENTY-ONE

A thousand queens, dead for nothing, and not one more shall die.

— PROCLAMATION OF QUEEN RIANNE CHARLOTTE LENORE, ASCENDED AND RETURNED QUEENSBLOOD OF RODARRI, 19 NOVA 1152 N.T.C.

1153 N.T.C. The Flame Pillar, outside the Hunger's Teeth Mountains.

Behemoths trailed the Shadows toward the continent's armies. Lexyra's breath caught in her throat. Impossible. None of the thousand queens in her bones had ever seen anything so terrible in all their centuries.

Batting a boulder out of the air, a behemoth whirled back to destroy one of her war machines. They stalked forward, cutting Theo and his small force off from the main army. A behemoth crushed a dragon fang wall under its clawed foot, before it bent down and swallowed three Rodarrians. They screamed the whole way down.

The emperor's blade came for Lexyra again. Strike after strike she met. Their feet slipped in the treacherous mud. They fought until each suffered from a dozen cuts. She glanced back toward the fray, watching their armies unable to hold their positions. They were going to be overrun.

Lexyra, Rianne, and all the queens in her bones, prepared for final death. They'd saved the Queensblood. Though their kin may still die, they would die of their own volition. Warriors. Generals. Ascensions would be no more. Their revenge was complete. They might not have been able to save the continent, but to die trying was as noble as death as they could hope for. Nothing more could be done.

"Fall back!" Avyllon's generals cried.

"Regroup!" Rodarri's commander-queens shouted.

Behemoths slaughtered hundreds in just moments. Not even the witches, sorcerers, and vampires could stand against them.

This was the end.

Blazing light erupted from the top of the stone pillar, sending shockwaves of flame pulsing into the clouds for miles.

Skin prickling, Lexyra could feel the protective Pillar shield pushing forward to extend to the coastlines.

Theo and the others did it.

They relit the Pillar. Somehow, they'd made it through.

"No!" Emperor Rexil roared.

Piercing screams filled the air as the Shadows began to fragment and disintegrate. The Mooncursed snarled and began to retreat through the enormous Way beside the Pillar. The Demorrans called for retreat.

With a shout that rumbled the ground, Teridar's armies charged.

Rexil glared at Lexyra. She lifted her bonesword, still dripping with his blood.

"I'll accept your surrender now," she said.

Without waiting for his response, she charged. Whillow's precise movements cut the air, slashing and slicing at Rexil with unmatched fury, driving him backward. Sweat poured down his face as he struggled to keep the Way open for his army with one hand. His sword arm struggled to keep up with Whillow's onslaught.

Lexyra, Vittoria, Whillow, Milah—each driving him back. He could not match their combined skill. His strength failed and a strike pressed through his defenses, wounding his sword arm.

"Your goddess can't save you from us," Vittoria whispered. "Your wards will not help you."

The Way grew smaller and dimmer as Demorrans shouted the retreat. Sweat poured from the emperor's brow. He backed away, glancing between Lexyra and the Way.

Safyrah and Noxanya sent bone darts from Lexyra's sword flying toward him, striking him with cursed magic. He stumbled, struggling to keep the Way open. Dark blood stained his purple and gold robes from half a dozen wounds.

"On second thought," Lexyra murmured, "I'll accept your death."

The emperor's Way collapsed in on itself, leaving the remainder of his army stranded in enemy territory and facing down their enraged foes with no escape. There would be no mercy.

The bone darts returned, and the bloodwitches prepared to send them through his wards again. Feigning before her attack, Lexyra drove her sword toward the emperor's heart. At the last moment, Rexil brought his blade up. The bonesword pierced his chest, just beside his heart. Blood poured out of his mouth.

A ragged, shrill scream pierced the air just as a small Way opened beside the emperor. He fell inside as it closed.

Hellsdamn it.

Rianne pushed to the front for a moment. His goddess must have saved him, but she would be hard-pressed to heal the cursed wounds ravaging his body.

Queensblood Rianne, ascended and returned queen of Rodarri, stood in a battlefield of enemy corpses, gripping her necromancer's bonesword forged from the discarded bones of her murdered ancestors. She cast a furious glare toward the horizon where her enemy fled. Rianne knew who she must be to save her people—a heartless, cruel monster. It already cost her future, her life, and soon would cost her soul.

Death was only the beginning, and this war had only just begun.

EPILOGUE

1153 N.T.C. The namesake capital city of Avyllon.

Aurienne wrapped a thick wool blanket around her shoulders and nestled against the cushions on the wide couch. Cool winds swept across her balcony, but the roaring heat on her back from the fire in her chamber kept the chill at bay. She overlooked her city. Steam from the heated pools turned to fog in the late winter afternoon.

From this height, she could see people wheeling their belongings on carts back to the previously uninhabited parts of the city. With the Pillars' full protection restored, people were returning to their homes. A small victory, and a costly one, but they'd managed to push back Rexil's forces. And they now understood the magnitude of the enemy they faced.

A quiet rustle behind her caught her attention and she turned to find Nesryn and the fox sitting on the balustrade.

"I'm glad to see you're awake," Nesryn said. "We weren't sure you'd survive. I can see the toll the battle took on you. It changed you."

The fox flicked its tail around its paws, golden eyes studying her.

"What I did shouldn't have been possible," Aurienne replied. "I'm still don't understand what happened."

"The land comes alive to protect itself, and magic as well," Nesryn said. "It's why I'm here."

A breeze caused Aurienne to wrap the blanket tighter around her arms.

"Now that I know Niamh is behind this, I understand what's been done. I know the magics available to our foes. The magic of the Shadows created the Mooncursed all those years ago—Shadow magic mixed with werewolf blood. Shadows should've been destroyed or banished, but she's found a way to bring them back, allowing her to make more Mooncursed, which can get through protective wards, at least for a time. And now, behemoths have come. We can't allow anything else to come through."

"From where?" Aurienne asked.

Nesryn's eyes darkened as she glanced at the fox. "Somewhere that shouldn't be possible."

The fox's fur gleamed with runes, and its ears twitched.

"She doesn't need to know," Nesryn said to the fox. "It doesn't change anything."

Aurienne blinked.

Is she communicating with the fox telepathically?

Theo stepped outside, two mugs of steaming cider in his hands. He sat beside Aurienne on the couch.

Nesryn stepped up onto the wide, stone railing. "I'm going to see what I can find out. You'll never claim victory by hiding here. We'll have to take the fight to Demorra."

The elf stepped off into the air, and in a flash of purple light, was gone through a Way. The fox also vanished, leaving Aurienne and Theo alone.

"What was that?" Theo asked, handing her a mug.

Her fingers brushed his, lingering on his hand. The touch drew a smile to his face. Settling against the cushions, she cradled the mug and leaned her head on his shoulder.

"Secrets coming to light. I suspect there's much more she's not telling us yet." She glanced up at him. "But let's not worry about it for a moment. The time for that will come."

He wrapped his arm around her and sipped the cider. A moment of peace filled her chest. Having given up fighting her feelings for him, she would take whatever time they had. He pressed a soft kiss to the top of her head.

Below, the quiet echo of children's laughter reached them amongst the familiar sounds of bustle. Waterfalls poured crystalline water into fresh pools, and fountains bubbled. The sounds of hammers on nails, and chisel on stone repaired the damage.

Her cards rattled inside the newly spelled bag at her hip, and she handed Theo the mug to dig within the blankets and remove them.

"What do you want to tell me?" she asked.

She shuffled slowly until the deck heated in her hand. Taking a steadying breath, she flipped the first card—one she'd never seen. A large stone and metal gate in a shroud of clouds held back flashes of light and darkness. A single, unknown word flashed across the bottom.

Etheria.

Afterword

Thank you for reading!

If you enjoyed *The Queensblood Crown*, please consider leaving a review on Goodreads or Amazon. Reviews, ratings, and word of mouth are so important for independent authors.

For more information about upcoming works and updates, visit my website www.alexbreewrites.com or follow me on Instagram @alex.bree.writes.

Want to stay up to date? Sign up for my author newsletter for exclusive updates, sneak peeks, and release news.

Alex Bree is a fantasy author and attorney living in Meridian, Idaho, with her husband, children, and dog.

Acknowledgments

The second book of any series is an evolving journey. There are lessons to implement, new ideas to try, and pressure to hit any successes the first book reached. There was so much I wanted to accomplish through the continuing stories of these characters I have come to love. I poured my heart onto these pages and hope you enjoyed it.

Korey, you are the best partner I ever could have asked for. I love you more than I could ever express in words. This book wouldn't exist without everything you do. You listen to all my insane musings, first drafts, editing and revising woes, bad poetry attempts, crazy ideas, and you never question when the writing process gets weird (and it does). To my children who inspire me every day, I love you! Hopefully, one day, when you're much older, you will read and love this.

My writing group partners are the backbone of this writing experience. There is so much that goes into getting a book out, and I appreciate all that you do (especially keeping me from spiraling). You're the first ones I go to when I'm deciding on the million things that go into a book—artwork, artists, editors, blurbs, chapter titles, website design, social media posts, fonts, formatting, obscure grammar questions, and everything else. A huge and ongoing thank you to A.J. Braun, Billie Grey, Loren Huxley, Jaci M. Lunera, Maia James, PC Nottingham, Tiffany O'Haro, N.C. Scrimgeour, Nico Vincenty, and Kaela Woodruff.

To my cover designer, Lisa Marie Pompilio, thank you for the beautiful covers that perfectly capture each character.

I also have some of the best friends a person could ask for! You are all amazing supporters and people, and I'm blessed to know you. Taylor, Jaime, Ruth, and Angela, you're amazing. Finally, thank you to my parents who always encouraged my love of reading and writing, and my brothers for their years of support.

www.ingramcontent.com/pod-product-compliance
Lightning Source LLC
Chambersburg PA
CBHW022010300726
48970CB00003B/827